THE STONE COLD THRILLER SERIES - BOOKS 4-6

A STONE COLD THRILLER BOXSET

J. D. WESTON

STONE RAGE

To come out on top, he must live undercover...

"What are we doing out here, Les?"

"This is where the boss said to meet them."

"It's pitch black, mate, I can't see anything. There could be fifty of them out there."

"Stop being paranoid," said Les. "Not like you to be jumpy."

"I'm not jumpy. I just don't trust them, the dirty, sly little-"

"We'll be out of here before you know it," replied Les. "Chill out. I used to bring the birds over here."

"Over here? What for? This place gives me the creeps. Can we at least have the heater on? It's freezing."

"Why do you *think* I brought them here?" said Les, turning up the Jaguar's temperature dial. "A bit of rough and tumble, Jay, they loved it."

"Is that what t.hey told you? How many of them came back for a second night of creepy love in the freaky field?"

"Not many," laughed Les. "Well, one actually, a few times. Sticky Sarah, we used to call her. She used to like that people could see in, dirty cow, voyeurism I think they call that."

"Sticky Sarah?"

"Yeah, she was a strange girl."

"Les, nothing about what you just said is normal. Firstly, why was she called Sticky Sarah?"

"Do you really want to know?"

"Probably not. When you say 'we,' can I assume that you weren't the only one to *experience* Sticky Sarah?"

"No, we all had a go. Well, most of us, apart from Little Lee. The poor fella was a slow developer. I have no idea how that guy survived childhood, he's probably still a virgin now."

"And when you say that Sticky Sarah used to enjoy being watched, do you mean to say that you brought her over here and banged her in the back of your car so other blokes could see in?"

"Yeah, dog walkers and stuff, she loved it," said Les.

"Did that not ever strike you as a bit weird, Les?"

"Not really."

Jay looked away from him in disgust. "I can't see shit out there," he muttered. "What was it anyway?"

"What was what?"

"The car, what car did you have?"

"Well, you know, I was young, didn't have enough money for my own car."

"Don't tell me you used your mum's car to smash Sticky Sarah around and have a load of dirty pervs stand around."

"No, no, no, I never," said Les. "I have got some decency."

"So, whose car was it?"

"I don't bloody know, do I?"

"You nicked it?"

"Yeah, of course, I did. Had a different one each week. I learned to drive in a nicked motor, my old man taught me."

"You what?" said Jay. "Your old man taught you to drive in a stolen car?"

"Yeah, he didn't know it was stolen, I told him I'd borrowed it off a mate."

"What if he got caught? How would you explain that?"

"Behave, Jay, I was fifteen years old. I didn't know any better."

"You're something else, you know that?"

Les laughed. "It's been a good old life, Jay. Had some great times, I have."

"Don't get all teary on me now."

"No, you know what I mean. Don't you ever wonder?"

"Wonder what?"

"You know, if you died, have you done all the things you wanted to do?"

"I have done most of them, Les," said Jay. "There are a few things still on the list though. One day I'll get around to ticking them off."

"What's that then?"

"Well, I might see if Sticky Sarah is still around and see if she fancies a bunk up while some old perv knocks one out."

Both side windows exploded in the car, sending glass all over the two men. Big hands reached in and dragged them through the car windows. Les pulled a knife and slashed blindly at the huge men who pinned him down on the grass. One of the men, a bald man with tattoos on his face, held Les' throat tightly and the other stopped his knife hand waving around by standing on his arm. A large knee came down onto Les' chest and, one by one, each of the fingers that held the knife were wrenched up, bent backwards and broken.

Les screamed in pain. He struggled, but it was useless against the size and weight of the man on top of him. Eventually, the last finger was snapped back like a twig, and the knife was taken from him.

The smaller of the two bald men that pinned him down held the knife curiously. He turned it in his hands, put the point in Les' eye, and slowly pushed down until the blade entered Les' brain and he fell silent.

Jay was on the other side of the car. Strong arms held him against the Jaguar's sleek paintwork. No words were spoken. Jay stopped struggling.

A tall, willowy man in a long overcoat stepped from the darkness into the pale moonlight. Jay could barely make out the features of his face but saw the glint of a scar that ran from the man's eye to his mouth, through his lips and down his chin to his throat.

The man gave a gesture to his men, who stood beside Les' body, to open the car boot. Opening it, they removed the sports holdall that contained four kilos of cocaine. They checked it and returned the nod to the boss.

Jay stared up at the man and spat.

"You will take a message to your boss."

"Fuck you, send a letter."

One of the men holding Jay landed a huge fist on his nose. Jay felt the bone break and tasted blood almost immediately.

"I am a reasonable man, but I am a businessman. It seems like your boss and I are in the same business. Competition."

"So run a sale or something. Isn't that what businessmen do?"

"It's an option," the man replied. "But I prefer not to cut profits for the sake of a few easy sales. I prefer to cut the competition." The man reached inside his coat and pulled out a long fillet knife. He flexed the blade and ran his finger along the thin steel.

"You will deliver the message for me?" asked the man.

"I'll tell him some ugly bloke from some shit stink part of Europe wants his balls cut off," said Jay. "How does that sound, wanker?"

"Hold him," the man said calmly.

The two men either side of Jay grabbed his hair and held him tight. The man in the coat stepped forward and ran the side of the blade across Jay's nose. With one hand, he pulled Jay's ear out from his head, and with the other, he sliced through the tissue and gristle in two neat, clean slices. Jay screamed and struggled against the two much larger men, but couldn't move. Spit flew from his gritted teeth, and his eyes were clamped shut as he fought the searing pain. He felt the man pull on his other ear, dull and hard. He felt the blade touch his skin sharply. Then he felt nothing but the burn of where his ears once were.

"Make sure he doesn't lose those, he may need them one day," said the man in the coat, as he wiped the blood from the blade onto Jay's jacket.

Jay's knees had given way, but his weight was easily supported by the two men. They dropped him to the ground face first, then kicked him to roll him over. Jay pulled his hands to his head, but his wounds were too tender to touch. Blood had run across his face into his eyes. He felt his arms being tugged outwards then felt a sharp point in the palm of his hand. He glared helplessly through the sticky blood to see one of the large men with a cordless drill. Then he felt the screw tear through his tendons, fixing one of his ears to his open hand with a long, gold screw.

CHAPTER TWO

A light rain fell like mist in the forest where Harvey Stone took his early morning run. His mind was clear, and his body had healed from the beating it had taken during the last job he and his team had worked.

They'd started out trying to intercept a robbery, things had escalated, and soon enough, terrorists had gotten involved. Harvey had been run over and later fallen from Tower Bridge wearing an explosive vest. He'd barely managed to avoid being torn to pieces by the blast and then had to fight not to let his body succumb to the fast-moving water that dragged him several miles down the River Thames.

Harvey had survived, and the team had succeeded. But they'd lost Denver, their driver, during the investigation, and each of the team was healing in their own way. The physical scars of battle often heal quicker than the mental scars, he thought.

Harvey leapt over an old fallen log, which he remembered from a run he had taken a few weeks previously. He never ran the same route twice, but often the crisscrossing paths intertwined in the deepest areas of Epping Forest, the forest that lay behind his house.

He ran with boots on for ankle support, and to make the challenge harder. Harvey didn't believe in running with bricks in a bag, but when he did run, he gave everything he had. Running with bricks in a rucksack was a military approach to training, and Harvey thought it doubtlessly worked, but would also cripple a man over time. Harvey wasn't a military man or even ex-military. He sat at the other end of that vocational spectrum, not quite as far along as the terrorists he had recently fought, but definitely on the wrong end.

Harvey had been raised by the leader of a well-known crime family, John Cartwright. John had fostered Harvey and his sister when they were young after their parents had apparently committed double suicide. Harvey had never believed the story of his parents' death and actively pursued the truth.

When Harvey had been twelve and Hannah, his sister, had been a few years older, he had witnessed her being raped, which led to her suicide.

The emotional damage the small boy Harvey took on changed his life forever. He fell under the wing of John Cartwright's minder who taught him how to channel his aggression, how to defend himself, and eventually, how to kill.

Three men had raped Hannah. The first man had been Harvey's first kill. It took a further twenty years for him to find the other two men and deliver their own retribution. That was when Harvey had removed himself from the circles of crime that sheltered him and stepped tentatively across the line into the world of crime-fighting. Harvey took that step armed with memories he'd rather not have and a list of people he needed to kill.

The list had two names. It was short, but it was a list that guided Harvey.

Harvey had been given two options after killing one of his sister's rapists, who he'd boiled alive in a copper bathtub until his internal organs had eventually cooked and his heart had stopped. The first option was prison, where he would likely serve the rest of his life and lose any opportunity to finish the list.

The second option had been to work with Frank Carver and his small team, which focused solely on fighting organised crime.

The choice had been simple, stay out of prison and work the list. Finding his sister's rapists had been therapeutic, cleansing and, above all, motivating. His list then focused on the mystery of his parents, who killed them and why, and his best friend and mentor, Julios, who had been shot by an unknown man. Then, during the last job, Harvey discovered that Julios had been the one to kill his parents. Harvey had been hit hard by the news. He'd been betrayed all his life. But the image of Julios standing over his parents' bodies had desecrated Harvey's earliest memories, memories of Julios training him, guiding him and sculpturing Harvey into the stone-cold killer he had become.

The list was nearly empty. He still hadn't discovered Julios' killer, but that was no longer a priority. Harvey had grown, he'd become part of the team, and had come to love his colleagues, something he never thought possible. He would find out how and why Julios had killed his parents, someday. But, for now, he was at peace. Frank Carver had removed the noose from Harvey's neck and set him free. Prison no longer loomed in the background; Harvey had paid his penance. Faced with the choice to stay working with his team, or to remove himself from everything tying him to the criminal world and live out his days in a small cottage in the south of France, Harvey had decided to stay.

He enjoyed the activity. He enjoyed the team, the banter

and the positivity that came from taking down gangs or stopping a tragedy. Harvey was healing in his own way, not from the wounds, mental or physical, that came from battle, but from the damage he had caused in his earlier life as a hitman for John Cartwright. The lives he'd torn apart so that John could grow richer. The fathers, brothers, and sons he had taken from daughters, sisters and mothers. He could never give those lives back, but with his remaining time on the planet, Harvey could do some good. He could make a difference.

The trees opened up as the forest grew thinner at the edge where the houses and roads ruled the landscape. The last obstacle was a steep hill, covered with a carpet of leaves and twigs. Harvey opened himself up and attacked the hill full speed, lifting his legs high, planting his feet hard and pushing his body up. His breaths came in short rhythmic bursts, and his arms pumped with each stroke. He broke the crest of the hill and jogged to the road, where he walked back to his house, breathing and stretching, and warming down.

Harvey leaned with his hands high on the shower wall and let the hot water run over him. He turned the water temperature up until it stung his skin then let his body get used to the heat before turning it up more. It was his morning shower routine. Within a few minutes, the shower was on full heat, and steam filled the bathroom. Then he turned the heat to cold, fast, removing the hot and replacing it with freezing cold water. His body tensed and grew red as the blood surged to the outer layers of skin to protect it.

He pulled a towel from the hook and walked to his bedroom. As usual, he dressed before drying properly, wearing a plain white t-shirt, black cargo pants and tan boots. Pulling the leather biker's jacket over his shirt, Harvey walked past the mirror without so much as a glance. He stuffed his SIG Sauer in his waistband and performed his routine of leaving the house. Every window was checked, and every door. He then took a mental snapshot of the rooms before leaving. Harvey had been trained to see if anything had been moved. Everything had a place, symmetrical, and easy to spot if he'd had an intrusion or something was disturbed.

Harvey used the interior door to his garage and locked it behind him. His motorbike helmet hung from a single hook on the wall in its protective black nylon bag. He pulled it off and hung the bag back up then started the BMW's engine. The garage door was operated from a small fob in his pocket. He rolled out, closed the garage behind him and pulled out onto the road.

Harvey rode slowly, enjoying the cool morning and minding the small puddles that had collected on the side of the roads.

It wasn't until he entered the M11 motorway southbound that he pulled his visor down and opened up the throttle. Less than twenty-five minutes later, he pulled up outside his colleague's apartment. He left the engine running, and lowered his boots to the ground, balancing the weight of the bike between his thighs.

Melody Mills led the team's operations; she made the plans. Guided by the team in their individual fields of expertise, she called the shots and reported to Frank. Melody stepped from the plush apartment block in long black boots, tight black leggings and a short leather jacket. She swept her long black hair over one shoulder and pulled on a helmet.

Harvey stood and held the bike upright as she swung her leg over behind him.

"Morning, Harvey." She gave him a firm squeeze to let him know she was comfortable, and he pulled off. The team's headquarters was a short ride from the Docklands, situated beside the Thames Barrier in Silvertown. As Harvey pulled onto the North Woolwich Road, he slowed then stopped to one side.

"What's up?" asked Melody.

Harvey was looking across the busy road at a burnt-out pub. Acrid smoke still hung in the morning air.

Melody followed his gaze. "Oh that, yeah that was on fire when I came home last night. It's a rough pub apparently, never went in there," said Melody.

"You know who ran it?" asked Harvey, raising the visor on his helmet.

"Haven't a clue," said Melody.

"For someone who works in organised crime, you don't know much, do you?" he jibed.

"Why?" said Melody defensively.

"That pub and the bookies next door was run by Carnell," said Harvey. "I hope for someone's sake that it was an accident, but I doubt it somehow."

"Carnell?" asked Melody. "Bobby Bones?"

"Don't ever let him hear you call him that."

"Why is he called that?"

"The only people that ever called him Bobby Bones called him it once, then never called him anything ever again. Or anyone else for that matter."

"You ever run into him?" asked Melody.

"Once or twice. He doesn't know me, but yeah, I had a run-in with a few of his guys once, a long time ago. Apparently, he's a decent guy, but you only cross the line once."

"I didn't even know he had pubs. Last we heard of him his boys did a cash transit over, they went away, and he didn't even show up for court."

"Yeah, that was last you heard of him, but that doesn't mean he's been quiet. He's a lively one. John Cartwright pushed him out of East Ham and Plaistow, and he ventured further into town. I know he's got a few bookies under his wing too. I'd have money that the fire was a hit, and he's not the sort of guy to take it lying down."

"Who'd hit him?"

"No-one this side of the water. He's a madman," said Harvey. "Let's go. Best not be seen staring at the charred remains of Bobby Bones' pub."

Harvey started the bike.

"I thought you said not to call him that?" said Melody.

"I said for *you* not to let *him* hear *you* call him that," replied Harvey. "*I'll* call him what I like." Harvey gave Melody a little wink in the mirror, lowered his visor, and pulled away hard. He felt Melody's hands dig into his sides as she held on tight.

CHAPTER THREE

Harvey pulled into the headquarters and parked his bike in its spot beside the team's new VW van and the Audi saloon. He killed the engine, waited for Melody to climb off, then kicked the stand down, and climbed off himself, putting his helmet in the bike's backbox.

Reg wasn't at his computer and Jackson, the team's new driver and engineer, was nowhere to be seen.

"Up here," called Frank from the mezzanine floor that ran the length of the right-hand wall. The mezzanine was home to Frank's office, a meeting room that was never used, and a break room where the team could eat, which was used as a meeting room.

Harvey and Melody joined the rest of the team in the meeting room, and Melody poured a coffee from the pot before sitting down.

"We ready?" asked Frank.

"Sure," said Melody. "I suddenly feel like we're late. Did we forget something?"

"No," said Frank, "but there have been some developments that we need to discuss."

"Great, a new case," said Melody.

"I like your enthusiasm, Mills. However, I'm not so sure you'll be as enthused when you hear about this one," said Frank.

He turned and faced the room, looking serious. "Are we all familiar with the Albanian mob?"

"Not on a first-name basis, sir," said Reg. "But I'm pretty sure we all know what they're up to."

"What are they up to, Tenant?"

"Hookers, coke, and protection, isn't it, sir?"

"Right, illegal prostitution, selling drugs and extortion," said Frank. "We've known about them for a long while, but you know as well as I do that unless we hit the main man, making arrests isn't going to stop the problem. We're better off concentrating our efforts elsewhere, somewhere we can make a difference."

"So do we have enough on him, the main man now?" asked Melody. "Is that what this is about?"

"No, Melody, we don't, unfortunately."

"So why the change?"

"Well, every now and then, the types of gangs we're talking about, not just Albanians but home-grown gangs too, will feel the need to stretch their legs, push boundaries and remind the firm next door that they are around, usually in the form of a little turf war." Frank hit the space bar on his laptop, which was connected to a large TV. An image of a dead man with a knife in his eye came up on the screen.

"Ooh," said Reg. "He didn't see that coming."

"He probably did, Tenant," said Frank. "That's a nasty way to go."

Frank hit the right arrow on the laptop's keyboard. An image of a man with his ears removed from his head and screwed to his hands appeared.

"See no evil, hear no evil?" asked Reg.

"No, it's not some intelligent criminal mastermind playing

games and leaving clues," said Frank. "I almost wish it was." He closed the image on the screen and returned his attention to his team. "This is the work of the Albanian mob. The men you see here are members of local firms, wanted for petty crimes, and on the watch list of the drug squad who are waiting for the big one to put them away."

"They weren't watching very hard, were they?" said Reg.

"Do you know how many individuals are on the watch list of the drug squad?"

"Yeah, I get it, loads."

"So what's the point of all this then?" said Harvey. "Where are you going?"

"Ah, Stone, a timely introduction. I'll answer your question in just a minute. But first I want to show you another photo or two."

Frank opened a photo from his desktop. It showed a row of shops totally burnt out. An ambulance was on the scene, and uniformed policemen stood outside to stop the public entering.

"I'm guessing that wasn't caused by a cigarette?" said Jackson.

"You're right," said Frank. "It wasn't a cigarette. See these flats here, above the shops?" The team nodded. "Who do you think lived in these flats?"

"Albanians?"

"No, Tenant, wrong. Ordinary people lived in those flats. Two office workers, a single mum with two small babies, twins in fact. A young couple due to get married." Frank paused and took the time to connect with his team individually. "They all died. Seven bodies, two of them less than a year old."

The room was silent as they all took the news in.

"Sad, isn't it?" said Frank.

"Who started the fire, sir?" asked Melody.

"A local firm started the fire, Mills. Killed their own, if you want to put it that way. According to the fire report, the cab firm downstairs was doused in petrol, as were the cars outside that belonged to the cab firm, and of course the firm belonged to our friends, the Albanians."

"So it's the local boys against the Albanians, is it?"

"So who exactly are *we* going after?" asked Harvey.

Frank took a deep breath and let it out slowly and audibly. "Both. This will be a long operation. We don't have access to the right people yet. But when we do, we'll be taking down the local firm and the Albanians, no prejudice. It will be messy, and we will be working with other teams to accomplish this."

"Carnell?" asked Harvey.

Frank looked at Harvey with raised eyebrows, questioning his comment. "No, Harvey, actually it's not. Not according to the reports from the drug squad, anyway. But what makes you say that?"

"His pub and his bookies up the road got burned down last night. We saw it this morning."

"Interesting, but hopefully unrelated."

"Something tells me it's not as unrelated as you hope," said Harvey. "Who's the local firm you think started the fire?"

"We don't know who's running it, yet," said Frank. "But they're smart, and they're tooled up, judging by the mess they've been making of the Albanians. The war is getting out of hand. Our job is to stop it, to prevent more innocent people dying and put an end to the mindless violence that has grown from the occasional dead thug winding up in the street to where we are now, with daily occurrences of violence and bodies."

"What's your plan, sir?" asked Melody.

"Well, first of all, we need to know who's running the cab local firm. Would you agree with that, Stone?"

Harvey didn't reply. He didn't need to. Harvey had learned from his mentor, Julios, at an early age how to communicate without words. Gestures, expressions, stares. He often found them to be more powerful than words themselves and allowed him to continue with his stream of thoughts without breaking into conversation.

"Then," said Frank, "we need to get involved."

"Get involved, sir?" asked Reg.

"He means, go in undercover," said Harvey.

"What, all of us?" asked Reg.

"No, Reg," said Harvey. "Just me."

CHAPTER FOUR

"You'll have an implant. It's a chip inserted under your skin so we can see where you are at all times," said Frank.

"No wires," said Harvey. "Too risky."

"Agreed," said Frank. "But we'll schedule regular meetings. I want a full briefing every day, and I want to see a legend before you do anything."

"A legend?"

"A profile; your name, what you do for a living, where you were born. You need to commit these details to memory. You'll be infiltrating some serious players, and if they catch wind that you're not who you say you are, you'll be torn apart."

"Do we have an in?"

"I was hoping you'd be able-"

"You was hoping to use my criminal past to get in?" said Harvey. "You do realise this is a rival gang to the firm I worked with, and there's a good chance I've done jobs on them already? You don't even know who the boss is yet."

"Are you known to them?" asked Frank.

"Only by name. I doubt anyone would know what I look

like. I did a pretty good job of staying downwind. I wasn't a face."

"Any ideas on how we can get in?"

"Yeah, I've got an idea," said Harvey. "Bobby Bones."

"Carnell?" said Frank. "He's not involved."

"Yeah he is, you just don't know it," said Harvey. "Listen, someone burned down his pub last night. Now that someone either is seriously stupid or is prodding for a retaliation."

"So you're going to get in with Carnell?"

"Not *in* as such, but close enough to paint us a picture," said Harvey. "He's got another pub down the road, and if that one isn't burned down as well, I'll go for a pint. But there is one thing."

"What?"

"He's a bastard, Frank."

"Carnell?"

"Yeah, if it comes on top, I'm taking no chances. I'll be carrying, and I'll shoot my way out. If he realises I'm with the police in any way shape or form, he'll skin me alive."

"Is that why they call him Bobby Bones?" asked Reg.

"Why don't you ask him, Reg?" replied Harvey. "I hear he loves to sit down and tell people about where he got the nickname."

"Tell us a story, Harvey," said Reg. "Tell us about Bobby 'Bones' Carnell and how he got his name."

Harvey looked across at Frank who rested on the table at the head of the room and nodded.

"Well, Reg," began Harvey, "rumour has it that when Bobby was a lad, some boys were picking on him. So he waited until he got one alone, beat him up and cut the boy's finger off."

"That's not so bad, considering what we deal with here," said Reg.

"He was about ten years old, Reg," continued Harvey.

"Then, a few weeks later he got another one alone, and he did the same thing, and then again with the last one. None of the three boys talked. They all told their parents they had accidents. Not one person pointed at Bobby, excuse the pun." Harvey pushed off the wall he'd been leaning on and walked to the centre of the room. "Bobby was left alone after that until he hit mid-teens, and he got into an older crew, did some robberies and got caught. Oddly enough, the witness that was going to testify lost all her fingers."

"Her?" said Melody. "He cut off a *woman's* fingers?"

"Yeah, some woman suddenly forgot what she saw and didn't stand up. Carnell walked free. It wasn't until he'd matured into doing bank jobs and running protection rackets that his fetish really took hold though. A rival gang, I forget the name, with a couple of heavies, came onto his turf, did a few of his blokes over. Bobby had them tied up in the butcher shop next door to his local pub. He made his own men watch as he cut strips of flesh from their bodies while they were still alive. Just hanging lumps of meat. Then Bobby cut their fingers off and put them in his pocket like they were pens. Rumour has it Bobby has all the fingers hanging in his office."

"Is that why they call him Bones?" asked Jackson.

"No, mate. They call him bones because he cut the leg off the first man, and beat the second guy to death with his femur." Harvey paused. "The fingers are just his trademark. The man is a bastard."

"And you're going to go and have a pint with him?" asked Reg.

Harvey didn't reply.

CHAPTER FIVE

"Can they sew them back on?" said the rich, articulate, grumble over the phone's speaker.

"They can, boss, but his hearing will be badly affected," said Tony.

"At least he wouldn't look like a freak. Has he told you who did it yet?"

"No, boss. He's been in surgery all morning having his ears removed from his hands."

"For god's sake. Who found him? Have we got that covered?"

"That's the most astonishing part, boss," said Tony, "he drove himself to hospital."

"With his ears screwed to his hands?" came the reply. "How did he steer?"

"I have no idea. But I checked the Jag, it's pretty beat up, and Les is still missing, so is the gear. I sent Jake over to the field to see if Les is around."

"And the other hospitals?"

"Nothing," said Tony.

"Well, I'm pretty sure I know who it was. But before we make a move, I need to be sure. He'll survive right?"

"Jay? Yeah, he'll just be uglier and a bit mutton."

"Tony?"

"Boss?"

"Go see his missus, will you? Sort her out, keep her sweet."

"Yeah, she's on her way here now," replied Tony.

"Couple of grand should do it."

"I'll sort it, boss."

Tony disconnected the call and walked back to the ward where Jay was. He caught hold of a nurse's arm.

"Excuse me, miss." The large African lady looked down at his hand on her arm. Tony removed it. "Sorry, can I ask you something?"

"How can I help?"

"My friend here, Jay Carter," he began.

"Oh, him." The lady gave Tony a look of contempt. "What do you need?"

"I'm worried whoever did this to him might come back and have another go, know what I mean?"

"No, I don't know what you mean."

"Well, the blokes that did it were pretty nasty. I reckon they'll be back to finish the job. Can we get him a private room?"

"You think this is a hotel, sir?" began the nurse. "We have very limited resources here, and I'm sure some patients have much more-"

"How much?"

"Excuse me?" she hissed.

"How much do you want? In your skyrocket, here you are, here's a grand, straight in your bin." Tony winked and slipped the bundle of twenties in her apron pocket. "Mum is the word, eh? When can we move him?"

The nurse held his gaze. She put her fingers into her pocket, pulled out the folded wad of cash and pinned it to Tony's chest with a long, brown finger. "You cannot *buy* a room here. Your friend is *not* in any danger and he, like the other patients we have, will be treated in an equal manner."

"Nothing we can do then?"

"Nothing you can do," the nurse said staccato.

"How about a drink? What time do you knock off, Gladys?" said Tony, reading her name badge.

"Visiting time is over. Say goodbye to your friend."

She turned and left Tony standing in the ward beside an old man's bed. The old man sat up with the covers over his legs and a newspaper laid across his lap. He looked up at Tony and smiled. "Hard to get that one," he said. "Gives a mean bed bath though." The old man winked at Tony, who chuckled and tapped the end of the bed thoughtfully.

"Good luck to you, mate," said Tony. He walked back to Jay's bed, slipping the curtain closed behind him.

"Jay," he called. Jay didn't respond. "Jay?" Tony gave his friend a nudge in his leg. Jay's eyes opened, but he was still under the effects of the painkillers. "Jay, I've got to go," began Tony. "Time's up, mate."

"Eh?" shouted Jay. "You what?"

"Shh," said Tony with his finger on his lips. He acted out what he was saying while he repeated himself. "I," he said, pointing at himself, "have to go." He made his fingers walk then gestured to the door.

"You going?" shouted Jay.

"Shut up," said Tony. He stood and checked behind the curtain to make sure a nurse wasn't around, then pulled a Glock handgun from his waistband and held his finger up to his lips again. Then he gave Jay a mobile phone. It was a cheap Nokia burner with one number on speed dial, Tony's number. "Anything you need, just call." He gave Jay a serious nod, then stood and pulled the curtain back just as Carli, Jay's wife, was walking through the ward.

"How is he?" she asked with concern on her face.

Tony pulled the curtain closed behind him and stood in the ward with Carli. "Listen," he began, "it's pretty nasty. But don't worry, we're dealing with it."

"Don't worry?" Carli cried. "He had his-"

"Carli, easy, hear me out." Tony held his hands up and then pulled another wad of cash from his pocket. "He'll be off work for a few weeks. Take this, it's from the boss, and if you need more, just call me, okay?"

"I don't want your money, Tony."

"It's not my money, it's the boss'. Just take it. It'll keep you ticking over."

Carli snatched the money from Tony's hand and brushed past him. Tony made his exit before Jay began shouting again.

He stepped out into the car park, lit a cigarette, and stood looking at all the cars. No sign of company. Two uniformed policemen headed towards the hospital's main entrance. They walked past Tony.

"Evening gentlemen," he said to them.

"Evening," one of them responded.

Tony pulled his phone from his pocket and hit redial. "Alright, boss, it's me, I reckon we ought to put a couple of blokes on the hospital."

"Do you think that's necessary?"

"If they come back for him, he won't stand a chance."

"If they meant for him to die, they would have killed him."

"So what was the point in cutting his ears off then?"

"That, Tony, was a message from them to me."

"Are we sending a reply?"

"They found Les, Tone."

"What's the news, boss?" asked Tony.

"Old bill found him this morning." There was a pause. "Stabbed in the eye with his own knife."

"Jesus, boss," said Tony with a grimace.

"Yeah, well, we aren't going to sit on our arses crying, Tone. We're going to make a plan. Meet me in the Spread Eagle tomorrow lunchtime."

"You want me to go see Julie?"

"I went to see Julie myself. Les was an old mate. But thanks, Tone, yeah. Get some rest."

Tony strolled across to his Ford in the far corner of the car park. He liked to park it away from the other cars so it stood out, and he could see if anyone was waiting in the cars nearby. He hit the button on the key fob, and the indicators flashed in the dim, early evening light.

Tony flicked his cigarette butt and watched the glowing lit tip spin through the air then extinguish on the wet tarmac. He opened the door of the car, climbed in and pulled it closed behind him. So much had happened, and he knew things were going to get a lot worse before they got better. If he was right, and it was the Albanians that had pulled the stunt, then things were going to get very messy. He sighed and laid his head back on the headrest for a moment before putting the keys in the ignition, triggering the detonator on the explosive device connected to the ignition coil.

CHAPTER SIX

Harvey swirled the remains of his pint at the bottom of his glass. It was one of the things he was dreading about going undercover. Not the danger, he could handle himself. Not the risk of death, he was ready for that provided it was quick, and he took the bloke with him. It was drinking alcohol; he hated the feeling of not being in control. But he would deter the people he was aiming to cosy up to if he didn't drink. It would raise a few eyebrows. So Harvey sucked it up and ordered another pint.

He was sitting at the bar of the Pied Piper on the edge of Canning Town. An old bloke sat on the end of the bar. A group of underage or barely legal kids sat in a booth in the corner. Three blokes about Harvey's age stood at the bar six feet away. It wasn't a particularly nice pub or even a big pub. But it had a bar, and that was all the clientele required. The types of people that drank in there did not require mirrors, marble or make-up. The men drank beer or spirits, and the women drank wine. Anything out of the ordinary would draw unnecessary attention, and the Pied Piper was not a pub where you wanted to be noticed.

Harvey ordered his second pint and waited patiently. He

was playing the part of a bloke whose girlfriend lived nearby. If he was asked, he'd complain that she was driving him crazy, and he needed to get out for a pint. The guy behind the bar turned the TV on. It was a decent sized flat screen mounted to the corner of the room so it could be seen from anywhere in the pub. Harvey wasn't into football, but he watched the game anyway. The red team were winning, the blue team weren't. *Good match*, he thought.

Harvey remembered the eighties when the football riots had escalated. West Ham fans would chase Chelsea fans along Green Street. Policemen and horses would line the road outside the Boleyn. It had been enough to put Harvey off the sport for life. He watched the players roll around with barely a scrape and felt ashamed that they were grown men. It was like watching kids play.

One of the men beside Harvey cheered when the red team missed an opportunity. "What, you supporting Chelsea now, Doug?"

"No, Trev, but if United win, then West Ham will be relegated, but if Chelsea wins, we'll stay in, just."

"I often wonder if it wouldn't be better to just go down a league. At least then we'd win a few games next season," said the one called Trev.

Harvey didn't look at the men, he just watched the match.

"Who you going for?"

Harvey heard the man's question but ignored him.

"Oy, dopey, who you going for?" said Trev.

Harvey turned his head to look at the man.

"What, are you special or something, mate? I asked you a question."

Harvey didn't reply.

"Jesus, we got a live one here, boys," said Trev, putting his pint down on the bar.

"The blue team," said Harvey without looking away.

"Oh, it talks, does it?" said Trev, looking to his two friends to see if they were laughing. "The blue team, eh?"

"Leave off, Trev," said Doug. "The bloke is just having a quiet pint. He doesn't want you in his face."

"Well, looks like you're losing, pal," said Trev.

Harvey didn't reply. He turned back to the TV, lifted his glass and eyed the men as he took a large mouthful of the rancid beer.

The door opened, and two big men stepped in out of the cold. They wore old, scruffy, leather jackets, faded jeans and trainers. Harvey watched them in the reflections of the window as they stood at the bar on the other side of Harvey.

One of the newcomers ordered two Stellas in an Eastern European accent.

"Cheeky bastard," said Trev quietly to his two mates. "Who the bloody hell do they think they are?"

"They're just having a beer, Trev, calm down. What's the matter with you tonight?"

"What's the matter with me?" ranted Trev. "Did you hear him order the beer? Bloody Albanians. This lot burned down the boozer last night and then come strolling in here for a swift half. I want to ram it down their throats, Doug."

"Calm down, it probably weren't *them*."

"How do you know that?" said Trev. "How do you know these pricks haven't come in here to size the place up so they can burn it down later?"

"I *don't* know that, Trev," said Doug. "But it's the boss' place, and we'd do well not to smash it up and get the mob down here. The boss wants this place intact. He said he's got a plan for the Albies."

"Shouldn't let them in," said Trev.

"Another pint please, mate," said Harvey. He nodded to the barman.

"Same again?"

"Yeah, mate. Please."

"Ain't seen you around here before."

"That's because I've never been in here before," said Harvey.

"What's the occasion?" asked the barman.

"What are you, a copper?" said Harvey.

"No, mate, just making conversation," said the barman. "Take it easy, eh?"

"Yeah, sorry, mate," said Harvey, going into full undercover mode. "The bird is upstairs in the flat with the hump about something. I had too much to drink to drive home, so I came over here to get away from her. Is that allowed?"

"Yeah, mate, of course. We've all been there. Ain't that right, boys?" The barman gestured to the three men watching the match.

"Yeah," said Doug, disinterested, "join the club."

"Where are you from?" asked the barman.

"You ask a lot of questions."

"Just being friendly, pal," said the barman. He held out his hand. "I'm Lee," he said.

Harvey shook Lee's hand but said nothing.

"I didn't get your name, mate."

"No, you didn't, did you?" said Harvey. "Best we keep it that way."

"Suit yourself," said the barman.

Harvey raised his glass to his mouth just as the man beside him accidentally bumped his arm. Harvey spilt beer down his t-shirt. He froze and stared ahead of him over the bar. He felt the eyes of the Albanian bore into him. Testing him.

Doug, Trev and their mate all fell silent.

"Barman," said Harvey, "fat bloke here owes me a pint."

"I understand English," said the big man in a thick Eastern European accent.

"Good for you. So where's my pint?"

"Maybe you should learn how to hold your beer. Barman, get him half, maybe he will find it easier to hold." The man slapped a twenty-pound note on the bar. "Keep the change."

"Boys, boys, boys, no trouble in here tonight, please," said the barman. "Take your argument outside. Trevor, do the honours, will you?"

"Gladly," said Trev, putting his beer on the bar. He walked towards the door and held it open. A cold breeze blew in, and Harvey saw in the mirror behind the bar that it had started raining outside. "Right, tweedle-dee and tweedle-dumber, out."

Neither of the Albanian men moved.

Harvey remained motionless.

"Did you hear me?" said Trev. "We don't want your kind in here. Out." Trev stared the pair up and down and took a step towards them. They immediately dropped their glasses and turned to face Trev.

The man closest to Harvey pulled his massive arm back to throw a punch. Harvey watched in the mirror, then raised his own left arm. He hooked it into the crook of the man's arm and stamped down on the back of his knee. The Albanian buckled as Harvey dragged his weight back, smashing the back of his head on the hard wooden bar. He crumpled to the floor out cold.

The other man stood shocked, then squared up to face Harvey and Trev, expecting a blow from either man.

"You speak English?" asked Harvey calmly.

The man nodded. He knew he was outnumbered.

"Take your mate, and go," said Harvey. "Don't come back."

Trev held the door open again, and the big man dragged his friend into the rain.

"Nicely done, mate," said Trev. "What's your name?"

Harvey considered ignoring the question. He stared at the man who ten minutes before had been picking a fight with him. It had all been part of the plan. "Gerry."

"Nice to meet you, Gerry," said Trev, shaking Harvey's hand. "This is Doug and the quiet one there is Sid."

Harvey nodded at them in greeting.

"I'm surprised you didn't just lump them when he spilt your pint."

"Waiting for the moment, weren't I?" said Harvey. "I can't stand Albanians."

"You waited long enough," said Trev. "I thought it was going to kick off. How do you know they were Albanian?"

"BO and cheap leather jackets," replied Harvey.

"Fair enough. Can I get you a beer, Gerry?"

"Tell you what," said Harvey, "why don't we let tweedle-dee and tweedle-dumber get a round?" Harvey held up the twenty pounds the big Albanian had left behind and gave a half-grin.

CHAPTER SEVEN

Melody woke the next morning with a message on her phone from Harvey telling her that the Albanians had made contact and he'd sent a message back to them. He expected things to heat up any day, but he would stay away from headquarters until it's over.

She rolled out of bed and stretched. She looked back at her girlfriend who was still sleeping, then dressed in yoga pants and a hooded sweater to go for a run. She ran along the river and into the old docks. There were no cars to avoid, and the relative peace meant she could let her head mull over the case.

She felt slightly helpless. Harvey was in the thick of it as usual, but it would be impossible for Melody and Reg to have his back if he was holed up in some pub. They relied on effective comms from Harvey but so far, all they had was the SMS he'd sent her that morning.

What did that mean? What message had he sent to the Albanians?

Before Harvey had left headquarters, Frank had insisted on Melody inserting a chip under the skin on his neck, so they could always trace his whereabouts. He'd spent most of the night in the Pied Piper, and knowing that Harvey didn't drink, Melody guessed that he would have been steaming drunk by the time he'd left.

Harvey had taken a tumble off Tower Bridge six months previously wearing an explosive vest. He'd taken down known-terrorist Al Sayan, but the explosion and the thought of him dying had rocked Melody. She had cried more than she ever thought she would. It was then that she realised she had feelings for Harvey. It was hard not to. He was a good man at heart; his moral compass was tuned. He was also a man's man, as tough as they come. He was desirable in every way, except for his very obscured past. She'd been with Frank when they had found the boiled remains of Sergio, Harvey's sister's rapist, and she'd seen Harvey at work. He was ruthless, yet he was gentle when he'd pulled Melody's half-drowned body from the ocean. He was cold-hearted and unforgiving, yet warm when Denver, the team's old driver, had been killed. He'd held her. Now Harvey was putting himself in danger yet again, and it didn't seem to phase him. Perhaps he'd never had someone to care for him. Maybe if he knew she cared, he'd stop and think. But if Harvey knew how she felt, the whole team dynamic would be changed, and she might lose him forever.

She ran on, pushing herself hard through the biting cold. The best she could do was to be there for him when he needed. She could watch Harvey's little icon on Reg's tracking screen as often as she could to keep tabs on him and make sure she was never too far away to help if he needed it.

She showered, dressed in her cargo pants, boots and tank top beneath a clean hooded sweater, and left her girlfriend asleep. It was still only five am. Melody drove a little two-seater Mazda convertible. The roof stayed up most of the year.

Her phone rang as she pulled out of her apartment and she snatched it from her pocket in case it was Harvey. It was Frank.

"Sir?"

"Mills, good morning," said Frank.

"What's the plan?" asked Melody.

"Have you heard from Stone?"

"Yeah, he says he'll stay away until this blows over, doesn't want to blow his cover."

"Okay. Next time you talk to him, tell him I want a daily debrief, not via you."

"Yes, sir, I'll tell him."

"Good. I want you to get down to Romford. Queens Hospital," said Frank.

"What's there?"

"Car bomb, known suspect. Remember the ears?"

"How could I forget?"

"Well, this guy was visiting him. He left the hospital got into his car and well..."

"Okay, sir. What are your thoughts?"

"My thoughts, Mills? I think this is getting out of hand and we're closing the proverbial barn door."

"My sentiments exactly. It's going to take some mopping up, sir."

"I agree. Sadly we have Stone in the thick of it, and he's not likely to be diligently mopping anything up. Whatever it is he's doing, you can be sure he'll be making a mess."

CHAPTER EIGHT

Four big men banged their pint glasses on the bar of the Pied Piper. It was a lock-in, and the doors had been locked five hours ago. They cheered loudly, and fistfuls of money exchanged hands. Harvey connected his sweaty hand with his opponent's, and they began to arm wrestle.

Harvey's fist gripped Doug's. Each man tried hard to get his fingers on top. Their hands were sweaty and slick, their shoulders and arms ached from the previous rounds, and Harvey, the undisputed champion, stared into the eyes of his opponent. His face remained impassive, his mouth unsmiling. He pushed hard; each inch of progress was locked off with Harvey's tired bicep. Move an inch, lock it off, repeat. Doug strained and squirmed, his feet fought for grip as he tried in vain to find purchase and an advantage. Harvey took a deep breath, released it slowly through his gritted teeth, then slammed Doug's hand onto the bar.

There was a loud uproar, money exchanged hands again, Trev hooted loudly, and the three other spectators sank their drinks.

"No more," said Harvey. "Home time." He feigned a little

drunken balance issue and looked at each of the men with one of his eyes closed.

"You think she's still mad at you?" asked Trev.

"Who?" asked Harvey, then he remembered the lie he'd told about his girlfriend being upset about something. It was the reason for him being in the pub in the first place. "Whatever. Catch you around boys."

"See ya later, Gerry," called Trev.

Harvey walked in the direction of some council flats. He took turns down a rabbit warren of alleyways and roads to make sure he wasn't being followed and then found a small cab firm on the main road to Canning Town. He sat in the back of the car and directed the driver to the row of shops a hundred yards from his home, where he stripped, showered and fell into bed.

He wasn't drunk. He'd managed to stay sober by drinking as much water as he could from the tap in the Pied Piper's bathroom. Each time he finished a beer, he'd excuse himself and drink more water than he had beer. He was happy that he'd made a good impression. Taking the Albanian down had been a decent way to infiltrate the firm, and then the drinking time had helped. Usually getting into a firm would take months, but Harvey didn't have months. The quicker he could get through this undercover piece, the sooner he could get back to normal, whatever that was.

He fell asleep wondering what exactly normal meant to him. Harvey's life had been far from normal before he'd been brought into the team. But ever since, they'd stopped a ring of sex traffickers, prevented a terrorist attack on St Paul's and saved a priceless jade Buddha from being stolen. During which, he'd been shot at and blown up, drowned, and now, he even had a dog. How did any of that happen?

He woke with a start and saw the bright light through his windows. It took a few moments for him to remember what had happened, and why he'd slept so late. It was early afternoon. There were missed calls and messages from Melody on his phone. He dialled her number. The number was stored, but for Harvey, it was easier to dial from memory than it was to go through his contacts list.

"Harvey, what's going on?"

"You tell me. I just woke up."

"You sound sleepy. You do realise what time it is, don't you?"

"Yeah, it was a late one, made some good progress with the firm."

"New besties?"

"You're my bestie, Melody. Where are you?"

"I'm at Queens Hospital in Romford. Remember the guy with the ears?"

"Yeah."

"Well, he had a visitor, one of his firm, a guy called Tony. Someone planted a bomb in his car while he was visiting."

"Tony?" said Harvey. "Not Tony Hunt?"

"Yeah, that's him, or was him," Melody corrected herself. "Did you know him?"

"I knew *of* him. He was one of Thomson's blokes back in the day. What was the name of the bloke with the ears?"

"Jay Robins," replied Melody.

"And the guy with the eye?" asked Harvey.

"Les."

"Les Fitzpatrick?" asked Harvey.

"Yeah, that rings a bell, I think so."

"It's weird, the boys I met last night haven't said a word about anyone called Tony, Les, or Jay, and the only talk of Albanians were the two that walked into the pub. I would have thought that a car bombing in the firm would have got around like wildfire. Maybe Bobby is keeping the news on the down-low. But it *does* sound like the remnants of Thomson's old mob.

Maybe Bobby Bones moved in when I took Thomson down a couple of years ago. Where's their manor?"

"All over. Stratford, East Ham, Bow. There's a few bars and pubs, most of the bookies. Anything cash with heavy foot traffic and they're involved by the looks of things."

"Bobby had a keen eye for an opportunity," said Harvey. "Most of those blokes were loyal to the letter. Thomson had been running Stratford for years, but not East Ham, that used to be John's."

"Your old man?"

"My foster father."

"So Bobby cleaned up," said Melody. "He did well."

"Yeah, but has he got the clout to keep these Albanians out? I doubt it. Most of these younger lot coming up are sloppy and into drugs. The Albanians are professionals, born into the life."

"We need to meet," said Melody. "We'll need a plan to put a stop to all this. We'll have to do something soon, the media are all over it. There's a crew here now. They love it; it's like Christmas for them."

"Stay away from the cameras, Melody. The last thing I need is for you to be recognised."

"What are you saying? What does that matter?"

"Well, I might need an angry girlfriend to get me out of the pub."

"Oh, right. What have you told them?"

"My girlfriend is a psycho. That's my excuse for staying in the pub."

"Right. So I may need to storm in and walk you out by the ear?"

Harvey laughed. "No, Gerry wouldn't stand for that. But I might need a bird if you know what I mean."

"Class, Harvey," said Melody. "Who's Gerry?"

"He makes a special appearance every now and then, gets

drunk with the guys, smashes them at arm wrestling and shows them how to deal with a pair of Albanian troublemakers."

"I'm not sure I could date a guy called Gerry," said Melody.

Harvey heard the smirk on Melody's face. "Yeah, well, I'm not sure I could date a psycho bird who drives me to drink."

"Touché."

"How's Frank?"

"Mad that you're not debriefing him."

"Good."

"What do you mean good?" said Melody. "Please call him after this call. He just moans at me when you don't give him a debrief."

Harvey laughed again. "Yeah that Gerry is a right bastard."

"Keep me posted," said Melody.

Harvey disconnected the call.

CHAPTER NINE

It was early evening when Harvey stepped back into the Pied Piper. The pub was busier. The same old man stood at the end of the bar, the same kids sat in the booth, but there were a few additions. The TV was off, and the jukebox was on, loudly playing the type of music that Harvey heard, but wouldn't remember two minutes later. Two women and two men stood at the bar laughing and joking. It clearly wasn't their first or last glass of wine that night.

At the end of the bar stood Doug, Trev, Sid, and the three other men who had joined them for the lock-in the previous night.

"He's back for more. What d'ya say there, Gerry, can I get you a pint, mate?" said Trev.

"Yeah sure. Thanks, Trev," replied Harvey.

"We were just talking about those two Albanians. Sid reckons they'll be back with their mates. What do you think, Gerry?"

"Wasn't it Albanians that burnt down the pub up the road?" asked Harvey.

"Yeah, we think so," said Doug. "How do you know about that?"

"Just some bloke at work, lives nearby and doesn't shut up, likes the sound of his own voice, know what I mean?"

"Yeah, well, best to keep that kind of info under your hat, Gerry. That was the boss' favourite pub, and he's not happy about it. They've burned down two of his pubs and three of his bookies in the past two weeks."

Harvey acted surprised. "What the hell? Why? I mean, if I can ask, I don't want to overstep."

"It's okay, Gerry. Keep it to yourself though, will you? It's going to kick off. The boss doesn't take this kind of stuff laying down."

"Yeah, no worries. We should get a bunch of blokes together and torch the bastards one by one."

Doug chuckled. "Well, that's not too far from the plan. Anyway, cheers." Doug raised his glass and Harvey chinked his own against the side of it.

Trev came back into the pub holding his phone. He walked directly to Doug. "Boss just called. He's on his way and said we need to clear this place. He's arranged something."

"Clear the pub?" said Doug. "What for? Any idea?"

"No, mate. Get Lee to turn the jukebox off, and I'll get everyone out."

Doug leaned across the bar. "Lee?"

Lee looked along the bar. "What's up? I'm serving."

"Well stop serving and kill the music," said Doug.

The music was cut shortly after, and Trev shouted over the moans and complaints. "Listen, I've been asked to clear the pub. So drink up, you all need to be gone in five minutes."

More complaints, tuts and dirty looks were aimed at Trev as he rejoined the group of men.

"You always have that effect on people, Trev?" asked Harvey, falling further into the character of Gerry.

Trev chuckled. "Yeah, although at least this time I didn't get a pint glass lobbed at me." He turned back to the crowd. "Four minutes, people."

Harvey began to finish his pint. "Have I got time for a quick shot? I'll neck it and be gone."

"Mate, relax, you can stay. You're with us. Get a pint, get me one too while you're at it," said Doug.

Harvey raised two fingers at Lee the barman in a peace sign. People began to filter out, and soon only the men were left in the quiet bar.

"They really listened to you this time, Trev. Amazing," said Sid.

Doug leaned towards Harvey. "Last time he did it a couple of geezers refused to budge, so Trev had to get all Jackie Chan on them."

"I didn't get Jackie Chan on no-one, Doug. It was more Chuck Norris." Trev performed a poor impression of Chuck Norris preparing to fight.

"Oy," said Sid. He raised his finger at Trev and looked him square in the eye. "One does not impersonate Chuck Norris. The man is a legend."

Trev laughed. "Yeah, apparently, when Chuck Norris goes to Rome, they do what he does."

"Apparently Chuck Norris can lick both his elbows at the same time," said one of the men.

"I heard Chuck Norris doesn't cheat death, he wins fair and square," said Doug.

The group were in high spirits considering the boss was coming, who Harvey presumed to be Bobby 'Bones' Carnell. True to Harvey's thoughts, the laughter stopped when the lights of three cars pulled into the pub car park and shone through the opaque glass in the door.

Doug leaned into Harvey again. "Do yourself a favour and just keep quiet. He's a nice guy, but he won't like hearing from you before an introduction."

"Yeah, no worries. I can leave if you want," said Harvey.

"No mate, stay, drink." Doug smiled and winked.

The doors of the pub opened and two men stepped inside, nodded to the group of men and held the door for Bobby Carnell to enter the room. He looked the typical East End gangster with a long Kashmir coat, thick horn-rim glasses and immaculate shoes. He walked to the bar where a scotch and soda waited for him. The two men that accompanied him stood beside him talking. Harvey noticed the word bones spelt out on the back of his hand in faded tattoo ink.

More cars pulled into the car park, and more men entered the pub who Doug seemed to know. He nodded at them. Then the man beside Bobby Bones caught Doug's attention and gestured to the doors. Doug tapped Trev with his foot. "Go and bolt the doors will you, Trev."

Trev nodded and disappeared into the throng.

"Quiet," somebody called. The room fell silent, and all eyes fell on Bobby 'Bones' Carnell.

"Thanks, everyone for coming," began Bobby. "I know you're all busy. I know Christmas is coming, and most of you have families to look after, so I'll be straight to the point." He sipped at his scotch. " In case some of you don't know my story, when I was a little boy, three bigger boys tried to bully me." He left a pause for the image to take hold in the minds of his men. "I waited patiently." Bobby's voice was gravelly, rough and very cockney. "Until one day, a few weeks later, I found one of those boys on his own. I gave the kid a hiding, and then some, and then I cut his finger off and stamped on his head one last time for good measure. Over the following months, I caught up with all three of them. They all got the same treatment, no favours, no matter how hard the last one pleaded. They all got the same hiding. And they all lost a finger. I've still got them in a jar as a reminder never to let anyone fuck me over." He took another sip of his drink and put the glass down. There was a fresh one waiting for him.

"Right now, gentlemen, I see the need to remind a few people not to fuck me over again, and I'll be honest, I need your help to do it." He stared around at all the men. His eyes settled on Harvey's for longer than necessary. Harvey stared back. Bobby moved on.

"Outside there are two vans and all the tools we need. We're leaving in two minutes. Drink up. We'll be back for supper."

"Tenant, where's Stone?" asked Frank as he walked down the headquarter's mezzanine stairs from his office. He stopped at Reg's command centre, which comprised twelve twenty-four inch screens mounted on the wall in three rows of four, and a super-computer Reg had named LUCY. It monitored the whereabouts of any GPS enabled device, which was typically phones that belonged to suspects, victims and the team, and tracking chips, one of which was inserted under Harvey's skin. There was another in his phone, in his watch, in his jacket, and on his motorbike.

"He left the Pied Piper five minutes ago, sir. I'm watching him now." Reg pointed up at the left-hand screen in the centre row. "He's not using his bike though, so I can only assume he's with a target."

"Mills," called Frank across the headquarters open space.

"Sir?"

"Has Stone contacted you in the past hour?"

"Negative, sir. I sent him a message but no response as yet."

"You told him to call in as I asked?"

"Yes, sir. He said he would."

"Get yourself ready," said Frank. "Jackson?"

"Sir?" Jackson was laying under the team's VW Transporter van, which served as a mobile operations unit. "Get cleaned up, you're heading out. Tenant, you too."

"Remember," called Frank over the noise of Jackson's tools being wiped and put away and Melody's cabinets being slammed shut, "we're observing only. We're not taking anyone down. But we are keeping an eye on our own. If Stone doesn't want to report in, we'll have to find our own information."

Melody dropped three large Peli-cases into the back of the van. One contained Steiner binoculars and a sighting scope. One contained night-vision goggles, and the other contained her prized Diemaco rifle. The Diemaco was Melody's favourite of the rifles they kept in the armoury and was her go-to weapon for long-distance.

Reg fired up the two computers in the back of the van and took his place at his bench, which ran the full length of the van's cargo area. Two screens sat atop the bench, and the rear windows were fully blacked out.

"We set?" asked Melody.

"Good to go," confirmed Reg.

Jackson fired up the engine and closed the driver's door. The computers in the back of the van gave Reg access over SSL VPN to LUCY, which meant he could control the headquarters doors, as well as the telephones, heating, and lighting. He hit the shortcut for the doors, and the motor above the concertina shutter jumped into life. The doors dragged across and Jackson reversed out.

"Where are we heading, Reg?" asked Jackson.

"They're at Old Street now. You know the way?"

"Yeah, lived here all my life, Reg. Just keep me posted if their position changes."

"Where exactly are you from, Jackson?" asked Melody.

"Me? I moved around a bit. Grew up in Essex, moved to East London, then out to Kent when my old man died. Landed a job at the local track and started driving."

"So how did you wind up on the force?"

"My old man was a copper. Mum always pushed me towards it, but I wanted to drive. So I guess it's a bit of both. Decent pension and I would say the hours are great but anything deeper than the Met, and the hours are messed up. I did a bit for SO-10, crazy hours. That's where I met Frank, and Denver too actually. He was a nice guy."

"You knew Denver?" asked Reg.

"Yeah, worked with him a few times on a few busts. Top bloke."

"Yeah, he was," said Melody.

"One thing I can't seem to work out though," said Jackson, "who do we work for? It's not SO-10 as far as I can tell, and it's obviously not SO19."

"We're unofficial. We're supposed to get status soon, but for the time being, all credit goes to SO-10. We're an unofficial arm."

"Expendable?"

"Yeah, in short. As long as we keep performing, we'll be made official. But it's slow going."

"Stone has joined the A1 towards Highbury," said Reg from behind.

"Highbury? Jesus. What is he mixed up in?"

"What's our ETA?"

"I'd say we're twenty-five minutes out," said Jackson. "What's he like?"

"Who? Harvey?"

"Yeah, bit wild from what I gather."

"Wild?" said Reg. "He's the nicest lunatic I know."

"Lunatic?"

"No, he's not," said Melody. "He's a nice guy. He just had a different upbringing and has a particular skill set that complements the rest of us."

"So, he's the one with dirty hands then?"

"You could put it like that."

"Is it me, or has he just got this stare going on? Like you ask him a question, he doesn't reply, but he doesn't need to. It's crazy."

"Powerful, isn't it?" said Melody.

"What about Frank?"

"Best boss I've had," said Melody.

"Yeah, he's okay, he's fair. He's good at letting us do what we need to do. I like that," said Reg. "Okay, the friendly chat is over. Harvey has stopped in a side street in Highbury. He's moving towards what looks to be a pub. Is this whole case going to revolve around pubs?"

"Whereabouts?" asked Jackson.

"Off Highbury Road, the Jumping Jack."

Jackson put his foot down and overtook the car in front. "ETA, ten minutes."

Melody checked her SIG and unboxed the binos. "Reg, find us somewhere to hole up. I've got an idea he isn't visiting old friends, and I need to get the suspects on camera." She held on as Jackson slid the van around a long corner.

"I've got it, there's a supermarket opposite. We can park up in the car park and get a decent view," said Reg. "What do you think is going to happen, Melody?"

"Well, he's with some pretty bad men, who just had their pub burned down, so I'd say it's not a housewarming party."

Fifteen men sat quietly in the two vans outside the Jumping Jack, each of them armed with a mixture of bats, short poles, machetes and knives. Harvey was in the first van. Nobody spoke. Each man was psyching himself up for what was about to happen. The man in the passenger seat, who had been stood next to Bobby Bones in the pub, turned in his seat and spoke quietly but firmly. "Trev, Doug, go in and make sure they're there. Order a pint and send me a text."

The remaining men waited a long two minutes before the text came through. He read the message aloud. "There's about thirty of them, but we'll catch them off guard. Turn right through the doors." The man looked around at the men sat in the back of the van. Most were staring at the floor or the ceiling, breathing hard, tensing up. Harvey stared back at the man, "In and out boys, the van is leaving in two minutes." He paused grinning. "Ready? Go, go, go."

The rear doors of the van opened, and the men filed out. Harvey stood fourth in line. The only two blokes he knew were already in there. Harvey had taken a bat from the pile of tools on the floor of the van. He carried his SIG and always had his knife on him. But he didn't want to stand out, so he chose the bat.

The first two men walked through the doors and held them open, leaving Harvey in number two position. He stepped through onto the typical worn, red pub carpet. His eyes hit the mirror above the bar, and he saw a group of big men behind the door to his right.

Harvey stepped around the door and swung at the first man. The table erupted as the Albanians stood up, and more of Bobby's firm appeared from behind Harvey in a chaos of swinging bats and blades. Harvey turned his attention to the far corner where more Albanians had risen and were making their way through the crowd, edging away from the fracas. A woman screamed and ran for the far doors, but a surge of large Albanian men forced her backwards.

Leaving the first fight, Harvey met the oncoming group head-on. He took the first down with a downward swing of the bat, then jabbed the second one with the butt of the handle. He heard a bottle being smashed and caught the movement in the corner of his eye; he ducked back, and the broken glass shot past his face. Harvey dropped down and shattered the man's knees. Another man kicked the bat from his hands, so Harvey instinctively drew his knife, stood up close to the man and drove the blade into his neck. A headbutt finished him off, and the man fell to the floor.

Harvey span and saw the doors opening; Bobby's men were leaving. The two minutes were up. But two more Albanians stood in Harvey's way. They were the last two men remaining. Doug held the door open. "Gerry, go, now."

Harvey stepped forward, blocked a wild punch and drove his knife into the first guy's throat. He pulled it out with a sucking sound as the second man swung for Harvey's face. Harvey dodged back quickly then lunged forwards, sinking the blade into the man's chest. He walked past the dying man and ripped the knife out, letting the Albanian drop to the floor behind him.

Another wounded Albanian rolled around on the carpet beside the front door. His arm was broken, and his nose had burst across his face. Harvey picked up the man's foot and dragged him outside.

"Cheers, Doug," said Harvey as he stepped outside, letting the man's head bounce on the hard pavement. He dragged him to the van, ignoring his moans and outbursts in a language Harvey didn't understand.

Harvey saw the familiar shape of a VW Transporter a hundred yards away in the car park of the supermarket. He could just make out the passenger door opening and a leg stepping down.

"Someone, give me a lift up with this, will you?"

"Who's that?" someone asked.

"I don't know, do I? I didn't stop to ask his name," said Harvey.

"We don't bloody want him in here."

"Yes, we do," said Dom from the passenger seat. "The boss will love that, nice work. Get him inside and let's fuck off before the old bill turns up."

"Go, we're in," said Harvey once he'd pulled the doors closed. He sat with his feet on the Albanian's back and removed his knife from its sheath to clean it on a rag from the van floor.

"Holy shit, Gerry," said Doug. "Think we found us a new man, Dom."

The man in the passenger seat turned around. "Is that right?"

"Did you see that in there?" said Doug. "He stabbed some geezer in the throat, then without blinking turned and stabbed his mate in the chest." Doug whooped. "It was legendary."

"Did we lose anyone?" asked Harvey, ignoring the remarks.

"Yeah, two fellas down. They're in the back of the other van."

"Serious?"

"One had his face slashed, the other is unconscious," said Dom. "Why do you ask?"

"Just checking the odds. Thirty against fifteen, none of them are standing, and thirteen of us are. Plus, we got a prisoner." Harvey leaned into the corner of the van. "Pretty successful."

"Yeah, well, it'll be successful in a minute when the whole place goes up."

"What do you mean, Dom?" asked Doug.

"While we were in there doing the renovating, Charlie here made a few gas alterations. Didn't you, Charlie?" Dom turned to face the rear of the van and smiled in the darkness.

"I'd give it two minutes max. As soon as someone lights their next fag, it'll be game over," said Charlie. He was older than the rest of the men, smoked roll-ups and had a hard, weathered face.

Harvey hadn't known about the fire. He needed to text Melody in case she went inside, but couldn't risk it, being so close to the other guys in the van. He was shoulder to shoulder with the man next to him, who would easily see what Harvey was typing.

The van pulled to the side of the road and stopped. "Sit tight, lads," said the driver. "Let's wait for the fireworks."

The second van pulled up alongside the first, and all the men stared out the rear windows.

Nothing happened.

A car drove past the two vans heading towards the pub, and from the supermarket car park came the dark square shape of the VW. It stopped and waited for the car to pass, then moved on again. It had just passed the pub when the gas ignited.

"There he is," said Melody. "I'd know that swagger anywhere. What's he doing?" Melody opened the door and stepped down to get a clearer view.

"He's dragging someone behind him," said Reg.

"He's looking right at us," said Jackson. "He is a lunatic. If the Albanians come back out of that pub, he is toast."

"He's okay. Just hang back, give him some space and let him do his thing."

"They were only in there a couple of minutes. What do you think happened?" asked Jackson.

"Judging by the people that ran out, I'd say it kicked off pretty well, and by the looks of Harvey, the local firm came out on top," said Reg.

"That won't be the end of it." Said Melody. "Follow that second van, Jackson. If those injured locals are going to be in the hospital for a while, it'd be a good place to catch up with them, get some answers. Let's go, Jackson, nice and slow."

Jackson pulled away, keeping the lights off until the vans were out of sight. They drove out of the car park and onto the road beside the pub.

"Don't stop here, keep going," said Melody, just as the pub windows blew out, causing the van to rock to one side. "Go, go, go." Flames licked the roof of the van, shattered glass rained on the bodywork, and Reg's blacked-out windows lit up as they pulled out of the blast just in time.

Jackson floored the van and accelerated to the end of the road.

"What the hell was that?" said Reg.

"What way did they go?" asked Jackson.

"Harvey turned right according to LUCY."

They heard the sound of sirens in the distance. "Okay, let's ease up, get our bearings."

"I was not expecting that," said Jackson.

"You get to expect the unexpected when Harvey is involved," said Melody, grinning slightly.

"You find that funny?" said Jackson. "I swear my eyebrows singed through the glass."

Melody laughed. "Relax, they just answered our questions."

"What questions?"

"Are we onto the right firm and will there be a retaliation?"

"A retaliation? The Albanians won't take this lying down. If there wasn't a war already, there is definitely one now."

"Good, we'll catch them faster," said Melody.

"And what if more people die?"

"Nobody wants that, Jackson."

"What about if Harvey is killed?"

"Don't talk like that."

"It's a possibility, Melody, not a wish."

"Harvey can take care of himself. Anyway, the question isn't about Harvey getting killed, it's about stopping innocent people dying as a result of the violence. Why the interest in Harvey?"

"There's no interest, Melody. I'm just being the caring team member."

"Well, how about we let Harvey do what he's good at, and we do our jobs and find him."

"Looks like they're heading back to East Ham," said Reg from the rear.

"Cheers, Reg," said Jackson. "Listen, Melody, I'm sorry. I shouldn't have overstepped the mark. I-"

"You didn't overstep the mark, Jackson. We're all a bit sensitive right now. We lost a good man a while back."

"Yeah, I get that. No hard feelings?"

"Whatever," said Melody. "Don't think too much on it."

"There's a great bagel shop near here, my treat."

"Ah," said Reg, "you've struck gold there, Jackson. Even Melody can't refuse a salt beef bagel."

Melody turned and smiled at Reg, then at Jackson. "Okay, but no more talk of-"

"Scout's honour," said Jackson, holding up his fingers in a scout salute.

"What about Harvey and his white van men?"

"Keep an eye on his location. We can't do much more than that. Besides," said Melody, "what's he going to do, torture the man? It's not the dark ages."

CHAPTER THIRTEEN

The Albanian hung by his bound wrists from a meat hook, swinging beside cow legs in the rear of Dave the Butcher's shop. He'd been stripped naked, and the breaks in his arms were visible against his skin; his body weight was pulling the break further apart, and the man's face was wrought with agony.

Dom, Doug and Harvey stood beside him.

"What a fat piece of crap," said Doug. "What're we going to do with him?"

Harvey was silent.

"We'll save him for the boss," said Dom. "He'll love this."

"Should I go, or what?" said Harvey.

"Go? Why go?" said Dom. "The boss will be over the bloody moon, mate. You just got yourself a job. No, Gerry, you're staying, mate."

A car door slammed a dull thud in the distance and footsteps approached. Harvey heard the door creak open but his eyes remained on the Albanian.

"Well, well, well," said Bobby 'Bones' Carnell. "What do we have here?"

"He hasn't said anything yet, Bobby," said Dom. "We thought we'd let you have the first go on him."

"First go, eh?" said Bobby. "Whose idea was it to bring him back here?"

The three were silent, then Dom spoke up. "Gerry here dragged him out the pub. I brought him here. Was that wrong, Bobby?"

"Wrong? Why would that be wrong? What we have here is a little talking parrot, and boy, are we going to make him sing. Right, where are the tools?"

"What do you need, Bobby?" asked Doug.

"Pliers," said Bobby, "to start with. Actually, no, scrub that, Doug." Bobby turned to Harvey. "Gerry, isn't it?"

Harvey didn't reply. He just leaned on the wall with his arms folded.

"Dom tells me you're a bit of a hard nut."

"You should have seen him in there, Bobby," said Doug.

"Anyone can take a few men down, Doug. You just need big balls. Have you got big balls, Gerry?"

Harvey didn't reply.

"Tell you what, Gerry, why don't you get this fat waste of skin to tell us who and where his boss is?" He paused to look at Harvey's reaction. "Reckon you can do that? Let's see what you're made of."

Harvey pushed off the wall and walked towards the Albanian, whose eyes opened wide when he looked at Harvey's expression. Harvey stood in front of him. He blocked out Dom, Doug and Bobby Bones. It was just Harvey and the Albanian in the huge slaughterhouse.

"Do you have a name?" asked Harvey in a dull, flat tone.

The man eyed him. Beads of sweat had begun to form on his temple.

"One more time, and then I'll get to work," said Harvey. "Name."

Harvey walked behind the man. There were scars across his back, long, deep, and thick, like he'd been whipped a long time ago. His right calf featured the flat white scar of a deep burn. Harvey had seen scars like that before. It was the type of scar that gave a sense of empathetical pain just by looking at the twisted and melted flesh.

The man rattled off a long garbled sentence in Albanian, and then said, "Aleksander."

"Aleksander? You look like an Aleksander." Harvey turned to Dom. "Do we have any wood?"

"Wood? What do you want wood for?"

"An old pallet or something. Can I get some wood, please?"

Dom followed the chain of command and turned to Doug, who left the room.

"You understand English, Aleksander?"

Aleksander didn't reply.

Harvey completed his tour of the Albanian and returned to stand in front of him. "English, Aleksander?"

Aleksander nodded. His angry eyes had softened, giving a window of weakness for Harvey to reach into.

Harvey hated every minute of the charade. It wasn't the first time he'd tortured somebody. But in the past, his victims had deserved every second of the ordeal. Aleksander was just a villain, same as Dom and Doug. Harvey didn't care if Aleksander lived or died, or any of them. He didn't care if the man spoke or not, but he had to make the man talk. This was an opportunity for Gerry to impress Bobby Bones. Getting Aleksander to inform on his boss would ingratiate Gerry into the boss' good books and then maybe he could put a stop to everything and get back to the team.

Harvey thought about how he missed his team. He'd never done that before.

"Are your family here, Aleksander? In London?"

Aleksander shook his head. "No."

"Are they in Albania?"

He nodded. "Yes, Albania, yes."

"And are you sending them money?"

He nodded again. "Yes, my mother and my sister."

"And your father?"

"He is dead," spat Aleksander. "He is traitor."

"So if you stop sending money home, what will happen to your mother and your sister?"

Aleksander didn't reply.

Doug came back into the room dragging two heavy wooden pallets. He let them fall to the floor.

"Can you break them up, please, Doug?" said Harvey. "I'm going to get a little campfire going to keep Aleksander warm."

Aleksander's eyes widened again.

"Do you like fire, Aleksander?"

Aleksander shivered with fear, and sweat began to run from his bald head down his unshaven face.

"You've been burned before, haven't you?" asked Harvey. "I saw the scar. Who did that?"

Aleksander didn't reply.

"Looks nasty." Harvey gauged the big man to be in his early forties. "Kosovo, right?"

Aleksander's eyes darted to Harvey's.

"I'm right, aren't I?"

"I saw the whip marks on your back too. You're a bad man, Aleksander, aren't you?"

"Fuck you."

Doug had smashed one of the pallets into firewood and stood back to watch the show. Bobby and Dom were enthralled by Harvey's calm composure, and the effect he was having on Aleksander.

"The thing is," began Harvey, as he bent down to pick up a few pieces of wood, "the Serbs weren't really organised enough, were they?" Harvey bent and began to arrange the wood. "I mean, they certainly weren't organised enough to capture one of the Albanian army and torture him unless, of course, you were a high-ranking officer. But if you don't mind me saying, Aleksander, you haven't really got officer qualities, have you?"

"You know nothing," said Aleksander.

"No, those wounds on your back weren't done by the Serbs, were they?" said Harvey, ignoring the comment. Harvey had learned over the years that momentum, building up tension and leaning on sore points was the key to getting somebody to talk. Harvey hadn't been trained to evoke information from a captive, he'd taught himself. Some men broke easily and disappointed Harvey. It may have taken weeks for Harvey to practise his mantra of patience, planning and execution, only to eventually capture the sex offender he'd been targeting and have him confess within a few minutes. Harvey preferred the chase. He found that the longer the tension built up, the more information could be sought. The deeper the confession.

"The Serbs weren't known for that type of thing, Aleksander, they were fighting a war. But the Albanians? Well, you guys have always been partial to a bit of violence, right? But why would the Albanians do something like this to their own? Unless, of course, you were absconding?" Harvey looked Aleksander in the eye. "Is that it, Aleksander? Did you run away like a frightened little boy?" Harvey let the man absorb his words before he spoke again. "You were captured by your own, weren't you? Big men capturing a frightened little boy."

Harvey stepped to the side of the room where a large roll of tissue paper stood on its end beside a sink, presumably for the butcher to dry his hands after he'd washed them. He pulled off a long stream of paper and rolled it into a ball.

"They hurt you, didn't they?" asked Harvey. "They hurt you so badly, you hate them now." Harvey bent to stuff the paper beneath the pile of wood, which lay beneath Aleksander's feet.

"In fact, you've never been back, have you?" Harvey stood. "I don't think you've seen your mother or your sister in all this time." Harvey paused to read Alexander's pained expression. "I'm right, aren't I? They're trapped there because you ran away, and you're stuck here because you're a coward." Harvey found a box of matches on the tiled window ledge. He opened the box and stopped, poised to strike the match.

"Tell me, Aleksander, are you going to be a coward now, or are you going to face your fears?"

"I will tell you nothing," spat the Albanian.

"You're shaking, Aleksander," said Harvey slowly and coldly. "That's the fear. When did you last shake like this? Was it when you ran away from the battle? Or was it when you ran away from your captors?"

Harvey struck the match.

I long thin stream of urine came involuntarily from Aleksander.

"There it is," said Harvey. "No-one can stop fear when it bites." Harvey held the match up in front of Aleksander. "There are just two things we need to know, and then all of this can stop, Aleksander."

Aleksander's eyes were squinted, his lip had begun to tremble, and he hung his head as far back as he could.

"Who's your boss?" said Harvey. The match burned out, and he dropped it to the floor. "It's okay, we have a full box."

"Stop," said Aleksander. His voice had risen an octave, and the fear had shaken his rough tone.

"No, Aleksander, I will not stop."

Harvey struck another match.

"Who's your boss?"

"Ah," gasped Aleksander.

"Don't cry, little boy. I know you're frightened, but tell me, and then all of this will be over."

"No."

"Aleksander, I won't waste this match."

"Luan."

"Ah, Luan. There we go." Harvey blew on the match, and the flame extinguished, leaving only smoke. Harvey dropped the match to the floor and pulled a fresh one out.

"Last name, Aleksander." Harvey sat the tip of the match on the paper.

Aleksander's head rolled forward, and tears fell from his fat face.

"Are those tears of shame, Aleksander?" asked Harvey. "No need for shame, you're just following your path and your daddy's path. He was a traitor too, wasn't he?"

Harvey lit the third match.

"Last name. Last chance."

Aleksander didn't reply.

Harvey waved the flame under Aleksander's face. The man's head sat bolt upright.

"I said, the last name?"

"Duri," said Aleksander quietly, and dejected.

Harvey puffed the match out and dropped it to the tiled floor. He pulled another one from the box and sat the tip on the striking paper again.

"Okay, last question," said Harvey. "Where do we find him?"

Aleksander didn't respond.

"So now you have two options, Aleksander. Option one." Harvey made sure he caught Aleksander's eye. "You tell me where I can find him, and you die a quick, clean death. There's honour in there, somewhere."

Aleksander didn't respond.

"Option two, and I don't like this one myself, Aleksander, but if you don't tell me where I can find him, I'll burn you alive." Harvey held his finger up. "And not only will I burn *you* alive, but I'll carry on looking, and when I do find Luan Duri, I'll make sure he knows that you informed, and I'll make sure your mother and your sister are punished back in whatever mud hole they live in."

Harvey moved closer and whispered to Aleksander. "How does that sound?"

CHAPTER FOURTEEN

"We seem to have a problem here, and I want solutions."

"They came out of nowhere, boss," said Ginger. "Too many for us to take on."

"Too many for you to take on? What are you, mice?"

"No, boss, Trig and me only just got away. They just burst into the club and pulled out knives and bats."

"And how many didn't get away?"

"Seven, boss."

"You left seven blokes to die? In my club? How would you like it if I left you to die? Maybe that's what I need to do?"

"This is out of control. They're going to slaughter us all," said Ginger. "They caught us off guard last night. They could hit somewhere else tonight. It's crazy. It's like they thought we deserved it. One of them actually said it was payback."

"Payback for what, Ginger? Why the sudden violence? I've been in this game my entire life, and believe me, it was nasty back in the eighties, but this is ridiculous. Where are the bloody police?"

"It's a retaliation, boss."

"A retaliation? Last thing I heard they killed Les, cut Jay's ears off, stole four kilos of coke, and blew up Tony. We haven't had time to retaliate ourselves yet."

"It's Bones, boss. Bobby Bones."

"Bobby Bones? What's he got to do with all this?"

"The Albanians hit his pub in Canning Town, burned it to the ground, his bookies as well."

"The one next door?"

"Yeah, the whole building was gutted."

"So what?"

"So Bones hit back, boss."

"He did what?"

"He retaliated. It was a bad one. One of our boys knows one of his boys, and well, cut a long story short, boss, Bones arranged for two van loads of blokes, all tooled up, to go in hard. Killed about twenty of them and then torched the gaff. A few got away with injuries and severe burns, and one is missing."

"Bones has him?"

"I think so, boss," said Ginger. "We reckon Bones has him tied up somewhere looking for answers. He's sick like that."

"Right, two things. Listen carefully."

"What's that, boss?"

"Tell me where I can find Bobby Carnell. We need to have a little chat. If he's going in hard, then we'll go in hard too. Make it public. In his pub is fine, he won't hit me there, not now. He needs me."

"What then, boss?"

"Well, once Bobby Bones and I have sorted out the Albanians, you and I will need to sort out Bobby Bones. He's cost me a lot of money so far, what with the missing coke and killing my men. I am *not* going to let him get away with it. Rule number one, Ginger, make sure everyone knows who's in charge."

"Seven dead bodies?" said Frank. "Where's Stone? Tell me he wasn't one of them."

"No, sir," said Mills. "No word from Harvey. His phone is off."

"Where is he, Tenant?"

"He's at home by the looks of things," said Reg. "Tracker says he rolled in at four am."

"Is he making progress, Mills?"

"He's inside, that's all we know."

"Tell him to inform us when an attack is going down. I don't care how he does it. But if he goes on another job without telling us, I won't be the one opening the cell door to let him out, he's on his own."

"I will, sir."

"Let's piece this together," said Frank. "Bobby Carnell and his boys hit the Albanians in Highbury. Two hours later, the Albanians retaliate and hit a club in East London, a club that doesn't even belong to Carnell. Why did they hit there?"

"The guy with the ears, sir," said Melody.

"Mills?"

"He wasn't one of Bones' men. Nor was the guy in the car bomb. Harvey said the blokes he's in with haven't mentioned any of it."

"Go on."

"It makes sense. It's *not* Bones' pub. There are *two* firms," said Melody, like she'd just solved quantum physics. "Bones is going after the Albanians for torching his pub and bookies, but the Albanians think it's the other firm. They keep hitting back at the wrong people."

"Somebody is going to be awfully upset at that."

"Who else have we got?" said Melody. "Who runs the club?"

"Unknown. No grasses, no info," said Frank. "It used to be John Cartwright up until he went missing eighteen months ago. It's been quiet since."

"That's what we need to find out. That's the missing link," said Melody.

"Tenant, find out who owns the East Ham club that was torched last night."

"Already done, sir. It's a shell company, Conspectus Group."

"Who's on the board?"

"It's not public. That'll take some digging."

"So dig," said Frank. "Mills, find Stone, take him for a walk, have the chat. No more cocking about. I want to know who's running the other firm, if there is one."

"Sir, I've been thinking," said Melody.

"Go."

"Let's find out from Harvey what the state of play is with Carnell. Reg will do some digging on the other firm, but it's the Albanians that need stopping. It's them causing all the violence. But if we take away Carnell and the other firm, the Albanians will overrun the East End, and we'll have more than just a few fires to put out."

Frank thought on that for a moment.

"You're saying we should let the local firms take care of the Albanians? And then move in once it's just local firms left to deal with?"

"Unofficially, sir."

"That's a crazy idea," said Frank. "If the public got hold of that information, we'd be hung."

"Well, we'd need to act quick. If we can somehow get Harvey to manipulate the play, so the Albanians are outed fast, we can pull Harvey out and remove one or both of the local firms."

"We need at least one. As mad as it sounds, having a strong underground keeps the streets in order. But what we can't have is two strong players fighting over territory," said Frank. "Tenant, go dig. Mills, go and find Stone."

Harvey sat on his kitchen stool with his laptop open in front of him. He ran a search for Luan Duri, the name Aleksander had given up, but the results were hard to filter. There appeared to be many Luan Duris. Searches for Luan Duri London, Luan Duri criminal, and Luan Duri Highbury all produced virtually nothing of interest. He needed Reg's research power.

The previous night had reminded Harvey of his past life. Not the pub fight, which had been unnecessary violence in Harvey's mind, but questioning Aleksander had stirred nostalgia. Harvey enjoyed breaking people down. He'd tortured many people and found that no matter how hard the person was, they all broke in the end, and they all had some kind of story to tell.

Aleksander's story had been one that many British people wouldn't understand and couldn't empathise with. The average person wouldn't be able to imagine being forced to leave your family behind and venture into a scary new world with no money and no job and no skills. As soon as his feet hit British soil, he would have been on the run, an illegal immigrant. It was no wonder that people like him turned to a life of crime.

Harvey was looking for information that would take the

Albanian boss down. The man was responsible for the deaths of a few men, probably many. There were a few that the team were aware of, but they'd need more on him. Harvey knew what was coming; he'd have to go and take a look, follow Luan Duri and find out for certain. If he could get his number, maybe Reg could get more information from it. If Harvey couldn't enable the team, there was no point being involved.

Aleksander hadn't been carrying a phone, but one of his men would be, and Luan's number would be stored on there. Aleksander had given up Luan's location, his office. All Harvey had to do was get close and be patient.

Patience, planning and execution, the three pillars of Harvey's training with Julios. He knew it sounded almost military, but the approach worked. Harvey had used it dozens of times. When Harvey was in his early teens, he'd found a police report of a boy he used to know from school. A bully. The boy was on the run for sex offences and had immediately sparked Harvey's interest. Harvey was always one to stand up for the small guys, to protect. But somehow, he'd failed to protect his own sister against the men who raped her. He'd been a young boy when it had happened. But still, the guilt played heavy on Harvey.

The boy who was on the run had also had run-ins with Harvey. He was a spiteful coward, and Harvey had slapped him about the playground when he found him picking on a small Asian kid. Harvey had roamed the streets for a few weeks looking for him. He'd waited patiently in places where free food may be on hand, and in sheltered areas within the forest when it had rained. His patience had worked out well. Harvey found him lurking in the woods near his parents' home and dragged the kid deep into the trees where nobody goes. That had been Harvey's second kill, and it awoke a thirst. It wasn't a psychotic desire to torture and hurt people; it was a desire from deep within to avenge the young girls who, like his sister, had been raped or abused. Harvey had seen first-hand how lives are torn apart, families are destroyed, and how life is never the same for these people.

From then, Harvey had an outlet for the urges he had. He would pay attention to the news and other media. He would watch for court cases involving sex offenders, and he would be patient, he would plan his attack, then he would execute it. Over the years, Harvey had refined his methods of getting information out of people. He had honed the skills Julios had taught him about stealth and death. Harvey knew which parts of the body could be removed to provide the most pain, but not kill the victim. Harvey also learned how to research people, and when the internet became widespread, his research became even easier. He suddenly found targets in the outlying counties; he could open up his field of vision and target those who most deserved to suffer.

What he needed to do now was to sit and watch Luan Duri. He needed to know where he went, who he was with; he needed to know his flaws, his weaknesses, his strengths.

Harvey stretched and rolled his head slowly from side to side. His body cried for a run, to limber up, to feel free again and breathe fresh air. He could still smell Aleksander's stale sweat.

The rain was loud against Harvey's kitchen window. It came in waves with the powerful gusts of wind. It wasn't a pleasant day for riding a motorbike. It was the type of day that never fully brightens up. The morning had been dark; the clouds had been low, and it had stayed that way until late morning. Harvey guessed it would stay that way until the evening too. But a dark day would work best for what Harvey needed to do.

Aleksander had said that Luan worked from a car breakers yard in Ilford, which was a ten-minute ride from Harvey's house in the dry. In the wet, it was maybe twenty minutes away.

Harvey pulled up the satellite imagery view on his laptop. The yard backed onto the River Roding, a Thames tributary stood adjacent to the train tracks that led from London out to Essex and beyond. Harvey knew the area. The tracks were raised, and a small arched bridge beneath the tracks provided access to an industrial area. There were other yards around Luan Duri's, another car breakers and a building materials supplier. Harvey saw the pallets of bricks and lengths of timber and noted how clean it looked compared to the array of crumpled, broken and beaten cars that adorned the muddy breakers yard next door.

Harvey noted the small cabin that was central to the property. It was accessible via a direct mud track from the gates. Alternatively, as Harvey was aiming for stealth, he would use the maze of pathways that led between the cars. He would need to watch for dogs and maybe take something to deal with them. The yard was a great location for Harvey. It was out of the way so he could spend days watching if he needed to, he'd just hole up in an old car. It was also quiet so nobody would hear the screams of anybody he came across that compromised the operation.

Harvey closed his laptop and dressed in black cargo pants, his tan boots, white t-shirt, black hooded sweatshirt and his leather jacket. He would be cold but would need to be agile, so he kept the layers to a minimum. Before leaving the house, he sent a message to Melody. *Got Alb boss' name, going for a recce.* He knew they would be watching him, so he didn't need to provide a location.

The ride to the junkyard was slow. The roads were slippery, flooded and busy with cars. Headlights reflected on the road's wet surface, and dark clouds loomed overhead. Harvey rode past the two huge gates to the yard. A trail of mud leaked from inside onto the pavement. The perimeter consisted of ten-foot brick walls, high enough to deter most people, but without barbed wire. Harvey parked his bike nearby between two cars that looked like they hadn't moved for some time. Before stepping off his bike, he checked his phone. Melody had replied. *We're watching you. Reg will update with more details.* Harvey stashed his helmet in the bike's backbox and strode confidently along the path to the yard.

One of the gates was open, presumably for customers to drive in, so Harvey slipped inside and ducked behind a row of cars. If he was caught, he would just say he was looking for a part. It was typical for someone to find the right model of car before contacting the management to discuss removing and purchasing it. But nobody approached him.

The rain continued to lash down, which made listening for oncoming footsteps difficult. Harvey stopped by a stack of scrapped cars in the second row. The car still had seats, and they were dry. Each row of cars had two layers. The top layer seemed to be newer, and in better condition than the lower deck. Harvey climbed inside and pushed the seat all the way back, reclining it as far as it would go, then pulled an old tarp from the back seat over him. If someone were to walk past, Harvey would remain still under the dirty old cover. His view of the cabin was near perfect, save for the door pillars of the car in the first row.

Harvey settled in for the exercise in patience.

CHAPTER SEVENTEEN

"I've got some bad news for you, boss," Ginger spoke into the phone.

"*More* bad news?" came the reply. "What is it now?"

"It's Malc, boss. He's gone missing."

"Missing? He's a full-grown man, not a ten-year-old kid."

"I know, boss. But his missus called, said she hasn't seen him since yesterday morning."

"Is he on a bender? He likes a drink that man. We're not a missing person department, you know."

"Yeah, but it's weird. His car is still in the boozer car park with keys in the ignition, but his phone and wallet are gone. It's just not like him, boss. His missus is worried, and well, you know things are getting a little hot lately, maybe it's-"

"Maybe it's what, Ginger? The Albanians? Why would they take him?"

"Maybe payback for the bloke Carnell took?"

"Carnell? This is becoming a royal pain in the arse, Ginger. Have you found that little bastard yet?"

"Yeah, I'm trying to set a meet-up, but apparently he's edgy right now. Our man has to pick the right time."+

"The right time? Who's calling the shots here? Me, not Bobby Carnell. He's got two choices, meet me and discuss the Albanians or I'll add him to the list, and he knows that's a battle he won't win."

"Yeah, but he won't be pushed around, boss, even if it kills him. Even if he knows we outnumber them by more than double. He's a stubborn man."

"Where's he based? I'm not dicking about here, I'll go see him."

"Pied Piper, boss."

"The Pied Piper? What's he drinking in that dive for?"

"The Albanians burned his other local down. I guess all his other pubs are too far away for a swift half."

"Right, tomorrow night we're going to pay Bobby Bones a visit. Go see Malcolm's missus, give her some money. Tell her we'll find him. If she gets hysterical, tell her to shut up, or we won't bother, she can find him herself. Someone needs to take control here."

CHAPTER EIGHTEEN

"Okay, I have some intel on the junkyard where Harvey is," said Reg, loud enough for everyone at headquarters to hear.

"What you got, Reg?" asked Melody. She was sitting in the reclining office chair with her feet on the desk and her laptop on her knees. The only noise in the open space was Jackson cleaning the van.

"I have the owner, his history, and his mobile. It's all we need to find out who he is and let us keep tabs on him."

Melody put her laptop down and walked over to Reg. "Show me."

"Right, Luan Duri, Albanian male, fifty-two years old. Formerly Albanian SHISH, which is the equivalent to the secret service. Retired with honours, then went missing when the new regime came into power. He's been hiding here for the past twelve years and is the owner of many businesses, mostly cash. Runs an export firm, probably stolen cars en route to Albania, and a few junkyards officially. Unofficially, the crime squad have him linked to some pretty serious players in the city, and he allegedly runs a protection racket in North London, which is believed to include the Jumping Jack, the pub Harvey blew up last night."

"Hey, Harvey didn't blow it up," said Melody.

"Okay, it's the pub he dragged a two-hundred-and-fifty-pound man out of before throwing him into the back of a van," said Reg. "Which one is worse?"

"Do we have this Duri's number?" said Melody. "Where is he?"

"Have a guess?"

"Oh God, don't tell me, he's in the yard where Harvey is sat?"

"Bingo."

"Okay, *I'll* message Harvey, and tell him to get out. *You* keep tabs on Duri, and do some more digging," said Melody. She pulled her phone out, and it immediately beeped with an incoming message. *Albanians have a blindfolded man inside the junkyard. He hasn't got long. Do I engage or watch them kill him?* Melody hesitated. Somebody's life hung in the air, and she needed to make the call. Save him and risk the operation or let him die? The man's death was by no means a guarantee of a successful mission, it would just allow the team more time.

"Sir," she called and waited for Frank's door to open. "Harvey is in the Albanian's junkyard. Reg has done some digging, and the guy is big time. Luan Duri, ex-secret service Albania. They have some guy blindfolded, and my guess is that it's not going to be a pleasant surprise."

"And you need *me* to tell *you* if you should compromise the investigation or let it play?"

"We should let it play, sir, I know we should. But will that come back and bite us in the-"

"We'll get a bigger bite if we expose Harvey now, Mills," said Frank. He eyed her and nodded. "Good call. Let it roll."

CHAPTER NINETEEN

Let it roll. Harvey read the message once then deleted it.

It was growing dark, and the rain was incessant. Harvey moved his feet and toes to keep the blood circulating. He was expecting the doors to open and the blindfolded man to be dragged out and dumped into the crusher. Harvey had seen that method of disposing of bodies before when he had worked for his foster father, John Cartwright. A junkyard was an asset for somebody dealing in stolen cars and dead bodies, making either one disappear was easy. Knowing a man with a junkyard was as good as knowing a man who ran a pig farm.

The lights were on inside the cabin, but the blinds were pulled down. Harvey listened for the cries of the man being tortured but heard nothing above the rain hitting the metal roofs of the scrapped cars and splashing in the thick mud. A black Range Rover was parked outside the cabin alongside an old BMW, the only two working cars in the yard.

The sky fell quickly to a cloudy dark night, almost in the blink of an eye. The lights inside the cabin stared like lifeless eyes in the night. A train rumbled past on the overhead tracks a hundred yards away, carrying commuters heading home from a long day in the office, reading books and newspapers, listening to music and thinking about dinner. It seemed funny to Harvey that none of the people on the train knew what was about to take place a few hundred feet away.

The train's rumble faded away, and Harvey heard the first cry. The initial attack was always the worst, Harvey had found. The body isn't ready for it. It might be a finger chopped off with bolt cutters or it might be a toe. The methods generally get progressively worse, and the screams become less as the body's senses are numbed by the continuous attacks. Harvey typically preferred to use words to break a man; most men's minds were much weaker than their bodies. But if they refused, Harvey went straight for the ultimate pain. He wouldn't let the body become accustomed to small stabs of agony. It was far better to go straight in with the big guns.

He thought about Aleksander. Harvey had been prepared to light the fire, but in the end, he hadn't needed to. What Bobby Bones did with him afterwards was up to him. Harvey had done what had been asked of him and left them to it. Chances are that Aleksander had fallen foul of Bobby's twisted mind and was minus a few fingers before a bag was thrown over his head.

A second cry sounded in the distance. It wasn't loud; it was muffled by the cabin walls and stacks of cars. But Harvey heard it clearly. It was a noise he'd heard a hundred times before.

The door opened, and the blindfolded man was kicked out onto the mud behind the Range Rover. He was naked. Two men stepped down beside him, and another stood at the doorway. An older man had one hand in the pocket of a long jacket; the other held a cigarette to his mouth.

Harvey couldn't see what was happening, but he heard the words of the old man, spoken slowly and clearly. "Let him go."

The two men bent and picked the man up from the mud then kicked him along the grimy track towards the gate. They laughed as he staggered blindly in the dirt. Even from forty metres away, Harvey could see that he'd soiled himself. The blindfolded man felt his way along the row of cars. He trod carefully, walking barefoot on broken glass and sharp, rusty metal car parts.

Then the old man at the door whistled loudly. A few seconds later, two large German Shepherds came running from behind the cabin. The first saw the blindfolded man instantly and began to bound across the mud. The second was inches behind. The sound that followed was truly horrific. The snapping and snarling dogs made short work of the naked man, and after less than a minute, the screaming and crying fell silent. Only the sickening growls of the dogs tearing lumps of flesh from his body remained, along with the ever-present percussion of the rain on the metal roofs.

"Call them off," said the older guy. "Take his head and deliver it to our friends." He pulled a long drag of his cigarette and flicked it into the mud before turning and closing the cabin door.

"Here he is," said Trev when Harvey strolled through the door of the Pied Piper. "Where've you been? Playing football?"

Harvey looked at his boots and pants. They were caked in mud.

"Crazy day at work, Trev. How's tricks?" asked Harvey. "Please Lee." He caught the attention of the barman.

"Not bad, Gerry. Crappy weather though. Took me bloody ages to get here."

Harvey took the pint from Lee and turned to Trev. "Where are the boys?" he asked.

"They're most likely on their way. Old Doug can't go a night without a drink, probably stuck in traffic."

Harvey lowered his voice. "Any comeback?"

"Nothing, mate," replied Trev. "Surprising really, but just goes to show what pussies they are." He took a big mouthful of his drink and nodded at Lee for a fresh pint.

"Nothing?" asked Harvey. He leaned in closer to Trev. "We slaughtered them. Are you sure they haven't done anything?"

"Positive, Gerry. What's up with you?"

"Nothing's up. It's just, well, they're not really known for being forgiving, are they? I'm surprised *this* place is still standing to be honest."

"Maybe they got wind that it was Bobby behind the attack, Gerry. Maybe they're busy running away."

"No, Trev. One thing I can guarantee you is that right now, they are *not* running away."

The door burst open, and a burst of fresh, cold wind hit Harvey. Doug and two other men walked in and closed the door behind them.

"Alright, lads?" said Doug, as he sauntered over to Harvey and Trev. "Blimey, it's brass bloody monkeys out there." He undid the buttons on his three-quarter-length leather coat and pulled off his scarf. "Please Lee," said Doug, catching the barman before he sat back down. "Here, Trev, you don't realise but you are standing next to a legend."

Trev looked around him with a confused look on his face. "Where? All I see is your ugly mug and this fella."

"You muppet. This fella here, Gerry." Doug slapped Harvey in the chest. "He's a nutcase, Trev." He leaned in and lowered his voice. "He had that fat Albanian singing in about ten minutes flat." Doug leaned away and took a long swig of his beer. "Ah, I needed that."

"What did he do?" asked Trev and then turned to Harvey. "What did you do then, Gerry?"

Harvey didn't reply.

"Don't tell me. You look like a nasty bastard with that stare thing you've got going on. I reckon you pulled out his nails or something?"

"Nope," said Doug. "Try again."

Harvey remained impassive as the conversation turned into a game. It wasn't a game, it was people's lives, and could easily be either one of them when the investigation came to an end. Harvey had given thought to the case, and how it would actually be closed off. He'd need to wipe himself off every memory that knew his true identity. When the time came, either he had to step out of it or clean up those who saw him turn. There was no chance he'd be stepping away, but he'd need to keep the cleaning to a minimum. These people clearly had big mouths. Most of them would need to be closed for good.

"Alright." Trev studied Harvey. "If he didn't pull his nails, I'd say genitalia?"

"What?" said Doug. "That's schoolboy stuff."

"Well, I don't know. There are a thousand ways to get someone to talk."

"One last go," said Doug.

"Okay. I'm guessing Bobby was there?"

"Yeah, he enjoyed it very much."

"I reckon Gerry here peeled the skin off him, his legs, I'd say?"

"Nope, none of the above, Trev, my old mate," said Doug, looking at Harvey proudly. "You want to know?"

"Go on then, enlighten me."

"He spoke to him."

"You what?"

"Words, Trev. That's all he did was talk to him, had the fucking bloke in tears, even pissed all over the floor."

"Behave, Doug," said Trev. He turned to Harvey. "Is that right, Gerry?'

Harvey didn't reply.

"You hard bastard," said Trev. "Always the quiet ones, Doug."

"Have you ever done that sort of thing before, Gerry? I mean, it didn't look like your first time."

"First time, Doug. I must be a natural or something."

"No way was that your first time, Gerry. I've seen a few men get information out of someone, and never in my life have I seen someone so afraid of a man's word. It was electric, Trev. You could have cut the atmosphere with a spoon, mate."

"Are we ready for a surprise attack from the Albanians?" asked Harvey, changing the subject.

"What? They won't come nowhere near us now, mate. They know who we are and they're scared."

"Is that right?" asked Harvey. "Did they look scared to you?"

"Not really. But that was the heat of the moment, wasn't it?"

"Do you really think they'll let this go?" asked Harvey. "Are we going in for another go?"

"Yeah, I think Bobby is setting something up, a final kick up the arse. Why's that? You want in?" asked Trev.

Harvey turned to Trev. He eyed him and studied his gaunt face with its weak jawline. "Of course I want in. I want to finish what we started. I'm not going to be happily sitting here with a pint waiting for the Albanian mafia to recollect itself, storm in here and clean up. Now's the time to hit them."

"You're keen," said Doug.

"Yeah, well," said Harvey, "if there's one thing I hate more than a liar, it's a bully." Harvey turned and sank his beer. "Please, Lee."

"Well, the boss will be pleased to hear it," said Doug. "He'll be here soon, so be sure to voice your opinion why don't you."

"If he asks, I'll tell him."

"Don't just wait for him to ask, tell him what you just said, Gerry." Doug put his arm around Harvey's shoulder and walked him away from the others. "Listen, a geezer like you could do well with Bobby. He's solid, right? Been around for donkey's, hasn't he?" Doug stopped them both by the jukebox beside the washrooms. "What you doing for work, Gerry?"

"I'm just helping a mate out at the minute."

"That's code for unemployed, Gerry. You can't kid a kidder. Look at yourself, mate. Now, look at me. If a bird walks through that door right now, who's she going to take home? You in your dirty clobber, or me with my nice clean shoes and Armani jeans? Me, of course. Birds don't want to have to bathe a bloke before she drags him into bed."

"What are you saying, Doug? It sounds to me like you're trying to push me into something here." Harvey let Gerry take control. The Harvey inside would have dragged the bloke outside and broken his arm just for touching him let alone insulting him.

"Easy, Gerry, no insult meant, mate. But you could do a lot worse than get a job with Bobby. He'll sort you out. You want me to have a word, or what?"

Harvey pondered on the question. Doug had played right into his hands.

"Yeah, alright then. What's involved? What's the pay like?"

"Gerry, mate, don't worry. You will be paid handsomely, and won't have to do much more than what you've done for him in the past couple of days. And if it's me that puts a word in, he's bound to agree. Did you see how impressed he was with what you did the other night?"

"Not really."

"Trust me, Gerry mate, you'll be fine. Look at you. I see loads of blokes come and go, and honestly, I can't remember the last time someone like you come along. You were made for this type of thing. I can't believe you've never done it before. Mate, you're a tiger, Gerry, a bloody tiger."

"Who's Dom then?"

"Dom? Oh, he's alright. He does all Bobby's legwork. Hard bloke, he earns well from Bobby."

"You reckon he'll be alright with it?"

"Mate, Bobby has got a boner in his pocket for people like you. Don't worry about Dom."

"What's he planning?"

"Who?"

"Bobby. You said he was planning something. What's he got in mind?"

"I'm not sure. I'm not privy to that kind of information until it's go-time. Know what I mean?"

"Alright. When's he coming?"

"He's coming tomorrow night. Come down, have a word, he'll probably make you an offer on a job. Do well, and he'll give you more work. Keep your nose clean, and he'll have you on the payroll, doing his collecting or something."

"Alright, Doug. Thanks, mate. I'll be here tomorrow. I best be off now though, she's doing my nut in. The last thing I need is for her to walk in here tomorrow gobbing off when Bobby is here."

"Yeah, no worries. Take it easy, Gerry."

Harvey turned and opened the door. A stiff, cold wind blew around the pub, and all eyes fell on Harvey. He stepped out and heard Doug call after him. "Oy, Gerry." Harvey turned and saw Doug leaning out the pub doors. "Remember, you're a tiger, mate. A bloody tiger."

"He's got a big mouth, Melody," said Harvey. "Big mouths are dangerous in my experience. He means well but doesn't know when to shut up sometimes."

"Invincible gangster syndrome?"

"I think so. It's like they glorify the thing, the lifestyle, the violence, and for what? Easy money? That's all these people want is easy money and a sense of entitlement. Like because they're hard, they're somehow better than most. It's hard to keep my mouth shut sometimes, but Gerry plays along. He's a rookie, right?"

"Right."

Harvey threw the ball for Boon, who bounded across the grass and misjudged the ball's bounce. It bounced over him, and he caught it on the second drop before running back towards Harvey. The pair were walking through the open fields of Wanstead Flats. It was a large open area with a few small lakes and plenty of space to make sure they weren't overheard or seen.

"How's he doing?" asked Harvey.

"Boon? Yeah, he's good. He's a good fit for the team, you know? Reg loves him, and he's getting to know Jackson. I think he's a little wary of Frank, but the old man dotes on him. He mostly sits by my feet in headquarters."

Boon, the dog, had belonged to a man that Al Sayan had killed on the banks of the River Thames. The dog had been named Boon by Harvey, who then gave him to Melody as a present.

"So, what's the plan here?" asked Melody. "What happens next?"

"Doug the mouth thinks he can get me a job with Bobby Carnell."

"Okay, so a career move for Gerry," said Melody. "Does Frank know?" She smiled up at Harvey.

"Not really a career move, but Gerry is scratching for work and Carnell likes what Gerry does, so go figure."

"And once you're inside?"

"Well, once I'm inside and trusted, it'll be easier to start going in wearing a wire. Then we'll have enough on him to take him down clean."

"How long do you think that'll take?"

"Not sure, but things are moving. All this booze is killing me. I'm supposed to go the Pied Piper tonight to talk to him. Doug will make the suggestion and Bobby will give me a job or two to test me."

"Oh for god's sake, Harvey. You're going to get yourself in too deep."

"Relax, I know what I'm doing. I've lived and breathed this stuff all my life. I'm more experienced than Bobby's boys."

"But Gerry isn't. How's the legend holding up?"

"Simple. Gerry is out of work, not afraid to get his hands dirty, and can look after himself."

"What if they ask too many questions?"

"All part of the profile, Melody. Gerry doesn't tolerate questions, and they won't push him. They've seen what he's capable of."

"Need I ask?"

"Best not to, Melody."

"I saw, you know?"

"You saw what?"

"I saw you drag that man from the pub and load him into the van."

"Yeah, why didn't you stop to help me lift him?"

Melody laughed. "Oh, you know, I wasn't dressed for it."

"Is that right?" replied Harvey. "I thought you were goners when that pub blew. None of us had any idea that had been done."

"Worried, were you?"

"Thought we'd killed you when I saw the van come round the corner. It was like slow motion."

"I hear concern in your voice."

"Of course I was concerned, Melody. Imagine the grief I would have got from Frank."

Melody elbowed Harvey. "You'd have been sad, and you know it."

"Yeah, you're right. Who would I tell all my troubles to if you were dead?"

"You don't really tell me your troubles, Harvey. You don't really tell me anything. It's okay, I get it. I understand why you don't open up."

"What do you mean? This *is* me opening up."

"You want to know something?" asked Melody.

"Go on."

"When that pub blew, it felt like the whole van was in a ball of flame."

"That's pretty much what it looked like too."

"I loved it."

"You what?"

"Honestly, Jackson thinks I'm crazy. I laughed, it was exhilarating."

"You hung from a plane without a parachute six months ago, and you think *that* was exhilarating?"

"I think I was just pleased to be alive. But it was funny to see the look on Jackson's face."

"Yeah, welcome to the team, Jackson."

They walked slowly, and Melody kicked the grass. The earth was soft from the previous day's downpour, and both their boots were soaked.

"You think about him much?" asked Melody.

Harvey knew Melody was referring to Denver, their teammate and friend who was killed by Al Sayan. "Yeah, I do as it happens. He was a nice bloke. You?"

"Every time I look at Jackson."

"Does Jackson seem out of place?"

"I'm not sure if it's because we're used to seeing Denver there, or, I don't know. But every time Jackson slides out from under the van, I expect Denver to grin at me."

"Time will tell, Melody. Think of the good stuff."

"I don't want to think about any of it, to be honest. I don't want to be reminded of Denver every time I look at Jackson. Is that wrong?"

"It's just your way of grieving, Melody. It'll get easier over time."

"How about the case?" asked Melody. "How do you see it playing out?"

Harvey let the words float around inside his head for a few seconds. "Something doesn't add up, Melody."

"You want to share that?"

"I watched that guy yesterday be dragged into the cabin in the junkyard. I heard his screams, and then once they got the answers they wanted, I watched the two German Shepherds tear him apart."

"Oh really, too much detail, Harvey."

"Then I heard Luan Duri tell his two boys to take the bloke's head and deliver it back as a message."

"Right?"

"I was in the pub last night, and not a dicky bird was said about it."

"Dicky bird?"

"Sorry, Gerry slips out sometimes. No-one said anything. I even asked if the Albanians had retaliated and both Doug and Trev said they hadn't."

"Oh god, I keep forgetting you're not up to speed on things. It feels like you've been on holiday or something," said Melody. "Frank and I have a theory that there are two local firms involved."

"That's exactly what I was thinking."

"Carnell hits the Albanians, they strike back at the other firm and repeat."

"But who's the other firm?"

"No-one knows. Whoever it is, has some loyal men. It's like they make a point of not being on the radar."

"So Bobby can expect a visit from both the Albanians and this other mob? Great," said Harvey.

"Frank wants to let it play."

"You what?"

"He wants to let the local firms take care of the Albanians, and then we'll take care of the local firms."

"There's going to be a lot of bloodshed."

"In his view, that's just thinning the numbers for when we step in."

"What does he want me to do?"

"Hang in there, do what you can, report back more often than you are, and stay alive."

Harvey nodded and stopped beside his bike.

"And what do you want me to do?"

Melody opened the door, and Boon jumped onto a blanket on the small back seat. She stepped closer to Harvey, reached up and put her arms around his waist. "I just want you to be careful."

CHAPTER TWENTY-TWO

"It's done, Luan," said Bardh. "I imagine right about now they will be discovering their friend."

"Good, they will retaliate. It's in their blood. And when they do, we will be ready."

"How many do we have?"

"We have thirty good men coming here right now, and another forty spread out across North London in case they strike there."

"Is thirty enough?" asked Bardh. "You saw what they did in the Jumping Jack."

"Those men were not carrying AK-47s. Trust me, when the local firm strikes here, it'll be the last thing they do." Luan paused to light a cigarette. "The crusher will be busy tonight." He smiled a cruel smile that showed his stained teeth.

"One of the men who escaped the fire is talking. He is in the hospital still but able to talk. His skin has melted from his face, and his hair is gone. He is *vigan* now. A monster."

"He doesn't need to concern himself with his future. He will be taken care of."

"He spoke of one man, Luan. A dangerous man, far more talented than the other thugs."

Luan looked up at the man from his desk in the cabin. "Tell me more."

"He moved with precision, like a dancer. With each step, he will strike, and with each strike, he will kill."

"You sound scared, Bardh. Where are your balls?"

"I do not fear death, Luan, as you know. But we must destroy this man. He is trained. It was this man that took Aleksander, and if there is one man left standing at the end of this battle, it will be this man. He killed many of our men."

"Do we have a name for him?"

"No, but if I am right, we will meet him soon. We have two men watching them, but until now, there has been no sign of this man."

"Do they keep him locked in a cage?" Luan smiled.

"He's special, Luan. He is a trophy."

"Then I want him found, and I want his head brought to me." Luan paused to take a drag on his cigarette. "With his balls in his mouth."

CHAPTER TWENTY-THREE

"Please, Lee," said Harvey. He was stood alone at the bar of the Pied Piper. Only the old man sat at the end of the bar where he always sat. The rest of the pub was empty.

"Quiet one tonight, Gerry," said Lee.

"Yeah, looks like it."

"Usually spells trouble."

Harvey didn't reply.

Lee set the pint down on the bar and leaned forward to Harvey. "So what's your story? You're not a local boy, are you?"

"We've had this conversation before, Lee."

"Yeah, you told me to mind my own business." Lee stood upright and folded his arms. "You know how long I've been running this pub?"

"I don't really care to be honest."

"Fifteen years. Fifteen years stood here behind this bar. Can you imagine that?"

Harvey didn't reply.

"The things I've seen, blimey, if these walls could talk. People come and go, Gerry. Always have and always will."

"I wish you'd go and let me think."

Lee ignored Harvey's comment and carried on talking at him. "There's always been trouble in these parts, you know? But it was always amicable. It was always done with a bit of dignity, know what I mean?"

Harvey stared at the pub door. A car pulled in, and the headlights shone briefly through the glass.

"Old school firms, now they had class, Gerry. Don't get me wrong, they'd cut your face off for looking at them the wrong way. But if you were on the right side of them, they'd take care of their own. It's not like that these days. It's every man for himself, dog-eat-dog. Sure, these boys all get along, they're on the same firm. But when push comes to shove, and someone has to go down, it'll be a scramble for the top and those at the bottom will be trodden on and forgotten."

Car doors slammed, and men's voices could be heard outside.

"Take my advice, Gerry. Don't get involved. You aren't the first one to get caught up in the bother, but get out while you can. You seem like a nice bloke, bit hard and a bit protective, that's fair. But do yourself a favour, turn away and don't look back."

The doors burst open, and Doug, Trev and two others walked in. "Oy oy, Gerry, you're keen tonight."

"How's it going, Doug? Trev?" Harvey shook the men's hands.

"Yeah, not bad, Gerry," said Doug. "Please, Lee." He made a circle with his hand indicating that he wanted a round of beers for everyone.

"What's new?" asked Harvey.

"Oh, this and that, Gerry. The wife is still gorgeous, and the dog's breath smells. Actually, no, that's the wrong way round."

Doug laughed at his own joke, slapped Harvey on the back, and picked up a beer from the bar. "And one for yourself, Lee, my old son."

"Cheers, Doug," replied Lee.

"Listen, Gerry, remember what I said last night? Bobby is coming down, he's got some news. Me and Trev reckon he's going to tell us what his plans are with the Albanians. I reckon we're going in hard, crack a few skulls."

"Sounds like fun," said Harvey. "Any idea what time he's getting here?"

"Any minute, mate. Just listen hard, and I'll talk to Dom to make sure word gets put his way, see if we can't get you a bit of work."

"Nice one, Doug. Appreciate it."

"No problem, mate."

The door opened, and more men walked in. Hard types, thought Harvey. Shaved heads, tattoos, gold sovereign rings and not one piece of un-scarred skin on show. They looked like the men that John used to have working for him in the eighties, the men that would be hanging around the house when Harvey was a child. Doug nodded at them. Harvey looked away for two reasons. Nobody liked to be stared at when they walk into a pub, and there was a small chance one of them may recognise Harvey if they had worked for John at any point in their criminal careers.

The TV was turned on and the football game was playing. Harvey pretended to be absorbed by it, but actually had no idea what was happening. He listened to the banter around him. He'd never learned how to deal with banter; he'd never been in the situation where allowing a man to insult you for any reason, even humour, was acceptable. Harvey had spent a large part of his life being invisible, barely existing. Anybody that had known him had known how dangerous he was and was highly unlikely to offer an insult, even in jest.

The pub was getting fuller. Gradually over the next hour, more men filtered in. They slapped friends on their backs and bought beers for everyone they knew. Then they insulted them. Harvey sipped his pint and observed the play.

When Bobby 'Bones' Carnell walked into the room, preceded by Dom, the bar fell virtually silent.

Bobby walked to the bar where a scotch and soda was placed in front of him and a pint for Dom. The noise crept back up to its original volume.

Harvey moved along to the end of the bar and stood behind a column in a relatively empty space. There was a small booth there that was hardly used. Harvey sat down with his back to the wall which gave him a clear view of the front doors. He pulled his phone out and messaged Melody. *BBC in PP. Will update.*

Harvey watched the dynamics of the firm. He knew that Bobby had more men than those in the pub. These were just the core, Bobby's most loyal men. There were about forty of them in total, plus maybe the same again not in attendance.

Harvey saw more headlights pull into the car park, four cars, judging by the waves of light that shone through the opaque glass windows. Harvey finished his drink and sat with an empty glass.

He watched the doors open, and six men walked in. They were all big guys with leather jackets, stony stares, and matching scars. The room fell silent. From where Harvey was sat, he could see Dom push himself off the bar where he'd been leaning and stride through the centre of Bobby's men.

"Is there a problem, boys?"

The new men stood silently either side of the door, three per side.

"Are you fucking deaf or something?"

The room was deathly silent. Lee flicked the TV off and led the old man around the bar out of harm's way. He limped around carrying his pint and disappeared into the back function room.

Then two things happened that shocked Harvey.

The door opened again, and before Harvey had even seen who it was, he saw the heads of Bobby's men tilt backwards to look at the giant man. One massive leg came into view, and then the barrel chest and thick jaw of Adeo Parrish. Harvey was transfixed. He was hidden in the shadows and couldn't be seen by the big man. Adeo was Julios' brother. Harvey had only met him six months previously during a strange series of events in which their paths had crossed. Adeo had been Stimson's bodyguard during the terrorist attack that had killed Denver and nearly killed Harvey. Adeo was the only one to have gotten away and *would* recognise Harvey if he saw him.

Harvey ran through his options. He was in a pub with more than fifty men between him and the doors, all of whom would slaughter Harvey if they found out he was working with the police and wasn't actually called Gerry.

He could take them on, but he knew that the odds were stacked heavily against him. He could shoot his way out, not a brilliant solution by any means. As he only had a magazine of fifteen in his SIG P226, he wouldn't get halfway through the firm before someone got lucky. Or he could hang onto every little bit of hope he could conjure up. But Harvey wasn't feeling lucky.

Adeo stepped to one side of the doors. His mass seemed to fill the room. The doors opened once more, and as if in slow motion, all eyes fell back to the door. A shiny brogue stepped through, and then the calm, confident swagger of John Cartwright.

He stopped and let the door bang shut behind him. Then, in the thick, gruff but articulate tone that Harvey remembered so well, he said, "Which one of you is Bobby Carnell?"

CHAPTER TWENTY-FOUR

"I am. Who's asking?"

Bobby's reply sounded light, weak and dulcet compared to the harsh grumble of John Cartwright's cacophonous voice.

"Do I really need to answer that?" replied John.

"Cartwright?"

"Mr Cartwright to you."

"And to what do we owe the pleasure, Mr Cartwright?" said Bobby, trying to sound large and confident in front of his men.

"Thought we'd have a chat. You can get your pets to stand down. We haven't come looking for a tear up," said John. "Yet."

The two men eyed each other with distrust. Harvey saw the men in Bobby's ranks discreetly sliding coshes and knives out of their waistbands.

"Alright, boys," said Bobby. "Stand down."

He turned back to John. "It's most irregular for men like you and me to step into another man's pub. But, seeing as you're here, let's keep it civil. What're you drinking?"

"I'll take a brandy, Remy Martin. Three ice cubes. No more, no less."

Lee heard the order and began to pour the drink. The two

men moved towards the bar, and Bobby's guys opened up the room. Men still drank, but nobody dared talk. Everyone was on high alert, waiting for a move from one of Cartwright's men.

"So, what's the topic, Mr Cartwright?" asked Bobby. "What exactly is it we're discussing?"

"Ginger?" called Cartwright.

A bald man with a red-haired goatee beard stepped away from the door and walked up to John. John nodded at him. Ginger pulled a canvass bag with a drawstring up and sat it on the bar. He began to pull the strings open.

The front ranks closed in, but John Cartwright held his hand up. "Easy, boys, calm down. It's not a weapon."

Ginger opened the drawstring and reached inside. He lifted his hand and pulled the bag away from the bottom to reveal a man's severed head. He dumped it on the bar in front of Bobby.

"Cheers, Ginger," said John, and Ginger moved back to his place by the door.

"Pretty," said Bobby and gestured with his head at the one that sat on the bar looking at him.

"One of my men," said John.

"Well? Isn't he looking for it or something?" replied Bobby. "I understand, John, that you are a grandfather in this world. I know you've been around since the good old days. But you know what? *That* makes *this* even worse." Bobby took a swig of his drink. "You come in here unannounced with half a dozen armed men." Bobby stared at each of the six men by the doors. "You're all carrying, aren't you?" Nobody replied. Bobby turned back to John. "They're all carrying, right?"

John gave a small shrug.

"And you bring this goon," said Bobby, gesturing at Adeo who stood far above any man in the pub. "What are you feeding him? Horses?" Bobby took another mouthful of his drink and gestured at Lee to pour another. "So you can see my problem, John. This is borderline taking liberties, mate."

"Considering this is your turf, I'll disregard your tone with me that once. But mark my words, Bobby Carnell, if you ever talk to me like that again, I'll cut you down myself." John spoke calmly and easily, unafraid even though heavily outnumbered. Harvey looked on with familiar admiration for John's control and presence. The man was born to do what he did.

John Cartwright had been missing for two years since he'd made a deal with Harvey. The deal was that Harvey was to kill the number one rival crime family. Their leader, Terry Thomson, was one of the most feared criminals Harvey had ever known. His habit of feeding people alive to his pet two-hundred-and-fifty-pound hogs had been common knowledge in the organised crime world. In return for the kill, Harvey would receive the name of the man that raped his sister, the first name on Harvey's list. John had left Harvey to do what he needed to do and hadn't been seen since.

Until now.

"The reason I'm here, Carnell, is simple. A little birdie tells me you've been having trouble with the Albanians?" John swirled the three ice cubes in his glass.

"Nothing we can't handle," replied Bobby. "Isn't that right, boys?"

A dull chorus of agreements emanated from the group of men.

"Is that right?" said John. He cocked his head and lifted an eyebrow.

"We've got them on the run, haven't heard anything from them in days. All mouth, no trousers I believe is the expression."

"Is that right?" said John again. "Has it ever occurred to you that they aren't very bright, Carnell? One English bloke is the same as the next English bloke."

"What do you mean?"

John nodded at the gruesome head on the bar. "You think that just fell off, do you?"

"No."

"How do you think it happened to come apart from the rest of him?"

Bobby sighed. "Albanians?"

"Correct, Carnell. Malcolm here was kidnapped from outside one of my pubs, taken somewhere and decapitated."

"Yeah but-"

"Do not interrupt me, Bobby Carnell, when I am talking."

Harvey had strong memories of John's hatred of being interrupted and recognised the structure of the sentence.

"I also lost a good man, and a dear friend, when the Albanians jumped their motor. They cut the other man's ears off, Bobby. Also, my number two, a very loyal man, Bobby, was blown up outside the hospital. And finally, I lost one of my clubs and *seven* more men. One of my favourite clubs, Bobby." He paused to take a drink then nodded at Lee for another. "Now you tell me what exactly you are going to do about it because it seems like every time you and your band of merry men here attack the Albanians, it is me who is taking the flack for it. And you know, I can strike back, Bobby. I could destroy them and you. But I value my men, they're loyal. So why should they put their lives on the line for something that you did, Bobby? Answer me that."

"We didn't know they were going after you, John," said Bobby quietly. "Sorry about your men." Bobby looked around the room at all the faces. He knew them all by name; he respected all of them.

"How would you have known?" said John. "But you do now, so tell me what the answer is."

"Seems to me like the Albanians have wronged us both, John."

"I'd agree with that statement."

"So we both owe them."

John nodded.

"Why don't we team up? I've got seventy or eighty men. You can pull that together I'm sure. Let's finish it."

John nodded again. "Who's your best man?"

Bobby looked around the room again. A few of the faces stood tall, pumped their chests out and looked at Bobby for recognition. A few others seemed to sink back into the crowd. "Where's the new boy? Gerry?"

CHAPTER TWENTY-FIVE

"Reg, it's Melody."

"Oh hey, Melody. It's been all of two hours since I saw you. How are things?" said Reg in a mock female tone.

"No time. I need you to scramble Jackson and pick me up."

"Okay," said Reg. "Let me guess, Harvey?"

"How long?"

"Thirty minutes."

"I'll be waiting outside."

Melody disconnected the call and re-read the message from Harvey. It was the first time Harvey had ever sent a message of this sort and Melody was worried for him. *In PP, BBC here. JC and Adeo just arrived!*

It had taken Melody a few minutes to work out who JC was. She knew Adeo from the Al Sayan incident, and that spelt trouble. Adeo had been there when the team had caught Stimson. He knew that Harvey was working with the police, and that left Harvey in an extremely uncomfortable position. But when she had put the name John Cartwright to the initials, her heart sank.

John wouldn't know that Harvey was undercover. But the risk of him spotting Harvey and blowing his cover as Gerry would raise immediate flags in Bobby Carnell's firm. Harvey would be questioned, and the trust he'd built up would be gone.

She changed back into her work clothes, cargo pants and boots, a tight-fitting t-shirt and short leather jacket, then filled a flask of hot water. It was going to be a long night, and she liked to be prepared. But mostly it was to kill time and stop her mind wandering while she waited for Reg and Jackson.

The van pulled up after twenty-five minutes, and Melody climbed in, barely giving Jackson time to fully stop the van. "Go. Pied Piper."

She turned to Reg in the back. "Do we have him on screen?"

"We sure do. He's still there. As are Bobby Bones and a few other numbers in the network we've been building up."

"Put your foot down, Jackson. If it kicks off, I want to be there."

"Melody," said Reg, "if it kicks off, you can't go in guns blazing. Harvey knew the risk."

"I want him to know we're here for him."

"He knows, Melody."

Melody climbed into the back with Reg and pulled open a Peli-case. She assembled a Heckler and a Koch MP5 and slotted the scope on top.

"What exactly are you planning to do with that?"

"You know what they call this?"

"A gun?" said Reg. He'd been trained in firearms but under duress and out of necessity. His choice of weapons was a blaster on his zombie-killing video game.

"Barking dog, Reg," said Melody, as she snapped a magazine into place. "You know why?"

Reg was silent.

"You'll know when you hear it. A few bursts with this and they'll scatter."

"Leaving us to pick up the pieces of Harvey," said Reg.

Melody looked Reg in the eye in the darkness of the van. She saw a glimmer of moisture in his eye and knew that he was using humour to cover his anxiety.

"Let's hope not, Reg."

CHAPTER TWENTY-SIX

Harvey stood up and stepped forward into the throng of men, who parted and made way for him to pass through. Some eyed him cautiously; others looked at him with contempt. They were perplexed at how a newcomer to the firm had suddenly earned the title of best man.

Harvey ignored Adeo, but out of the corner of his eye, he saw the recognition. His eyes widened, and mouth fell open, but to his credit, he remained silent. John had his back to Harvey and was drinking his drink. He looked up and caught Harvey's stare in the mirror behind the optics in the bar. John remained motionless.

"So, you're Gerry, are you?"

Harvey didn't reply.

"Gerry what, Son?" John spoke the last word slowly and decisively.

Harvey ignored the hidden greeting. "Sloan."

"Gerry, this is John Cartwright, show the man some respect, eh?"

"It's okay Bobby. He looks like a bright boy, he'll learn some manners," said John. He remained with his back to Harvey, swirling the ice cubes in his drink as he'd always done. "Bobby here tells me you're his best boy. Is that right?"

Harvey didn't reply.

John stood silent for a moment.

"If I was to tell you to do a job for me, Gerry, would you do it?"

"Tell? Or ask?" Harvey had seen the trick question coming from his foster father. John hated weakness; his favoured men had all earned John's respect by standing up for themselves. They had never been rude, but they hadn't been pushed around either.

John nodded.

"Sorry, John, he's new," said Bobby.

John raised his hand and shook his head.

"If I told you that we have a problem with the Albanians, and I needed someone to take them out, would you be willing to help?"

"If you asked nicely, John."

Bobby slapped his forehead in disbelief. His eyes were popping out of his gaunt face.

"Okay, I'll ask nicely, Gerry."

"Probably then," said Harvey. "But I'd do it on *my* terms, and *my* terms only."

"I'm really sorry, John," started Bobby. "Dom, take him-"

"Leave him be," said John. He turned with his drink to face Harvey. Harvey stared at the old man's face. He hadn't seen him for two years, but he hadn't changed much; he looked older, but his hard features bore the aged skin well. He was clean shaved as he always was. Old school habits.

"What might those terms be, Gerry?"

"I go in with your best man."

"*My* best man?"

Harvey didn't reply.

"You think the two of you can pull it off?"

A murmur built up among the men, then quietened when Harvey turned to Adeo.

"Him."

John downed his drink and placed the glass symmetrically on a cardboard coaster that sat on the bar.

"When?" asked John.

"Now. We leave now and come back when it's done. These blokes can all go home to their wives and kids."

"What? And what do expect us to do while you're gone, Gerry?" asked Bobby. "Twiddle our thumbs and wait for the heroes to come home?"

Harvey didn't reply.

"And if you don't come back?" asked John.

"I'll be back," said Harvey.

CHAPTER TWENTY-SEVEN

Harvey drove. Adeo filled the rest of the space in the front of the BMW that Dom had given to Harvey. They drove in silence. Neither one acknowledged the identity of the other.

Harvey felt his phone vibrate in his pocket, a message from Melody probably. He saw the square outline of the van in the rear-view mirror and made sure that Adeo hadn't spotted him checking. The team were a card up Harvey's sleeve, and would likely come in handy in the very near future.

They pulled off the A406 North Circular Road and slipped into the back streets of Ilford. As they passed under the railway bridge, Harvey pointed out the yard on the left.

They parked a few hundred meters further on than the gate. Parking in the evenings was difficult; commuters were coming home from work and spaces went like gold dust. Harvey reversed into a spot, using the car's parking sensors to get into the tight space.

He killed the engine.

"Before we go in, I want to make one thing clear."

Adeo looked back at him with his hand on the door handle.

"We do this my way. That's the only way we'll get back out again. If you deviate, you're on your own."

"You think you're better than me?"

"I was trained by the best."

"There's one thing you haven't considered, Harvey Stone," said Adeo as he pushed the door open and heaved his mass out of the car. Harvey climbed out and leaned on the car roof opposite the big man. They stood face to face. For Harvey, it was like seeing Julios stare back at him with his unemotional eyes and stern frown. "Who do you think trained me?"

The team's VW van passed behind Adeo as the two men stood facing each other across the car.

"The junkyard is set out in rows," began Harvey. "The cabin is in the centre. The crusher is behind it. There're rows of cars on the left, rows of cars on the right, rows of cars at the back and front with a space leading from the gate to the cabin. Plenty of places for them to be hiding. Luan Duri is the main man, an old guy in a long jacket, smokes too much. I don't know how many there will be."

"You've been here before?" said Adeo, his brow furrowed.

"You think I'd come here without a plan?"

"So much of Julios in you."

"I'll take that as a compliment."

"Are we going over the wall?" asked Adeo.

"If the gate is locked, yes. Can you handle that?"

Adeo didn't reply.

The pair walked off towards the gates. The road was quiet, and they were blessed by a dark night. Harvey checked the parked cars all along the front to make sure there weren't any lookouts. All the cars were empty.

The gates were wide open.

"Keep walking," said Harvey. The pair marched past the

open gates and slipped down the side of the property between the yard and the embankment that led up to the train tracks.

"That was a trap," whispered Harvey. "Last time I was here, only one gate was open. It's like they're expecting us to walk in guns blazing."

Harvey pulled an old wooden pallet from a deep puddle and stood it beside the wall. Without a word, he climbed up, reached up to the top of the wall and pulled himself up. He lay on the wall and looked back down at Adeo.

"One last thing," whispered Harvey. Adeo had one foot on the pallet and was preparing to pull himself up. "I hope you like dogs."

Harvey flashed Adeo a warning smile and lowered himself down to the floor.

He pulled his knife from its sheath on his belt and took the time to listen for any movement. There were voices in the open space near the cabin. Several men were huddled around a fire inside an old oil drum, like hobos.

Harvey felt rather than heard Adeo land behind him; the ground shook slightly. But as Harvey turned, Adeo stood upright. It hadn't surprised Harvey, Julios had been as big as Adeo and had been far more agile than he looked.

Harvey made a circle motion with his hands, indicating to Adeo that they would split and work the perimeter, meeting up on the far side of the yard. Adeo gave an imperceptible nod and turned away from Harvey.

Harvey watched him for a few seconds. It was like having Julios back. Harvey had never been afraid of anything. But for the twenty years that he'd been trained by Julios, he'd worked with him for close to fifteen of them, and there was a certain level of comfort knowing the big guy had his back. Working alone had never been an issue, but having a solid and reliable partner was invaluable and mitigated much of the risk.

Harvey began to make his way around the ring of cars. He checked inside every one he came across and looked through to the next row if he could. Inside the cars made an ideal place for someone to wait, as he had done himself just two days previously. There was some banging in the distance, metal on metal, followed by a long scrape of something heavy being dragged across concrete, like a car part.

Harvey found the first guard napping on the passenger seat of an old Ford Escort. Harvey effortlessly flicked the tip of his blade into the man's neck and severed his windpipe. He left a wound less than an inch long, and the man woke immediately, fighting for air and drowning in his own blood. Harvey held the man's mouth closed until his lungs filled and he stopped moving.

Harvey continued on his walk. He stood at the back wall of the property behind the cabin and the crusher and saw the open cage where the two German Shepherds lay. He crept silently; he was out of sight of the dogs but smelled cigarette smoke. The hushed voices of two men came from behind the next car. Harvey waited, watching them talk quietly. They were big men, but relaxed and off guard.

Harvey made a plan.

He found a small steel nut on the floor and tossed it behind the men. They both span around. Harvey watched as one signalled for the other to remain where he was and be quiet. Then the first one slipped away. He hadn't taken five steps when Harvey's garrotte slipped over the man's head, and Harvey silently dragged him into the shadows.

The first man crept back along the wall towards the corner where Harvey stood. Harvey saw his vague shadow and heard his heavy boots.

"Hello?"

Harvey could smell the cigarettes on the man's breath.

"Kush eshte atje?"

The big man came around the corner slowly and hesitantly. Harvey slipped around the car and came up behind him. When the man's foot kicked the soft body of his friend, he bent to see what it was. He then stood up and took a deep breath ready to alert everybody. Harvey's knife came from behind him. One slice across his throat and the big man fell to his knees, choking on his own blood.

Harvey left the two dead men in a pile in the shadows and made his way quietly along the wall, where Adeo met him.

"What took you so long?" whispered the big man.

Harvey ignored the comment. He knew that if Julios had trained him, Adeo would understand that the delay was due to obstacles. Given that Adeo had taken nearly the same time to make half a circuit, Harvey guessed that he had also come up against only two men maximum.

Harvey signed to move into the next ring of cars and complete another half circuit.

They went back the way they had each came to maintain familiarity. But the second ring of scrap was far more challenging without the benefit of the shadow the wall provided. Harvey felt he could be seen through the windows of cars in the inner circles.

He moved slowly. His eyes picked up the slightest movement, the flutter of a discarded wrapper on the floor as the breeze blew across it, the flap of a loose seat belt. Harvey was directly behind the cabin once more when movement in the corner of his left eye stopped him in his tracks.

One of the dog's ears had stood up. It was lying down, relaxed, but one ear was raised and turned like a satellite towards Harvey. He remained dead still. Voices came from near the cabin as two men walked loudly towards the spot where Harvey had dropped the two smokers.

The dog's head turned and his eyes locked with Harvey's. He didn't move. It stood and walked briskly out of its open cage and turned in Harvey's direction. Its ears were pinned back as it closed in.

The two men came briefly into view between two cars then disappeared into the shadows.

Harvey heard the low guttural growl of the dog as it approached with more urgency. But Harvey stood his ground. He held his knife by his side ready to strike the dog between its front legs if it attacked.

He knew Shepherds, and if it had been trained well, it would go for his arm or throat, more likely the throat. It would use its weight to bring Harvey down then sink its teeth into the soft tissue of his neck.

The other dog moved in behind the first. Both dogs stood in front of Harvey. Their hackles were up and their ears pinned back. The first dog was the alpha. The second would follow the first dog's lead. Harvey stared at the alpha, unafraid. The showdown lasted thirty seconds, no more. Then the alpha broke eye contact, and its ears dropped. The second followed suit.

Harvey was now lead dog.

He dropped to his haunches, and the dogs came to him like they were old friends.

Harvey stood and shooed them away. Then, before he knew it, they pounced behind him and pinned a large Albanian man to the ground. The man struggled as the lead dog tore into his throat. He punched out, but both dogs held on, and he finally gave up. His body fell limp, and the dogs sat by their quarry.

Harvey stared the first dog in the eye and held its cold gaze. Its mouth was black with blood in the dark night, but there was one more man in the shadows somewhere. Harvey stood motionless and let the movement come to him. The shadow on the car in front grew darker as somebody moved past very slowly.

The dogs were too noisy when attacking, so Harvey had them sit and stay using two movements of his hand to the more aggressive of the dogs. The second followed suit. They sat and watched Harvey slip silently behind the man and pull the steel wire cable tight around his neck. The man was strong and fought back with defensive judo moves that Harvey recognised and countered. All the while, he maintained pressure on the steel wire. The large Albanian managed to use his bulk to turn and face Harvey, so Harvey leaned back and slammed his forehead into his nose. Dropping the wire, he snapped the man's head to one side, who dropped like a stone at the feet of the German Shepherds.

Harvey signed for the dogs to stay and slipped into the shadows between the two cars. Adeo was waiting for him again and stepped out of the darkness when Harvey approached. This time there was no jibe at the delay, and Harvey saw Adeo's blood-stained hands.

There was one more row of cars to get around before the cabin.

Adeo stepped closer to Harvey and ducked down beside him behind the cars. He signed with a bloodied hand that he'd seen a risk. Harvey looked back at the open space in front of the cabin. The men had set up a tripod-mounted flamethrower either side of the alley of cars that led from the gates to the cabin. One man stood on either side, ready to incinerate anybody that came up the alleyway.

The flamethrowers didn't pose a problem to Harvey or Adeo. But from where the men stood, they wouldn't get close to the cabin without being spotted.

"How many men inside the cabin?" whispered Adeo.

Harvey shrugged. Adeo leaned in close to Harvey. "Once

we're inside that cabin, there'll be no more hiding. We'll have seconds to take them out."

Harvey shook his head. "Too risky." He chanced a glance around the edge of the car in front to make sure the men were still there and then ducked back to Adeo. "We need to draw them out. We have the advantage out here."

"And how do you plan on doing that?"

Harvey stood, drew his SIG from his waistband and stepped into the open space. He fired twice, one round in each of the men's heads.

CHAPTER TWENTY-EIGHT

"Was that gunfire?" asked Melody, cocking her head to one side.

"I don't know," said Reg. "It's a pretty industrial-"

"Shh," said Melody. She was listening for more fire.

"You asked," said Reg.

"Oh, this is killing me," said Melody with her head in her hands. Her MP5 lay across her lap ready to go at a moment's notice. "Reg, can you get Frank on the loudspeaker?"

Within a few seconds, the van filled with the sound of a ringing phone.

"Tenant, what's the news?"

"Sir, it's me. You're on loudspeaker," said Melody.

"Go on."

"It's just an update, sir. Harvey has been inside the yard for more than thirty minutes."

"Any action?"

"We just heard two gunshots."

"You thought we heard gunshots," said Reg.

"Did you or didn't you hear gunshots, Mills?"

"Ninety-nine percent sure, sir."

"Same gun?"

"Definitely. But I couldn't hear it clear enough to make out if it was a SIG."

"Spacing?"

"Double-tap, of that I'm sure."

"Then it's Stone. Those Albanians will be using AKs, forty-sevens or seventy-fours."

There was a silence while Frank made a decision.

"Sit tight, wait for the chaos. If I know Stone like I think I do, the whole place will erupt any minute."

"Copy that, sir."

"Mills?"

"Sir?"

"Thanks for the update. Make sure our boy gets out in one piece." Frank disconnected the call.

CHAPTER TWENTY-NINE

The door of the cabin was kicked open, and two men ran out brandishing AK-74s. They spat a few rounds in Harvey's direction then ducked behind some cars. Harvey didn't take the bait. Instead, he dipped back down to Adeo.

"The surprise is up, but this isn't over until Luan Duri is face down in the mud," said Harvey.

Adeo nodded and stood. He pulled his own weapon from a discreet holster beneath his arm. He slid the action back and let it slide forward to collect a round.

Harvey ran between the cars to the far wall behind the cabin. Adeo ran in the opposite direction. Taking a quick glance back toward Adeo, Harvey saw him disappear around the corner near the gates. Harvey moved off towards the two men he'd dropped earlier.

Voices rang out in the night, confused shouts in Albanian, along with the occasional bursts of automatic fire. These weren't trained men. If they were, they wouldn't be shouting. A man was framed in the window of a car; he was waiting in the shadows. Harvey took him down with the butt of his SIG then finished the job with a swipe of his knife through his throat. He knelt beside the dying man, looked around, then stood to make his way towards the rear of the cabin. He caught sight of something in the corner of his eye and turned to find the two dogs sat perfectly still, exactly where he had left them. Harvey gave a light whistle, and the dogs ran to his side. He chanced a glance up to the cabin window and peeked inside. The back of the old man's head was in clear view. He was sat at a desk giving orders to another guy with tattoos.

Harvey checked around him; he was alone. He turned back and raised his weapon. Then the lights went out, and the sound of chairs scraping along the cabin's thin floor came through the walls.

Adeo, Harvey thought. He must have tripped the switch. Harvey had had a clean shot, but couldn't risk missing now by firing into the darkness. He moved to the corner of the cabin. A roar of automatic fire came from less than ten metres away, but Harvey couldn't see its source. He stole a quick look around the side of the cabin and saw a man firing from the hip like he was in a movie, walking backwards out of Adeo's range. Harvey fired once and took the man down. He considered taking the AK but thought better of it. They were too cumbersome, and he intended on being out of the junkyard in less than two minutes.

From where Harvey stood, he saw the gates and Adeo's massive shadow moving closer to the open space. One Albanian had dragged his friend away and now manned one of the flamethrowers. Harvey took careful aim, released a single round and hit the five-foot-tall orange gas bottle directly. The bottle exploded with such force that before the flames had taken form, Harvey saw the man being blown like a leaf in the breeze towards the cabin.

More shouts filled the silence between short bursts of the automatic weapons. Car lights lit the alleyway to the gates where Adeo was waiting, and the roar of a powerful engine overshadowed the chaotic shouts. A small part of Harvey hoped it was Melody with her MP5. But it wasn't the team. It was a BMW that tore through the gates and aimed directly at the massive bulk of Adeo. The big man had no time to react. He threw himself onto the bonnet of the car, lifting his legs clear of the bumper, and slammed into the windscreen. He bounced over the roof and landed heavily in the mud. The car slid to a halt as Adeo rolled on his back and clutched his chest.

Harvey slipped back into the shadows. The dogs followed.

The cabin spewed out men, more than Harvey had imagined had been in there. He couldn't understand the language of the shouting, but he got the gist. The gates were slammed and locked, and he watched as Adeo was dragged unconscious into the cabin and the door was closed.

Men began to spread out, searching the grounds for Adeo's accomplices. The lights came on in the cabin, and the ground around him lit up. He pointed to the cage and gave a verbal command to the dogs. "Go." The dogs trotted off and lay down on the ground. By the time they had turned to watch him, he had slipped further into the depths of the ranks of cars.

Harvey shivered; the adrenaline was wearing off. Footsteps came from his left. The Albanians were more confident in their search now and they walked in pairs. Harvey stepped out just as two men drew close. He slotted one in the neck and jammed his finger into the eye of the other. He whipped the knife from the first man and plunged it into the chest of the second. The man gasped. His eyes looked up at Harvey, big and white, pleading, understanding. Harvey twisted the blade and jerked it out, letting the man fall to the ground.

Shouts began to come from the cabin, not Adeo's but foreign. An older man's voice. Luan.

Harvey strode along the side wall of the property. Two men crept around the corner in front of him. One looked behind as the other breached the corner, using tactical manoeuvres. These two were military trained, not like the others he had come across. Harvey raised his SIG and took them both down with two shots. The shots seemed to wake the dead. Shouts rang out from all directions across the yard, and scattered footsteps approached from all directions. Harvey turned one more corner, looking for a place to duck into and gather his thoughts. He turned and stepped into the muzzle of a waiting AK-74.

CHAPTER THIRTY

Harvey stared down the barrel into the man's eyes. He was calm, not breathing heavily, and wasn't excited. It wasn't his first time; he was a pro and would probably be ready for an attack from Harvey. Harvey dropped his SIG to the ground and raised his empty hands.

"Walk," said the man.

Harvey didn't move.

"I told you to walk, so walk."

"Where am I walking?" Harvey was waiting for the footsteps of more men, joining the man to celebrate their capture, but none did. He was alone, which told Harvey that the only other men were in the cabin.

"Just fucking walk or I'll drop you right here."

A three-round burst from Melody's barking dog turned the man's cold expression into shock, horror and pain. He twisted and dropped to his knees. Harvey picked up his SIG and put the gun to the man's head. He looked up at Melody and pulled the trigger.

"What took you so long?"

"Ah well, you know, traffic, the weather," said Melody. "I'm glad you're okay. Let's get out of here before-"

She was cut off by the noise of two engines starting. They ducked into the line of cars and watched as the BMW and Range Rover sped out the gates and into the night.

"Reg, come back," said Melody into her earpiece.

"Go ahead."

"Two vehicles just left the yard. Can you track them? BMW and a black Range Rover."

"Yeah, I see the Range Rover. I have his plate. Let me see what I can do."

Melody turned back to Harvey. "Are you coming with us?"

"Wait in the van. I need to check the cabin."

Melody looked through the cars to the cabin. It was shielded by piles of scrap. "You think he's still in there?"

"Adeo? Probably not. But we might find something else in there."

"I can't read you, Harvey."

"Don't try then."

"Are you going to save Adeo or kill him yourself?" She handed Harvey a fresh clip for his SIG, knowing that he would be running low.

"To be honest, Melody," he said, sliding the new magazine into place, "I haven't decided yet."

"It would be nice to get some arrests at the end of this, not just a pile of bodies." Melody gestured at the yard which had men lying on cars, feet and legs sticking out from between piles of junk and one flamethrower with its docile flame tapering off into the air.

"He knows too much. I can't risk him talking. Wait in the van. I'll be out in a sec."

"No, Harvey. I'm coming with you. I've already missed most of the action. At least let me search the cabin with you."

Harvey sighed. "Okay, let's move. In and out. One minute."

The pair ran to the door of the cabin. The lights were on, but there was no movement inside. Melody stood to one side of the door, her MP5 held ready to fire. Harvey kicked the door in, sending it across the floor inside. Melody was in and aiming her weapon at all the blind corners. Harvey stepped in behind her. There were two rooms, both of equal size, approximately four metres wide by six metres. The first was a mess room with a long central table and chairs, presumably where the men would sit and drink coffee and smoke. Two large filing cabinets stood to one side containing scrap records and logbooks of some of the cars that passed through, probably the bare minimum to keep the taxman and law at bay. There were calendars of topless women on the walls, and overflowing ashtrays on the tables, plus empty Vodka bottles dotted around like ornaments.

The second room was Luan's office. A large, glossy desk stood in front of a cushioned, leather reclining chair. There were two less comfortable chairs on the guest side and a potted plant in the corner.

There was no paperwork in the desk drawers, no photos on top, and no sign of anybody being in there, only the smell of cigarette smoke and the musky scent of old sweat.

"Jackson, be ready to go in two," said Melody into her comms.

"Copy," came the reply.

"Dead end," said Melody. "Let's hope Reg managed to get a track on the Range Rover."

"This isn't his main office. This is just a convenient spot for him to work when he's in the area. He's got a main office somewhere else, somewhere slightly more welcoming," said Harvey.

"I'd also say he's got somewhere *less* welcoming for Adeo, and that's where they're heading."

"I'd agree with that," said Harvey. "Let's move."

"Wait," said Melody, then she lost her momentum and added weakly, "are you going to tell me about it?"

"About what, Melody?"

"You saw your foster father, after all this time. I thought, well-"

"There's nothing to think about. He's a villain, I'm not. I've paid my dues."

"You think he'll blow your cover?"

"If I go back without Adeo, maybe. Otherwise, I'm doing him a favour. I just need to make sure I corner him, have a chat, get a lay of the land. I'm sure he'll realise that I'd be slaughtered if he lets on that my name is not Gerry and I've been lying to the firm. I can't imagine he'd want that to happen. But he didn't get where he is by being nice, did he?"

"Let's move," said Melody, and turned to the door. She stepped down the three small steps as Harvey followed then heard the familiar sound of an AK being cocked.

"Drop your weapons," said the man.

Harvey gave a long slow whistle. "You're good," he said.

"No games. Drop them."

Harvey heard the sound he was waiting for, the scatter of mud and light rhythm of dogs' feet bounding across the yard. Movement caught the man's eye, and he turned to see two airborne fifty-pound German Shepherds with bared teeth.

The dogs took him down with no effort and tore through his throat with the savage, carnal ferocity of wolves.

Harvey nudged Melody as she stood and looked on in horror.

"Let's move."

CHAPTER THIRTY-ONE

"Talk to me, Ginger," said John Cartwright. He was sitting alone at a table for two in an Italian restaurant on the Isle of Dogs. The waiter had just delivered his lobster linguine. He sipped at an expensive glass of Chianti and waited for his new number two to deliver the update.

"It's Adeo, boss. Gerry just walked out with some bird. No sign of Adeo."

"Talk me through it."

"Well, they were in there about half an hour when the place erupted. Sounded like a bloody movie. Two cars came tearing out, and the bird walked in carrying a machine gun. I haven't got a clue where she came from. Then there were a few more shots, and the pair of them walked out like they just had dinner."

"Did anybody follow the cars?"

"No, boss, we're on our own here. We expected to see Adeo and that Gerry bloke come running out."

"Do you think Adeo is down?"

"I just poked my head in the gates and saw two massive dogs. Nothing else moving. He's either dead or in the car."

"Well, if we lose Adeo, I want Bobby and his firm taken care of and dumped in the river, Ginger."

"Sorry, boss."

"Don't apologise to me, Ging. But make plans. Make sure we're ready to jump the lot of them as soon as I give the word."

"Will do, boss."

"What about the bird? Who is she?"

"Dunno, boss. She looks serious. She's got filth written all over her."

"A cop?"

"Who else has automatic weapons like that? Besides, it's the way she held it. Like she'd trained, you know what I mean?"

"Are you following them?"

"Yeah, they just walked up the road. I'll find out where they're going and get back to you."

"Make sure you do, Ginger."

CHAPTER THIRTY-TWO

"This is more like it," said Reg as the van pulled away. "The whole team back in the van, just like the old days."

Melody didn't reply. The statement reminded her that Denver wasn't there.

"How are you getting on with finding that Range Rover, Reg?" asked Harvey.

"Done. Easy. LUCY is tracking it now. I just traced the plates back to the dealer, hacked the dealer's firewall and-"

"Another time, eh Reg? Sorry mate, it's been a rough night."

"Reg, where am I heading?" asked Jackson.

"A12, Jackson, all the way," replied Reg. "Looks like they've stopped in some kind of recycling plant off Pudding Mill Lane."

"Mark the exits for me, Reg. I'll take a look in a minute. Jackson, can you call out the ETAs? Melody, how many spare clips you got for the SIGs?"

"Two each."

"So, four for me then. You're staying in the van."

"No, I'm not. I just sat outside and listened to world war three going off in that yard."

"You'll blow my cover. I need to go in and get Adeo

and get out. If I have help, he'll know I'm still old bill. At least if I work alone, I may be able to convince him otherwise."

"For God's sake, Harvey."

"Sorry to interrupt, people, but we have a tail," said Jackson. "They've been on us since we left the yard."

Harvey was sat on the floor of the van behind Melody in the passenger seat. "Melody, how close?"

"Two hundred metres give or take."

"Reckon you can make the shot?"

"What? Harvey, we're not on a random killing rampage."

"No, we're running an operation to stop organised crime. Can you make the shot or not?"

"No, Harvey, I won't do it."

Harvey pulled his SIG from his waistband. "Jackson, take us somewhere quiet."

"What are you doing, Harvey?" said Melody.

"Stopping organised crime, Melody. What does it look like I'm doing?"

"I know a place around the corner. We'll be there in one minute," said Jackson.

"Reg, on my three."

"No," said Melody. "Stop, everyone. Just stop."

"No time, Melody. We're in this now," said Harvey.

"Thirty seconds," said Jackson.

"Reg, be ready with the door."

"Harvey, what are you doing?"

"Melody, do you trust me?"

"With my life. But this is stupid."

"Ten seconds."

"Get that barking dog of yours and be ready to jump out on my one." He'd turned and spoken the words carefully at her, looking her directly in the eye.

Melody made the MP5 ready and sat with her hand on the door handle. "Frank isn't going to like this."

Harvey felt the van turn right. Trees hung across the road, and only old warehouses stood either side.

"Three."

Jackson eased off the accelerator pedal, and the van began to slow. The car behind drew close.

"Two." Reg pulled the handle on the rear door and shoved it open as hard as he could.

Harvey fired twice at the car's radiator, and angry steam hissed from the grill.

"One."

Melody dived out of the passenger seat and covered the car with the MP5.

Harvey began to slide out of the van. "Tyres."

Melody gave two three-round bursts and took out the front and back right tyres.

Harvey strode to the driver's door and ripped it open with his weapon on the driver. He reached in and dragged the man to the tarmac. Harvey stood on the back of his neck and aimed at the passenger. "It's Ginger, right? The man with the head in the bag?"

The man nodded.

"You've got three seconds to get out the car before I finish you right here. Try anything dumb, and she'll open you up. One."

The man opened the door.

"Two."

He slowly stepped out with his hands raised.

"Three. Good. When I give you an order with a time limit, do it faster. Next time, I won't be so lenient." Harvey's eyes never left the man who stood close to Melody. "Reg, ties."

Reg grabbed a bundle of zip ties and climbed out of the van. He passed them to Harvey.

"I don't want them, zip this up," said Harvey. He had full control of the situation. "Put two or three on, they're going in the back with you." Once Reg had pulled the man's hands behind his back and had the first tie pulled tight, Harvey released pressure off his neck and walked round to Ginger.

"You're considering running."

"No, I'm not, honest I-"

"Yeah, you are. I saw you looking about."

"I didn't, I weren't-"

Harvey fired a round into the man's foot. "No running."

The man fell to the ground with an inaudible whimper.

"Reg, tie this one up." Harvey walked back to the driver. "Up." The man struggled to roll over with bound hands, so Harvey leaned down, grabbed his collar and gave him a yank to help him stand. "In the back."

Once Ginger had been loaded up, Melody climbed into the passenger seat, and Harvey sat on top of the two men. He pulled the door closed. "Gerry says go," said Harvey, reminding the team not to use his real name. "ETA?" he called.

"Less than five minutes out."

He tapped Reg on the shoulder. "Show me the exits, mate," said Harvey, keeping the use of names out of the conversation. "And good work back there, nice and quick."

Reg turned smiling, and said, "Thanks, Ha-"

"Exits," said Harvey, warning Reg not to use his name.

"Here we are," said Reg, diverting his sentence. "One main gate at the front, a smaller gate at the side in a quiet street, and nothing at the back except a high wall and the canal. The satellite is live, so I've scrolled back a few hours and found this daylight shot from earlier."

Harvey memorised the layout of the site. It looked to be fairly large, maybe a few acres, with a group of three buildings in one corner. There were heaps of scrap metal, white goods and piles of randomly assorted recycling shown on the satellite imagery.

"Okay, driver, side entrance please."

"I'm coming with you," said Melody.

Harvey didn't reply.

"You hear me, Gerry?"

Harvey was tightening his laces. "You're taking these two in."

"You can't go alone, Gerry."

"One minute," said Jackson.

"Track me, follow me, do what you need to do. I'll let you know if I need help."

"And how do you plan on doing that?"

Harvey nudged Reg again. "Got an earpiece?"

Reg passed Harvey an earpiece from a small bag on his bench. Harvey removed the hygiene wrapper and slotted it into his ear. He hit the tiny button twice for the channel to stay open without the need for the push-to-talk. "Take these guys in. Come back for me," said Harvey, looking Melody in the eye to reassure her without embarrassing her. "Driver, what's the ETA on HQ and back?"

"Forty minutes, including drop off time."

"I'll be out in thirty-five. If I'm not, come looking for me."

"Ten seconds," said Jackson.

Harvey banged his SIG lightly on the head of one of the men beneath him. "While I'm gone, I'd like one of you to do me a favour." He spoke slowly and clearly. "I want you to tell these nice people where I can find John Cartwright." One of the men struggled as the van came to a stop. Harvey nodded for Reg to open the rear door. "Because I promise you if you wait for me to get back and I have to ask you, it's going to hurt a lot more, and for a lot longer. Is that understood?"

No reply.

Harvey bent down between the men's heads and offered a growling whisper. "I said, is that understood?"

The men waited for a few seconds then both nodded.

Harvey stepped off the back of the van and reached up to close the door. He caught Melody turning in her seat, watching him with worry in her eyes.

He winked and closed the door, then turned and stepped into the waiting open gate.

CHAPTER THIRTY-THREE

Reg opened the sliding shutter doors of the team's headquarters using LUCY's console. Jackson pulled the van in and the shutters slid back in place.

Melody opened the van's sliding side door and spoke to the two men. "Out."

"What are we going to do with them?" asked Reg.

"Find me some handcuffs, Reg," replied Melody. "Come on, you two. Out."

The two villains slid backwards out of the van and stood.

"Where are we?" asked Ginger.

"No questions, just move. See that column over there?"

A steel girder supported the mezzanine floor. It was bolted top and bottom.

"I'm sure you know the drill. Stand with your backs to the beam," ordered Melody.

Reg returned with two sets of handcuffs from Melody's filing cabinet. Melody raised the MP5 to her shoulder and aimed at the two men. "Okay, cut the ties, and cuff them back to back around the column."

"No problem, I've been tying people up all night," said Reg.

"Driver?" called Melody. "Can you cover these two while I get some ammo?"

Jackson walked over to Melody, took the MP5, and placed the butt into Ginger's shoulder.

"You've fired one of these before. That looks natural."

"I've been known to help out here and there," said Jackson with a smile.

"Good to know. Make sure those cuffs are tight and uncomfortable."

The team were ready in under five minutes.

"Okay, you two, Ginger, wasn't it? And what's your name?"

The man didn't reply.

"You want to tell me where we can find John Cartwright?"

"Not really, Miss," said Ginger.

"It'd work in your favour if you did."

"Is that right? I'd have my throat slit, and even if I went away, he'd get me on the inside. I'm not telling you nothing."

"Well, I'll tell you right now, this is the easy option. If you talk, I can get you in witness protection. Nobody can find you."

"Yeah right, you don't know John Cartwright."

"Oh, believe me, we know John Cartwright better than anyone."

"No, save your breath, lady. You've got twenty-four hours to charge me, and I want my legal rep if you do."

Melody laughed. "Honestly, look at us. You really think that conventional rules apply here? You two aren't who we're after. You're small fry, not worth the paperwork. The number of men Gerry put down tonight, two more wouldn't make a difference. So your options are simple. Talk to me, or *Gerry* will make you talk."

"You talk like he's some sort of legend. Who is he? Ex-SAS or something?"

Melody laughed again. "No, but you're right, he is a legend."

Melody stood and turned to walk away. "But I'll tell you this, Ginger."

Ginger looked up at Melody. "What? Tell me what? He's going to pull my fingernails out?"

"Fingernails? No." She walked back to him and looked him in the eye. "If you don't tell Gerry where we can find Cartwright, he won't stop at you. He'll find your family."

"Behave. He wouldn't be allowed, he-"

"Who do you think he is, you idiot? He's not the police, he's one of you. He's a villain, a lifelong villain. He's been killing people since he was twelve years old, and he's pretty good at it. Piss him off, go on, I dare you. I guarantee he'll bring your wife here and let you watch him."

"You're talking out of your arse, bitch. No cops can do that."

Melody laughed. "We're not cops. We don't exist. Look at where you are. Not very nick-like is it? Wake up, Ginger. You're in for a rough ride, and your ticket to surviving is slipping away."

Melody turned to Reg. "Can you stay here and keep an eye on these two? Any problems, use your weapon."

"Me? But I-"

"Keep calm. They can't go anywhere, but better safe than sorry. Besides, we need you on LUCY."

Reg looked slightly dejected. "Okay, I guess."

"Driver, we ready to go?"

"Let's do it."

Melody spoke softly into the comms. "Gerry, no need to reply, but our ETA is..." She looked at Jackson who mimed fifteen minutes. "Fifteen minutes. That's one-five minutes. Click three times if you need something."

Jackson put the van into reverse and pulled out of the unit. Ginger's eyes met Melody's as she disappeared from view.

"That was impressive," said Jackson. "Powerful."

"That was desperate, Jackson."

Jackson put the van into first and pulled away as the sliding shutters closed. "How do you mean?"

"If they *don't* talk to Harvey, he'll rip them to shreds. I was *trying* to save their lives."

CHAPTER THIRTY-FOUR

Harvey surveyed the dark recycling plant in front of him. The satellite image he'd seen on Reg's screen mapped the scene out for him. The three buildings were in the far right-hand corner, and there was no sign of movement. Harvey took a path around the edge of the plot alongside the high wall, keeping to the shadows and moving slow, always listening and watching. It was during these times that Harvey's mind was most alive, like a Neolithic man walking through the African bush, always alert for dangers, always having an escape route, and most of all, always having a plan.

The few times he had to cross open land, he encountered no trouble. The lack of security told him two things. Firstly, Duri was not expecting to be followed or tracked, and secondly, the site had limited men. The scrapyard had been full of men. He and Adeo had taken a lot of them down. Now Harvey just needed a plan to tear his way through the rest of them.

He came upon the buildings. They were laid out in a large L-shape, with the third building far longer than the rest. Harvey supposed this to be the offices. The other two structures were smaller, ten metres by twenty, Harvey thought. He stood between the outer wall of the compound and the first small building. It smelled damp, and the windows were opaque with wire mesh. Harvey took a guess that this was the toilet and shower block. The next building had lights on in one of the rooms. Harvey stepped slowly up to see in, but the room was empty. It was a small office for two people. Two old telephones stood on two old desks, with two battered old chairs behind them.

There were no nude calendars, no empty bottles of vodka and no overspilling ashtrays. He felt around the window. It was locked. The area was fairly rough, so security would be quite high. Yet the gate had been left open, possibly because of the speed at which they were travelling, and possibly because they weren't planning on staying long.

He heard footsteps on the boarded floor inside. Heavy boots. A door slammed shut somewhere, and men's voices vibrated through the thin walls, but Harvey couldn't understand the language.

At least two, Duri and one other.

Then Harvey heard voices from outside. Two more. The tone of the first on the inside suggested hierarchy. One was sharper and shorter, the other more appeasing. The two voices around the corner sounded more conversational, equals.

Harvey chanced a glance around the corner. Two men stood smoking. An AK-74 leaned against the wall behind one of them. The other had one hand in his pocket. They were relaxed, confident that nobody would come. One of the two men took a casual look around him. Harvey ducked his head back and heard the men walk away. He watched them disappear into the middle of the yard, then turn behind a pile of white goods.

Harvey followed.

He stepped quietly onto patches of dry mud, around

puddles and through muddy tyre tracks. It was pitch dark in the yard, and Harvey could hear nothing.

Until the lights came on.

Two powerful spotlights atop an earthmoving machine forty metres in front of him lit the ground where Harvey stood, followed by the roar of its powerful diesel engine starting up. Harvey froze. He was in plain sight. Another pair of spotlights lit him from behind, and another diesel engine began to cough into life. As if in sync, lights came from either side of him. The air was filled now with the spitting and deep throaty growl of four engines. He had nowhere to run.

The mechanical squealing of the machine's heavy iron tracks joined the ensemble, and the bass-like rumble of thirty tons of heavy machinery filled the lower spectrum of sound. Hanging chains from the heavy steel bulldozers rattled in percussive shudders as the enormous machines slowly closed in on Harvey.

The ground was now well lit and Harvey saw the silhouettes of many men filling the gaps between each machine. Each perfect human shape was scarred with the unmistakable barrel of a Kalashnikov.

Harvey growled at his own stupidity under his breath. Patience, planning and execution, his mantra. He'd acted hastily to save his own life. But by doing so, he now saw no other option than to lay down his weapon.

He held fast as long as he could until the machines were each just ten metres away. He was boxed in by the steel, diesel-powered monsters, and the grit and tenacity of the Albanian mafia.

The engines were cut, and the silence that followed the deathly chorus seemed to linger as if in appreciation.

"You are a brave man," said a voice, the old man's voice, Duri.

Harvey didn't reply.

"Stupid, but brave." The man in the long coat stepped out of the glare of lights and towards Harvey but stopped three metres in front of him. "Did you really think that just two men could destroy us? Do you see what we have built here in your country?"

"All I see is a bunch of immigrants on a piece of land that nobody else wants."

"Ah, we see things with different eyes though, do we not?" The man began to walk in a circle around Harvey. Harvey stayed perfectly still, all too aware of the twenty AK-74s that were aimed at him.

"You see, where *you* see wasteland, *I* see opportunity. Where *you* see the unwanted items of the rich. I see a profit for the poor people of Albania, my homeland." He spoke the last two words softly, with affection.

"I don't care about the waste, have it. But you overstepped the mark, didn't you? You couldn't help yourself, right? You just wanted one more piece of the pie. Well, that pie belongs to us. London? We might let you live here, and yeah, we let you send your money home. That's just humanity. But each time you stand on someone else's toes, you disrupt a very delicate balance."

"How poetic. You like poetry?"

"Not particularly."

"It's a shame. Poetry is a beautiful way to capture our history. So many great poems describe times long ago that we strive to understand today. In fact, poetry is the only record of certain historical events and is the basis of our knowledge. Like a verbal tapestry."

"Please tell me I'm not standing here in the mud talking about poetry with a pikey? Is this how it ends? I thought I'd have a more peaceful death if I'm honest."

"'Tell me what they'd write about you. The poets."

Harvey didn't reply.

"Tell me who you are."

Harvey didn't reply.

"You'll talk, of that I'm sure. I have skills. I was taught by the best."

"We share an enthusiasm for encouragement. Aleksander spoke too. I was amazed at how quickly he spoke if I'm honest. A big bloke like that reduced to tears and pissing himself."

Luan glared at Harvey.

"Tell me who you are."

"I'm going to need a little more encouragement than that, Luan."

"You want encouragement?"

"Do it."

"You want to piss your pants like Aleksander?"

"Make me. Let's play."

"You're a crazy fool."

"Yeah, maybe. But let me make one thing clear. When the tables turn, and it's you who needs encouragement, I'm going to make you sing. Bear that in mind, and we'll see who sings loudest, eh?"

Luan laughed. "Such control." He stopped laughing, took on a serious grimace and stared into Harvey's eyes. "I look forward to breaking you." He nodded to the man behind Harvey.

Harvey felt the butt of a rifle slam into the back of his head. Blood rushed to his brain, he tasted iron, and darkness enveloped him.

CHAPTER THIRTY-FIVE

Harvey woke stripped naked in a windowless room with rough concrete walls. His wrists were bound with a harsh manila rope, which was fixed to chains that hung from a steel eye bolt in the concrete ceiling above. A single lamp to his right barely lit the ten-foot-square room, and a single chair sat opposite him where Luan Duri sat calmly, staring at Harvey.

"Good morning," said Luan.

Harvey's head throbbed, and his back was aching like he'd been dragged across the concrete floor.

"Did you sleep well?"

It was pointless to try to work out where in the compound he was. If he was actually still in the compound. His watch had been removed; he had no idea how long he'd been out for. All Harvey could do was prepare himself for what was to come. To survive.

"You interest me," said Luan. "I do so wish to know your name. It would make the conversation so much more engaging if I knew who I'm talking to."

Harvey didn't reply.

"You'll tell me. Eventually."

Luan stood and walked around the back of Harvey.

"So, perhaps we can start with something easy. We do, after all, have all night. Longer if need be." Luan leaned over Harvey's shoulder and spoke quietly into his left ear. "Tell me about Aleksander, our mutual friend. Tell me how you made him talk."

Harvey didn't reply. He felt something cold and hard trace the muscles on his back.

"You take good care of yourself."

Harvey felt the point of a blade in the small of his back.

"Tell me," whispered Luan.

"I didn't touch him," spat Harvey.

"Oh, come on. The silence I can deal with, but lies, I cannot tolerate liars."

"He spoke freely against you."

"Did you...encourage him?"

"I didn't need to."

The blade slid up Harvey's spine and stopped between his shoulder blades. "One of the things I enjoy about what you call encouragement is the exploratory elements. I regard it as a lesson in science. For example, I once opened a man and removed various parts of him. I did it slowly, of course, such matters require delicacy, or else the heart will fail and spoil my fun."

He leaned over Harvey's right shoulder and whispered. "Shall we have a science lesson?" He stopped. "Do you notice you are missing some items?"

It was then that Harvey realised the earpiece had gone. The blade ran further up Harvey's back until it found the wound where the tracker that Melody had inserted had been. It had been removed.

"You see now why you interest me?" said Luan. "More so than the giant in the next room, your friend."

Luan stepped in front of Harvey. "Do you want to know what I think?"

"Not really."

"I think you're with an agency. SO-10 maybe? SOCA?"

Harvey didn't reply.

"I have been in Britain long enough to know that even SO-10 are not permitted to kill without approval. Yet you, my friend, well you created quite a body count in my yard, didn't you? I'll admit that they were not perhaps my best men, good men are hard to come by, but you made it all look so effortless."

Luan paced around Harvey once more.

"If you're holding out for rescue, then I am afraid I have bad news for you. Everything you owned, your clothes, your phone, your little devices, are all on a journey a long way from here. So you may be here some time."

Luan stepped close to Harvey and looked deep into his eyes. Then Harvey felt Luan's hand on his genitals. "How about our science lesson? I'm done talking. Now it is your turn." Luan squeezed hard. Harvey bit down on his lip and breathed out hard through his nose.

Luan released his grip. "Impressive. You're a real man's man, aren't you?"

Harvey didn't reply.

"I think I'll start with something smaller," said Luan. "I'll save the best for last." Luan licked his lips slowly. "An ear maybe? Or a toe? What do you think?"

"I think you're writing a cheque you can't afford, pal."

"Is that so?" Luan looked thoughtfully around the room then stepped into the shadows. Harvey heard the clatter of tools on a bench. Then Luan stepped back into the light holding an axe handle.

"Did you miss me?" said Luan and then swung the bat.

"Fast as you can, Jackson. I don't want to miss the party," said Melody. Jackson opened up the throttle on the VW van.

"Reg, talk to me. How's he looking?"

"Well, he's on the move."

"He's moving? Where?"

"In transit, now. His phone, tracker and earpiece are all moving east."

"What's he doing? Can we get him on the comms?"

"Without the antenna on the van, the earpiece relies on GPS or satellite. Looking at the keep-alive report, he went dark ten minutes ago, and is now heading east at fifty miles an hour."

"Be my eyes, Reg," said Jackson. "Where am I going?"

Melody was taken back by the phrase 'be my eyes.' Denver used to say that in times just like the one they found themselves in.

"Head to the North Circular Road. You can cut in or out of town from there. I'll keep you posted."

"We're screwed if we lose him, Jackson."

"Then we better not lose him." Jackson looked across at Melody. She was a tough girl, but she clearly had feelings for

Harvey. They'd shared so many adventures already that somehow she loved him. Jackson was good at reading people. He was intuitive to people's feelings.

"Reg, it's Jackson."

"Go ahead."

"Put me through to a Chief Superintendent Fox with the Hackney Police."

"What are you doing?" asked Melody. "This is 'covert. We can't call it in. Do you know what we did back there?"

"Trust me, Melody. Fox owes me."

"I'm working on it. It's out of hours, so I'll need to find his mobile, and they like to hide those. Fortunately, I like to find them, and... here it is. Sit tight caller."

The communication was routed to the phone call and the van's loudspeaker.

"Fox." The voice answered abruptly.

"CS Fox, it's Jackson."

There was a long silence. "I wondered when you'd call it in."

"I wouldn't if I had a choice, sir."

"I hear you're on the dark side now?"

"Dark in terms of visibility, but always on the side of the law."

"Okay, what is it? And why?"

"A bird, sir. I'm afraid I can't tell you any more than that."

"I can't just release a chopper without good reason, Jackson. You know that."

"I thought we had a deal, sir."

"We did have a deal."

"And you owe me."

"I do owe you, but I was expecting maybe you'd use that to release a friend who was caught drink driving or something."

"I'd never ask you to do that, sir. You know my view on DD."

"But you can second a police helicopter without good reason? Where are you taking it?"

"Sir, do you trust me?"

"I used to."

"It's covert, sir. If I could tell you, I would, I'd even call you in to help. There's enough glory in this one to hang a few medals off your tunic."

Fox gave a heavy sigh. "I suppose you want me to clear the bird with ATC too?"

"It'd save a lot of embarrassing questions, sir."

"Give me five minutes. Call me back."

CHAPTER THIRTY-SEVEN

"Dom, tell me where we're at."

"Bobby, they're cleaned out. Our men are inside now. We've hit every bookie they protect, and we've got men outside all the pubs."

"Any resistance from the owners?"

"One or two. Most turned around easy, happy to be looked after by natives, as it were."

"Good, good. I want twenty good men in the area, I want to be seen, and I want the locals to know that Bobby Carnell now runs the manor, and they no longer need to fear the Albanians."

"You reckon John Cartwright will strike?"

"No, Dom, I don't. Right now John Cartwright is probably sitting feeding his greedy face, more concerned with what Gerry and his goon are doing. Leave Doug here with me. He can run things while you're expanding the business. Once the Albanians are out of the way, Dom, I'll sort you out, mate. You've done well."

"Cheers, Bobby."

"Remember, any sign of an Albanian in the area, and you take them out. From what Sid said, Gerry and Adeo created an absolute bloodbath, said it was like a scene from a film. Pretty soon, they won't have the men to do anything about it, and they'll have to go elsewhere. Home hopefully. Make some friends, Dom, buy some drinks, work out what local boys we have there, get them on board. You know how it works. Don't say too much, but work out where the extra hands are if we need them."

"Will do, Bobby. But listen, mate, I've been thinking. This John Cartwright, he's old school, right?"

"Yeah. So?"

"So how many times has someone like Cartwright walked brazenly into another firm's boozer, stared the main man in the eye and pretty much forced him to do something, like take on another firm."

Bobby was silent.

"You see what I mean, Bobby? I reckon once the Albanians are gone, he'll come after us."

"Behave. He's not looking for a war between us. He keeps to his turf we keep to ours. Respect, Dom, that's what it's all about."

"Yeah, but we're not keeping to our own, are we? Here I am on the border of North London, making sure the Albanians don't come back. It's going to piss him off, Bobby."

"So, we take John Cartwright out. I am not backing down, Dom. Don't get weak."

"I'm not getting weak. You know me, Bobby. I'm just sitting here piecing it all together."

"Right, well while you're sitting there, piece together a plan so we can off Cartwright. I'll get some boys in East Ham to have a look at where he's dug in."

"What about Gerry, Bobby? I don't trust him."

"Gerry who, Dom?"

CHAPTER THIRTY-EIGHT

Harvey fought for breath. Luan had just finished another round of wild swings on his back, and his lungs had taken a beating. He could taste blood. His legs had given way from the repeated strikes to his balls, which were now swollen and angry red. He hung from the chains and revelled in the break.

"Pretty soon I will move to something a little sharper," said Luan. "Are you sure you wouldn't like to tell me your name?"

My name, thought Harvey. *What the hell is my name? Am I Gerry now? Harvey Stone wouldn't be here. He was smarter than that.*

"I'm talking to you," said Luan.

Gerry may have gotten me into this mess, but it'll be Harvey who gets me out.

"Bardh," called Luan.

The door opened after a few seconds. A man with a shaved head and tattoos on his face opened the door.

"Boss?" said Bardh in a deep grumble. He wasn't a particularly big man, not compared to Adeo or Julios, but he looked fit and strong. His skin hugged his unshaved face, and his dark features were prominent in the dim light.

"Bring me the goon, Bardh."

The door closed.

"You're going to enjoy this," said Luan.

"Am I? I can't say I'm thrilled right now."

"Well, I'm going to enjoy it anyway."

The door opened again, and four men brought Adeo inside. Two held Kalashnikov assault rifles, while the other two manhandled him into the room. Someone brought steps in and fixed chains to the eye bolt in the ceiling beside Harvey.

"Now leave me," said Luan. "Go find some food. I can watch them. Bring me something."

The door closed, and Luan sat on the single wooden chair in front of Harvey and Adeo. He reached into the inside pocket of his long coat and pulled out a fillet knife. He held the weapon with ease, clearly accustomed to handling that particular knife. Luan flexed it and studied the edge for nicks and small chips on the finest part of a blade, but there were none.

"When I was a boy, my father taught me to fish," said Luan. The statement wasn't particularly aimed at either one of the two men that hung from the ceiling like carcasses of game. It was an opening line for his story, and he spoke like John Cartwright had spoken of Harvey's parents. Like it was rehearsed. A speech. Verbatim.

"We had a small house in a small village with a river that carved its way through the fields like a snake. My mother was always at home, always something to do, cleaning and cooking or sewing. She made our clothes, you know. We had chickens for eggs, and we grew vegetables, potatoes and such. Money was tight and food was expensive. The horror of the war still hung in the air, and people clung to memories of lost children, parents, family. It was a dark time in a bitter and cold winter. Nobody looked to the future, the present was hard to ignore. But my father was a strong man. He taught me to hunt and to fish, so often we would sit in a small rowboat on one of the many lakes, and we would sit and talk and catch fish. We never caught too many, only enough to feed us and occasionally we would catch one for our neighbour. To trade. My father never spoke of the war. I always imagined it was because the horrors were too much for a child to learn of. But since, I have learned that it was he who performed the horrors, and so I surmised that he had been ashamed of his acts. I wonder if he could see me now, if he would see how I understand. Maybe he would have told me those things he did. Maybe he would have taught me. Father and son, sharing a kill. There's something poetic about that, isn't there?"

He looked at Harvey who had been studying his face as he told the story.

"I told you, poetry runs through our very existence. I'm sorry, Adeo, I was referring to a conversation that we had before you arrived. How rude of me."

Luan dropped his head again and continued with his story. "My father did teach me how to use a knife. This very knife in fact. It was his own, and then he passed it to me. A man bonds with his knife, doesn't he? There's something special about a well-crafted knife that surpasses any connection a man may have with a gun or a rifle. My father showed me how to gut a fish. Then he showed me how to clean it by opening it up. When I was an expert at both, he showed me how to use my knife to cut the fillet from the bone. At first, I found bones in my food, sharp reminders that my lessons were not over. But after some time, I was practised and moved on to chickens, and then bigger and tougher animals."

Luan looked up at Harvey who stared back.

"Am I boring you?"

Harvey didn't reply.

"There was a family in our village, rough people, and dirty.

They stole from the villagers, and the father went to prison. Soon the family became so poor the mother could barely feed her children. I found her eldest son in our house one day. My mother was feeding the chickens and my father was out somewhere working the fields with other villagers. The boy was older than me by a year, maybe two. I stepped into the kitchen, and he turned to face me, unafraid but ashamed. His pockets were full of the fruit my mother had picked, and the bread she had baked. The boy turned to walk away, and I let him. I watched him leave, and he looked back at me as he closed the door of our house. I followed that boy through the windows as he walked around the side, and then to the front, where he disappeared into the narrow lane that led to their house. I checked my mother was not around then I slipped out of the house after him. His shame had been forgotten in our kitchen. He walked along eating our fruit, skipping puddles of rain. He looked like a boy who hadn't care in the world. No father had ever taught that boy to fish and gather food for his family. No father had ever shown that boy that life can be bearable with a little hard work, that obstacles are there to face on your own, and that stealing from another is not the answer."

Luan paused and looked back up. "That was my first time. My first kill." Luan held the blade lovingly. "I took all those lessons my father taught me and went to work. I fought the boy and knocked him down with a rock. I dragged the boy into the thick bushes that lined the sparse fields. I cut him open like a carp, and I removed his insides. I filleted the boy, and I ate his liver."

There was a long silence before Harvey spoke.

"How did it taste?" He felt Adeo's eyes on him and caught the cold snarly smile of Luan Duri. Just the corners of his mouth upturned.

"Delicious," said Luan. "Like the first meat I ever really

tasted."

"And you ate more?"

"They were desperate times. Food could not be wasted."

"And they were hard times too, weren't they? A killer could not be caught or he would surely pay the ultimate price."

"You listen well," said Luan. "Can I ask, have you tried it? Human flesh?"

Harvey didn't reply.

"You were doing so well. But you may be pleased to know that my little anecdote is now over. It is now your turn to entertain me with your own stories. I am sure that you both have many, so I will do a deal with you." Luan rose and dragged the chair into the corner of the room. Then he walked behind the two naked men. "Each of you will tell me one story, something horrific. *I* will judge. *I* will decide who dies first. But this I will not tell you. I will not tell you what I am looking for. Am I looking for gruesome? Or am I looking to see who has the strongest morality? I may be looking for a story to tell my grandchildren or I may be looking to see who deserves to die first. But I will tell you this, the winner will die fast and relatively painlessly. The other, well, not so fast and not so painlessly. Is that understood?"

Adeo nodded. Harvey just stared at the floor.

"Begin."

Harvey lifted his head and sensed Luan close behind him, urging him to talk.

"I had a sister once," began Harvey, "when we were young. She died." Harvey closed his eyes and dragged the memories he'd fought so hard to bury back to the front of his mind. "Some bad men took her and raped her. She was just a child, barely fifteen. I was twelve at the time, and I'll never forget the night it happened. I heard her screams, and I heard their breath destroying her with each stroke. I sat in the shadows and listened, helpless. She killed herself a few days later. She stole a knife from the kitchen and took it to her room, where she stabbed herself in all the places they had touched. Squeezed. Penetrated."

"This is good," said Luan. "Do go on."

"I found the first man six months later, and with the help of a friend, I took him down. I made him suffer. Eventually, I killed him. I felt a small amount of peace for Hannah. But I hadn't finished. It took me twenty years, but I found the next man. He'd been close all along. I'd seen him every day, and every day as I grew stronger, and the twelve-year-old boy grew into a man, he feared that the day would come when I found out his dirty secret and would bring more peace to Hannah."

Harvey took a moment to push the memory of Jack aside and bring forward the memory of Sergio. "Sergio was a coward. A numbers man with long bony fingers that were in every little nook and crack. He knew everything and controlled everything with his knowledge. I boiled Sergio alive in an antique copper bathtub. I watched his eyes turn pale white, blinded as the liquids inside them boiled. I watched as, one by one, his organs failed. Cooked. Ready to eat."

"Like a boil in the bag?" Luan smiled.

"Like a boil in the bag, Luan. As he died, he gave me the name the last man who had been there, the last man who'd raped my sister. Again, I hunted and found him. I took him to the very same place where I had boiled his friend alive. He was a villain, a cold-hearted villain with little sense of morality. We never saw eye to eye. He ran a sex trafficking ring, bringing on girls from Albania, Lithuania and other places. He sold them for sex and charged his punters for the pleasure of killing."

"And this man's name?"

"Donny."

"Donny?" said Luan.

"Donny Cartwright."

Luan stepped in front of Harvey with his head cocked in interest and Adeo's eyes bored into Harvey.

"I saved the girls and took Donny to the basement where Sergio had boiled."

"Go on." Luan was getting excited.

"I left him there with the girls he had sold. He was torn to shreds by ten angry women who had narrowly escaped death. They emerged from the dark stairs with his blood on their hands and faces. Donny Cartwright had been mutilated beyond recognition."

"There is honour in your story."

Harvey didn't reply.

"You're a cold man, but you have a warm heart." Luan nodded. "You should hope now that Adeo here is not such a storyteller."

He turned to Adeo who hung his head, then raised it and turned to face Harvey like Luan wasn't there.

"I worked once for a man. It was mostly collecting money and breaking bones. But sometimes my partner and I were asked to take care of people, men who got in the way, or who over-stepped the mark. We would make them disappear, quietly and quickly, with little mess."

Harvey held Adeo's gaze as he told the story. Adeo wasn't struggling to remember the details, they were fresh in his mind like they'd hung there waiting to be told.

"Leo was a strong man, a practised killer. He was feared throughout the East End, but he was also one of those men who carried his presence well. He was respected. He was gentle to those who needed a softer touch, but he could be brutal. Leo had this gift. He could make people talk. He'd barely touch them and they would tell us everything we needed to know. He'd deliver death slowly, drawing out the pain and savouring the screams like a king savouring the finest wines. I liked Leo, everybody did. But one day, our boss, a powerful man, called me into his office alone and told me to finish Leo."

"Finish Leo?" asked Luan.

"Kill him. Leo had failed the boss. He had made his own judgment call and allowed a woman who had wronged the family to live; he'd allowed her to escape. The boss found out. Of course, I followed my instruction and lay in wait inside Leo's house, hidden in the darkness of the shadows. I waited all night for him to return, something I was accustomed to. But Leo was a dangerous man. I had one chance, and if I failed, he would have killed me. When he stepped past me in the darkness, I reached out and cut his throat. One slice. No turning back. His wife, Olivia, had been standing behind him. I hadn't seen her."

"That was a mistake," said Luan.

Adeo stared at the ground and nodded. "She fell to her knees and screamed, louder than I ever heard a scream before, piercing and haunting. She was beautiful, even in her anguish. Leo had been the envy of the firm." Adeo looked up and stared at Luan. "I cut her throat too. I laid her on top of Leo so they may die together with the knife in her hands, and I ran." Adeo let his head fall back. Harvey saw a thin shiny trail of tears stream from his eye. "A small girl sat on a chair by the front door beside a baby in a hamper."

Harvey snatched his head up and lurched at Adeo. His rope snapped tight. "You bastard!" he shouted and swung his legs to connect with Adeo. But Adeo stepped away to the limit of his rope out of Harvey's reach.

"*Untie me*, Luan," snarled Harvey. "Untie me *now*."

"You're in no position to-"

"*I said untie me.*" Spit flew from Harvey's lip. His wild eyes were wide with anger and hatred.

"I picked up the children, and I ran from the house."

"No!" screamed Harvey. "Stop."

"Neighbours had heard her scream. They gathered in the street and saw me run from the house," continued Adeo.

"No more, you bastard," Harvey yelled. He was snatching at the rope, pulling it in all directions, looking for a weakness in the fixing.

"I like this," said Luan. "Carry on, Adeo." He looked enthralled at Harvey's rage.

"I was known to the people that saw me leave the scene. We all were; we ran the place. My brother took the rap for me, and then travelled back to Portugal, while I hid in Britain with some allies far away from this place."

Harvey fell limp and hung from his bindings. His arms stretched awkwardly upwards. His head hung towards the cold, hard ground.

"Is that your story, Adeo?" asked Luan.

Adeo nodded.

"So, you are a coward? You ran and let your brother take the blame. Are you ashamed?"

Adeo nodded once more. "If it is my time to die, then it was time to tell my story." Adeo looked at Harvey then let his eyes fall to the floor.

"I have decided," said Luan, "which one of you shall die slowly and painfully and which one of you shall die fast." Luan ran the blade along Harvey's chest and took a long, deep breath.

"Adeo, you will suffer in the most horrific manner of deaths. You shall be opened up and gutted like a fish while you still breathe the air of this world. I shall feed you your own liver."

Adeo inhaled sharply but held his face taut and let his cold stare land on Luan's smiling, chilling expression.

"It has to be me," said Harvey quietly.

"Excuse me?" said Luan. "Did you speak?"

"Let me do it."

CHAPTER THIRTY-NINE

"Reg, this is Melody. Come back."

"I hear you, Melody. Where the bloody hell are you? It's so noisy."

"Well, surprise, surprise, Reg, Jackson has a chopper license."

"Oh no, not again."

"It's okay, Reg, we haven't stolen this one. We're in the air now. Where are we going?"

"Looks like Harvey is heading out to Southend on the East Coast."

"What the hell is he doing there?"

"Maybe he fancied a go on the arcade machines?"

"No, this is wrong, Reg."

"The trackers don't lie, Melody."

"Southend, Jackson," said Melody.

"Any idea what he's driving, Reg?"

"Well, the satellite imagery shows that the Range Rover is missing from the junkyard. So I checked with the car's GPS and can confirm that it is also heading towards Southend."

"He's got style," said Jackson.

"He's out of his mind," said Melody. "Okay, Reg, we'll touch base when we're closer."

"Okay," said Reg. "I'm setting up a beta version of LUCY's mobile app on your phone. Wait a minute then you'll find the icon on your screen. You should be able to get a real-time visual of Harvey's chips."

"Perfect," said Melody. "I'll wait one minute then get back to you if I have any issues."

The A127 was a dual carriageway that ran from Romford out to the East Coast, snaking its way through the Essex countryside. Melody waited a minute as directed by Reg, then found the new app on her smartphone home screen. Reg had made the icon a simple L-shape with a stereotypical, cartoon burglar wearing a stripy shirt and a mask over his eyes hiding behind the L.

The app opened into a typical map view, but a drop-down on the left showed various names that Melody could select. Her name was there along with Jackson's, Reg's and even Frank's. Of course, Harvey's name was there too, so she hit the little check sign next to the names Harvey and Melody. The map showed a *Waiting* sign, then the letters M and H appeared on the screen. H was travelling along the dual carriageway with M approximately two kilometres behind.

"We're close," said Melody to Jackson. "Another two kilometres. Let's take it wide and flank him just in case."

Jackson nodded and turned the chopper south-south-east.

"Reg, come back."

"Go ahead."

"LUCY works fine. We're on him now. We'll let you know when we have him on board."

"Copy that, Melody."

"You do not honestly think that I would cut you down and then arm you?" said Luan.

"You don't need to arm me," said Harvey. He spoke from the very pit of his stomach, staring down at the floor in a mix of disbelief and realisation. He'd accepted long ago that it had been Julios who had killed his parents. He had abandoned any subconscious inclination to hold on to his memory. But Harvey had been wrong, misguided, and now the truth had been laid out in front of him. Adeo was the killer. Adeo was the man he'd been hunting all this time. He had stood side by side with Harvey, protecting him, and now hung from chains in a bunker beside him.

"Let me be the one. I've earned it. I accept death. In fact, it couldn't come sooner, but only once I've finished this."

"No," said Luan coldly. "Why?"

"I was that child, Luan. They were my parents." Harvey fixed Luan in his stare. "I've been chasing this man all my life. So if I'm about to die, at least give me the honour of killing him."

"Interesting," said Luan with consideration. "But I have a better idea." He walked to the bench, rolled up the leather pouch that contained his tools and held them under his arm. Luan opened the door and placed the tools outside then stepped back inside the darkened room. He pulled his handgun from inside his coat and spoke loud and clear.

"You will both fight," said Luan, "to the death."

Harvey looked around and saw only the chair as a potential weapon. "The man who stands at the end will be shot dead. Quite painless."

"Are you going to cut us down?" asked Harvey.

"Oh no, this you must figure out yourselves," said Luan. "Good luck, gentlemen." Luan closed the door.

Before the lock had been turned, Harvey caught sight of Adeo's leg reaching out to kick Harvey. Harvey lifted his legs and hung from the bindings. He had to get free. If Adeo broke free before him, he would be killed.

With all his remaining energy, Harvey hung from the rope and chains and hoisted his legs up, so his feet were above him on the concrete ceiling. With all his might, he pushed his legs against the roof. But it was no use; the eye bolt was screwed into the thick concrete. He saw Adeo beside him using his immense weight and working the rope back and forth to create friction. Harvey began to do the same with his feet against the ceiling. Pushing down, he ran the rope back and forth until a thin blue smoke began to form. His arms and shoulders ached and burned from being held up in the air. His wrists started to bleed as they rubbed against the harsh manila bindings. But slowly, fibres in the rope began to break.

Harvey glanced across at Adeo who had worked up a rhythm and was making progress. He chanced a wild kick and his heel connected with Adeo's nose, but he continued unde-terred. Determination was set on his face.

Harvey worked harder than before. He knew that when the rope eventually gave way, he would crash head first to the floor, but that was inevitable. He heard the splitting of fibres, but not his own. It was Adeo's rope, who was now frantic. His massive bulk hung from the chains, and smoke rose steadily from the bindings.

Harvey doubled his efforts. He chose a longer action to get the most friction. The blood had gone to his head, and he dizzied with the effort, but something inside pushed him on. Some carnal survival instinct told him that if Adeo broke free first, Harvey would die.

He began to hear his own rope splitting.

Adeo's chains rattled beside him.

Smoke, thick now, rose like a flame.

Adeo growled with the effort.

Harvey's breathing fell in time with his rhythmic action; short, sharp stabs of concentrated breath.

Metal clattered.

Faster.

Concrete dust reached Harvey's nostrils.

He pushed harder with his legs against the ceiling.

Adeo stood beside him. His weight had finally ripped the eye bolt from the ceiling. He stood beside Harvey with his wrists still bound, and a heavy lump of chain swinging from the rope.

Harder.

Adeo swung the chain.

Faster.

The steel ring on the end of the chain connected with Harvey's back. He lost his momentum, and his breath stung. Harvey's legs screamed to drop down and give up. His shoulders burned.

Slam. Another blow to his back from the chain.

Blood from his wrists ran down his arms, and flaps of skin on either hand were held open by the harsh rope.

Crack. His shoulder blade took the brunt of the next blow. He worked the rope faster despite his body screaming in pain. He saw the chain being swung back for another blow then finally the rope gave. Harvey fell to the floor and smashed his forehead on the hard concrete. Somewhere, in some other part of his vision, he saw Adeo swing widely and miss. Harvey rolled; he needed distance. Adeo's chains crashed into the concrete beside his head, and Harvey scrambled to his feet. The blood ran back into his limbs. His wrists stung like fire, and his right eye began to swell from hitting the floor. He ducked another of Adeo's wild swings and charged at the big man, catching him off balance. They both stumbled to the ground and Harvey landed two good head-butts before Adeo threw him off like a doll. Adeo's nose was broken, and blood ran out freely down his face. He smiled a cruel smile and licked the blood from his lips.

Harvey grabbed the wooden chair, and prodded the big man like a lion tamer, using the chair to block his swinging chain until Adeo wrapped the chain around its legs and wrenched it out of Harvey's hands.

Then Harvey stopped. He calmed himself. Maybe it was the memory of Julios and the discovery of his innocence; he hadn't killed Harvey's parents. He *had* been a friend. He remembered Julios' words, the same as he had done a thousand times before. *Patience, planning and execution.*

Harvey waited. He dodged Adeo's wild swings. He planned, analysing Adeo's moves until he spotted a weakness. Most large men like Adeo had protective muscle against their internal organs, which rendered kidney shots or any attempt to wind them useless. The key to fighting larger men was the throat or the groin.

Then it happened. Adeo took a wild downward swing that would have smashed Harvey's skull. But Harvey sidestepped, and with an open hand, he jabbed out at Adeo's throat. One fast jab, in and out. Adeo gasped for breath. The human reaction to the loss of airflow is panic. Adeo was no different. He reached up to his throat with his eyes opened wide. Harvey reached out again with both hands and forced his thumbs into Adeo's eye sockets. He pushed hard until both thumbs were up to his knuckles inside Adeo's skull. Then Harvey forced the big man against the concrete wall.

Adeo still fought for breath. He tried to grab Harvey, but he was weak with panic. His attempts were futile. Harvey lifted the big man's head and delivered a headbutt with no effect. He tried again and again until Adeo's nose was a flattened mess on his face. Harvey removed his thumbs. Adeo's eyes searched around uselessly. He was blinded, stumbling and regaining his breath, when Harvey struck once more. The final blow was a perfect uppercut that dislodged Adeo's jaw. The big man fell against the wall with his arms up in defence.

Harvey smashed the wooden chair against the wall and picked up one of the broken legs, an eighteen-inch length of smooth wood that had been lathed perfectly round. One end was broken, pointed and sharp. Harvey stretched his neck right then left, each time waiting for the satisfying click of the joints. Then he moved closer to Adeo who held onto the wall with panic etched across his blind face.

Harvey stood over Adeo in the dim light. He felt power surging through him as if it was fed from Adeo's diminishing will to live. Adeo dropped to his knees then fell forwards onto all fours. Harvey placed his foot on Adeo's back and forced him to the ground. The big man gave little resistance.

"You should know, Harvey," rasped Adeo. "You should know that your father was a good man."

"I have no doubt, Adeo."

"Do you ever wonder where you get your talent, Harvey?"

"Your brother trained me."

"Yes, he trained you, as he trained me. But you have something inside you, a fire, Harvey. It's in your blood."

"I was just a kid."

"You were a little monster, Harvey. You were always wild. But you were also fair and warm-hearted. It's from Leo I think."

"It didn't do *him* much good, did it?"

"He died well, Harvey. It is a game we all play, a line we all walk. But we know that one day death will step from the shadows."

"Am *I* standing in the shadows now, Adeo?"

"No, Harvey, you are not. But then, you were never one to follow the rules."

"Are you ready, Adeo?"

"It was John that gave the order, Harvey," said Adeo. "Remember that. John gave the order, but it was me that carried you away." Adeo's eyes searched blindly for Harvey. Then, as if accepting defeat, they cast down to the floor. Adeo lowered himself to his knees and hung his head. "Do as you must."

Harvey pulled Adeo's head back by his hair and placed the chair leg in his mouth. "Bite."

Adeo closed his mouth around the leg. His teeth bit into one end of the chair leg. The other end rested on the floor. Adeo knew what was coming.

"I'll always remember it, Adeo."

Harvey stamped down on the back of Adeo's head and forced the chair leg up into Adeo's brain.

CHAPTER FORTY-ONE

————————————

"There he is, Jackson. Ten o'clock. He's pulling off the main road."

"Where does that take him?"

"Nowhere. Looks to me like a dead-end, just an old farm."

"Okay, I'm going to take us down lower."

Jackson eased forward on the collective which changed the pitch of the blades. The chopper descended slightly, and Jackson maintained an altitude of fifty metres, swinging the bird around to the car's right-hand side.

"I can't see much," said Melody. "Looks like he has a passenger."

"Unless he's tied up in the boot."

"The thought crossed my mind too, Jackson. But I don't believe it. Whatever is happening, Harvey is in control."

The car came to a stop at the edge of a field, and Jackson descended more to bring the chopper down on the grass beside it. The passenger window rolled down, and the muzzle of an AK-74 thrust out and began to let off short bursts at the helicopter.

"Whoa, abort," said Melody. A few of the rounds glanced off the fuselage.

"Holy crap. What did you say about Harvey being in control?"

Two men climbed out of the SUV and took aim at the helicopter. Jackson banked right and took the chopper well clear of the gun's effective range.

"Now what?"

"Put me down somewhere. The only way out is back along that lane, so get me in front of them."

"You asked for it."

Jackson took the chopper down in the field a few metres from where the narrow lane met the busy dual carriageway. Melody saw the lights of the car turning in the distance; it was coming back. "Get up high, I'll disable the car." She took a quick glance at the LUCY app on her phone and saw that Harvey was stationary where the car had stopped. "Harvey is up there. Go check he's okay, I'll take care of these guys." Melody cocked the MP5, slammed the door and ran off towards the lane to cut the car off.

She stood in the tree line as the headlights grew closer. Then she stepped out and fired off a full magazine in three-round bursts. The left-hand tyres blew out, the windscreen shattered and the car ploughed into the drainage ditch on the side of the track in a puff of steam. Melody changed magazines and stepped up.

"Out of the car, now," she yelled.

There was no reply. The driver was slumped over the wheel. Then the passenger door opened, and the AK opened up. Melody dropped to the ground, rolled, aimed, fired, rolled, aimed, fired. The shooting stopped. Melody lay still. Then gravity took over the body of the passenger; it slid from the car and slumped awkwardly onto the ground.

Melody got up into a crouch and made her way carefully to the back of the car. She kicked the AK away from the dead man and surveyed the damage. Melody's first burst had taken the driver out. He'd been hit in the neck and the chest and stared at her with dead eyes. The second man had been hit in the face with her last burst. He wasn't a pretty sight.

Her phone began to ring. It was Harvey. Melody hit the green *answer* button.

"Thank god, we thought they were dumping your body."

"Melody, it's Jackson. Nothing here but a pile of clothes and Harvey's belongings."

Bobby 'Bones' Carnell stood at the bar of the Pied Piper with Doug and Trev. He drank his scotch and soda down in one hit and put the glass on the bar.

"Yes please, Lee, and a beer for the boys too."

"Cheers, Bobby," said Doug. "So no news then?"

"Yeah, loads of news, Doug," said Bobby. "It's a fast-moving world out there. Gerry and the big fella have apparently annihilated the Albanians, and Dom has moved into their pubs. We've regained some lost ground. So the future's looking bright, mate."

"And Gerry?" asked Doug.

"What are you two an item or something, Doug?" replied Bobby. "That's the second time you asked about him."

"I just thought he would be an asset to the firm, Bobby. He's pretty handy."

"He's a fucking liability is what he is, Doug, my old son." Bobby took a large mouthful of his drink and put his glass back down neatly on the coaster. "Doesn't follow orders, he's a wildcard. Sure, he's handy to have in a row, but when the game is strategy, I need men who do then ask, not ask then do their own thing. He's too bloody unpredictable."

"So are we going to just forget about him?"

"Oh no, Dougy. I'm not that callous. He did, after all, get me the Albanian, which in turn gave us the name of the boss and their whereabouts."

"So we're going to take care of him then? I know he's hard up at the minute, that's all."

"I didn't realise you were so soft, Doug."

"I'm not soft, Bobby. It's just that, well, he did us a turn. I thought the least we can do is slip him a few quid."

"Tell me, Doug, how much do you know about this Gerry fellow?"

"Not much. He was pretty quiet."

"And how many times did he come in here?"

"A few."

"And he drank with you every time?"

"Yeah, he was a decent bloke."

"So, right now, some bloke we don't know is out there somewhere, and knows a lot more about us than we do about him?"

"Well," said Doug, "if you put it like that."

"I do put it like that, Doug. If the Albanians haven't chopped him up into little pieces and fed him to the fish, your first job is to find him and take care of it. Is that understood?"

"Ah, that's a bit-"

"Is that understood, Doug?"

Doug paused. "Yeah, Bobby, I get it."

"Good. The firm is expanding, Doug. Now's a good time for you to move up the ranks a bit. Dom has got his own firm in North London now. I need a good right-hand man down here. Stop being a pussy and show me what you're made of."

The door to the pub opened and a familiar but unwelcome face walked in. The ambient noise fell quiet.

"Bobby, you might want to see this," uttered Doug under his breath.

"Carnell," said John Cartwright.

"You're brave coming here alone, John," said Bobby, turning and leaning on the bar.

"I hope that's not a threat, Bobby?" said John. "What're you going to do, slot me in front of all these people?"

"They're all friends, John. They won't see anything if I tell them to look away."

"Besides," said John, ignoring the power play, "while all this is going on, I'd say having an open channel is pretty healthy. Your boy is out there with mine."

"I hear they were welcomed with open arms."

"They were welcomed, Bobby. I don't think open arms is an accurate evaluation."

"As long as they get the job done, John. That's all that counts, isn't it?"

"You heard from your guy? Gerry, wasn't it?"

"Yeah it was Gerry, and no, we haven't heard from him. You heard from him, Doug?"

"No, Bobby," replied Doug. "Not a little-"

"You don't seem too bothered by it, Bobby," said John.

"Well, he'll be well remembered, John. I was just telling Doug here that we should get a plaque engraved and put up behind the bar." He sipped at his scotch. "Drink, John?"

"No, Bobby."

"Lee, brandy, three ice cubes please," said Bobby, ignoring John's answer. "You heard from the big bloke then, John?"

"No, but I will, I'm sure of it."

"Is that right, John? And what if you don't? What if it's all gone a bit Pete Tong and they're both cut up into little pieces?"

"Then, Bobby," spat John, "you and I will need another plan. That would give the Albanians all the confidence they need to start spreading their dirty little feet."

"Oh, I wouldn't worry about that, John."

"And why's that?"

"Well, right now, all the Albanians have is a few old junk-yards and some pubs in North London that nobody else wants. Plus probably some protection and knowing them, they've also got their dirty little mitts in some dirty little brothels as well. But that's not my cup of tea, John."

"You've moved in?"

"Early bird and all that, John," said Bobby with a smug grin.

"You want to make sure someone doesn't knock that grin off your mug, Bobby. It doesn't do to try and get one over on me."

Doug put his beer down. "You need to watch your mouth, John."

"Am I talking to you? No. You'll know when I'm talking to you because I'll look at you. I might even throw you a biscuit and pat you on the head too, so shut up and sit back down."

Doug looked at Bobby, who shook his head. "Sit down, Doug. Listen, John. There's no need for all this. I was faster off the mark than you. Maybe it's time you got out of all this. You've done well, you're well known, respected even. Maybe you're a bit long in the tooth for it, mate. It's a young man's game."

John downed his drink and put the glass back down on the polished wood. He moved closer to Bobby and spoke quietly.

"We either do this together, Bobby, or not at all. I'm in your manor, I respect that. But do not overstep your mark."

"Goodbye, John," said Bobby. "Shut the door on the way out, will you?"

"Is that the way you want things to be?"

Bobby didn't reply.

John turned and walked out of the pub. He left the doors open.

"He's got to go, Doug," said Bobby.

"You're going to off John Cartwright?"

"No, Doug, my old son," replied Bobby, "*you* are going to off

John Cartwright. Now close the door, will you? It's bloody freezing."

Doug took in the statement and walked to the doors. Killing John Cartwright would go down in history within the confines of the criminal world in which they operated. The man had survived countless attacks and had run most of the East End for longer than many of Bobby's men had been alive.

Doug pushed the door closed, but as he turned, the doors were kicked open again behind him. Two men stepped inside. The first shot Doug in the face; the second emptied his handgun into Bobby 'Bones' Carnell. They looked around the pub. The few drinkers sat in booths with their mouths hanging open. There was no other reaction. No more of Bobby's men.

The two men stepped back outside and climbed into the waiting van. The first man dialled a number on his phone.

"Jasper?"

"Boss, it's done. He's down."

"Good work. Get the boys and go seize his assets. It's time people started knowing that John Cartwright is still around. I've been laying low too long."

CHAPTER FORTY-THREE

"Nicely done," said Luan. "I didn't think it would be you still standing."

Harvey didn't reply. Luan was talking through a little slot in the heavy steel door.

"It's almost a shame to kill you. You fight well."

Harvey leaned against the wall. He was ready. It had taken him more than twenty years to find every man on his list. But he'd done it and now found himself with two more names to add.

Someone had shot Julios two years ago during a gun deal with the Thomsons. Harvey had chased them, but they got away. The man may take some finding. John Cartwright had also been placed on his list, a name Harvey never thought would be there. But he'd given the order; John was responsible for the death of Harvey's parents and knew he must pay the price.

Harvey thought about the story John used to tell him about his parents, how he'd found Hannah and Harvey on a bench seat in his pub. Harvey had been in a hamper with a note. His sister had sat next to him. The note had said that his parents had killed themselves. John had told the story verbatim for years.

But now Harvey had discovered the truth and he could see why John had lied. His father had been a dangerous man, and Harvey had inherited his keen sense of survival, his raw power and ferocity. John had known all along that he had been breeding a killer.

And now that killer was about to turn on him.

The unmistakable thumping of a helicopter beat the air above the bunker and Harvey tore himself away from his thoughts of how to kill John.

"Who is this?" asked Luan.

"Are you expecting company?" asked Harvey.

The door opened, and Luan stood with his handgun pointing at Harvey.

"Do not try to make any moves. I will cut you down. I see I have toyed for too long with you."

"If you're going to point that at me, you better know how to use it, Luan."

"I was firing guns before your daddy's vermin seed found its spawn," spat Luan. "Out, and keep your hands where I can see them."

Harvey stepped out of the dark room and into the night. The cold bit into his skin and his bare feet sank in the thick brown mud.

Harvey felt Luan's fillet knife against his throat and the gun in the small of his back. He was a pro; nobody could fend off both attacks. If Harvey reached for the knife, Luan would fire the gun. If he reached for the gun, Luan would slash his throat.

The chopper hung in the air fifty metres away. Harvey heard Jackson's voice loud and tinny over the tannoy fixed to the underside of the helicopter's fuselage.

"Let him go, Duri. We'll take it easy on you."

The bright spotlights fixed on either side of the chopper's windshield shone directly on Harvey and Luan, blinding them both. Only the faint outline of the rear rotor could be seen on the edge of the silhouette. Jackson fought the controls against the strong wind and descended some more. The slight variation in the helicopter's stability gave Harvey a brief glimpse of Melody. She was in the back with the door open and one foot on the skid. Presumably, her Diemaco was aimed at Luan.

Harvey battled in his head. Knife or gun?

The knife would surely kill him; the gun needed reaction time.

"It's not so easy, I'm afraid," shouted Luan.

"Don't make me do this," Melody shouted back.

"I won't make you do anything."

Harvey felt the blade cut skin.

"Make your move," Luan cried at the chopper.

Harvey reached up and wrenched Luan's hand from his throat, twisting it away then bending over in one smooth motion, pulling Luan over his back. The handgun flailed in the air as Luan fought to stay upright and tumbled over Harvey's shoulder in a slick judo throw.

Luan landed, rolled and stood in one smooth motion. He lifted the gun to point it at Harvey. He opened his mouth to say something, and the front of his head exploded.

Melody stepped down to the ground. She aimed her weapon around and cleared the area before stepping up to Harvey.

"Cold?" she asked.

Harvey didn't reply.

"Who's this?" asked Melody.

"Luan Duri," said Harvey. "The main man."

"And Adeo?"

"Inside."

"Alive?"

Harvey didn't reply.

"So no survivors?"

"None worth mentioning," replied Harvey. "Mind if I get some clothes before we carry on this chat, Melody?"

"I didn't think of you as the shy type, Harvey."

"Let's go. Whose chopper?"

"Jackson called in a favour."

"Don't suppose it has a spare change of clothes inside?"

"Want my jacket?" Melody said with a smirk.

"No. Luan won't be needing this anymore." Harvey began to remove the long coat from Luan Duri's dead body.

"You're going to take a dead man's coat?"

"Melody, I'm naked and it's November."

A few minutes later, Harvey joined Melody and Jackson in the chopper.

"Right, let's get this bird back to Hackney," said Jackson. "I think we just about pushed our luck here."

"Headquarters, Jackson."

"No time, Harvey," said Melody.

"Headquarters, Jackson," said Harvey. "You can land on the roof."

"Harvey, Frank wants to talk to us before we do anything else," said Melody. "Let's get this back to Hackney first, eh?"

"Do I have to flag a cab?"

"What's the rush?" asked Melody. "We got Duri."

"We got Duri, but..." Harvey couldn't talk. If he mentioned John Cartwright, Melody would know instantly that he'd go on a rampage. "They're still out there. The firm will wonder where I am."

"Bobby Bones?"

"Yeah, he's a bit of loose cannon that one."

"So not John Cartwright then."

Harvey didn't reply.

"Harvey, something has happened. What is it?"

"Jackson, can you get me back to base, mate?" said Harvey, ignoring Melody's question.

"Not leaving me much choice in the matter, are you?"

Harvey stared out the window.

"What happened in there, Harvey?" asked Melody.

Harvey didn't reply.

"Okay, save it. But we'll talk back at HQ." Melody was turned in her seat. She put her hand on his leg. "I'm your friend, remember?" She remembered that he was naked under the long coat and took her hand away. "Just don't bottle it up. Let me help you, Harvey."

"You wouldn't get it, Melody."

"Maybe, but try me. See if I do get it, and I if I do, I'll help you, whatever it is. Alright?"

Harvey turned and stared at her. "Do we still have those two muppets at HQ?"

"Ginger?"

"Yeah."

"Yeah, they're still there," said Melody. "Frank has been on at them. They won't talk."

"Yes they will," said Harvey. "We just need to ask the right questions."

CHAPTER FORTY-FIVE

Harvey and Melody stepped out of the helicopter onto the roof of the team headquarters. The wind tore off the river, whipping at Harvey's coat and biting into his skin. A small door led them to the washrooms, and another took them to the main area beside Reg's workstation.

Harvey walked straight to his desk where he kept a sports holdall with a change of clothes.

"Good evening," said Reg. "You're home early."

"Hey, Reg," said Melody, eyeing Harvey. "What's the news?"

"Oh you know, this and that. Nothing as exciting as what your news will be. Do tell." Reg sat back in his reclining leather office chair waiting for Melody to fill him in on all the details.

Melody took a glance across at the two men handcuffed to the pillar. "Let's talk in a bit, Reg. Where's Frank?"

"I'm here," said Frank. He was stood on the mezzanine floor looking down at Melody. He had a serious look on his face and spoke quietly. "Debrief in ten minutes. Get a coffee, do what you need to do, and get yourself into the mess." He disappeared into his office.

Harvey finished dressing. He tossed the long coat onto the

back of his desk chair, walked over to Melody's desk and pulled a thirty-metre length of climbing rope from where it hung on the wall then stopped at Reg's desk.

"Keys."

"What keys?"

Harvey didn't reply.

"Oh, you mean the keys to the handcuffs? Sure here they are." Reg pulled open his desk drawer, but before he could lift the keys out, Harvey's hand was inside the drawer. Harvey strode over to the two men. He formed a loop at the end of the rope and put it around Ginger's neck before unlocking the handcuffs. The driver sat looking up at Harvey looming over them with a scared look on his face. Then he watched as Harvey dragged Ginger away.

"Reg, doors please."

Reg looked at Melody, silently asking if he should open them. Melody nodded reluctantly and watched the top floor to make sure Frank wasn't watching.

Harvey continued to drag Ginger across the smooth screed floor and out into the night. The man struggled to his feet and was led along the walkway to the riverside. His damaged foot from where Harvey had shot him earlier had been cleaned and dressed in a bandage. Without stopping, Harvey hoisted Ginger over the railings and held him above the raging river below. Iron rungs were fixed into the side of the river wall for the men who serviced the Thames Barrier so they could get in and out of boats. Ginger's undamaged foot stood precariously on the edge of one of the slippery rungs.

"Where's John?"

"John?"

"John Cartwright."

"I don't know. Don't let me fall, please. It's just a job. I didn't-"

"I need an address."

"I don't have an-"

Harvey let go but allowed the rope to play through his hands. Ginger splashed down into the river, and the immense current immediately dragged him downstream. The rope pulled taut, and Ginger fought hard to keep from going under. Harvey dragged him back to the side, where Ginger's frozen hands clung to the rungs.

Harvey pulled up on the rope, forcing Ginger to climb unsteadily up the slippery, iron ladder.

"Where?" said Harvey when Ginger had reached the top. Harvey held the rope tight with one hand and held Ginger by the scruff of his neck with the other. Ginger coughed up some river water and let it run down his face.

"He'll kill me. You don't know him as I do."

Without warning, Harvey landed his forehead on Ginger's nose.

"I know him better than anyone. You've got three seconds. Three."

"No, please."

"Two."

"I can't."

"One."

"Okay, stop."

Harvey finished fixing Ginger back to the pillar alongside the driver and took the stairs up to the mess where the team held their meetings. Frank was already stood at the head of the room and Melody had taken her place by the coffee machine. She held a coffee between both hands, savouring the warmth of the cup. Reg sat on one of the two couches playing on his phone.

"How long until Jackson is back?" asked Frank, ignoring Harvey's entry.

"He'll be another thirty minutes. He'll be coming from Hackney," said Melody.

"Okay, well let's start without him. I'll fill him in later."

Frank sat on the edge of the large dining table that served as the meeting table. In all Harvey's time there, he hadn't seen anybody actually sit and eat there.

"I'll keep it as brief as I can," began Frank. "The chief has been on to me. Stone, can you tell me who you've been talking to? What firm is it? Just to clarify."

"Carnell."

"Bobby Carnell?"

"Yeah, you knew that."

"Just for the record, that's all," said Frank. "In the Pied Piper pub? Am I correct?"

Harvey didn't reply.

"Am I correct, Stone?"

Harvey nodded.

"Bobby 'Bones' Carnell was shot dead in the Pied Piper this evening. Anything you want to tell me?"

"Not really."

"So it wasn't you?"

"No, Frank, I was busy having the life kicked out of me in a concrete bunker buried in some junkyard." Harvey pointed at his swollen eye.

"The chief told me, and I'll paraphrase, the team is creating too many toe tags and not enough arrests."

The room was silent. The chief had the power to shut the unit down. The team had already had several warnings following previous cases and were told to bring more suspects in. The chief had said they were abusing their powers.

"Fourteen men have been found dead in the Ilford scrap yard, Stone," said Frank. "Fourteen?"

Harvey didn't reply.

"Are you not capable of *arresting* anybody?"

"You brought me in to do what you can't do, and I'm doing it. If there's a problem just say the word."

Frank looked disapprovingly at Harvey. "Where's Luan Duri?"

"Lying face down in the mud in Bow."

"Dead?"

"That was me, sir," said Melody. "He was about to execute Harvey."

"Well, you should have bloody let him," barked Frank. "We haven't had *one* arrest worth anything in this investigation. Those two clowns downstairs are nobodies. Crime isn't going to come grinding to a halt by taking *them* off the street, is it? We probably can't pin anything on them anyway. Do you see what I'm saying here? We need to do more police work. Leave the SAS crap to the bloody SAS."

The room was silent once more.

"So where does that leave us?"

"Just one more firm left. Seems like somebody did all the hard work for us, sir," said Melody.

"I want John Cartwright in handcuffs and with a pulse. I don't care how you do it, but I want him." Frank glared at Harvey with a look that told Harvey that he didn't care about the relationship between him and Cartwright. "Are you up for this, Stone?"

Harvey stared at Frank. He pushed off the wall where he'd been leaning and stepped over to him.

"Have you any idea what I've been through tonight, Frank?"

"Yes, I can see by the body bags."

"You need knocking down a few pegs, standing there in your nice suit with your hot coffee dishing out *I wants*. I've had enough of it, Frank. I've been shot at, hunted down, had guard dogs set on me, stripped naked, tortured and beaten. Then the final straw was that I was this close, Frank." Harvey held up his finger and thumb an inch apart. "I was this close to being executed, and you expect me to stand here and listen to you dribble on about how there are too many toe tags and not enough arrests? Why don't *you* get out there and see how you get on? These men are dangerous. They don't just put their hands up and let you put the cuffs on, Frank. They fight back. They shoot. They do anything they can to survive another day." Harvey spoke softly. "So finish your nice hot coffee. Go back to your nice, warm office, and stick that in your crappy little report."

Harvey stepped away and opened the door to head out.

"Where are you going, Stone?" asked Frank.

Harvey stopped, turned and glared at Frank. "I'm going to get John Cartwright, and if you want him alive, you'd better go out and get your hands dirty."

"Stone, if you do this, it's over. I can't protect you."

"You're right, Frank," said Harvey. "If I do it, it's over."

"How do you plan on finding him?"

"Easy," said Harvey. "I know where he is."

"Tenant, I want Stone on that screen, and as soon as he steps out of line, we call it in. No more games. This isn't a bloodbath. We're supposed to be police."

"He's only got one tracker left, sir, his bike," replied Reg.

"And where's his bike?"

"Currently doing one hundred and ten miles an hour down the A13."

"Well, where are all his other chips? We put one in his neck, didn't we? What the bloody hell happened to that?"

"Duri cut it out, sir. Took his phone off him too."

"And his jacket? Tell me we have one in his jacket."

"Nope," said Reg. "Looks like he pulled that out when he came back."

Frank turned to Ginger who was sat shivering on the floor cuffed to one of the upright pillars that supported the mezzanine. "You. What did you tell him?"

Ginger looked away, then turned back to Frank. "I d-didn't tell him anything."

Frank stared hard at the man who was visibly freezing. "Full immunity."

Ginger cocked his head.

"You haven't got anything on me anyway, so immunity from what exactly?"

"You work for John Cartwright."

"Never heard of him."

"That's strange because we have a gun that matches a double homicide in the Pied Piper that took place earlier today, only moments after John Cartwright left the pub."

Ginger closed his eyes in disbelief. "Is that right?"

"The prints on the weapon match yours exactly, Ginger," lied Frank. "And an eyewitness put your silent mate here on the scene too. He held the door. I could probably get his prints off that too if I needed to." Frank paused. "Do you understand the severity of the situation, Ginger?"

"Yeah, you want me to grass."

"You tell me what you told our friend, and maybe John Cartwright survives," said Frank. "You fail to tell me, and I'll see to it that you spend the next ten years sharing a cell with the biggest, friendliest, and loneliest category A prisoner I can find. He'll warm you up, Ginger."

Ginger hung his head. He cast his eyes up to the man opposite him, Clive, who shook his head and mouthed, "It's not worth it."

"No deal," said Ginger.

Frank stood over him then squatted down beside the pair.

"You both just made the biggest mistakes of your lives."

"It doesn't matter. If we grass on John, our lives won't be worth living anyway."

"If you grass on John, Ginger," spat Frank, "you'll be saving his life. Did you see my friend who just left here? Of course you did. Look at you. Have you any idea what he's capable of?"

Ginger sat and looked at the floor. "He won't get away alive." He mumbled.

"You what?" said Frank. "What did you say?"

"You didn't honestly think I'd give him John Cartwright's home address, did you?"

Frank stared in disbelief. Melody strode over to Ginger and kicked him hard in the kidneys. "Where have you sent him?"

Ginger just smiled. Then his shoulders began to bounce as he chuckled to himself.

"Tell me where he's going, Ginger," said Frank gravely.

"Why don't you ask your mate? He'll be strolling through the door right about now. I do hope they don't recognise him." Ginger grinned up at Frank.

Melody leaned down and landed a clean right hook into Ginger's jaw.

CHAPTER FORTY-EIGHT

"Boss, it's Jasper."

"What's the news?"

"We're hitting them hard. I've got three crews out there right now cleaning up. By this time tomorrow, nobody will even remember Bobby Carnell."

"Good work," said John. "Carnell said he'd taken over the Albanian's turf too. What's the name of the guy that wiped his arse, Jasper?"

"Dom, boss."

"Dom, that's it. Okay, it'll be him taking care of North London, and you know what? He can keep it. We've got no interest there. Our roots are here. But we need Dom to know that we're doing him a favour. He might be useful later on."

"Send him a message, Jasper. Find out where Bobby Carnell's body is being stored and get yourself up there."

"Boss?"

John spoke quietly, with a cruel intonation. "Cut his right hand off and send that to Dom. Tell him to stay up there, and we'll all live happily ever after. But if he tries to stretch his legs in East London again, it'll be the end for him *and* his family."

"There's something poetic about that, boss, considering Carnell's fetish for fingers."

"Yeah, if he's got brains he'll pay attention. He might even become an ally one day. But if he hasn't got brains, and doesn't do what he's told, then that's the gene pool at work."

"The gene pool, *right*."

"Any news on Adeo?"

"Nothing, boss. The Albanians are quiet."

"Ginger said Adeo and that Gerry bloke went to some junkyard the Albanians ran. Said it was a bloodbath."

"You think he's alive?"

"Something tells me he's not, Jasper. Shame, I've known him for thirty-something years. But it wouldn't be the first mistake he made."

"I don't believe it," said Jasper.

"What?" asked John.

"What if I told you that Bobby's guy just rocked up here?" said Jasper, pleased with his discovery. "He just parked opposite me in the car park."

"Gerry?"

"Yeah, looks like him. Face like a slapped arse. He's on a motorbike just sitting in the dark outside the Basement Club in Barking. Looks like he's waiting for someone or something. I'll call the boys, and in about ten minutes he'll be dragged into the back of the van and dumped in the river, boss. Leave it with me. I'll take care of-"

"No," said John, a little too abruptly. "Don't touch him."

"Boss? He might know about Adeo."

"I guarantee he knows about Adeo, Jasper, but do not let the boys anywhere near him. I also guarantee that even if they do succeed in getting him into the van, it'll be him who's dumping them the river. I'll be there in thirty minutes. I do not want him touched."

CHAPTER FORTY-NINE

"Let's go, Jackson. We'll take the Audi, it'll be quicker," said Melody.

"Mills," said Frank.

"Sir?"

"A quiet word," said Frank, opening the shutter doors and stepping outside into the frigid air.

"We're already behind him, sir."

Frank gave her a look that told her that the talk was non-negotiable.

They walked slowly towards the river then stopped once they were out of earshot of Jackson and Reg.

"It's a delicate situation, Mills."

"Yeah, but I'm keen to look after Harvey. He's mad right now, but he's an asset, sir."

"He is, Mills. He's good at what he does, but he's a liability."

"Can I speak freely?"

"Always."

"With all due respect, sir, you could have gone easier on him. The night he's had would have probably have killed the pair of us. Your words and tone was the last thing he needed.

Harvey is in a position where the most powerful villain out there knows he's up to something. If John finds out that Harvey is working with us, he'll never be able to step foot in East London again."

"Yeah, that's a predicament, alright. You think that's the only reason he's going after Cartwright?"

"What other reason is there? I spoke to him about it, and there doesn't seem to be a relationship between them."

"I got that impression, but I also got the impression Stone respects him. There are not too many people out there that Harvey respects, you know that?"

"Yeah, I do."

"He respects you, Mills. You make a good team."

"I admire his strength and control."

"Control? Did you see him leave here?"

"That wasn't him out of control, that was Harvey taking himself out of a situation. I'd bet money he's found somewhere to sit and think before he acts."

"Patience, planning and execution?"

"Exactly, sir."

"If he kills Cartwright, that's it, you know that?"

"Yeah, you said."

"You don't understand, Mills. If he kills Cartwright, the balance will shift. Cartwright is the glue that holds the world out there together. Ever wonder why nobody holds up the off-licenses or local businesses? Did you ever wonder how, in a place where terrible violence happens nearly every day, old ladies can still leave their homes and go play bingo or collect their pensions? The firms might be a royal pain in the arse for us, but trust me, they keep a lot of the crime down. Now tell me, out of the three firms involved in this investigation, which one is still going strong?"

"Cartwright."

"And of those same three, which one didn't we know of until today?"

"Cartwright."

"Exactly. He's a villain, Mills. But if Harvey takes him away, there'll be chaos as smaller, younger and bloodthirsty firms strive to take control and petty criminals begin to take the piss. We'll have more deaths on our hands than we can deal with. If the chief doesn't shut us down anyway for this fiasco, then he'll shut us down for sure when there's a dead body or two showing up every day."

"I understand, sir."

"If Cartwright dies, I can't go on. I'm on the home run towards retirement. I haven't got it in me to learn a new way of doing things. John Cartwright is the last of the old school villains, Mills."

"And you're the last of the old school cops."

"Exactly. I'm tired, Mills. I want to hand over the reins on a high note. Retire in peace, as it were."

"I get that, sir. However, I also think that maybe the time for people like John Cartwright is over. We don't need the carnage, but maybe some fresh blood might do some good."

Frank raised an eyebrow at Melody's comment. "You should see if my chair is comfortable, Mills."

"Sir?"

"My desk chair, see if it's comfortable. I have a feeling you'll be sitting there sooner than you think."

CHAPTER FIFTY

"Where did it come from?" asked Dom.

"We don't know. Nobody saw anything."

"Cartwright."

"Cartwright is down, Dom. He's barely got enough men to make him a cup of tea."

"No, don't you believe it, mate. Cartwright is playing the game. He's on a rampage. He's got men in every one of our pubs from East Ham to Bow."

"So why send us this?"

"It's a message."

"A message? They could have just called instead of sending Bobby's hand."

"Cartwright is drawing a line in the sand."

"What do you mean?"

"If he wanted us, we'd be laying in some dark street right now or buried in Epping Forest. It's not *us* that he wants. He just wants his manor back."

"So we're stuck up here now? I can't stand this place."

"For the time being, mate," said Dom. "We need to leave

Cartwright alone. Let things settle. We're building up numbers. When the time is right, we'll make our move."

"What about the lunatic? Gerry?"

"Gerry?" asked Dom. His mind had trailed off miles from where he stood. Dom was a strategist. He was thinking about John Cartwright and something his dad had taught him when he'd been a boy. Bullies had ripped his shirt and stolen his lunch money, and he'd wanted to get revenge. His dad had told him to make friends with them; retaliating would be futile. For a young teenage boy full of pubescent emotions, the advice had seemed absurd. But as he thought about Cartwright and the position he now found himself in, the strategy made perfect sense.

John would be an ally, a good ally to have. But the things Bobby had taught Dom countered his father's words. Bobby had groomed Dom for the job he did. When Dom had been much younger, Bobby had shown him first-hand how to deal with someone who stepped on his toes or pushed him too far. Bobby was respected for it.

Dom had two choices, and both had severe consequences. Stay out of the East End, let John Cartwright have his manor back and risk losing all respect from Bobby's men, who were his own men now. Or he could strike while Cartwright's numbers were down and his men spread out. Dom knew that they were taking over Bobby's turf. Now might be the only time he could get in an attack. The choices weighed heavily on his mind.

"The hard nut, Dom."

"Yeah." Dom snapped back to the chat with his friend Cole. "He managed to make a name for himself pretty quick, didn't he?"

"Apparently Bobby liked him. He said he had a certain cold style. Even made the Albanian bloke cry and didn't lay a finger on him."

"Do we know anything else about him?"

"No, Dom. It was Doug that found him and made the intro-duction. He met him in the Piper, apparently."

"When exactly was that?"

"A few days ago. The day after the Dockside Arms was burned down."

"Convenient, don't you think?"

"What're you saying, Dom?"

"I'm saying that I wonder if this Gerry is really who he says he is. Did you see how he spoke to Cartwright? And how he ignored Bobby?"

"He's a hard nut, Dom."

"No, there's more to it than just hard. It's like he was somehow above it all. Like none of it really mattered."

"You reckon it was him that killed Bobby?"

"No, it was two men according to Lee the barman. He didn't say it was Gerry and I'm pretty sure he would have if it was."

"So what are you thinking?"

"I'm thinking a lot, Cole. I'm thinking that this bloke shows up out of the blue. Three or four pubs are burned down, all of which belong to one firm or another. Blokes are being killed left, right and centre and another one had his ears cut off, and I haven't seen one flashing blue light."

Cole jerked his head at Dom in surprise. "You don't think-"

"I don't know for sure. It's just a theory. But it's just a bit odd, that's all. Don't you think?"

"I think you're paranoid, Dom."

"Maybe, Cole. Get the word out to the boys, will you? Bobby is dead. I'm taking over."

Cole smiled. "You've got some balls, Dom, I'll give you that."

"Tell them we're meeting in the Rose and Crown tonight."

"You going to give a speech, Dom?"

"No speeches, Cole. Tell them to come tooled up. We're

going to pay John Cartwright and his boys a little visit. We'll start with that crappy little club of his, what's it called?"

"The Basement Club."

"Yeah, that's it," said Dom. "I want every bit of firepower we've got. I'm going to wipe John Cartwright off the face off the earth."

"Call your pet dog off," said the voice on the other end of the phone. Frank was silent. "Did you hear me?"

"I heard you, but the play is rolling. If I call him off, there'll be questions."

"So use your imagination."

"It's too far gone."

"You stand to lose a lot more than I do, Carver. You know that?"

"And if I don't?" said Frank.

"An anonymous phone call to your superiors, maybe?"

"You don't have anything on me."

"Phone calls, Frank. Records of our conversations," said the voice. "Plus a certain murder of my friend Mr Parrish."

"He was a wanted murderer. That little incident got me a reward."

"I'm not talking about legal action, Carver."

"Stone?"

"What do you think he'll do if he finds out it was you that killed Julios all along?"

Frank gave the question time to settle.

"What makes you so sure he works for me? What makes you think I have any control over him?"

"Oh, Frank, you don't control Harvey Stone. Nobody does. But if you're any good, you can steer him."

"How do you know he works for me?"

John laughed. "Frank, I don't like to blow my own trumpet, but I didn't get where I am without being a *bit* smart. He's a cop. Harvey very likely didn't go to police training after being almost invisible for most of his life. If he turned, then he was coerced. And if he was coerced then, my friend, there's only one dirty cop I can think of who would try a stunt like that. As soon as I found out it was you who shot Julios and Harvey had gone to the dark side, so to speak, well, two and two, Frank. Keep your friends close and your enemies closer. That's what you've been doing all this time, isn't it?"

"What do you think he'll do if gets his hands on you? You did, after all, have his parents killed. I doubt he'll even give you time to talk."

"What makes you think I killed his parents?"

"You're not the only one who can add two and two. Harvey told me how you used to tell him the same old story. How you found him and Hannah-"

"In my bar, on a seat." John finished. "I'm his father, Frank. I'm sure I can appeal to his good nature. That puts me in a pretty strong position. With one phone call, I can have you arrested. You'll lose your pension and probably go away for a spell at Her Majesty's pleasure. I'm sure you'll be welcomed inside, Frank. Lots of old friends who'll want to say hi. Or I can set Harvey on the right path. You know, tell him a few truths about his dirty cop boss. I'm sure he'll go easy on you. Maybe he'll even make it quick. But I doubt it."

There was a silence as both men played the possibilities out in their heads.

"So this is goodbye, Frank. May the best man win."

John Cartwright disconnected the call.

Frank walked slowly towards the doors to headquarters.

"Mills, keep me informed," said Frank.

Melody was loading the Audi with her Peli-cases. One contained her MP5, another had her Diemaco sniper rifle, and the last had a mixture of surveillance equipment. Boon was following her around the workspace and sniffing at the boxes.

"Will do, sir. You heading home?"

"It's been a long day, Mills. This old dog needs some rest. And that old dog needs a walk." Frank gestured at Boon.

"He'll get one soon enough."

Frank hesitated, looked her in the eye, and smiled weakly. He glanced around the headquarters then turned and walked to his car.

Melody watched him leave then called Jackson again. "We're moving."

"Harvey is outside The Basement Club in Barking. At least his bike is. Obviously, I can't tell if he's actually gone in for a dance or not."

"We'll know soon enough, Reg," said Melody. "Listen, did Frank seem off to you?"

"You mean did he seem grumpy and miserable? Isn't that normal?"

"No, I mean..." Melody stumbled for words. "I don't know. He said some weird things."

"Like what?"

"I can't say. But can you keep an eye on him?"

"Yeah, sure. Want me to listen to his calls?"

"No, Reg, just, I don't know what I'm saying, sorry. I'm tired, and nothing seems normal anymore."

"Normal?" Reg laughed. "This *is* normal, Melody."

"Let's go," called Jackson.

Melody climbed into the passenger seat of the saloon and leaned out to pull the door closed. "Reg?"

Reg spun in his seat to face Melody. He smiled as if reading her thoughts.

"Thanks, Reg," she said.

CHAPTER FIFTY-TWO

Harvey hated the loud, obnoxious beat of dance music. It dulled his senses. Mixed with the dark shadows of the basement club, his ability to control risk, make a plan and execute it was narrowed. But Harvey had no plan other than to find John Cartwright and take him down.

One of John's men had seen Harvey in the car park. He'd sat watching Harvey. Harvey had seen the faint glow of a mobile phone against the man's face and was sure he was sending an update on Harvey, maybe to John himself. It didn't matter. In fact, it helped Harvey. John now knew where to find him. Two things could happen. John would somehow know that Harvey had turned, and was undercover; he'd be torn to pieces. Or John would find him and they'd talk, then Harvey would kill John. He couldn't see any other option. Nobody in John's world could know about Harvey's involvement with what was essentially the police. Official or unofficial, it would make no difference to hardened criminals.

Harvey found a small booth in the corner of the club. It was on the ground floor with the main entrance in full view and a staff door to Harvey's left. He felt the stares from the men that prowled the room. He'd definitely been recognised.

Opposite and to the side of Harvey were three larger booths. It was the type of seating shown in the gangster movies that Harvey's foster brother, Donny, had been thrilled by as a child. Glamorous looking women would be sat either side a coke-sniffing, over-confident hoodlum who would be drinking champagne and slipping folded wads of cash to staff, valets and girls every five minutes. The scene in front of Harvey was very different. Each booth sat five or six men, all holding bottles of beer, smoking cigarettes and trying to look as tough as possible. They were joined by the guy Harvey had seen sitting in his car on the phone. In a series of silent gestures, nods and head shakes, the men in the room decided not to make a move on Harvey.

It amused Harvey to watch the scene play out. He could see what they were doing, he understood what they said, and he realised the reasons why. They might as well have just spoken out loud. John Cartwright was clearly on his way.

Harvey played out the plan in his head. He would take John away from the club somewhere quiet, somewhere they could talk. Harvey had questions; John would give the answers. Then Harvey would let him die. It would be quick. John deserved that for the way he'd raised Harvey and Hannah. He'd provided as well as he could for them. But for the lies, the deceit and for killing his parents, John must die.

John Cartwright strode through the main doors at the front of the club and grinned at the girls who flashed their smiles and flicked their over-sized eyelashes his way. He was in his element, thought Harvey. He'd always been one for the women. When Harvey's foster mother had left John, a series of blonde bombshells enjoyed his company. They typically spent more time in the washroom racking up lines than they did with the old man. But the next day, he always had a spring in his step.

There was no eye contact between John and Harvey as John made his way through the room, stopping at any table he passed to introduce himself or greet acquaintances. That's all they were, acquaintances. Men like John Cartwright didn't have friends. They just knew people, the right people.

"Mind if I sit?" asked John, finally reaching Harvey's booth.

"It's *your* seat."

John slipped into the small booth and nodded at the group of men sat opposite. Harvey remained silent. He followed John's eyes to the men and then back to John. A few seconds later, a brandy with three ice cubes arrived at the table. It was served on a new cardboard coaster with a serviette folded in a neat triangle next to it. A small dish containing three olives finished the demonstration of power and control.

"So," began John, "Gerry, is it?"

"What's a name?"

"Where for art thou, Gerry?"

"Seemed like a safer name to use than Harvey Stone."

"What happened to France? You were always dead keen on France. Thought you'd stay out there."

"Something called me back."

"I'm guessing it wasn't Bobby Carnell that called you back, Harvey."

"It's complex."

"Try me."

"You wouldn't understand."

John Cartwright sat for a moment in silence. He studied Harvey as only a father can. "I'm proud of you, Harvey."

"What is it you're proud of?"

"Just you, mate," replied John. "Your strength, your will. It's infectious."

Harvey didn't reply.

"So, to business then, shall we?"

"Business?"

"I presume that *is* why you've come to see me? To have a go at me on behalf of Bobby Carnell?"

"Bobby can go to hell, John."

"Thought you two were pals?"

"Not really. He's a means to an end."

"That's lucky, Harvey."

"Lucky for who?"

"You, Harvey."

"Why's it lucky for me?"

"Because I shot him earlier."

Harvey didn't reply.

John sipped at his drink like he'd just told Harvey that school was cancelled the next day.

"So it's just you then? You won."

"Did I? Win, that is?"

"Carnell is dead and the Albanians won't be giving anyone more trouble for the foreseeable. You cleaned up, John. Congratulations."

"Yeah well, I'm not exactly singing and dancing about it just yet."

"What's the problem?"

An explosion rocked the room. The sharp crack of the detonator was followed by a deafening boom that rocked Harvey's eardrums. The two swinging front doors were torn off their hinges, and the tables surrounding the grand entrance to the club were blown across the room. Lights blew out and, just for a moment, the scene played out in slow motion for Harvey.

Bright headlights focused on the entrance, blinding anyone who tried to run out of the club, which had begun to smoke and smoulder. Flames were building in several small fires, and smoke was already beginning to fill the room.

Silhouetted against the bright entrance were the legs and

torsos of men who stormed the club. John's men in the booths opposite Harvey sprung from their seats and reached for weapons, bottles, knives, chairs, anything they could find. But the attackers were prepared. Shots rang out in a riot of recoil and frantic untrained firing. Many of the men had apparently seen too many films and emptied a full clip into the smoke and confusion. Girls fell to the floor, cut down in the crossfire. Wrong place, wrong time.

Within moments, the attackers were moving towards the rear of the club. Harvey instinctively ducked John's head down. When the gunfire had passed, he wrenched him from the booth to his feet.

Covering John, Harvey turned and kicked in the staff door. There was a cloakroom on Harvey's left and kitchens to his right. He knew that every kitchen had to have a fire exit, so barged inside to the shock of two staff. He held John's head low and kicked his way through the fire doors. Immediately, the flash of a muzzle and the sound of automatic gunfire traced a line of bullets towards Harvey. They'd been waiting for people to burst through the fire doors. They'd been waiting for John.

Harvey pulled John back inside and ducked beside the door. He grabbed a large, sharp flat knife from where it hung on the wall. Using the blade as a mirror, he confirmed that he was outnumbered and trapped.

Then he heard the familiar sound of Melody's barking dog. The MP5 had such a unique growl as it spat 5.56mm rounds from its muzzle in bursts of three. Harvey took another glance in the blade. He could just make out the man who'd been firing the AR from his hip now shooting back towards the car park. Harvey pushed John against the wall, told him to stay there then made his way outside. He raised his SIG, and took down the man with the AR, then bent to pick up the weapon. Other men had fallen back and were concentrating fire on Melody. Harvey finished the magazine in short bursts to keep the attackers' heads down. He whistled to John and gestured for them to go. "Where's your car?"

John fumbled for his keys then hit the button on the fob. The lights on a silver Bentley Continental flashed once, and the interior light gracefully grew brighter.

"Let's go," said Harvey.

Melody was fifty feet to Harvey's left, half in and half out of the VW van. Harvey figured she would have her Peli-case open beside her with magazines being reloaded and lined up for her by Jackson.

Harvey didn't acknowledge the team. Instead, he opened the passenger door of the Bentley and helped John duck inside. He then climbed into the driver's seat.

Harvey slammed the car into drive, span the wheel and accelerated. The rear end span out almost immediately and the vehicle began to move sideways out of the car park. Harvey corrected the over-steer with short, sharp twitches of the wheel. Men stood like rabbits in the headlights as the Bentley lurched towards them. Rifles clanged into the side of the car, metal on metal, and heads bounced off the tempered glass windows, bone on glass.

Sliding the car towards the exit, Harvey quickly spun the wheel onto the opposite lock, allowing the rear to skid out noisily onto the tarmac road. Harvey found second gear and held it. The rear wheels span and filled the road with smoke. Gunfire dotted the car's bodywork as the tyres found traction and the massive torque sent the car up to seventy miles per hour in less than four seconds, a long time when men are stood on the road behind firing automatic weapons.

"Where are we going, Harv?" said John, rising up from his ducked position in the car.

"For a drive. Keep your head down."

"They're my guys, Harvey. I can't leave them."

Harvey didn't reply.

"Harv, they're my blokes."

"Not anymore they're not, John," said Harvey coldly. "They weren't prepared. Most of them will be dead by now."

"So much fucking death, Harvey," said John. "I thought the eighties were bad."

Harvey dropped the speed down to fifty to avoid attention from the police then settled into cruise control.

"It's a shame," said John. Harvey glanced across at him. "I liked that club."

"I would've thought you'd prefer something a little more classical?"

"Well, something a little more classy, for sure. But the birds there were always good and willing."

Harvey didn't reply.

"Plus, it used to be Thomson's, which somehow sweetened it for me. Know what I mean, Harv?" John paused. "Where are we going anyway?"

"For a walk."

"A walk?" replied John. "It's the middle of the night, and it's November."

"So we'll walk fast."

"The house?"

Harvey didn't reply.

"You've been back, haven't you?"

"A few times."

"I knew you'd bring me here."

"It's nostalgic, John."

"So many happy memories, eh?"

"Just memories, John."

"You know I still own it?"

"I heard you couldn't sell it."

"Yeah, lawyers manage the estate now. Keeps me under the radar. But they do checks on all the assets every six months."

Harvey didn't reply.

"It's funny," began John, "they keep finding bodies in the basement there, you know?"

"Sergio, John."

"Yeah, the basement. Must be something that draws people there to off someone."

"Is that right?"

"Cross my heart, Harv. Apparently, last time they found some rag-head down there. No wonder no-one wants to buy it."

Harvey didn't reply. He turned the Bentley's steering wheel and manoeuvred the car through the gates of the old house. The tyres crunched on the gravel, and the headlights cut a bleak path through the gloomy fog that rose from the unkempt, overgrown lawns. The large house stood like a forgotten friend and emerged from the mist as they neared. Two front windows halfway up the two curved staircases inside stared like black eyes in the night. The large wooden double doors hung open like a gaping mouth. Horror, frozen in time.

"Look at the state of the bloody place," said John. "Hard to imagine all the good times we had here, eh?"

Harvey didn't reply.

John climbed out of the car and pulled his coat around him. Harvey turned the engine off and followed suit. He stood with his leather biker's jacket flapping in the wind and his white t-shirt glowing in the faint light.

"Shall we have a look around?" asked John, and he began to walk off.

Harvey walked with him to one side, but close enough that they only had to talk quietly. It was like the fog enclosed them in a tiny space, where only they could hear or see each other.

"You were always quiet," said John. "As a kid, you were great fun, but you were always reserved. It was nice. You weren't noisy, not like Donny when he was that age. But I always thought you'd grow out of it."

Harvey glanced across.

John returned the glance and held Harvey's stare. "You never did." He smiled the smile of an old man who'd seen it all and knew that life held few surprises for him anymore.

"They called me, you know," said John. "When they pulled Donny out. I heard mixed stories, none of them pleasant. But I knew you were involved. I'm not sure how, but I just knew."

"What did you hear?"

"He'd killed some young girls or sold them or something. Something bad."

"Did you know about him and Sergio?"

John paused then said softly, "No. No, I didn't. I was his father, Harvey, but when I heard, I didn't disbelieve it. Not for one second. I knew he was guilty as soon as they told me. I'm so sorry."

"You watched me struggle for all those years?"

"You wouldn't understand."

"I do now. I've had what you might call a moment of clarity, John." Harvey took a lungful of the moist air. "You watched me struggle to find Hannah's killer for all those years, and never helped because deep down you always knew, didn't you?"

John looked at Harvey, pleading with his eyes. "I couldn't change it. The lies had gone too far."

"Tell me where Leo and Olivia are buried."

John stopped in his tracks.

"You see, John, what amazes me is how inhibiting you were. Not only did you fail to tell me who killed Hannah, who killed my parents and why, but you stopped me from finding out, didn't you?"

"No, Harvey, I-"

"Save it, John. I've been away for two years now, and not only have I found the men that killed Hannah, but I also found the man that really killed my parents." They walked on a few steps in silence. "It was there for me all along, John."

"Donny?" said John.

"I watched him die."

"Adeo?"

"He confessed before I killed him."

"So that's you done then, Harvey. You must be happy. That list of yours is all ticked off, and you can go sit on that beach of yours, eh?"

"Not yet, John. I still have a few loose ends to tie up."

"Yeah, I'd like to disappear somewhere hot," said John. "Sit by the pool and fade into old age in style. But..."

"But what?"

"I never could sit still. I'm surprised you can, to be honest."

"I like to read."

"What do you read?"

Harvey gave him a look to ask if they were really now talking about what books they read. "Books. Whatever. Anything that distracts me from reality."

They had completed a slow full circle of the house and stood at the bottom of the few steps that led to the front door.

"So you reckon you're going back to France, do you?" asked John.

"When I'm ready."

"Who are you looking for? What's the hold-up?"

"Julios."

"Oh, I see," said John. "He was more of a father to you than I ever was, wasn't he?"

"You both played different roles."

"You mean I paid for everything, and he taught you everything."

"I'm happy, aren't I?"

"I don't know, Harvey. Are you? You've had a face like a slapped arse for as long as I can remember." John smiled. "I'm sorry it came to this, Harv. I really am."

John raised his handgun and pointed it at Harvey.

Park further down the lane, Jackson," said Melody. "We can walk back up. When was your last firearms refresher?"

"It's due again anytime."

"You feel comfortable with a weapon? It's your choice."

"Yeah, sure."

"Good. Denver tied a polycarbonate holster to the underside of your seat. You've been armed all along."

Jackson reached down, found the SIG P226 and pulled it out, smiling. "My choice, eh?"

"Nearly your choice."

Melody pushed the Diemaco's magazine home and chambered a round. She was satisfied with the smooth, well-oiled action and flicked the safety on. Pulling down her night-vision goggles, she stepped from the van, closing the doors quietly.

The grounds of the house spread out all around her. She'd always been impressed by the property, but in the mist and gloom, it had an eerie feeling about it. It held the memories of too much death.

Harvey had told her once how, as a child, he remembered the house being warm and full of the small things that made a home, vases, flowers, pictures, children, parties and the rest. But after Harvey's foster mother, Barb had left, the house had grown cold. The cook resigned and the house lady began to fade away. Sadness enveloped the old wooden beams. Thick dust lay on the rugs and the window sills. John's office was clean, and the bedrooms were clean, but the rest of the house began to fall into disrepair.

Melody and Jackson stepped quietly through the long grass, moving slowly and listening for the deep rumble of men's voices. They heard nothing. It was as if the mist retained the sound within. Melody used her night-vision goggles and found the two men stood at the front of the house. She remained motionless; she was two hundred feet from the big grand entrance. In the green, animated view of the NV goggles, Melody could easily see John's confident but smaller frame against Harvey's rigid and athletic posture. Though she couldn't hear them, the scene didn't look heated. They seemed to be having a normal, calm conversation.

Maybe Harvey had changed his mind. Maybe he couldn't go through with it. There was no shouting. No flailing arms releasing frustration. Just two calm men in control of their emotions. Father and son, almost.

And then John raised his gun.

CHAPTER FIFTY-FOUR

John Cartwright held the shiny Glock tight with both hands.

"It didn't have to come to this," said Harvey.

"So why bring me here?"

"I changed my mind. I owe you more than that. You did raise me."

"I thought that we agreed that it was Julios who raised you?"

"Whoever it was, you're the one who fostered me."

John pulled the hammer back on the weapon. "You took away my only son."

Harvey was surprised at the statement. "He *raped* my sister, *your daughter*." He spoke the words with a distaste in his mouth.

"He was sick. There was always something wrong with him, only child stuff, I guess. But he was still my son, and you took him away."

"He was a *monster*. He was bringing girls in from Europe and selling their deaths with sex. It's one of the sickest things I've ever come across, John."

"No Harvey, you're sick. How many sons or fathers or brothers have you taken away?"

Harvey didn't reply.

"Tell me who the monster is *now?*"

"Tell me where they're buried."

"Who? Leo and Olivia?" asked John. He laughed. "They're buried right here, Harvey."

"Here? Under my nose all this time?" said Harvey, stepping towards John. "You gave the order, didn't you? You bloody killed them. All those times I asked you about my parents, and you told me that same old cock and bull story about-"

"Finding the pair of you in a booth in my bar in East Ham. We did everything ourselves back then, you know, even served drinks when the bar staff were busy."

"That's the one," said Harvey. "I was in a hamper."

"It was for your own good, Harvey."

"I was going to let you walk away."

"Then you're dumber than I give you credit for."

"Where?"

"In the orchard."

"Where we used to play?"

"They're not the only ones, Harvey," said John. "You'll be surprised at the secrets this place holds. Plus there's always room for one more in there."

"You're really going to kill me?" Harvey was incredulous. "Of all the people in the world, it boils down to this, does it? Killed by my own foster father."

"You killed Donny. I can't let it go."

"You killed my parents."

"Touché," said John. "You're a cop."

Harvey was stunned. He hadn't been ready for John to know the truth.

"That's right, I know *all* about it. How you left Donny here for the women to tear him to bits. How you brought Stimson down, and I know all about the terrorist. What was his name, Al Sayan?"

"Who told you about all of this?"

"It doesn't matter, Harvey. The fact is that you turned. You have to understand that, as uncomfortable as it makes me to say this, I can't have a foster son as a copper. Think of the damage it would do. One of us has to go and, as I'm the one with the gun, well..."

Harvey inhaled deeply through his nose and stared down at his foster father.

"I do love you, Son."

Harvey didn't reply.

"I love you enough to complete you before, you know."

"Complete me?"

"Julios, Harvey," said John, "or Edgar Parrish as he was known before he took the rap for his little brother. See Harvey, that's what brothers do for each other, help them, stick up for them. Not leave them in a basement to be torn to pieces."

"You know?"

"Who killed Julios? Of course, I know, Harvey. In case you've forgotten, *I* run the East End. You don't get to sit in *my* chair at *my* desk without knowing a few people in the right places. Even if some of those places are a little *questionable*."

"How did you find out?"

"I know people, Harvey," said John. "You get all sorts of information. Especially when one of your closest friends is shot dead during a gun deal."

"They're not friends, John. They're on your payroll."

"Well this guy is not on my payroll," said John. "But he was close with Terry Thomson before you shot him."

Harvey thought back to the night Julios had been killed. The black Range Rover that had sat in the clearing, watching.

"I wouldn't call him a friend as such, but we've both looked out for you along the way."

"You both?" said Harvey. "Who? Who was it?"

John's face curled into a tight smile. "Frank."

Harvey was winded, dizzied.

"Do you know how much it costs to keep someone like you out of prison, Harvey? Money. Lots of money and lots of friends in high places. So don't make this harder than it already is. You've got your closure. Now turn and look me in the eye."

Harvey turned slowly, still taken back by the shock. Frank. All along, it had been Frank. That's how he'd kept the noose so tight, because he had all the answers. Harvey had been played all this time. The one person left on his list had been stood beside him all along, just as Sergio and Donny had been.

Harvey straightened and turned completely to face John.

"Anything you want to say?"

"No. Just do it." Harvey held his arms out wide.

"Goodbye, Son." John's finger began to squeeze the trigger.

Harvey didn't reply.

Something metallic clicked far off in the mist to John's right. He glanced away momentarily.

Harvey raised his own weapon and aimed it at John's head.

John turned back to Harvey, his own weapon still aimed at his son.

"It's you or me, Harvey," said John.

Harvey squeezed the trigger, but his hand shook.

"You can't do it, can you?"

Harvey breathed through pursed lips, clenched tight against his teeth.

"If you're going to do it, Harvey. Now's the time."

Harvey brought his other hand up to steady the aim, but they both shook visibly. He lowered the gun and stared at John, who strengthened his stance.

"I can't do it," said Harvey.

CHAPTER FIFTY-FIVE

"Shh, you hear that?" whispered Melody.

Jackson nodded in the dim light and pointed to Melody's ten o'clock. She pulled the night-vision goggles towards her eyes and tracked a lone man creeping silently across the lawn from where Harvey's little groundsman's house stood derelict and graffitied. The man was trained. He moved well and was patient. He reached within one hundred feet of Harvey and John Cartwright then dropped to the ground. It was then that Melody saw the shape of the rifle. The man quietly folded down a bi-pod and moved into the prone position, pulling the rifle into his shoulder. Melody flicked back to John and Harvey. Harvey held his hands up like he was welcoming death. John's silhouette aimed the gun like a man who had been around guns. His stance was strong despite his age.

"Who is it?" whispered Jackson.

"I don't know. But we can't disrupt the state of play now."

"Harvey is going to be shot."

"No," said Melody. "He wouldn't let himself get shot."

"He's looking pretty close."

"No," she said. "No, Harvey would at least try." She pulled

the scope back to her eye and found the pair of men in the rifle's night-vision scope. John had straightened up. He was ready to fire.

The shadowed figure to their right slid the rifle bolt home. Melody heard the dull metallic click. She whipped the rifle to her right and saw the man taking aim.

Turning back, she refocused on Cartwright. "Do something, Harvey," she whispered. "Don't just stand there."

Relief washed over Melody as Harvey raised his gun. The two men faced each other, each with pointed weapons.

"Come on, Harvey," she whispered.

Then a sickening feeling clawed her gut as Harvey lowered his gun, and time stood still as John re-aimed his own. Harvey looked defeated. His arms hung limply by his sides. Melody watched like a voyeur. She aimed but begged silently for Harvey to move. Then the silence was shattered by the report of the stranger's rifle.

The green-hued night vision turned bright white as John's hand clenched, pulling the trigger on his handgun. The vision refocused in time for Melody to see John Cartwright drop to the ground. He seemed to fall backwards in slow motion as gravity overcame his body.

Melody snatched at the rifle and aimed at the stranger. She saw as he reloaded and shifted his aim onto Harvey, preparing to shoot once more.

"Harvey, get down!" she screamed.

The man's head popped up and searched the mist for her. Melody saw as his eyes must have found her, and his rifle began to swing around onto her location.

Melody had already aimed. She released the shot. The 7.62mm round rang out clearly in the mist, louder than the other two shots that had fired. The echo seemed to last forever.

She rolled to her feet, bringing the rifle up with her. Jackson followed as she made her way to the stranger she'd just killed.

She stopped and looked at the body of the man who lay on the ground.

"Oh god."

CHAPTER FIFTY-SIX

Melody and Jackson stood over the body, a dark shape in the mist that rolled across the wild, unkempt lawns of John Cartwright's old house. The body lay face down and still on the butt of the rifle. Jackson used the toe of his boot to raise the man's hip and roll him onto his back. Melody had the man covered should he pull a weapon from underneath him, but he was clearly dead. The side of his head had been ripped apart with the exit of Melody's round.

"Going to be a tough one to explain," said Jackson.

Melody dropped to her knees and fought to hold back her tears. She bent and rested her head on Frank's chest until a sob came from somewhere deep inside her. She didn't know if it was shame, guilt, or the death of a friend and mentor.

"Melody," said Jackson, "let's go."

"You didn't know him," she replied. "Not like I did."

"Melody, he was in up to his eyeballs."

She straightened and turned to face Jackson, who stood over her, unemotional with a hardened face.

"We were watching him," began Jackson, "for months now.

He had calls with known suspects and perverted the course of justice to suit his own well-being."

"No, not Frank," said Melody. "He wouldn't-"

"Terry Thomson, Melody. We have audio recordings of the calls."

"But he'd never-"

"But he did, Melody." Jackson's voice softened. "I know it's not easy to hear, but-"

"What do *you* know? Who *are* you?"

"Let's just say that my transfer to Frank's team wasn't a coincidence."

Sirens grew louder in the still night air, and the mist seemed to try to cover the dead with its spreading wispy limbs.

Melody stared down at the body. Frank Carver's emotionless face stared back at her. There was no expression of surprise, anger or hate. Just peace.

"We need to find Stone."

"You don't need to do anything," hissed Melody. "I'll find Harvey."

"He's wanted, Melody."

"He was cleared. You can't. Leave him."

"Who cleared him?"

The question hung in the air.

"Frank."

"You think that's legit?"

"Let me find him. If anyone is going to bring him in, it'll be me."

Jackson nodded faintly.

"Goodbye, Frank," said Melody under her breath before she stepped away and headed to where she truly dreaded to step.

John Cartwright lay flat on his back with his arms outstretched like an extra in a low budget gangster movie. He stared up at the sky with an open mouth held in a grimace.

Melody wondered what his last thought had been. He'd been about to kill his son. He'd betrayed his own, something that Melody knew wouldn't sit right with many of the old school firms.

Melody searched the area for Harvey, but he'd gone.

"You've got twenty minutes to find him and bring him in. I won't be able to hold them off any longer," said Jackson.

Melody walked around the spot where Harvey had stood. There were no tracks visible in the darkness, and the stone steps that led to the two large front doors were empty and cold. Melody turned to watch the headlights of two police cars burst into the grounds and follow the gravel driveway to where she and Jackson stood.

"What's that?" asked Jackson.

Melody followed his gaze to the house. A dim light came from inside. It was soft at first, but by the time the police had found them in the fog, the dim light had turned to a flickering flame. Just briefly, at the rear of the house where the stairs of the basement opened out into the kitchen, Melody thought she saw the shape of a man. Harvey. He stood there facing her, motionless as the fire grew, then vanished.

"Harvey," Melody called out. "Harvey, it's over."

Harvey didn't reply.

The small fire grew into a hungry blaze that chewed through the ancient wooden house, consuming its secrets of the past. Before long, the glow and heat of the fire held the mist at bay, and the spinning blue lights of police cars, ambulances and fire engines lit a riot of chaos and colour in the night.

The thump of helicopter blades suddenly became audible over the growing noise of the fire.

"Go find him, Melody," said Jackson. "I'll hold them off as long as I can."

Melody sprinted into the mist to the rear of the house. The

large empty pool lay like an animal trap in the poor light, and the weathered outbuildings looked sad and derelict in the glow of the fire. She caught sight of movement ahead on the tree line. It was Harvey. It was as if he was waiting for her to spot him before he disappeared into the trees.

Small branches gave way as she burst into the orchard. Lines of trees that had once been well maintained were now overgrown with plants and trees that fought for light. She stopped, looked and listened. It was silent inside the orchard. Only the faint trickle of a stream could be heard.

"I guess I owe you thanks," said Harvey.

Melody turned and found him stood beside a tree.

"No," she said. "No thanks needed."

"You saved my life again."

"You would have done the same."

"Was it Frank?"

"What makes you think that?"

"Was it Frank, Melody?"

"Yes," she said, her voice at breaking point.

"I always thought he was dirty. John confirmed it."

"Don't say that. He saved you."

"He saved himself, Melody, or tried to, at least. He was on terms with John and Terry Thomson. He knew all along who killed Julios."

"It was Frank, wasn't it?"

Harvey didn't reply.

"Are you coming easy?"

Harvey sighed audibly. "Am I being arrested?"

"It's Jackson," began Melody. "He was onto Frank. He's holding them off, so if you come quietly-"

"If I come quietly, there'll be no fuss, is that right?"

"Don't make this hard, Harvey."

"Hannah and I used to play here as kids."

"It's nice. You were lucky."

Harvey laughed. "Lucky, eh?"

"Privileged?"

"Closer, I guess. I was for a while anyway," said Harvey. "They're buried here, you know?"

Melody looked at him in the darkness. "Do you feel closure, Harvey?"

"Closure?"

"You found the answers you were looking for. Do you feel like you can rest now?"

"In prison, you mean?"

"It doesn't have to go that way, Harvey. Think of all the good things you've done with us. That has to stand for something."

"Think of all the bad things I've done along the way, Melody."

"You're not a bad person, Harvey."

Harvey didn't reply.

"Come with me. I can make sure they go easy on you."

"Take care of yourself, Melody."

A huge fireball lit the scene behind Melody as the roof of the great house caved in, and the blaze reached up for the cool air. Melody span around and watched the spectacle.

"That's the end of an era, Harvey."

Harvey didn't reply.

"There are a lot of memories going up in flames."

Harvey didn't reply.

"Harvey?"

Melody searched the darkness. The space where he had leant against the tree was empty. No movement caught her eye.

Harvey was gone.

Melody stood at the head of the mess room where Frank used to stand. Reg sat on the couch where he always sat and Jackson perched on the arm of the other chair. Boon sat obediently at Melody's feet and leaning against the wall beside the door where Harvey used to stand was the chief.

Melody glanced over to the chief and he answered her unspoken question with a gentle nod. She turned to face Reg and Jackson then sat on the edge of the table.

"Our brief was to reduce the growing violence among the territorial gangs in the East End. Namely, to bring the Albanians' spread to a halt." Melody looked up at the ceiling, unable to hold Reg's gaze for any length of time. "I think we can safely say we achieved that. Luan Duri is down, and most of his men are either dead or on the run. Many are believed to have escaped the UK borders." She turned to the chief. "We have eyes on the remainder of the Albanian firm and will make sure they do not try to spread their wings." Melody reached back and hit a key on her laptop. The large screen mounted on a mobile TV stand came to life, and Luan Duri's face appeared upon it.

The chief nodded his approval.

Melody hit the right-hand cursor on the laptop, and Bobby Bones' photo appeared. "During the operation," Melody continued, "Robert Carnell, AKA Bobby 'Bones' Carnell, was believed to have been shot dead by members of John Cartwright's firm. Dominic Fox is believed to have taken over Carnell's operations but has been pushed out to North London, Highbury, to be precise. We have eyes on him to make sure he stays there, and the profiles of all known associates have been passed on to the Organised Crime Division."

"Good, Mills," said the chief, and waited for her to continue.

"Now, let's move on to John Cartwright, father of Donald Cartwright, who was recently killed in a human trafficking operation. John has been on the watch list of the Organised Crime Division and its predecessor organisations such as SO-10 and SOCA for more than forty years. He was taken down by the very man that kept him out of our reach, the same man that diverted our attention and ensured that John Cartwright's very existence was in the shadows." Melody hit the right-hand arrow on the laptop's keyboard one last time and Reg gasped at the image.

"Frank Carver has been under the surveillance of the Organised Crime Division and internal affairs for two years." Melody paused to allow her throat to open itself and for her emotions to calm. She took a deep breath. "Frank Carver was guilty of perverting the course of justice and was responsible for at least one murder." She paused. "Edgar Parrish, AKA Julios." Melody stared directly at Reg who sat aghast at the news. "I recently received confirmation that Carver was the killer."

Melody turned back to the chief. "I'd call this operation a huge success."

Reg began a small clap at Melody's debrief. It was in jest,

but Jackson joined in, and the chief added three small claps before pushing himself off the wall. Reg and Jackson stopped and stood. Boon walked beside them as they left the room. As Melody stepped in behind them, the chief held his hand out to stop her.

"Stay, Mills. There's something I'd like to discuss."

CHAPTER FIFTY-EIGHT

Harvey Stone lay on the edge of a long golden beach in the small town of Argeles-sur-Mer in the south of France. The empty beach stretched out before him, and long grass blew in the soft breeze behind him. It was midday, and the heat was at its peak. He lay with a book by his side, closed neatly with a ten-euro note to mark the page. His eyes were closed to the bright sun but its rays brought life to his skin, and the soft, cool breeze cleansed his body of old memories.

He felt the sun fall into shadow on his eyelids.

"You're in my light."

"I am the light."

"Are you? Any danger you could shine somewhere else?"

"You're a hard man to find," said the woman.

"I'm not exactly hiding."

"I followed you all the way from Essex."

"I wasn't exactly running either."

Harvey felt the woman step around him then watched her in his mind as she stood gazing out to sea.

"How do we do this, Harvey?"

"How do we do what? It's the end, isn't it?"

"It doesn't have to be."

Harvey didn't reply.

"I could use a man like you."

"Someone who doesn't mind getting his hands dirty?"

"Among other things."

"I thought they were already dirty? Are you bringing me in?"

"Not necessarily."

Harvey opened his eyes and craned his neck forward to see Melody stood silhouetted by the sun. Her hair blew softly in the breeze and rested on her shoulders, and her short leather jacket flapped against her side.

"Two choices," she said.

"Let me guess, one bad, one worse."

"I wouldn't say that."

"Well, what then? I'm a busy man, can't you see?"

"First choice. You come back to London with me. The chief offered me Frank's job. I can have you cleared as an operative, you know."

"I'd report to you?"

"You always did, really."

"Second choice?"

Melody dropped slowly to her knees, leaned forward onto all fours and crawled up Harvey's body. Her eyes fixed on Harvey's. She stopped inches from his face.

"This," she said, and kissed him.

Harvey didn't reply.

The End

STONE FREE

When Angie Turvey turned on the lights and laid eyes on her dead neighbour, who hung from Angie's living room wall with six-inch nails through her wrists and ankles, she knew her life was about to change forever.

Emirates flight EK5110 landed at Dubai International Airport at twelve thirty in the morning. Among the business class passengers were Angie Turvey and her eight-year-old daughter, Anya. Angie held her daughter close as they made their way past the flight crew and onto the gangway. She pulled her Louis Vuitton carry-on case behind her, and her daughter pulled her own small bag beside her. The girl's little, pink carry-on contained only a stuffed dog that resembled her own Yorkshire Terrier in London, some colouring books and pens, plus a photo of her with Mickey Mouse and her mum and dad at Disney World. The photo was in a small, wooden frame with the cartoon mouse on the top right corner. Her father had placed it in there without her knowing to keep beside her bed in the family's Dubai villa. He wanted to remind his daughter that he wasn't far away, and even though he couldn't join them on this particular trip, he was thinking of them both.

The chauffeur-driven limousine doors locked automatically with a reassuring, soft click as the car began to move, and the child lay her head on her mother's lap to sleep.

"No, baby, we need to get home," said Angie. "If you sleep now, I'll have to carry you, and I have the cases to carry too."

"I will help you, ma'am," said the driver, with a glance in his rear-view mirror.

"Thank you, sir, but that won't be necessary." She nudged her daughter. "Why don't you tell me what we're going to do on our first day of our holiday, Anya? We're nearly home."

"Tomorrow?"

"Yes, what would you like to do first?"

"Can we play in the sea?"

"Of course we can. Maybe we can have pancakes and then lay on the beach for a while. Would you like that?"

Anya nodded. "Can we also play in the swimming pool?"

The mother took a sharp breath in. "You want to play in the pool, and the sea?"

Anya nodded and gave a little giggle. "Yes, and I want juice with ice."

"Please?"

"Please."

"That's better. I asked Julie to stop by and drop off some basics, so we should be able to make breakfast. But we'll need to go shopping at some point, okay?"

"Shopping?"

"Yes, Anya, we need to buy food for the holiday."

"Okay, but after swimming?"

"Of course. We'll have a nice morning then we'll go buy some food, and if you're a good girl, you know what I'll get you?"

"What, Mummy?"

"Ice-cream."

The girl beamed up at her mum and looked out of the car window.

"But you have to stay awake for another ten minutes, okay?"

"Okay, Mummy."

The Mercedes pulled up outside the villa on frond H of Dubai's prestigious Palm Jumeirah. There was a double garage which contained two cars, a blue Porsche that Angie's husband drove when he was in Dubai, and a larger BMW SUV that was big enough for the whole family, plus shopping and luggage.

"There we go, that wasn't so bad was it?" said Angie as she opened her door. "You'll be in bed in just a few minutes."

The driver walked to the rear of the vehicle to extract the cases, while the mother helped her daughter from the car. She tipped the driver one hundred dirhams and watched as he pulled away. The street was quiet. Each frond of the man-made, palm-shaped island had security at the entrance. The security guards allowed only residents and named guests to enter. The tight security had been one of the features that swayed her and her husband to take the villa. It also limited the amount of traffic on the narrow roads.

There were only fifty villas on each frond, and most of their neighbours were never around. Julie, who lived in the house next door was the only nearby permanent resident. The house on the other side of the Turvey house was rented to holidaymakers, and during the cooler winter months, had a variety of people coming and going.

The mother dragged the large case and the smaller carry-on, while her daughter pulled her own little bag to the front entrance. The large wooden door swung open, and she noticed that Julie had left the lights and the air-conditioning on for her. She made a mental note to thank her for the gesture.

She closed the door behind her and put the cases down.

"Right then, Anya, how about you get off to bed? Do you want me to come and tuck you in?"

Anya nodded and pulled her stuffed dog from the little carry-on.

"Okay, well go get changed, and I'll be up in a sec, okay?"

"On my own?"

"You want me to come with you?"

"It's dark up there."

"Okay, well come on then. I'll come and turn the lights on, but you have to go straight to bed, okay?"

She settled Anya into bed and stroked her hair until she fell asleep then closed the bedroom door behind her and walked down the stairs, hoping that Julie had left a bottle of wine in the fridge.

The stairwell took her back down to the large hallway where her cases were. She left them there and walked towards the rear of the house to the kitchen, which was halfway along the hallway on the right-hand side. She found a bottle of Pinot Grigio in the fridge, silently thanked Julie, and poured herself a glass.

The housekeeper had been recently and cleaned the kitchen, so she relaxed, leaned against the hidden fridge, and took a long tired glance around the immaculate kitchen with its Carrara marble surfaces, and top of the range appliances. They'd done very well. Her husband had taken promotion after promotion, and they had been able to afford a modestly luxurious lifestyle. But she smiled at the fact that she still preferred to drink cheap wine from her crystal glasses.

She shoved off and walked out into the hallway, turning right into the huge lounge and dining area at the very back of the huge, five-bedroom villa.

Angie kicked off her designer boots and reached for the light switches on the wall to her right.

The first switch lit the chandelier above the twelve-seater, lignum vitae dining table in the dining area to her left. The second switch powered the ceiling-mounted spots that were spaced equidistantly around the edge of the room, and on one wall lit the large, three-metre square oil painting by contemporary artist Leonid Afremov.

On the opposite side of the living room, the spots lit the naked and broken body of Julie.

Her head hung limply, and her wide eyes stared as if she'd died in fright. But the blood all over her skin, and the bruises on her face told Angie that Julie had put up a hard fight, and lost. She'd either bled to death or died from internal injuries.

The crystal glass smashed on the tiled floor.

Anya suddenly began to scream from her room.

Then from behind Angie came a chilling, gravelly voice.

"Welcome home, Mrs Turvey."

Harvey Stone woke at his usual five am, in his usual naked manner, and climbed out of bed onto the ancient hardwood floor before stepping into the en-suite.

The old farmhouse, built in the typical French manner using a tasteful blend of stone and timber for the structure with a slate gabled roof, offered little protection against the brisk winter air outside. There was no double-glazing, and most of the doors were ill-fitting wooden panels that swelled with the summer humidity and shrank to allow the draughts through in the much cooler winter months. But Harvey loved the house. It was everything he needed and nearly everything he owned.

He padded to the kitchen to be greeted by his dog, Boon, then stoked last night's embers in the wood burner. He added a few logs and some kindling then set about putting the kettle on to boil. He found his shorts on the couch and slipped them on; they had been pulled off the previous night when things between Melody and him had gotten lively, and they'd moved their sins to the bedroom.

Harvey leaned against the kitchen worktop, which was wooden and polished to a smooth finish that was flawed only by the century of use it had seen. The old farmhouse still had some work to be done, and although each morning he surveyed the interior, he knew his efforts were needed on the exterior; work on the interior was for the summer. Until then, the roof needed fixing, and gaping holes in the rotting window frames needed caulking. Harvey wasn't really a handyman, but he'd been retired for six months and found the work filled his day nicely.

The kettle started to boil and began its low warning whistle. Harvey took it off the stove and poured the water into the French press. He gave the coffee a minute then added it to the waiting tray and walked back to the bedroom with Boon at his heels.

Melody lay on her side facing the window. The thick duvet clung to her hip, and her naked back welcomed Harvey. He set the tray down on the dresser beside the window and poured coffee into the two mugs. He added fresh cream to Melody's coffee and left his own black.

"There's my man," said Melody. "You made coffee already?"

"You were sleeping."

"Coffee can wait. Why don't you come back to bed?"

"I'm going for a run," said Harvey, and Boon's ears pricked up.

Melody raised herself up onto an elbow to take the mug of coffee from Harvey. "One day, I'm going to teach you how to use long sentences." She smiled up at him as he reached down to kiss her.

"One day, I'm going to teach you that I can't be changed."

"Made of stone, right?"

"Something like that," replied Harvey.

He pulled on a t-shirt, socks and his running shoes while Melody read the news on her phone.

"What's the plan for today then, mister retired man?" asked Melody, looking up at him from inside the covers.

"Windows and maybe see about getting someone in to sort the roof out."

"Don't you want to come to town with me?"

He stepped across the room to her, bent and kissed her on the forehead. "I'll see you later."

"Is that a yes or a no?"

Harvey didn't reply.

He glanced around the house, pulled the front door closed behind him, and checked it was locked. Then Harvey jogged the two hundred yards from the door and along the muddy driveway to the lane that connected the small farmhouse to the beach road at one end and the town of Argeles-Sur-Mer at the other. He sped up to his usual pace and settled into his breathing rhythm. The lane was quiet and dark, and soon the horizon showed the pale, misty blues of the morning Mediterranean.

The only other movement was Boon, who ran in the fields alongside him. A few cars passed sporadically, and each time, Harvey moved from the lane's hard tarmac surface to the rough, bumpy grass hillock to the side. The cars were locals judging by the plates, but the third car had UK plates. It wasn't unusual as tourists often ventured to Argeles-Sur-Mer as a reprise from the less tranquil Riviera further east.

He reached the beach and ran through the long, wild grass that grew on the edge onto the soft, clean sand that led down to the sea. Harvey ran every morning, and each morning he ran a different route; it was an old habit he'd been taught by his mentor Julios to avoid people planning an attack. Many of the routes he took across fields, through the town or through the nearby forests found their way onto the beach eventually, usually as a last sprint before he headed home. Each time he ran on the beach, he'd see the same old guy, stripped down to nothing and swimming in the ocean, no matter the temperature.

"You are early this morning," the man called, holding his hand up in a wave, completely unabashed by his nudity.

Harvey nodded as he passed, and lifted his hand to acknowledge him, and then put his head down and pushed himself harder. He didn't plan his route, he just ran where his legs took him and avoided the places he'd run recently. Harvey turned off the beach before he came to a small village and headed into the fields opposite. As he crossed the road, he caught sight of the small, blue saloon with UK plates. It was parked outside the coffee shop that he and Melody used. Harvey bounded across the field and into the wild forest that lay behind.

An hour later, he turned into the driveway to his farm and slowed to a walk with Boon at his heels. Melody stood in the kitchen clutching a fresh coffee when he opened the back door and they walked back inside.

"Hey, you want more coffee?" asked Melody, reaching down to pat Boon.

"No, I'll take a shower, and get started outside." He headed out of the kitchen.

"Erm, Harvey?"

He stopped and turned to look at Melody.

"Aren't you forgetting something?"

"No, I rarely forget anything."

"My kiss?"

Harvey smiled and stepped across the terracotta-tiled floor, then landed a kiss on her lips.

"You're all sweaty," Melody said. "I *like* it."

"Are you wearing that today?" asked Harvey.

"What?" said Melody, looking down at the loose-knit sweater and jeans. "What's wrong with this?"

"You're going to get dirty."

"Dirty? How?"

"Outside helping me."

"Who said anything about helping you? I'm going into town."

"Oh right. Are you going to walk there in those shoes?"

"Walk? No. I'll take the car."

"Is that right?"

"Yes," said Melody.

"Okay then," said Harvey as he left the room pulling his shirt off.

"Harvey?" called Melody, as he turned the shower on to let the hot water pull through.

"What?"

"Where are the car keys?"

Harvey didn't reply. He smiled to himself, stepped into the shower, and let the hot water run over him.

"Harvey?" Melody was at the bathroom door, leaning against the door frame. He looked up at her. "Did you hear me?"

Harvey switched the water off and ran his hands through his short hair.

"Hand me a towel."

"Where are the keys?"

"Hand me a towel." Harvey broke into a smile.

Melody reached in and took the towel from its hook on the wall. "Where are the keys?"

"Towel."

After a long pause, Melody said, "Keys."

Harvey stepped from the shower cubicle. Melody took a step backwards.

"Give me what *I* want," he said.

"Give me what I want."

"You want keys?"

"Among other things," replied Melody with a smirk.

Harvey walked slowly toward her, as she stepped slowly backwards into the bedroom. The backs of her legs found the bed, and she let herself fall onto the duvet. Harvey strode up to her and looked down. But a movement caught his eye, and he froze. At the far end of the driveway, parked on the lane, was the blue saloon he'd seen twice already that morning. Harvey moved away from the window.

"Stay down."

"What?" said Melody, confused. "What's wrong?"

Harvey began to dress in cargo pants, boots, and a fresh t-shirt, keeping an eye on the car with frequent glances out the window.

"Who's there?" said Melody.

"That's the third time I've seen that car today."

"So what? Probably just tourists."

"UK plate."

"*So?* Tourists," replied Melody.

"No, it doesn't sit right."

"So is the fun over?"

"Get your rifle on them," he said. "I'm going out there."

Harvey slammed the door closed and stepped out onto the muddy driveway. He strode directly down the centre of the track, his eyes fixed on the shape of the driver behind the driver side window. Two more shapes moved in the back totalling three people in the car. He reached within fifty yards of the car when it suddenly pulled away and headed off in the direction of the beach.

Harvey stopped and watched it drive away. He turned back to Melody who was at the bedroom window waving him back.

"You see that?" asked Harvey as he stepped back inside.

"I saw a car with three people in."

"Parked outside our house in the middle of nowhere."

"They're probably lost," said Melody.

"Lost? There's nothing to find."

"Maybe they're looking for somewhere to camp."

"They weren't campers, Melody."

"Ah, forget about them, Harvey," said Melody. "Let's enjoy the day."

"And if they come back?"

"If they come back..." She stepped up close to him and pulled his face down to hers by his shirt. "I'll set my man on them." She kissed him hard on the lips.

Harvey responded by kissing her back briefly then pulling away. "What did you have in mind?"

"In mind?" she said.

"You said you wanted fun. What do you want to do?"

"Oh, why don't we start with breakfast?"

"I could eat," said Harvey. "Where?"

"Why don't we go to the little cafe in the village by the beach?" replied Melody. "I feel like I need something fruity."

"Something fruity, yeah?" said Harvey.

"Mmm," replied Melody, licking her lips seductively.

Harvey saw through the charade. He saw where she was taking the conversation. "First, we train then we eat."

Melody's arms flopped to her sides as Harvey stepped away, and he smiled to himself when he heard her sigh behind him. He whistled for Boon who came running in from where he'd been sleeping on the spare bed.

Their mornings typically involved training of some description. Some mornings they sparred in their barn, where Harvey had set up a few floor mats. Other mornings, they ran together and worked out. Harvey usually led the training, but Melody had recently been teaching him how to shoot a rifle. She had explained to him that a handgun, like the SIG Sauer P226 they had used when they worked together, was not effective at long range, and the automatic MP5s they had used were barbaric and unwieldy in comparison to the skill required to tame a 7.62 sniper rifle. Long range shooting required elegance, practice and precision, and the Diemaco rifle she preferred was the perfect partner for a sniper.

"Let's go, boy," said Harvey, as the dog skipped around in two tight circles by his feet.

Melody pulled on a tight and short leather biker jacket and took the rifle from the gun cabinet in the hallway. "Right, boys, let's go."

The three stepped out into the large field at the rear of the house. Three bales of hay marked the firing position, and a wall of hay, exactly one thousand metres away, marked the target.

Melody had trained at Bisley, one the UK's finest shooting grounds, where volunteers would wait in a bunker below the target, ready to pull the target down, call the shots, and paste a new target on. But in Harvey and Melody's field, they didn't have that luxury. They simply replaced the targets after finishing the session, so a new target was ready whenever they felt the urge to shoot.

Long-range target shooting was Melody's speciality, and for Harvey, there could be no better tutor. She slapped his hand if he gripped the rifle stock, and would tell him to let the rifle lay on his open hand. If he snatched a shot, she wouldn't even call it from the scope, she would simply tut.

Harvey had learned a lot, and as he dropped to the prone position, Melody didn't utter a word to help him. He lay down and got comfortable. The rifle lay across his open left palm and the butt was pulled in tight to his shoulder, finding the sweet spot to absorb the massive kickback from the rifle.

Before he even lowered his head and found the target through the scope, Harvey calmed his breathing. He placed the box of rounds beside him so that he could reload without dropping the rifle.

"Groups of five at five inches, five shots in the head, five in the chest," said Melody. "Take your time. How's the wind?"

"Two knots, maybe three," replied Harvey.

"So, what are you going to do?"

"Take a test shot and see where it goes?"

"Negative, Stone," said Melody playfully. "You have a live shooter situation. He has fifty people pinned down and you're their only chance of escaping. What are you going to do?"

Harvey closed his eyes and felt the tiny clicks of the scope as he adjusted for the wind.

"You happy with that, Stone?"

"I'm good," said Harvey. "If I miss, I'll just walk over there and beat the-"

"Live firing on my command," said Melody. "You have one minute to take the shooter down, soldier." She paused as Harvey lowered his eye to the scope. "Go."

Melody waited patiently for Harvey to find his rhythm. She was pleased with his progress and looked on lovingly as, for once, he was out of his comfort zone. He fired off the first round.

"Gently," said Melody.

The second round was snatched.

"Squeeze," she said.

The third shot was perfect. Harvey remained totally motionless until he'd fired off all ten rounds. Melody waited patiently for him to finish and give her a report.

"Shots fired. Target is down," said Harvey.

"Is the weapon safe?"

"Yes."

"Lower the weapon and stand away from it. Collect your shells and place them in the bin behind you."

Melody enjoyed the formalities of shooting. But more than

anything, she maintained the same level of safety and communication at their own home range, as complacency would more than likely cause a fatality.

"How do you think you did?" asked Melody, as Harvey stood and clicked his neck both sides.

"One group of three to the head, one group of five the chest," Harvey replied.

"And the other two?"

"Wild."

"Ready to go again?" asked Melody.

"I will be, give me a-"

"No time for that, Stone. The man you took down has been replaced. You now have fifty-seconds on target two. Five by five, head and chest, on my command."

Harvey dropped to the floor, raised the weapon, and lowered his eye.

"Is the weapon safe?" asked Melody.

Harvey checked the safety.

"Mistake. You dropped your eye, and you haven't even reloaded yet."

Harvey cursed and reloaded. The end of the muzzle of the rifle moved around as he struggled with the magazine.

"You just lost your position, Stone. Look at the end of the rifle, keep it still, keep your cool, take your time. You've got this. It's precision, it's accuracy, it's a skill, and I've seen you do it before."

"Okay," said Harvey with a little frustration. "Leave me to it."

Harvey slid the fresh magazine into the rifle as gently as he could and felt it click. He didn't hit it home with his hand. He remembered Melody's words. This is a weapon for the skilled sniper. It is not an AK-47, and he was not a terrorist. He kept his body still as he brought the rifle to his shoulder. His palm opened flat, and the rifle lay on top. Melody spoke to him again.

"That's good. The weapon is part of you, no part of lying there should be uncomfortable. It sits naturally in your shoulder like it was made just for you. It rests on your palm like it's weightless. You don't look through the scope, the scope shows you what you want to see."

There was silence as Harvey controlled his breathing once more.

Then softly and calmly, Melody gave the order. "Target is at one thousand metres, Stone. It's a live shooter, and only you can bring him down. Five by five on my command."

She paused. "Begin."

When Harvey had finished, he remained still until instructed to move by Melody. He wasn't one for obeying orders, but Melody insisted on effective communication on the range, and shooting was her game, not his. He was the student.

"Shots fired. Target is down."

"Is the weapon safe?" asked Melody.

"Yes."

"Lower the weapon and stand away. Collect your shells and place them in the bin behind you."

Harvey did as instructed and waited for Melody to ask how he thought he did.

"How about that breakfast?" asked Melody.

"Yeah, sure," replied Harvey. "But aren't you going to ask how I thought I did?"

"Do I need to ask?" said Melody. "Your posture was perfect. Your grip was exactly right. You were breathing like you were reading a book instead of shooting a gun, and your timing was impeccable." She looked up at him with her hands on her hips. "If you didn't get five by five that time, I'm going to buy you a catapult. You want to go check?"

Harvey looked at the target, a small dot at the edge of the field.

"It'll still be there when we get back, won't it?" He whistled for Boon and collected the rifle from the blanket on the ground.

A few minutes later, once the rifle had been locked away, they made their way along the long muddy driveway.

Boon ran ahead, but never strayed too far, and never ran in the road. Harvey had seen his owner killed by a terrorist the year before and had rescued the dog. It was Melody who took care of him mostly, feeding him and talking to him, but the dog saw Harvey as the alpha and hung on his every word.

They walked side by side along the lane, with Boon scampering along in the fields alongside them. The morning was fresh, but the pale blue sky promised a day of pleasant sun.

Harvey was quiet, not broody, but just deep in thought. Melody eyed him. She understood him well. It had taken a long while, but she could read Harvey, although, often, that wasn't always a good thing.

He'd come a long way, she thought, from the hitman she'd met a few years before to who he was now. Melody had seen him turn, seen him struggle with his past, and fight the system only to overcome his restraints. She admired the way he hadn't given in to the system that could have locked him away for the rest of his life. Instead, he'd bent the steel framework of conformity to suit himself, and managed to come out clean. He'd left the past behind. Although gnarly hands had held him and thick chains had bound him to the criminal world, he'd broken free and come out fighting. She likened him to a magnificent sailboat that crested the high waves of the rough stormy seas and crashed into the deep troughs that threatened to swallow him. He'd weathered the storm all his life and was now enjoying the gentle breeze that pushed him along the calm, blue waters.

"Do you miss it?" asked Melody.

"Miss what? The team or the work?"

"Both, I guess," replied Melody. "It was a big part of our lives."

"Yeah, but let's face it, it couldn't have lasted much longer."

"Why not? We were doing well."

"*Doing well?*" said Harvey, incredulous. "We reported in to a bent cop, you were kidnapped and nearly drowned, I was shot at, tortured and nearly blown up, and Denver-"

"Yeah, what about him?" said Melody.

"Do I need to say it?"

"No. No, I guess you don't."

They turned out of the lane, crossed the road and stepped onto the beach. Boon was there playing in the long grass and waiting for them.

"We had the skills though," said Melody.

"Yeah, we had the skills, but not the numbers, and certainly not the direction."

"So you don't miss it?"

"No," said Harvey. "No, I don't think I do. I was ready to relax and enjoy my retirement a long time ago."

"But you're young and capable."

"And tired, Melody. Tired of the games, the lies, and most of all, I guess I'm tired of death."

There was a silence between them, as they both thought about the people they'd known that had been killed, the targets they had killed themselves, and the victims that had suffered horrible deaths.

"I'd go back," said Melody.

"You what?"

"I'd go back. Don't get me wrong, I love what we have here, but if the opportunity came knocking, I think I'd open the door."

"I thought you wanted to write?" said Harvey.

"I do, but I miss the thrill of the chase, the research, and the satisfaction of stopping..." She paused. "I don't know. It's just speculation."

"You do what you have to do, Melody. I'm staying right here."

"I gave up a lot to come be with you."

"I didn't ask you to, Melody. *You* made that choice."

"I know, I'm sorry. I shouldn't have brought it up."

"You have freedom of speech," said Harvey. He gave her a smile. "I'd support you, you know that. But I don't have the will anymore."

Melody took his hand. "Maybe you don't have the will because there isn't any danger?"

"What's that supposed to mean?"

"Oh, come on, Harvey. I saw you in action. The more peril there was, the more dangerous you got."

"I did what had to be done."

"You did some crazy stuff, Harvey."

"Whatever, we're alive, aren't we?"

"I guess. And what are the chances of opportunity knocking at the door out here?"

Harvey stopped, and Melody turned to him.

"Pretty good, I'd say," said Harvey.

"Sorry? What?"

"Blue saloon outside the café."

Melody spun and saw the car parked outside the small café.

"You're paranoid."

"I hope you're right."

"Are we going inside?" asked Melody.

"You're damn right we're going in."

CHAPTER THREE

"How did you sleep, Mrs Turvey?" said the man with the gravelly voice. He swept his side parting of fine silver hair to one side and watched as Angie Turvey struggled against her restraints. "I do hope you won't be a nuisance, Mrs Turvey," said the man. "I'd hate for you to end up like poor old Julie there."

"You sick bastard. Let us go," Angie whispered, trying not to wake her daughter, who had cried herself to sleep beside her on the large U-shaped couch.

"No can do I'm afraid. Wheels are in motion. But fear not, it'll all be over in a few days, and you'll be free to leave."

"A few days? Let her go," hissed Mrs Turvey, gesturing at her sleeping daughter. "She's done nothing wrong."

"No, but she's valuable to me," said the man. "The question is, Mrs Turvey, how valuable are you both to good old Mr Turvey?"

"What's my husband got to do with this?"

"It's too early for all this. Why don't we have coffee first? I'll make it." He grinned, then stood and walked to the kitchen like the house was his own.

Mrs Turvey sat and studied her restraints. Her wrists were

bound by layers of thick duct tape, as were her ankles. She thought about hopping to the garden, but couldn't get far even if she *could* get up from the soft couch.

The second man was younger and of Arabic descent, not local, maybe Egyptian, thought Mrs Turvey, He was sat in a chair by the dining table working on a laptop, making sure to face the screen away from her, so she couldn't see what he was looking at.

"I had a thought, Mrs Turvey," said the older man as he re-entered the room. "I know you but you don't know me." He set the tray of coffee down on the coffee table, then sat and interlocked his fingers. His arms rested on his thin legs. "My name is Caesar Crowe. My friend here is Omar. Under normal circumstances I can assure you, you'd be pleased to meet me, Mrs Turvey. But I do empathise." He paused. "These aren't ordinary circumstances, are they?"

"You mentioned my husband. What do you want? I can get it, whatever it is. Is it money? I can get anything you want from us."

Crowe laughed a loud, hearty laugh. "No, Mrs Turvey, I do not need your measly wealth." He turned to Omar at the dining table. "Omar?"

"Four hundred and fifty-eight thousand in cash, another one point two million in assets," said Omar, without looking up from the screen.

"You see, Mrs Turvey, you're only worth one point seven million." His voice turned from mock friendly to cold and harsh. "My boat is worth more than that."

"So what *do* you want?" said Mrs Turvey. "Something we own?"

"Getting warmer." The fake warmth returned to Crowe's voice.

"I can't think. I don't know. Tell me, I'll get it, you can have it, whatever it is. Just let us go."

"This is a fun game." Crowe sat forward more and leaned over the table. "Why don't you keep guessing?"

Mrs Turvey's imagination ran in circles but kept coming back to the same conclusion.

"You want me?" she asked, averting her eyes.

The silver-haired man gave a hearty laugh, and then in a flash, the humour vanished from his voice. "Let's hope it doesn't come to that, Mrs Turvey."

Harvey stepped past the parked blue saloon car, told Boon to sit and stay then pushed open the door to the cafe. The little bell fixed to the top of the door frame rang lightly, loud enough to alert the waitress of a new customer, but not loud enough to disturb the customers who were already seated.

There were eleven tables each with four wooden chairs set out in true French cafe style, which was, in Harvey's mind, far too close together, and the tables themselves were too small for four people to eat at comfortably. In the right-hand corner sat an elderly couple. Harvey had seen them before. The old man from the beach sat to the left of the door, watching the world wake up. Three men in cheap suits sat at the centre table. They all looked directly at Harvey and Melody.

"Let's sit," said Melody, and gave Harvey a gentle tug on his shirt. They sat at their usual table by the window to the right of the door, Harvey with his back to the wall. The waitress beamed at them as she strode from the counter to their table. "Bonjour," she said. "Are we fine today?" she asked.

"Good morning," said Melody. "Two coffees please." Then she added, "Merci," and smiled apologetically.

"Merci. I shall be right back with your coffees." The waitress left the table and reopened the view to the three men, who continued to stare at Melody.

"Is there a problem here, boys?" asked Harvey. Melody rolled her eyes.

"Subtle, Harvey, so subtle," she murmured under her breath.

The man who was sat in the centre of the three whispered something under his breath to the men either side of him, then stood and walked the ten steps to Harvey's table. He was in his late forties, slight, with intelligent eyes that lay underneath thick, bushy eyebrows.

"Miss Mills?" he asked, looking at Melody.

Melody nodded inquisitively. "Who's asking?"

"We thought so, but couldn't be sure. Apologies for putting the frights on you outside your home earlier."

"You didn't put the frights on anyone, buddy," said Harvey.

The man looked uncomfortably at Harvey. "I'm sure," he said. "Erm, may I?" He gestured at one of the spare seats at the table.

Melody nodded her head and allowed the man to drag the chair out. He sat himself down and pulled in close to the table so he could rest his arms on top and talk discreetly. His fingers interlocked, and his gaze held Melody's in a fatherly manner. Harvey noted the monogrammed cuffs on his shirt with crossed rifles on his cuff-links.

"Miss Mills, my name is Gordon, Ian Gordon, and I believe we have a common friend, a Mr Jackson?" He raised his eyebrows with the question.

Melody drew a deep breath and sat forward.

"Go on," she said.

"Well, Miss Mills, I understand that you were previously working for-"

"We all know where Melody worked," said Harvey. "We all know her history, so cut to the chase and stop wasting our time. What's all this about?"

Gordon glanced back at Harvey. "Quite so." He fumbled for the words. "Miss Mills, Mr Jackson has requested you join him in London. There's a situation that he believes you are perfectly suited for; you have a particular skill set, were the words Mr Jackson used. My colleagues and I have been sent to find you and to kindly request that you consider this an opportunity."

"Three of you?" said Harvey. "Heavy-handed, isn't it?"

"With all due respect, Mr Stone, we were warned that there may be some resistance, and believe me, for the time being, it's best if we agree that you were not part of this conversation and that I, in fact, did not meet or even lay eyes on you."

"Is that why you drove off?" said Harvey. "You didn't want to incriminate yourselves?"

Gordon turned back to Harvey with a hint of frustration, but he held his cool. "We drove off, Mr Stone, for two reasons. Firstly, yes, association with you is not recommended, not for our sakes, but for your own. Secondly, and far more importantly, behind you in the window, your partner here, Miss Mills, had a 7.62 calibre Diemaco snipe rifle aimed at us. And given her accuracy record with the weapon, we believed it would be more appropriate, and far safer, for us to instigate initial contact in a public place, such as a cafe."

"So here we are," said Harvey.

"Quite right," replied Gordon. "May I continue please, Mr Stone?"

Harvey sat back, put his arms behind his head, and gave a slight nod. He eyed the other two men in his peripheral vision. They were feigning being relaxed. If they were who Harvey thought they were, they'd be carrying, and ready to jump into action in a fraction of a second.

"So, Miss Mills," continued Gordon, "I'm afraid I really can't say any more than that at this point. But if you'd care to join us for a briefing, I'm sure Mr Jackson will be able to fill you in on the rest of the details."

Melody held Gordon's eyes. "You want me to come with you to London based on a request from someone I used to know to do a job that I know nothing about?"

Gordon stood and replaced the chair under the table. He straightened his tie, adjusted his cuffs, and gave a cursory glance to his colleagues.

"Miss Mills, I believe we both know that you'll be there. You know the place. But I must stress, time is of the essence." Gordon glanced at his wristwatch. "We'll see you there at eight am tomorrow." He gave a tilt of his head and a confident smile. "Au revoir."

The three men left the cafe, climbed into the blue saloon, and drove off slowly.

Melody and Harvey sat in silence as the waitress brought their coffees. "Apologies for the delay, I did not want to interrupt."

"Merci," said Melody.

Harvey straightened in his seat and sat forward. "You've got twenty-two hours to get packed and into London. We both know you're going, so just go."

Melody felt the uncomfortable pause.

"You're not okay with this, are you?" replied Melody.

"It doesn't matter what I am. If it's what you want, then stopping you doing it isn't a solution that's going to work out well for either of us, is it?"

"I don't *have* to go," said Melody.

Harvey smiled and leaned forward. "What we have is great, Melody. But you're young, this could be the chance you need. Don't let *me* hold you back."

"But *you're* not holding me back. *I* am," said Melody. "I'm holding myself back because *I* want to be with you. *I* want the all the things we planned for, the things we talk about, the house, the lifestyle, and if you hadn't noticed, I want you."

Harvey ignored Melody's hidden plea for an emotional response.

"Where were those guys from?" he asked. "They seemed a little more serious than Frank ever was."

"I'm guessing MI6," replied Melody. "If they're on orders from Jackson, they must be."

"*Jackson?* MI6?"

"Must be. When the team split up, we all went in different directions. Rumour has it, Jackson was MI5, and was transferred."

"Just remember me, Melody."

"You're talking like it's *over*."

"Well, it probably *is*."

"Why is it?" Melody's face dropped. Her eyes watered. She reached over and squeezed Harvey's hand tight.

"If us ending is what it's going to take to get you to go and earn yourself an amazing career, Melody, then we're over. Go home, get your stuff, and go."

"You don't mean that," snapped Melody, louder than needed. The old couple in the corner turned at the sudden outburst, and then looked away in unison.

Harvey stood, left ten euros on the table, and walked to the door.

"I'll take the long way home. Be gone when I get back." He paused to look at her one last time. "Good luck, Melody. You earned this."

Harvey called for Boon to follow and let the cafe door close behind him. He turned left toward the village and was out of sight by the time Melody had gathered her senses and walked out into the empty street.

"I knew you'd come," said a familiar voice. Melody looked up from her phone. There were no messages from Harvey. She'd checked at every opportunity since arriving in London the previous night.

"Jackson, hi," said Melody. "It's good to see you."

"I wish it could be under more accommodating circumstances," said Jackson.

Melody found her throat closed. She murmured a quiet, "me too."

"You okay?" asked Jackson.

Melody took a long breath. "I'll be fine, just memories."

"Yeah, memories, eh? Who needs them?" said Jackson in an empathetic tone, before switching to a more professional voice. "Let's go. We have a space on the fifth floor for ops."

The reception inside the Secret Intelligence Service building on London's Southbank had a corporate look with shiny marble floors, and a cleansed feel but with security unlike anything Melody had ever seen. On any other day, Melody would have been in awe of the security, and filled with wonder at the secrets the grand building held. But it was all she could do to keep Harvey from the front of her mind long enough to hold half a conversation with Jackson.

Jackson led her through security, where she was given a pass to enter the security barriers, and then had her bag screened.

They took the lift in silence. Melody was fully aware of Jackson's desire to ask after Harvey, and Jackson was fully aware of Melody's desire to ask how he came to MI6.

As if by intuition, Jackson spoke. "This could have been yours, you know?" he said. "You'd have fit right in. Someone like you could have made waves."

Melody continued to face forward.

"My wave-making days are over, Jackson. I'm happy enough." She doubted the words even before they left her lips. "Besides, you burned your way through MI5. I'm sure someone had their eyes on you long before the team split."

Jackson was saved by the doors opening. They stepped out into a quiet corridor. Melody expected a hive of activity with phones ringing and people running in every direction. Instead, the corridors were as corporate as the reception had been, shiny and clean, but bland.

The large control room with screens lining the rear wall, however, was humming with activity. Jackson closed the door behind them both. A few people looked up from their desks, others kept their heads down. It looked as if everyone was too busy to be inquisitive. Melody knew the layout. Comms were in the centre of the room, two researchers sat at one end of the room with Gordon and the two men who had accompanied him to France, and techs were sat beneath the wall-mounted screens. Melody's eyes glanced across the screens and finally rested on a familiar interface. It was LUCY, a hardware and software solution designed and built by the tech guy from her old team, Reg.

"Is that–"

"LUCY?" said Jackson. "Of course it is, LUCY doesn't go anywhere without her owner."

The chair beneath LUCY span round and Melody laid eyes on her old friend.

"Reg, oh my God. How are you?"

Reg beamed and put his blueberry muffin on his desk. He stood and the two of them hugged. Melody felt her throat close once more. It felt good to see Reg; the two had grown quite close, and then everything had changed. They hadn't seen each other for six months.

"Okay, break it up," said Jackson. "You'll have time to catch up later. In the meantime, Mills, you'll need to be briefed."

"See ya later, alligator," said Reg with a smile.

Melody smiled weakly at Reg and followed Jackson into a glass meeting room.

"Excuse the fishbowl. It won't take ten minutes to bring you up to speed, but you'll need to sign the Non-Disclosure Agreements." He slid her a pile of papers, neatly stacked with highlights beside each signature box.

"You're aware of where you are?"

"MI6?"

"It's more than that. The building is called the Secret Intelligence Service building, so it has few more tricks up its sleeve than just us. And you're aware of who the boss is?"

"No, I'm not up to date," said Melody honestly.

"Okay. Well, there are tiers and arms and all the complexities of a government organisation." Jackson gestured at the room outside. "This particular arm reports into a man called Bernard Turvey."

"Okay," said Melody, "and he's head-hunted me?"

"No, Mills, I've head-hunted you."

"So where does Turvey fit into all this?"

"He's a good man, plays the game, runs risks, wins mostly,

and he's respected, at least in this room he's well respected. Maybe not so by his peers. But that's a good thing, for him anyway."

"He's in trouble?" asked Melody.

"It's sensitive, Mills."

"Hence the secrecy act," said Melody, nodding at the pile of papers.

"He has a wife and daughter. The daughter, Anya, is eight. The wife is thirty-nine. They flew to Dubai two days ago, where the family own a holiday home on Palm Jumeirah. They haven't been seen since. No contact."

"So it's a missing person case? Bit heavy for you guys?"

"The neighbour, a family friend, is also missing, last seen heading to the Turvey's house to drop off some groceries." Jackson paused to let Melody build the scene in her head. "Have you ever heard of Caesar Crowe?"

"No, not that I remember anyway."

"Long time criminal, thinks of himself as an international mastermind, slippery, if you know what I mean?"

Melody nodded.

"We received a message from him with certain demands. Failure to complete the demands will result in the death of Turvey's family."

Jackson made the statement with an air of nonchalance that took Melody by surprise initially. But the truth *was* that it was black and white.

"What are the demands?" asked Melody. "Cash?"

"Slightly more serious than that I'm afraid." Jackson sat forward and looked Melody in the eye. "In two days' time, Bernard is due to give a speech for a charity he chairs. The speech will be televised and broadcast around the world on the usual media platforms. It's all in aid of the DWC's annual donation stunt, but the allocation of funds is set to change the lives of millions of people. The donation is well received and is long awaited by all accounts."

Jackson hesitated and watched as Melody's brow furrowed, trying to figure out where she came into the situation.

"Following his speech, Bernard Turvey is to put a gun to his own head and kill himself. Live across the planet."

Melody's jaw dropped. She was stunned. "I never-"

"None of us *expected* it, Mills," said Jackson. "But the fact of the matter is if he doesn't go through with it, his family dies. Either way, they'll never see each other again."

The situation rolled around Melody's mind, but she didn't reply. There was nothing to say.

"Melody," said Jackson, the charm and friendliness lost from his tone, "we need you to take Crowe out."

Melody dizzied at the thought of what was happening. The realisation of where she was and what she was being asked to do came crashing home.

"Are you okay, Mills? You seem a little distracted," said Jackson.

"Yeah," said Melody, "I'm fine."

"Fine? What did Harvey think of you getting involved?"

"I think it's best for both of us if we leave my private life out of this," replied Melody, a little harsher than she meant. "I'm sorry, it's just-"

"It's okay. It's a sensitive case, but if you have your own issues, now would be a good time to say so. We can try and find someone else."

"I don't have issues, Jackson. Just drop it, okay. I'm in."

"Glad to hear it. You'll be in and out in no time, all being well. Now go see Ladyluck, and she'll provide the details of your alias. She's the girl on the end desk."

"An alias?" replied Melody. "Is that necessary?"

"Melody, you're a former operative for several variations of

British covert ops and armed police. The moment you step off the plane, you'll have eyes all over you. It's best if you're an unknown. I believe you'll be a Miss LeFleur. Ladyluck over there has an entire profile on you. Memorise it on the way to the airport. Oh, and Melody..."

Jackson hovered, waiting for her to respond, and for her eyes to meet his.

"It is *imperative* that the local government do *not* become aware of your presence."

CHAPTER SIX

"I want to talk to him," said Mrs Turvey. "I have to tell him-"

"Tell him you love him?" said Crowe. "How touching. But Angie, come on. Just imagine how hard it is for him right now. Can you imagine the suffering he is going through?"

Angie Turvey sobbed aloud. "I have to at least..." Her voice trailed off into a high-pitched whine.

"I'm a patient man, Angie, but please, let's keep the language to English. I don't understand whatever that is."

"You sick bastard. What's he ever done to you?" spat Angie.

"Mummy, I'm scared. What's wrong?" Anya had woken and found her hands bound just like her mother's.

"Nothing sweetheart. It's okay."

"But you're upset. What's happening? Why are we tied up?"

Angie looked up at Crowe. "Can I take her away to talk to her?"

"Ha, honestly? No, Angie, you can't."

"How am I supposed to talk to you about all this in front of her?"

"Talk about what, Mummy? What's happening?" The girl broke into a wail.

"That's just it, Angie, you're not. There's nothing to talk about."

"Is something wrong with Daddy?"

"No, baby. Nothing's wrong, please, adult talk okay? Go back to sleep. There's nothing to worry about."

"Everything is wrong, Anya," said Crowe. "You might as well know the truth."

"Don't you dare say a word to her," hissed Angie. "That's not your place. It's bad enough."

"Your father has been a very bad man, Anya."

Crowe's voice was that of an educated man with clear pronunciation, and the holier-than-thou tones of the upper class. An English, public school boy in his youth, Crowe had fallen from grace and had been lurking in the criminal underworld ever since. He used his education, wit and cunning to manipulate his newfound peers who, in his mind, all suffered from a severe lack of intelligence, which made them mere tools in his plans, as opposed to partners, colleagues or equals of any description. Caesar Crowe had no equal.

"Stop it. I swear to God I'll-"

"What did Daddy do?" asked the child.

"You'll what? Hurt me?" Crowe laughed once. It was a short, sharp laugh, empty of emotion. "Do you want to know what your daddy did, Anya?"

"No, please stop. I'll do anything, just...please," cried Angie.

"Mrs Turvey, I can assure you, you have nothing I want." He eyed her with distaste. "However, Omar here might have a different opinion."

"Please, Mr Crowe, not my daughter. Don't touch my daughter. I'll do what you want. Do what you want to me, but leave her."

"Relax, Angie. Nobody is going to touch your daughter. Do you think we're sick?"

Crowe smoothed his shirt and picked a loose thread of cotton from his trousers.

"Why don't you take her to the bedroom and let her have a lie-down, Omar?"

Omar strode across the room, and Angie caught his eye. "Don't you touch her, just, don't." Her face softened. Helplessness washed across her eyes. "Please, not her."

"I promise I will not hurt your daughter," said Omar genuinely.

"Thank you," whispered Angie.

Omar bent and picked Anya from the couch. She lay over Omar's shoulder like a sack, unable to manoeuvre into a comfortable position.

Angie felt helpless watching a stranger take her daughter away, but somehow the look Omar had given her was as reassuring as it could have been. Besides, Angie didn't want Anya to hear anything about her father from Crowe. As soon as Omar had left the room, Angie whispered to Crowe. "Please let her go. She can't see all this. It'll scar her for life."

"You want me to open the door and let her walk out?"

Angie let her head hang. She was cried out and exhausted. "Why, Mr Crowe? Why us?"

"Simple," said Crowe. "Your husband killed my family. He stole everything we had, and he ruined my life. So now..." Caesar Crowe smiled a cruel smile, and his cold grey eyes glistened. "*I'm* going to ruin *his* life."

"Your flights are booked, visa on arrival. We have an ally who will meet you at the airport. From there, he'll take you to get equipped, though I believe Tenant also has a few tricks up his sleeve that you'll take in your hand luggage. Nothing out of the ordinary."

Melody shot a glance through the glass partition to Reg, who sat drinking coke at his desk, leaning back with his keyboard on his lap and his feet up on a stool. Reg must have sensed Melody's look, as he turned in his seat, smiled and waved.

"Who's the ally?" asked Melody.

"Bob," said Jackson.

"*Bob?*" replied Melody. "Is that his full name or is there more to it than that? Maybe another syllable or something?"

"That's all you'll need to know. He's taking a pretty big risk getting you armed out there, so the less you know about him, the better. He'll find you at the airport."

"So he's not operational?" asked Melody. "He's not helping us?"

"He's engaged elsewhere. We have a small team out there.

The entire population of the country is only nine million, so the team tends to reflect that." Jackson held her gaze. "You'll be on your own, Mills."

"No local help? Police? The UAE has pretty effective security council from what I hear."

"Mills, it's important that we stop this man. I'm sure you empathise with the sensitivities?"

"Of course. It's a shocking demand."

"What's also important, politically, is that the Dubai government don't find out that we're there."

Melody didn't reply. She stared at Jackson, interpreting what was not said, rather than what was.

"That's why you chose me, isn't it?" said Melody. "Because if I'm caught with a weapon, or for whatever else, there's no tie."

"Mills, it's not-"

"Am I using my own passport? Or will I be masquerading as some fictitious do-gooder out on a lonely holiday in the desert?"

"Have you finished?" said Jackson.

"No, I'm just getting started."

"Well, I'll finish it for you," said Jackson, taking control of the briefing. "There's a long-standing treaty between the UAE and the UK governments. We're allies, but recently that tether has been under some pressure. Officially, we're supposed to request permission to send in an operative. But that takes time, which as you're well aware, we do not have."

"And if they do find out we're there?"

Jackson stared hard at her. "We're not there, Mills. We don't even know you. If the Dubai government gets wind of what we're doing, it won't be us trying to patch things up, it'll be the PM and the foreign minister. And if it comes to that, well, I'm sure you can use your imagination."

There was a silence that was broken by the door to the control centre being opened. The hum in the room dropped and people lowered their heads. A man stood in the doorway wearing a sharp suit and brogues. On any other day, he would be the image of success and confidence. But on that day, his posture was weak, his eyes sunken, and his crop of jet black hair looked as though it had been hastily made good, rather than groomed and styled.

Jackson caught the man's attention, and he made his way to the door of the fishbowl meeting room where Melody and Jackson sat. Closing the door behind him, he turned to look down at Melody.

"Sir," said Jackson, "this is Mills, the operative we spoke about." Jackson turned to Melody. "Mills, this is-"

"Bernard," the man cut in. "Bernard Turvey. I'd prefer if we kept this informal. You're not an MI6 asset, rank is of no importance here. What is important is that my family are made safe."

Melody shook Bernard's hand, and he sat beside Jackson. "I presume Jackson has briefed you?"

"Yes, sir. We were just getting to the details of the operation."

"Good," said Bernard. "I'll stay. There's not much to it for an operative of your calibre. Are you aware of the Palm Jumeirah in Dubai?"

"Sir, are you up to this?" asked Jackson. "We can handle it."

"The last time I looked, Jackson, *I* ran the operations."

Jackson nodded slowly. "As you wish, sir."

"I am aware of the Palm Jumeirah, sir, yes," said Melody.

Jackson pulled an aerial photo from the stack of papers in the centre of the desk and pointed to the frond H, which was on the south side of the man-made island.

"You can see here that each frond represents a branch of the Palm. Residential villas line both sides of each frond, giving each villa its own beach access. The beaches are private and accessible only from the villas themselves, or by sea. Frond H is situated here." Jackson used his pen as a pointer. "And the Turvey villa is located here." Jackson circled the villa before moving to frond G. "We have secured the rental of a holiday home on frond G, which is here." Jackson pointed again at the adjacent frond and circled another villa. "As you can see, it's not directly opposite the Turvey villa, but it's very close. It's a three-hundred metre swim across the water at high tide. Villa to villa, you're looking at an eight-hundred-metre shot."

"You want me to take him out?"

"No, Mills. We *need* you to take him out," said Jackson. "As soon as you arrive, you need to formulate a plan then get the surveillance running. Tenant will gear you up. After that, you'll have just under twenty-four hours to take him out."

"Is he alone?"

"We don't know. We assume accomplices, but these will be financially motivated if there are any. Take out Crowe, and they'll lose interest."

"What if I take out Crowe and the accomplices do something stupid?"

"Mills," said Bernard, "don't *let* them do anything stupid."

"Bob will arrange a Diemaco for you," said Jackson, "your weapon of choice, and he'll set you up in the villa. From there, you're on your own. See Tenant before you leave for your comms and surveillance gear. See Ladyluck, and she'll set you up with your ID and travel documents, all expenses paid, but be sensible. You know the rules. Any questions?"

"Yes," said Melody.

Jackson raised his eyebrows, waiting for her to speak.

"Hypothetically, if I fail?"

Bernard swallowed and took a breath. Melody saw his tired eyes redden and shine as he fought to hold his emotions back. "If you fail, Mills, I'll be on stage in two days' time holding a Sig to my head, and saying goodbye to my family."

CHAPTER EIGHT

It had been less than twenty-four hours since Melody had left. Harvey was out running and had stopped on the beach. Boon stood far ahead looking back at him, wondering what his master was doing. He trotted back to Harvey, who then dropped to his haunches to stroke Boon's head.

Melody had left a note for Harvey on his bedside table, and for the first time in Harvey's life, he just couldn't shake the thought of a girl from his mind. He'd always been the one to end the few relationships he'd had. But this time it was different. With previous girls, he'd ended things because they were so far removed from the life he'd led, the life of a killer. It didn't matter how much he'd liked them, there just wasn't a way to explain to them what he did. He couldn't even tell them it was just trans-actional, it had been business; it was his job. They would never have understood, and would always wonder where he went late at night, which led to questions, which led to lies, deceit, and ultimately the end of the relationship. But he'd met Melody *because* of what he'd done for a living, and she'd fallen in love with him despite his past. He thought on that point. Fallen in love.

The note had been succinct and direct. Melody told him that she didn't believe they were over. It had all been too good to throw away. She'll be back when the job was done if Harvey would have her.

"What do we do, boy?" he asked Boon.

The dog just buried his head into Harvey, as if questioning why he'd stopped stroking him.

Harvey wanted her back, but also knew that he couldn't be the one who stopped her from reaching her potential. Melody was a great operative. He'd had every faith in her when they'd worked a job together. But questions ran through Harvey's mind. What if in ten years' time she regrets staying with him? What if someone comes after Harvey? An old enemy or a released prisoner. What if?

They had enjoyed a great six months together since they'd left the very unofficial team that had targeted organised crime in London. One of their colleagues had been killed by terrorists. Then an internal investigation had uncovered Frank Carver, their boss, as being dirty. The time to leave had been right for Harvey, but Melody had higher aspirations. She had worked her way up through the ranks and shone. Harvey stared at the sand. He couldn't be the one to hold her back.

When he stepped back into the house and closed the door behind him, the place felt emptier than ever before. Dishes sat on the draining board in the kitchen, pictures hung on the wall, and cushions were placed neatly on the little two-seater couch opposite the wood-burning stove. They were all reminders of Melody. Harvey would never hang pictures, and he'd never buy cushions from little boutique stores. He'd always lived a simple life. Possessions had never been high on his agenda. But now he'd had them, now he'd had Melody, he found he wanted them. He wanted her.

What if she was hurt? What if she was killed because she

was sent to do a job that he could have stopped? If she didn't do it, someone else would. Let them, Harvey thought. Let Melody stay safe.

There were no messages on his phone from Melody, and he hadn't sent any to her, despite the part of his mind that fed memories of her into his thoughts. He'd wanted the change to be as easy as possible for her. Harvey stood in limbo between the bedroom and the living room. Boon stared up at him, sensing his master's unease.

Then, without any further hesitation, the decision was made. Sitting on the edge of the bed, with Boon at his heels, he lifted his phone and dialled a number he'd memorised.

Jackie and George were retired British expats enjoying the autumn years of their life on France's southern coast. Melody and Harvey had met them in the village and Melody had said they seemed kind, genuine and trustworthy, and the foursome had informally arranged to go to dinner, with no date set. Harvey made the call. They agreed to look after Boon for a few days, and when he got back from his trip, they'd all go to dinner. Harvey hoped it would as a foursome.

Less than two hours later, Harvey was on his motorbike blasting through the lanes, and then onto the motorway that would take him to Calais. He'd made the journey many times before. In the past, he'd stop at an Air B&B or bed-and-breakfast to make the journey last two days, both for comfort and to enjoy the road. But this time, he rode directly to London, only stopping for fuel, toilet and water breaks.

He made the journey in fifteen hours, and climbed off the bike sore and stiff.

The winter days in London are short, and night falls quickly. Workers arrive to work in the dark and leave in the dark. This worked in Harvey's favour. He'd waited an hour for his target to show, and the dark would allow him to get close without being seen.

The man walked down the steps of his office onto the Albert Embankment and turned to head towards the train station. Harvey followed on foot. Vauxhall Station was a five-minute walk, and as Harvey shadowed the man, he made a plan. It wasn't until the man stepped onto the packed train and reached up for the handle to steady himself that Harvey stepped up behind him. The doors closed with a hiss. People fought for space to read their newspapers and books. Others stared at their phones. Harvey moved in closer to Reg and spoke quietly in his ear.

"Don't turn around," said Harvey. "Where is she?"

Reg startled and began to turn.

"I said, don't turn around," said Harvey. "Where is she?"

"You missed her," said Reg. "She's on her way."

"Where, Reg?"

"I can't say. I signed the-"

"Reg."

"Dubai. But you didn't hear it from me."

"You have her location; tell me where to find her."

"Harvey, you can't, the assignment, it's serious."

"Even more reason for me to go bring her out of there, don't you think?"

The train braked hard as it reached the next station, and when the doors opened, Harvey found himself blocking the exit. He stubbornly stayed where he was, forcing other passengers to move around him.

"Are you going to move or what, mate?" said a construction worker in dirty jeans, heavy boots, and a thick jacket.

Harvey didn't reply.

The man put his head down as soon as he made eye contact with Harvey and edged around him.

"Still got your charm, Harvey," said Reg, as more people replaced the ones that disembarked.

Harvey and Reg moved to the far side of the train to stand out of the way of the hurried commuters.

"It's good to see you, Harvey."

Reg's words were met with Harvey's stony face. "I need to find her."

"Her flight left a few hours ago, Harvey," said Reg. "I'm sorry. I can't bring her back."

"How long has she gone for?"

"It's a two-day op," said Reg. "I can call you as soon as she's back if you want?"

"You can do better than that, Reg," said Harvey. "Set me up with comms and give me access to her tracker, and I'll go find her myself."

"Seriously, Harvey, it's out of the question."

"Have you forgotten exactly what it is I did for a living, Reg?"

Reg shook his head. "How could I forget that?"

"Right, comms and tracker. Where and when?"

"I'm not going to win this, am I?" said Reg.

Harvey didn't reply.

"Tomorrow night. Same place same time?" said Reg.

"That's too late. I'll be twenty-four hours behind."

"I can't get the comms until tomorrow morning."

"What about her tracker?"

"You could just download the app."

"The app?"

"Don't worry, it's encrypted," said Reg. "It'll give you access to LUCY. From there, you'll see where Melody is."

"What's your stop?"

"It's the next one."

"Okay, we're going outside, set me up with the app."

"You're really going out there?" asked Reg. "You could compromise the whole operation."

"Reg, when have you ever known me to do anything stupid?"

"Well, there was the time you jumped out of the moving van onto the moving taxi and got yourself run over. And, of course, there was the time you jumped into the Thames wearing an explosive vest. And-"

"Reg, stop," said Harvey. "I'm not going out to get involved, I'm going out there to watch Melody and make sure she stays safe."

Reg nodded slowly. "The company man inside me hates this. I want to call this in."

"But?"

"But the friend inside me wants to go look after her. This one is serious."

The train braked again, and the doors hissed open. "Shall we?" said Reg. "Let's go ruin my career."

They walked to the top of the steps and surfaced at Clapham Common.

"Okay, give me your phone, I'll set it up," said Reg.

"Not here," replied Harvey. "Have you forgotten who you work for? There's a bench on the common near the church. Take my phone, walk clockwise around the grass, and I'll meet you on that bench." Harvey handed Reg his phone.

Reg looked at Harvey's phone. "Wow, you really need to update this beast, Harvey. I'm surprised it even-" Reg turned around to face Harvey, but he was gone.

By the time Harvey was stepping onto the plane and taking his seat at the very back, Melody had already landed and was walking confidently through terminal three of Dubai International Airport. She scanned the crowds that were waiting for loved ones or colleagues to arrive but saw nobody she recognised and nobody that wore the serious look of an operative. She didn't imagine the mysterious Bob would be standing and holding a card with her name on, but she thought she might have been able to spot an operative.

She exited the terminal and looked around. It was winter, but the air was still warm compared to the frigid bite of London's perpetual breeze. Decorative fountains welcomed newcomers to the country, along with rows of taxis and limousines.

"Excuse me, do you have the time?" said a voice.

Melody turned to see a short, stocky western man stride towards her. She glanced at her watch. "It's two am," she replied with a smile.

"Okay, thanks," said the man. "Get in a cab, and then check

your pocket," he added under his breath and disappeared into the throng of people. Melody did just that.

"Just drive," she said to the taxi driver. "I'll tell you where shortly." She turned on the interior light and pulled a piece of yellow notepaper from her pocket. The scribbled writing was just an address. She expected nothing more.

"Al Warqa," Melody said to the driver. "Street sixteen."

The cab driver nodded and fought his way across three lanes of traffic onto a faster road, then accelerated to one hundred and twenty kilometres an hour. His driving was erratic and not at all relaxing, as if the driver was keen to drop her off so he could get another fare; passenger comfort was not high on his list of priorities.

In the early hours of the morning, the roads were clear. A glance at the compass app on her phone told Melody she was heading east. She knew that the Palm Jumeirah was south and west of the airport. She kept an eye on the compass and the GPS, and soon, as the buildings grew smaller and fewer, the dark landscape outside was represented by yellow desert on her phone's map.

Villas lined the street, each of them hidden away behind tall walls. She directed the driver to stop three hundred yards from the villa on the address and waited for him to pull away before walking to the front gate. The empty street felt open and insecure; she felt an element of vulnerability. The gate was open, so she stepped inside onto the forecourt and pushed the little gate closed behind her. The villa was a single storey with a large, wooden double door, which was ornately decorated. It opened as she climbed the few marble steps, and Melody stepped inside.

Melody was immediately hit by the coolness of the house. High ceilings and sparse windows kept the Arabic houses cool, and the constant air conditioning maintained the temperature.

The marble continued throughout the interior, along a wide hallway which led into an open space where the man who had asked her the time at the airport stood waiting.

"Miss LeFleur?"

"You'd be in trouble if I wasn't," replied Melody.

"Welcome to Dubai. I'm Bob," said the man. "Apologies about the airport, can't be too careful, you know?"

"It's okay, I enjoyed the ride."

"Drink?" asked Bob. "Wine, whiskey or water?"

"Is the water safe to drink?"

"Safer than the wine." Bob smiled. "It's all bottled."

"I'll take a water then, thanks."

"Relax," said Bob. "You want to take a shower before we get down to business?"

"When are we leaving?"

"For the Palm? In a couple of hours, you'll need to beat the traffic," said Bob as he stepped into the kitchen.

Melody looked around at the Peli-cases stacked up against the walls. Bob came back into the room and followed her gaze.

"Not for you," he said. "Your kit is in the next room." He passed Melody the chilled water.

Melody nodded. "Thanks."

"Take a shower," said Bob. "The spare bedroom is through that door. There're towels and stuff. When you're done, I'll brief you and get you kitted up."

Thirty minutes later, Melody was sitting crossed legged on the floor of the majlis, an area with floor cushions around the edge where locals socialise. Two large, intricately designed rugs covered the majlis floor. Bob handed her two large Peli-cases; one was long and slender and one was the size of a small suitcase.

"Seven-point-six-two Diemaco with rounds and scope in one case, and SIG Sauer, comms, binos, and bugs in the other," said Bob, as he lowered himself to the floor with a bottle of beer.

Melody popped each case open and checked the kit. She trusted Bob, but if she didn't check and a mistake happened, she wouldn't be in a position to point fingers.

"Do you have a map for me?" she asked.

Bob reached across and handed her a thin folder. "All the info we can give you."

"Do we have eyes on the house at all?"

"None. The location isn't even confirmed, but it's the best we have."

"The location isn't confirmed?" said Melody.

"Apparently the demands were sent over an encrypted line via a dozen different locations worldwide. HQ didn't even have a position until some tech guy decrypted the message and traced it back around the world."

Melody thought of Reg and had faith in his ability. "I'm pretty sure it's fine then. Did you see the villa I'm going to hole up in?"

"Yeah, I rented it. I had a good look around. No nosy neighbours, it's mainly holiday rentals on the Palm. There are some permanent residents but not many. The Turveys' house is supposed to be on the other side of the water, and about four or five houses along. You'll need to do a recce yourself."

Melody put the file down. "Doesn't seem like there's much concrete here."

"There's not," said Bob. "But what can we do?"

"Are you joining in the fun?"

Bob shook his head. "No chance. I can't blow my cover. You'll be on your own, I'm afraid."

Melody nodded. "What's the situation like here?"

"Situation?"

"In Dubai? Do you see much action?"

"No, we're forbidden to operate here. I'm just keeping the place warm," replied Bob, easing himself back. He was clearly comfortable with his posting.

"You must be bored then. Don't you want to get involved?"

"Not really, we've got too much to lose. I'm guessing Jackson explained the tension?"

"Yeah, he said we couldn't get caught," said Melody.

"No, he said I can't get caught," said Bob. "You can do as you wish. You're not tied to anything."

"How am I getting there?"

"I'll take you. That'll be the last you see of me. After that, you're on your own." Bob finished his beer and reached for another from a six-pack beside him.

"Are you on your own out here?" asked Melody.

"Listen, LeFleur, or whatever your name is," Bob said, sitting forward to hold her gaze, "you seem nice, you're pretty, and I hear good things about you. But don't go cocking this up. Stop asking questions and get your head in the game. *You don't need to know* how many there are of us out here *or* what our real names are, and when I drop you off, you'd do well to forget you ever met me. I'll be civil and professional. I suggest you do the same. There's more than just your own life at stake here."

Melody absorbed the hit with raised eyebrows and slammed the peli-cases shut. "So now I know where I stand, why don't we hit the road?" said Melody. "I've exhausted this resource, time to move on and get the game in play."

"Don't take it personally, LeFleur, and trust me, the game is already in play. You're coming up to bat in the last quarter. All eyes are on you, girl."

CHAPTER TEN

"Sir, I just had a check in from Mills. She's in the villa and setting up," said Reg.

"Good, let's get eyes on her if we can," said Jackson. "I want to see what we're up against."

Reg began typing effortlessly fast into his keyboard. He was using the chat feature he'd added to LUCY, his creation.

"Sir, she's just prepping for a recce. She's setting up the camera with night vision, so we'll see her swim across."

"Right, everybody, listen in," said Jackson, addressing the whole room. "Up until now, we've been going on hearsay and chasing our tail. We now have an asset in place, and pretty soon, we'll have audio on the Turvey house. We need voice recognition ready to go. Get the databases up. We need eyes and ears on the local police. I want to know the moment they get wind of something. We cannot be found operating in Dubai, people. Lastly, I need everyone switched on. If you need coffee, go get it now. If you need the washroom, do what you've got to do because once that audio is on, and the clock starts counting down, you won't have five minutes to spare." Jackson paused.

"We've got this. We can stop him, but timing will be critical. So keep alert."

There was a hustle as people prepared for the long shift. Some had already been there for more than a full day; others had taken the time to get some rest. Jackson approached Reg who sat with his feet up and his keyboard on his lap.

"What are you up to, Tenant?"

"I'm lining up access to the Dubai roads authority, the RTA. From there, I'll be able to follow someone by road, for example, Melody, as she runs to the airport."

"Ok, good. Is that live?" asked Jackson.

"No, I'm just setting up the access. Once we're in, there's a good chance of being caught and the web traffic being traced back here. So we won't use it until we need it."

"Good. How long will it take to initialise a connection?"

"Depends. All I can do for now is prep it ready to go. Likewise for the security council. I can get all sorts in there, but until we need it, I don't see the need to make a grand entrance and announce our arrival."

"Good stuff," said Jackson. "How's Mills doing?"

Reg flicked his mouse across two of his screens and revealed a high-quality camera view of a small stretch of water with large houses lining the far side. "That's the Turvey's house there," said Reg, "the one with the kayaks on the beach and the swing set."

"Is that the best we can do?" asked Jackson. "We're not going to be able to see much of Mills."

"Hopefully nor is our man, Crowe, sir," replied Reg.

"If she's as good a shot as you say, this will be over in the next few hours. As soon as the sun comes up, I want that audio recording, and I want Mills in place ready to pull the trigger."

Jackson left Reg to it and headed to the small glass meeting room. He closed the door behind him and pulled up the recently dialled numbers on his phone. The ringtone was halted by a strong, elderly man's voice. "Jackson, fill me in," came the reply.

Jackson pictured the old man sitting on the floor above with a tumbler of brandy, his old squashed and pitted nose, huge eyebrows, and a smugness that came from a life of entitlement.

"Sir, all assets are in play," said Jackson. "Mills is in place. We're setting up audio tonight. Our man Omar will venture outside on our signal and take Melody by surprise."

"Good. What about Stone?"

"He's en-route, sir."

"For sure?" said the old man. "We can't have any mistakes here."

"For sure, sir. Gordon tailed him and Tenant to Clapham Common last night. Tenant set him up with Mills' tracker. Stone left shortly after."

"Good. Remember how we need this to play out," said the old man. "I need Crowe taken out and Stone either implicated or dead. God knows we might just get out of this with our hands clean, and leave Dubai to take care of Stone."

Jackson felt a pang of uneasiness grip his stomach. He understood that Stone was a liability, and he understood that the old man held a grudge against Stone and wanted him finished. He also understood that the old man held the keys to Jackson's own career. Life wasn't always fair. There had to be winners and there had to be losers. Jackson didn't plan on being a loser.

"Leave it to me, sir," said Jackson, and he disconnected the call.

"Can we at least have some light in here?" asked Angie Turvey. "I don't even know what time of day it is."

"You don't need to know the time of day," replied Crowe. "Why don't you tell me about your husband?"

"Where's my daughter?"

"She's safe. She's with Omar. He's great with kids; he has two of his own."

"Two of his own? How can anybody have their own kids and put someone through this ordeal?"

"Easy," said Crowe. "Money. Now tell me about your husband."

"My husband? What do you want to know? It sounds like you know enough already."

"Au contraire, Angie. Tell me about *him*." There was a finality to the last word. It sounded almost spiteful with Crowe's over-pronounced diction.

"He's my husband. He's a good man."

"He's a good man, is he?"

"Yes, yes he is. He chairs a charity in London. He helps thousands of people."

"How does he help them, Angie?" Crowe's voice had turned soft with an inquisitive tone.

"He re-homes people that need twenty-four-hour specialist care. He provides medical aid. He, he-"

"It sounds a lot like Mr Turvey knows how to spend other people's money, and make himself glow with the sheen of an angel while doing so, Angie. Tell me, does Mr Turvey ever get hands on and help these people? Does he wipe the drool from their chins? Does he hold their hands when they shiver and shake? Does he clean their soiled clothes when the treatment has its way?"

"How can he? He just organises-"

"What does he organise, Angie?"

"Help. He organises help for the people."

"Does he do the organising? I must say I find it hard to picture Mr Turvey in his fine suit, waiting on hold for a hospital clerk to respond to his call. It sounds like the type of task someone else might do for him, doesn't it, Angie? Someone like, say an assistant, or secretary. Does he have one of those? An assistant?"

"Yes, of course he does. He's far too busy to-"

"Far too busy to what, Angie? Come to little Anya's school play? Or her dance class, perhaps? What do you say, Angie? Is he too busy to take care of his wife?"

"You bastard," spat Angie. "You don't know anything about us." She struggled against the duct tape that had been wrapped around her ankles and wrists, then, like the time before that, and the time before that, she stopped fighting, and her body crumpled in defeat.

"Oh, Angie, what a performance," said Crowe. "Julie there was the same, of course, but *she* had something to fight for. *She* had a loving husband."

"*Bernard* is a loving husband."

"Ah yes, Angie. But who is it he is loving? Ah, *that's* the question, isn't it?"

"You're going to pay for this."

"Yes, probably, but you know what? I'll have a damn fun time while they try to catch me."

"You know who he is, so you know who he works for?"

"Yes, I do, and I happen to know that the United Kingdom's secret services are not permitted to operate here in the UAE without specific instructions and permission. The Sheik would not be at all happy if our boys in blue were found to be carrying out an investigation on UAE soil, let alone sending a bunch of armed SAS abseiling off the rooftops. Besides, Angie, Omar re-routed the message around the planet before it was delivered. They'll still be looking for where the message came from by the time old Bernie gets up on stage for his last performance."

"He'll find a way. He knows pe*ople."

"Yes, he does," said Crowe. "I must say, you're especially kind to him, given all he's put you through. Do you ever think about him with the other girls, Angie?"

"Shut up. Stop saying that. There *are* no other girls."

"Oh, that's strange," said Crowe. He turned to face the hallway. "Omar," he called softly, like he was summoning his puppy.

Omar crept down the stairs and stepped into the room a short while later.

"How's little Anya doing?" asked Crowe. His feigned concern sickened Angie.

"She's fine. She's sleeping," replied Omar.

"Oh good," said Crowe. "She's had a hard day, hasn't she? Poor little mite."

Nobody replied.

"Omar, would you happen to have the photos of Mr Turvey and those Russian girls to hand? You know the ones."

"Yes, they are here where you left them." Omar walked to the dining table and picked up a blue cardboard file. He handed them to Crowe.

"Now, what do we have here?" said Crowe, as he flicked through the A4 printed photos. "Ah yes, here we are. Here's Mr Turvey enjoying drinks and dinner with another of the charity board members, I believe. Do you know this man, Mrs Turvey?" He pointed to the man opposite her husband.

"Yes, he's a friend," replied Angie. "That's Eddie McIntyre."

"And who is this by his side?" asked Crowe.

"I don't know," said Angie, looking down at the floor.

"Pretty, isn't she? I bet she cost a few quid. What do you say, Omar? Pretty? Expensive?"

"Both," replied Omar from the dining table. He was working on the laptop, but Angie still couldn't see what he was doing exactly. She considered waiting for her chance and getting to the laptop herself. A mini-plan formed in her head that she'd post a help message on social media.

"And here they are going into the Dorchester Hotel, Angie," continued Crowe. "Wasn't that where he took you, Angie, all those years ago?" He tutted. "That's just plain rude."

"He has problems," said Angie. "I know what he does." Her head hung low, and her foot began to shake involuntarily. "I need to sleep and I need to pee."

"Oh, but we're just getting to the good stuff, Mrs Turvey," said Crowe with sickening enthusiasm. He held up a photo. "This one's my favourite. I thought I'd save it for last."

CHAPTER TWELVE

For Harvey, being crammed in a seat for nearly eight hours on a passenger jet was horrific. He didn't touch the in-flight entertainment and used the time to plan instead. Many scenarios emerged in his mind's eye, but one scene continued to force its way to the front among countless others, the plan of what he'd say to Melody. But each time he came close to preparing a speech, he could only imagine her being hurt by someone else. Then his mind wandered to handing out cruel punishment to whoever was harming Melody. He couldn't help but feel it was all wrong, that she shouldn't be there.

So in the end, his plan always came back to patience, planning and executing. It was the mantra of his mentor, Julios. There would be no speech, there would be no apologies, there would be no hurt. Melody would not even know Harvey was there unless she needed help. Then he'd be there, ready to step in. Until that moment, he decided he'd be a shadow, a skill he'd been honing since his early teens.

Harvey stepped off the plane onto the gangway. He didn't have a carry-on, nor did he have any checked luggage, just the clothes on his back. Passport control was interesting, so many different nationalities, all waiting to visit Dubai. Harvey wondered if he was the only one there who didn't want to see the sights.

When he reached the exit to the terminal, hundreds of people stood waiting for loved ones to arrive. Harvey strode through the crowds, aware that only Reg knew he was even in the country. Ideally, Harvey would have rented a motorbike, but the journey and the chaotic terminal had gotten the better of him, and he settled for a taxi. The cab ride gave Harvey time to study the LUCY app on his phone that Reg had installed. He hit the drop down, selected 'track' and was presented with only one available operative to track. But it was the only tracker he needed, Melody's.

She was a thirty-minute drive from the airport on Palm Jumeirah, on one of the branches of the tree-shaped island. Harvey knew the Palm Jumeirah to be an area where wealthy people lived and holidayed. He presumed there to be tight security in place.

As the cab drove him along the Palm, Harvey saw the entrances to fronds A and B, then C and D. They all had tight security. The guards themselves, lit dimly by the small light from their little cabins, didn't look particularly terrifying. But it would just take one of them to raise the alarm and the game would be up. He couldn't chance it. He'd need to circumvent the security.

In the end, the taxi dropped Harvey a few hundred yards from the entrance to frond G, where the tracker icon on the LUCY app showed Melody to be. He zoomed in on the icon, which was accurate within three metres. She was on the beach out the back of the house.

Harvey found a spot between fronds G and H where he could easily scale a wall, make his way through the landscaped vegetation, and drop down onto the beach. He stayed amongst the shrubbery for a while and practised his old habit of waiting a standard full minute before making his move. He sat at the point where fronds G and H met, with each of the private beaches in front of him, one bearing left, the other bearing right.

There was no sign of any activity. The app showed Melody to be another six hundred yards along the beach to his left. He wondered why she would be housed there. It didn't make sense. The place had so much security that fast getaways and staying invisible would be almost impossible. She must have a target, Harvey thought, and he'd have money that the target would be one of the houses on the opposite beach. But which one? The villas were all very well maintained, not Harvey's style, but he could see the appeal.

He dropped down onto the beach of frond H. The app told Harvey that Melody was still on the beach of frond G, just across the water. But she wouldn't see him in the dark on the opposite beach. He walked close to the shore so the incoming tide would remove his prints. Most of the houses looked empty, except a few. An Asian family sat at a dining table in one house, another just had a solitary man in shorts watching a movie, oblivious to Harvey outside. More houses had lights on. One had all the curtains closed, others had lights on but no sign of activity. Nothing seemed out of the ordinary. The tide had already begun to wash away his boot prints by the time he walked back along the beach, trying to piece it all together.

Harvey reached the place where the two beaches met, climbed over the rocks that separated them, and began to walk along frond G as if he was a holidaymaker out for an evening stroll. Halfway along, he glanced at LUCY and found Melody's icon to be halfway across the water. Keeping to the shadows at the back of the beach, he sat and watched for movement on the water.

He knew Melody was a strong swimmer. She could probably manage a fair amount of the three-hundred metre swim underwater. Harvey heard no splashing, saw no dark shape in the water, but knew she was out there somewhere.

On the beach outside the house, Harvey stood where LUCY had originally pinned Melody's location. The house next door had a row of thick trees and bushes, an ideal spot for him to wait and observe. It wasn't long before wet footsteps on the sand announced Melody's return. She trudged up the steps in a black wetsuit and neoprene booties then pulled the suit off and hung it to dry over the small table and chairs beside the pool. Harvey looked on from the shadows of the bushes. He was desperate to call her name or go to meet her. But he couldn't. He'd just be the distraction that caused the mistake. He was better off being an observer, a guardian. If she needed help, he'd be there. If she didn't, then he'd stay out of the way, and find the right time to tell her what he wanted to tell her.

Harvey saw the bedroom light come on at the rear of the house and knew she would be taking a shower to wash the salt off her skin. He needed more facts. He needed to know when she was going across again, so he could cross in advance and be waiting, ready. There was a small balcony at the rear of the house, adjoined to the bedroom where he presumed Melody was showering. He took the opportunity to climb up onto the ground-floor window ledge and leap up to grab the balcony, pulling himself up with ease. Once he'd confirmed that Melody was nowhere in sight, he climbed the balustrade and tucked himself into a dark corner. He chanced a glance back into the room and could see the Peli-case with the Diemaco. Another smaller case was open with a SIG, binos, night vision and a few other accessories laid across the bed.

He played out her operation in his head. She must have swum across to plant some audio or video feeds then she came back here to get set up for a long-range shot. The bathroom light went off. Harvey tucked his legs up close to his chest to stay small. The bedroom light went out.

Then the balcony door opened.

Harvey listened for movement. He smelled the familiar scent of Melody's shampoo escaping from the balcony door, luring him like a child is lured with a trail of sweets.

The sound of a table being dragged across the tiled floor told Harvey that Melody was still in the room. He closed his eyes and pictured her. If her task was to take a shot at a house on the far side of the water, she would be pulling a table up in front of the balcony to lay on and take the shot. She would have her comms on the table with her, and her binos to mark the distance. Once she was set up for the shot, Melody wouldn't move until the target presented itself.

Harvey stared out across the water to the house that she had been to. It was the house he had seen on his walk with the lights on and curtains closed. He knew her style. She would have planted audio against the glass of the house's sliding doors. The sound would carry well through the glass. He sat in the darkness, and watched the house with her, like a voyeur.

He heard Melody get comfortable on the table. He heard her prepare herself for the long haul. A shot like the one she was going to take would require concentration and focus. It felt good to be so close to her. A small part of him wished he could just reach out to her, or even say something. Then she spoke.

"I thought you wouldn't be able to stay away," said Melody. "Too tempting for you?"

Harvey's head turned, his mouth opened, but she spoke again.

"Phase one complete, Reg. Audio is on," said Melody.

Harvey didn't reply.

"I'm in position but the curtains are closed," she began. "Audio is loud and clear, but right now it's just getting snores and the hum of the air conditioning. Sounds like someone's sleeping downstairs. With any luck they'll wake up and open the curtains. Until then, I'm blind and without a shot."

The tinny voice replied something inaudible to Melody.

"I am sitting tight. I'm dug in and ready. How long do we have until the speech?"

There was a pause while her handler spoke, then, "Sixteen hours? You better hope those curtains open before then, or else we'll need a plan B."

Another pause.

"Copy. Will report back hourly. Out."

Harvey sat and listened to the one-sided conversation. Sixteen hours until a speech? He couldn't put the pieces together. The only thing Harvey could possibly do to expedite the issue would be to go and do something to make whoever it was open the curtains. He'd need Melody to leave first; he couldn't get off the balcony without her knowing he was there.

Harvey sat and waited. Sixteen hours. He'd done worse, he thought to himself, and in far worse conditions than by the beach in Dubai.

Jackson closed the door to his modest office. The walls were painted white, which was standard throughout the building. He'd personalised it with a few photos of him with his unit in Afghanistan, stood alongside a Challenger tank in full combats, and armed to the teeth. Another photo on his desk was of his family and their pet retriever laying together on the ground in the garden of their Sussex home.

He pulled his personal phone from his pocket and dialled a number from the recent call list. It was answered almost immediately.

"Jackson, update me," said the old man's voice with no pleasantries or salutations.

"Mills is in position, audio is set up, and we have ears. Not much to report until they wake up and open the curtains."

"And Stone?"

"Tenant put a tracker on his phone. He's hiding a few metres away from Mills."

"You brought Tenant into this? I thought I told you to keep this on the down low?"

"Tenant is helping his friend. He doesn't know we're onto him. He's not stupid. He'd know we were after Stone all along."

"So, what's your plan?"

"We stick with plan A until we have no option. It's the cleanest takedown."

"So Mills takes the shot and high tails it out of there, and we send in our asset to pick up Stone?"

"Yes. As long as somebody opens the curtains and Mills can take the shot, the play will roll, and we'll be clean."

"And plan B?" asked the old man in a long, tired mumble.

"Three hours before the speech, we send Mills over and she gets caught. Stone steps in and takes out Crowe."

"Sounds like there's more potential with plan B," said the old man. "It doesn't rely on somebody opening the curtains."

"It's messier. Plus, we'll lose Mills. She could be an asset, sir. I'd like to try and keep her alive and out of prison."

"Okay, let it roll."

Jackson left his office and stepped into the operations room. Reg was sat at his desk watching Melody and listening to the audio traffic that was being broadcast from the tiny audio bug that Melody had planted. The audio was sent over satellite link to the operations room and was being played through the ceiling speakers. The heavy breathing of a sleeping man was slightly humorous at first, but soon it had become background noise, and Reg was able to focus on Melody. Whenever nobody was looking, he would change the tracker view from Melody to Harvey to make sure he was in position then switch back to Melody.

"Tenant," said Jackson, "how's Melody doing?"

"No change," said Reg. "Sun up in one hour."

"Okay. You know her well, right?"

"We worked together for a few years," said Reg.

"Okay, I want you to handle her," said Jackson. "We have fifteen hours until the speech, which means in twelve hours' time, if those curtains haven't opened and she hasn't taken the shot, she'll need to get herself over there to do the job manually."

"Manually?" asked Reg.

"Manually, Tenant. She'll need a plan in place before she goes. Give her the heads up so she can work on it."

"You're sending her in alone?" said a female voice from behind Jackson.

"Ladyluck, when I talk to you, you'll know it because I'll look at you."

"Sorry, sir, but, we don't even know who's in there, and it's my job to ensure the safety-"

"It's your job to sit on your arse and obey orders, Ladyluck," snapped Jackson. Then his voice softened. "I'm not going to let anything happen to her. She'll be fine. She'll formulate a plan, run it by me, and we'll help where we can."

Jackson turned back to Reg. "Tenant, you look like you want to tell me something."

"Erm, no, sir," said Reg. "I'll, err, get her onto the plan then."

Reg watched Jackson walk away and met Ladyluck's confused look. Jackson was acting out of character. Reg knew it. Ladyluck knew it. The whole room knew it.

"Wakey, wakey, Mrs Turvey," said Crowe. "Today's the day I've been waiting a long time for."

Angie stirred on the couch. Omar lifted his head from the dining table where he'd slept with his face buried in his arms.

"Come on, get yourself up. One way or another, today will be the last day you see your lovely husband." He smiled cruelly at the woman who was struggling to sit upright.

"I need the washroom, and I want to see my daughter," said Angie, offering no compromise. She raised her head and locked eyes with Julie's deathly gaze, who hung from her wrists with her head hanging forward.

Crowe thought about it for a moment. "Use the downstairs washroom. Omar will wake Anya when you're done."

Angie pushed off the couch to her feet and hopped across the floor to the washroom.

"Angie, darling," said Crowe. She stopped, held onto the hallway door frame, and turned to him. "Don't do anything I wouldn't do." He winked at her.

She hopped the last few steps to the washroom where she closed and locked the door before sitting down. Angie held herself together for a few moments then all her emotions came flooding out at once. With her face in her hands, she tried to stifle her sobs; she didn't want Crowe to hear her crying. But she couldn't stop. The pictures he'd shown her of Bernie and the girls had been bad enough, and she'd pretended to brush it off. But the photos of the other men in his bed were disgusting, horrifying even. It was suddenly as if she didn't know Bernie at all. She'd suspected him of cheating a few times. But she always knew he loved her and cared for her with everything he had. In some crazy way, she could understand the other girls, accept it almost, but she couldn't accept that he'd cheated on her with other men.

A part of her didn't care. A part of her just wanted him to be there to tell her it was all over, and they were going to be fine. But something gripped her heart and squeezed her chest. It pulled to remind her of the impending agony, tugging on her insides.

She thought of Anya. One way or another, her daughter was about to be heartbroken. Angie held her tummy, remembering how precious it was when Anya was inside, and how they'd sworn to protect her from the world, from bad people, people like Crowe. She had to get through this. She had to be positive and stay sharp. She'd wait for the next opportunity, and then strike, anything to delay the inevitable. Maybe if she hurt Crowe or Omar, the balance would shift. First things first, she'd get Anya in her arms and ask to have the tape removed. She couldn't do anything with her hands and feet bound.

Angie finished, pulled the chain, and then hopped out of the washroom. She leaned on the door frame and waited for Crowe to address her.

"What do you think you're doing standing there?" he asked, his tone reminiscent of an old school teacher, scolding and cold.

"I need to stretch my legs. Can you just remove the tape, please? I haven't been a problem, have I?"

Footsteps on the tiled hallway floor behind her caused Crowe to stare past Angie. She turned to find Omar coming down the stairs.

"She's gone," said Omar.

"Gone?" said Crowe in his sharp, aggressive tone. "How *can* she be gone?"

Omar lifted his hand and showed two pieces of duct tape that had been gnawed through. "She must have got out of the window."

Crowe stepped up to Angie. She turned to move away, but he struck her in the face, sending her to the floor. With her hands bound, Angie was unable to stop herself falling. Her face bounced off the hard tiles, and she felt the sharp dagger-like stab of a broken cheekbone.

"You bitch. You put her up to this, didn't you?"

Angie tried to move but was stuck laying on her bound arms. "No," she mumbled, with her face against the floor. "How could I?"

Crowe kicked her hard in the kidney then turned to Omar. *"Don't just bloody stand there,* go find her. Bring her back," he screamed.

Omar turned and left, closing the front door behind him. Crowe focused his attention on Angie once more. He reached down and grabbed a handful of hair, pulling her face from the floor.

"Get up, bitch," he snarled, and pulled harder, dragging Angie to her feet.

"You want me to remove the tape? I'll remove the tape for you." He slapped her once more, sending sharp stabs of pain into her cheek. Then he pushed her toward the back of the couch. She stumbled forward, and her elbows hung onto the leather.

Crowe bent to rip the tape at her ankles and snatched it clean off her skin with two hard tugs.

"How's that?" he asked. Then, without waiting for a reply, he kicked her legs open and put his hand on the back of her neck. "Let's see what Mr Turvey has been neglecting all these years." Crowe reached down with his free hand and raised the back of Angie's dress. "Not bad, Mrs Turvey," said Crowe.

"Get off me, you pig," said Angie, as she began to struggle against Crowe's grip.

"Now, now," he said, "don't you think you owe me a little something for my troubles? We can do this now, or we can do this when Omar brings your dirty little bitch child back here. Maybe she can watch?"

Angie kicked back and up with the heel of her foot and connected with Crowe's genitals. He doubled over behind her but maintained his grip.

"You're beginning to get on my tits, Mrs Turvey," he wheezed. "There's only one thing left for you."

He dragged her to the floor then grabbed her hair and pulled her across the smooth tiles to where Julie hung, her body already stiffening.

Crowe kicked Angie. "Get up."

Angie didn't move; she was frozen in horror.

Crowe sent a full-fisted punch to her eye and knocked her flat against the floor once more.

The harsh sound of curtains being ripped back and the slap of Crowe's open hand against her bare skin woke Angie from her unconscious state into a semi-conscious world where nothing made sense, and every part of her body hurt. Her mind span. A dull ache throbbed inside her head. A sharp pain stabbed her face and aches tugged in her tummy for Anya. She hoped Anya had gotten away and was getting help. She hoped the ordeal would soon be over. Dark dizziness overcame her, and Angie awoke with a splitting headache. Hard sunlight pierced her eyes, blinding her, but she was upright. She was tied up and hanging by her wrists. She closed her eyes and focused on the dark, turning her head away from the light. When she reopened them, she found that she'd been bound once more. She had been tied in a crucifix, naked, and face to face with Julie.

The room where Melody lay upon the table by the balcony doors was west facing. The sun quickly began to light the houses on the far side of the small channel of water that separated the fronds as it rose behind her. She took another look through the binos at the Turvey house and shuddered to think of what might be happening inside. A career of dealing with some of Britain's sickest minds had left her with a bad taste and a vivid imagination of what people are capable of and the lengths they will go to get their way.

She was aware that as the sun rose, she would be visible from the other houses on the opposite frond, the Turvey's neighbours. So she rolled off the table and stretched then pulled her own curtains closed, leaving enough of a gap for her to see only the Turvey house.

A sudden image of Harvey sprang to her mind as she stood by the balcony door. She paused with her hand on the curtain and thoughts of the operation slipped from her mind. How nice it would be for Harvey to be with her now, and Boon. They'd watch the glow of the sun warm the calm Arabian Gulf and light the sand coloured houses in hues of orange and yellow.

Melody took the opportunity to use the washroom then returned to resume her position on the table. She'd rolled up a blanket to lean on, which had unravelled during the long night. Pulling it off the table, she began to roll it up again, ready for round two. She stared through the gap in the curtains, her mind split between Harvey and the job in hand.

It wasn't until she was placing the rolled-up blanket on the table that her mind registered the movement she had just seen inside the floor-to-ceiling sliding doors of the Turvey house. She spun around and peered through the gap. Reaching for the binos and finding the magnified doors, she took a breath then rolled onto the table. The slightly angled view of her elevated position gave her a side image of somebody tied to the wall beside the double doors, somebody who looked to be naked and struggling. It had to be Mrs Turvey. The curtains had been opened.

Melody's heart began to race. So she took deep breaths to control the rise and drop of the scope. She flexed her fingers, blinked and readied herself for the man she'd been hunting to step into view.

The curtains blowing in the breeze that rolled off the water were the only movement Melody saw. Each time the curtains moved, she was sickened by the sight of Mrs Turvey's pink and vulnerable skin. She waited, tense and ready to strike, her finger poised over the trigger, daring not even to swallow. She focused on her small shallow breaths, in through her nose and out through pouted lips, blowing the cool air onto her fingers.

Time stood still. It was as if she were in the room with Mrs Turvey as something struck her, and her body recoiled toward the opened door as far as her restraints would allow.

Melody now knew where the man was standing. He was behind Mrs Turvey and behind the wall, out of sight.

She slowly reached up to her ear-piece without moving the

perfect positioning of the Diemaco that lay cradled in her hands, ready to wipe one more evil human off the earth.

She pushed the button on the ear-piece and held it until she heard a tiny beep which meant that the comms channel would stay open, disabling the push-to-talk function. Reg would be able to hear everything she said, and she'd hear everything he said. There was a small delay as her voice was encrypted, transmitted up to a satellite, then bounced around the earth to another satellite above London, where it was sent down to a receiver, decrypted and broadcast over the ceiling speakers as sound waves.

"Contact," she said. It was one word that woke a room of tired operatives into a heightened state of awareness. "I have eyes on Mrs Turvey."

Jackson paced across the room to the mic which sat to one side of Reg. "Mills, tell us what you see."

"The rear doors are open. The curtains are pulled back. But the only movement has been Mrs Turvey so far. No sign of any male."

"We have movement at the front of the house," said Reg. "I'm on the satellite, but I'll have to be quick before I'm discovered." There was a pause while Reg identified what he could see. "IC6 male walking to the front door. He's inside."

"He's definitely inside?" asked Jackson.

"He's gone from view," said Reg. "Mills, you should see movement any second. I need to cut the video feed."

"I'm all eyes," said Melody, slowly and quietly. She tried to keep her heart from pounding. She'd spent hours in the prone position facing targets, both wooden and human. She knew she could make the shot, but with Mrs Turvey and potentially the daughter around, there was no room for error. It would need to be a clean shot.

"Hold on," said Melody. "I see something, a leg. I have his leg. Mrs Turvey is blocking the view."

"Can she move?" asked Jackson.

"Looks like she's tied up to something. I can't see what."

The room in London went from being a hive of activity as operatives hurried to bring plans forward and ready themselves for their part in the play to dead silence, as every ear hung on the words Melody was saying.

"Damn it. He moved too quick. I have one IC1 male inside. It looks like he's talking to somebody out of sight."

"Could be the IC6?" said Jackson.

"Okay, he's moving back," said Melody.

"Description?" asked Jackson.

"Silver hair, smart, fifties."

"Crowe," said Jackson. "Take him down."

"Hold on," said Melody. "He's moving into view."

Crowe pulled the curtain back and began to step outside.

"Executing in three..."

Crowe reached outside the doors and seemed to take a breath of fresh air.

"Two."

He looked out across the water, then side to side.

"One."

Crowe quickly pulled his head back in and slid the door closed.

"Shit," said Melody.

"Mills?" said Jackson. "Take your time."

"He's gone. The door's closed."

"Tell me you're kidding."

"No, he just came out to close the door."

"You missed your chance, Mills," said Jackson. "I thought you said you could handle this?"

"With all due respect, I don't see you out here."

"Stop right there, Mills."

"I'll stop when I want to stop. Right now, I'm about to send a 7.62 round across the water at eight hundred metres per second, and I have inches to spare before I kill your boss' wife, and God knows, maybe his daughter too. So I'll take my sweet time, and make sure I get it right, sir." She closed off with finality.

"That's it, Mills, you let it out," said Jackson, smiling. "How do you feel?"

"With all due respect, Jackson, keep your mouth shut and let me run the play. I'm here, you're not."

"Anything you say, Mills," said Jackson, calmly and strangely pleased with her outburst.

"Hold on," said Melody. "I see movement."

"Tenant, get that screen up, satellite."

"Okay, but you have a thirty-second window before they trace it," said Reg in a playful warning tone.

"Just get it up," said Jackson.

"Oh, Christ," said Melody.

"Mills, talk to me," said Jackson.

"It's the little girl," said Melody. "She's standing right outside the doors."

The sound of a magazine slotting into a SIG handgun, followed by the smooth action of the weapon being armed and a round sliding into place was a familiar sound to Harvey, especially when it was done with the speed and control of an expert weapons handler like Melody. It was a sound he hadn't heard for a long time, yet would somehow never forget.

He'd heard Melody's last words and was himself staring at the little girl stood innocently at the French doors. He was unable to move until he heard the doors crash open and Melody's boots squeak across the tiled floor and out of earshot. There was no way Harvey would get across the water before her if he leapt from the balcony. In fact, even as he stood to enter the room, he saw her bound down the stairs beside the pool onto the beach. She sprinted across the sand, took two large steps into the water, and dove in.

Harvey watched as she reappeared twenty-seconds later halfway across the channel. He moved inside and lay himself down on the table.

By the time Harvey made himself comfortable and found Melody in the rifle's telescopic scope, she was striding out of the water. The little girl stood at the glass doors, unseen by Crowe and Omar. She turned in response to Melody calling her, but then quickly turned back and peered in through the glass.

Melody bounded up the steps into the Turvey's rear garden. She crossed the small lawn and was just metres away from picking the little girl up in a swoop when the doors suddenly slid open. But nobody appeared. Harvey couldn't see the figure who had opened the doors, but his finger felt for the trigger. Melody had frozen. She crouched down to the girl and stroked her hair. Melody was talking to someone inside the house, someone out of Harvey's sight. Harvey kept his focus on the open doors. He could see pale skin, and the unmistakable form of a woman struggling against restraints, the mother, he guessed.

Harvey could see how unwavering Melody was even from the distance he was at. She kept control as much as she could. But it wasn't until the handgun pointed out from the open door that Harvey knew she was no longer in control. She was in serious trouble.

The gun was followed by an arm. It had tanned skin but not like the glowing tan on a westerner, so Harvey wondered if it belonged to a local. Then a shoulder appeared. From this range, Harvey's chances of hitting an arm were slim. He'd need the head. The torso would be better, but a head might be doable.

Harvey ran through the checklist Melody had taught him. He remembered her words. *"Even in the tensest moments, when the target is speeding by, the checklist must be complete before you pull the trigger. That's the only way you'll know for sure that you gave it all you had."*

A glance with his free eye caught the large flat leaves of the palm trees outside, barely moving. The water was still. The rifle was loaded, safety off. The butt of the weapon was firmly pressed into his shoulder. His eye was a good three inches behind the scope. His breathing was checked.

Melody stood with her hand on the head of the girl.

"Move, damn it," whispered Harvey.

She was blocking his view. Harvey remained focused on the arm and shoulder, waiting for the torso or head to step into his cross-hairs.

His breathing increased, and he checked it with three long, deep breaths. Melody moved again, directly in his field of vision. The small cross in his scope planted firmly on the back of Melody's head. He daren't move but he eased his finger away from the trigger. He knew Melody liked a hair trigger. Barely a strong a breeze would be enough to bring the hammer down.

And then, in a moment of coordinated synchronicity and luck, the arm became a shoulder then a face, and Melody reached down to protect the girl.

Harvey fired.

CHAPTER SEVENTEEN

Angie didn't hear the shot. She only saw the chaos that ensued.

Before the shot, she saw Anya suddenly at the door looking scared. Her eyes were bright red, and she had scratches down her bare legs. Angie had tried to shoo her away, to get her to run, to find somebody. But the little girl had just stood there confused as to why her mummy wasn't opening the doors to pick her up. Angie had mouthed for her to run away, get help, but the scared eight-year-old girl had been too afraid to move. She hadn't budged.

Then there had been a woman. She was wet as if she'd come from the sea. Angie had been momentarily filled with hope, a sudden moment of heart-lifting joy that had been cut down when Omar too had seen the movement. He'd stepped up to the sliding doors, hidden behind the curtain, and waited for the woman to get close to Anya. Then he'd snatched the door open and aimed his gun outside. Anya had cried for her mum, loud and shrill. Omar had shouted for the woman to get down on the ground. The woman had shouted back insults at Omar. All the while, Crowe had stood out of the way beside Angie, smiling as the events unfolded.

Crowe pulled a handgun from his waistband and quietly put it against Angie's head. Angie immediately froze, scared to move a muscle. The feeling of the hard steel against her temple and knowing a bullet was inside just waiting to end her life was terrifying. She wasn't afraid of the pain. She wasn't afraid of dying. But she *was* afraid for Anya.

Then, without warning, Omar had flinched as if he'd seen something behind the stranger. The woman had bent to grab Anya, and the back of Omar's head cracked open. Blood spattered across Angie's face, the floor and the walls. His body slumped the ground, half in and half out of their holiday home.

"Mrs Turvey, are you okay?" said the woman. "I can't see you. Are you hurt?"

"Mummy," screamed Anya.

"Don't say a word," whispered Crowe in her ear.

"Mrs Turvey, talk to me," came the woman's voice again.

"One false move, bitch," said Crowe, "and they both get it."

Angie heard the woman talking to Anya from behind the wall. "Stay here, okay? Do not move." There was a pause and the racking of a weapon. Angie recognised the sound from movies. "I'm coming inside. I know you're there, Angie. Trust me. Everything's going to be okay."

A booted female foot stepped onto the tiled floor.

"That's far enough," said Crowe.

The woman stopped.

"Let her go, Crowe, this isn't worth it."

"Drop the gun."

"Crowe, let's talk about this. You're surrounded. There's armed police all around you."

"There'll be one less if you don't drop that weapon," said Crowe confidently.

The woman threw the gun onto the couch.

"Good. Now step inside and bring the girl."

"You don't need her. Let her go," said the stranger.

Crowe laughed. "And let her run to the police? You should have done your homework, missy. You clearly have no idea who I am."

"I know who you are. You're Caesar Crowe. You're a criminal whose career is about to come to a grinding halt."

"Stop stalling. Get inside and bring the girl."

Angie watched as the woman bent down to pick up Anya.

"I'm watching you," said Crowe.

"I was just picking up the girl. You can't expect her to walk over-"

"Over what?"

The stranger looked at the floor where Omar's body was slumped.

"Oh, I see," said Crowe. "Yes, that might be a little disturbing for her. Close the door."

Angie made eye contact with her daughter, who looked up expecting to be hugged. But Angie couldn't move.

"Well this is fun, isn't it?" said Crowe. "The four of us. How about you new girls take a seat?"

The stranger didn't move, but Anya hugged her leg and hid her face from Crowe.

"It wasn't an offer," said Crowe. "*Sit down.*"

"Why don't you let Angie go, or at least let her get dressed?"

"Why don't you do as you're told and sit down?"

"Maybe I don't want to sit," said the woman.

"Oh, you'll sit. Even if I have to break your legs, you'll sit. Who are you anyway? And what are you doing here? Who sent you? Was it *Bernie?*"

"Bernie who?"

"Don't play games with me. I'm smarter than the average bear."

"Oh, you're smart, Crowe. I have no doubt about that. But

smart isn't going to stop you from being tossed in a cell to live out the rest of your sorry life."

"Who says it's going to come to that?" replied Crowe. "MI6 send a whining little bitch to stop me. Is that it? Is that all they think of me?"

"MI who?" asked the stranger.

"Don't play games. I won't tell you again. I know it was MI6 that sent you. But maybe they sent *you* because you're not a real operative. I'm right, aren't I? They can't operate here, it would get all..." Crowe gestured with crazy hands, waving his gun around. "Political. Am I right? So they sent you. Probably some little upstart with a smart mouth and knows exactly what to do with it. Hmm?"

"You're wrong, Crowe."

"I'm wrong, am I? About what? You having a smart mouth or you being keen to get up the ladder?"

Crowe moved away from Angie and strode over to the woman, who moved Anya behind her out of his reach.

"I bet you banged your way from office to office, licked your way through your exams, and rode the promotion pole until you could fuck no further?" He sniffed at Melody like an elderly man might enjoy the scent of a wild flower. "Well, I have news for you, little lady." Crowe walked behind her, and Anya moved around to her front, then he softly whispered in the stranger's ear. "This is the end of the ride for you." The woman tensed and Angie guessed Crowe had the gun in the small of her back.

"Put the gun down," said the stranger. "No pads, just you and me. We'll see whose end is coming."

"Not long now until we all have a little face to face with our friends in England, ten hours and fifteen minutes to be precise. During that ten hours, you have two choices. You can make life hard and die painfully. Or you can sit down, be good, and pray that Mr Turvey completes his end of the bargain."

She walked away from him towards the sofa, taking Anya with her, and disappeared from Angie's view.

Angie heard the duct tape being ripped from its roll. Four times, she heard the screech of tape being pulled out then the rip. Angie knew it meant that both Anya and the woman had their wrists and ankles bound. Now they were all prisoners. Crowe walked to the sliding doors, pulled Omar's body inside by his belt, slammed the door and snatched the curtain closed once more. For a brief moment, he was exposed to whoever took Omar down and Melody waited for the shot. But the moment had been too fleeting.

"Nothing like a little privacy, Angie. Now, where were we before we were so pleasantly interrupted?"

"Oh my God, sir, we need to get her out of there," said Lady-luck. The rest of the room sat horrified at what they'd just heard over the comms. "She had no business going inside. And did I hear right, someone just got shot?"

"The time for your opinion is not now, Ladyluck. We'd all appreciate it if you kept it to yourself for the foreseeable future. Now is the time for planning, and taking down Crowe." Jackson turned to Reg. "Tenant, how are we doing with the live feed?"

"Which one, sir?" said Reg. "The house or the charity gig?"

"Mr Turvey's speech. We need to make sure that we have control over the live feed. We can't have a live suicide all over the media."

"You think he'll go through with it, sir?" asked Reg.

Jackson gave the question consideration. "What would you do if the two people you loved the most had a gun to their heads and all you had to do to save them was to pull the trigger yourself?"

"Hard to say, sir. How do you even try to empathise?" replied Reg.

"All we can do is communicate, and work as hard as we

damn well can to bring Crowe down, preferably before Turvey takes the mic."

Reg opened his mouth to say something, but stopped, and turned away.

"Tenant? What is it?" asked Jackson. "You've been acting funny for a few hours now. If there's something you think I should know then now would be a great time to say so."

Reg turned his head back. "It's just that Melody is a friend. I feel like we're not doing everything we can to help her. Surely the Dubai government can send in their boys?"

"Okay. So do you want to call the Prime Minister, wake him up, and ask him to get on the blower to his counterpart in Dubai? Can you imagine how that call would go, Tenant? First of all, the fact that we even have operatives over there goes against the treaty that somebody far more intelligent than ourselves dreamed up and worked hard to get put in place. Secondly, if we send in troops, either our own or the UAE's, Crowe will terminate Mrs Turvey and the kid. We have our hands tied, Tenant. Whatever we do, we need to be smart and it needs to be covert, and van loads of blokes with automatic weapons are not covert. I need you switched on, Tenant. Are you switched on?"

Reg nodded slowly. "Yeah. Yeah, I'm switched on."

"Good," said Jackson. "Don't worry, we'll get her out."

Jackson left the room, and Reg opened a discreet chat window with Harvey. He typed out a message that read, '*M has been caught. She's being held with the mother and daughter. Clock is ticking. Options are minimal.*' Then before he hit send, he deleted the long message, looked around once more to make sure nobody was watching his screen, then simply typed, '*M is in trouble.*'

The scope of the Diemaco gave Harvey a clear view of Melody bending down to pick up the girl then stepping inside the house. He saw her toss her weapon. He still had no idea of how many men were in there, or how much danger she was in. Harvey knew that Melody could handle herself. They sparred frequently, and although Harvey usually came out on top, Melody was a tenacious fighter who rarely backed down.

He knew Melody would be wondering who took the shot. Harvey had no idea if other operatives were waiting for a signal or prepared to step in. A calm disposition was one of Harvey's many traits. The ability to keep a cool composure when the pressure was on was key to staying alive in many cases. He thought back to his training as he always did, when his mentor, Julios, had taught him the three steps to a successful mission. Patience, planning and execution.

Aware of his own abilities, Harvey had a good idea that he could steam into the house, take out whoever was holding Melody, and get them both out alive. He couldn't however, be so sure about collateral. Melody was trained and would act as soon as she saw her chance. But somebody untrained, like the little girl, would likely be hurt or killed in the attempt. Harvey remained still. He lay prone on the table Melody had set up, with the curtains drawn, leaving just a small gap for him to keep an eye on the house.

Two plans formulated in Harvey's mind. Whatever was occurring in the house had the pressure of time. Pressure meant mistakes. He'd wait for that mistake and be ready to act. Plan B was for when plan A had run out of time. He studied the house, and like all the other villas, it had a flat roof with air conditioning units and water tanks. The climb up would be easy, as he could walk carefully along the pergola, and up the maintenance ladder that was fixed to the side of the house. There was space for him to move about on the roof and, given the chance, he could drop down onto the second-floor balcony. If the house across the water had similar windows to the house he was in, Harvey would be inside within seconds. From there, he could take whoever it was by surprise.

He made the decision to stick with plan A until nightfall, then plan B would come into play.

A small vibration in his pocket signalled an incoming message. He pulled his phone out and saw the screen displayed a little silhouette of a cartoon spy that Reg had created to differentiate alerts from the LUCY app from other apps. The alert simply read, "*M is in trouble.*"

Harvey didn't reply.

He lay still, almost catatonic. His arms were locked, so the weight of the rifle wasn't pulling on his muscles. He could be ready to fire at a moment's notice. But as ready as he was to take the shot, he knew deep down that as the sun sank lower in the sky and the red and orange hues of warm light washed over the house, he would be leaving soon and pushing plan B into action. Shadows of palms grew long across the water until they eventually merged with the blackness of the sea. Lights from nearby houses cast an unnatural glow over areas of the beach but left strips of shadow between the structures. Harvey made the weapon safe, laid it down, and rolled off the table.

Harvey had decided he wouldn't swim the channel, he would run around it. It would take longer and be much further. But for what he had to do, being wet would be a hindrance.

The run took a little under twenty minutes. Again, Harvey ran in the soft wet sand near the shore so the incoming tide would cover his tracks. The whole time he was running, he thought about Melody. Harvey considered this fact: he'd never really been in love before. He guessed it was love, although he had no comparison. But he also didn't like being without her. He couldn't imagine life without her. He liked the feeling. Although it came with its own set of vulnerabilities, it felt right. The timing was good; maybe settling down and letting Melody have a career of her own wasn't such a bad thing. He could still do the things he wanted to do. Of course, he'd worry, just like thousands if not millions of other husbands and wives around the world who worried about their spouses when they went to work. Firemen, policemen, soldiers. Melody and Harvey would be no different. Maybe he could just keep an eye on her. Maybe that would be his way of staying sane.

Harvey stopped a few houses down from the large villa that Melody had disappeared inside. Standing on the edge of the beach, he pushed all thoughts of Melody and their future behind him and basked in the shadows, allowing his senses to take stock of the situation.

A few small fish splashed in the water nearby. Larger predator fish were chasing them, maybe. Heavy palm leaves scraped against neighbouring leaves in the gentle breeze. But nothing else moved. He studied the rear of the house. Traces of light outlined the rear sliding doors, but the rest of the house was dark. Above the doors, a small red LED blinked, a movement sensor. Harvey checked the house next door where there was no blinking LED and the lights were all out. His plan adjusted.

Making his way through the rear garden of the adjacent house, he reached up to the top of the wall that adjoined the Turvey house and pulled himself quietly up. The pergola, a wooden structure designed to provide shade, was just a few steps away along the wall. Its thick wooden beams took his weight easily.

Once on the Turvey property, Harvey worked his way toward the roof access ladder, which was fixed to the side of the house.

The steel rungs were cool to the touch and wet from the humidity of the night. A short while later, Harvey was on the Turvey's flat roof, ducked down behind one of the four air conditioning units that stood near each corner.

He waited a full minute before making his next move. The standard minute was longer than most people had the patience to wait. If he'd been heard during his climb, the standard minute wait was long enough for anyone looking to give up and put the noises down to an animal or a bird.

The first-floor balcony was a fifteen-foot drop from the roof. It had looked less through the scope of the rifle, but it was still doable. Harvey lowered himself down. He guessed his feet were still roughly seven or eight feet from the balcony, but just four feet from the balustraded handrail that ran around the edge. He twisted his body to see his feet below, then hung from one hand. Then let go. His feet found the wide stone handrail easily. He bent his knees to absorb his weight and flung his arms out to balance. Straightening, he checked his surroundings once more and dropped to the floor.

A hard look at the glass door on the balcony told him the curtains were open, but the lights were off. It was too early for people to be sleeping, so the room should be empty. If it wasn't, he'd need to use plan C, extreme violence and a controlled chaos of attacks on the men. It was a last resort and one that did not guarantee success.

Harvey was unarmed. He was going up against an unknown number of men who must be armed, else Melody would not have given her own weapon up so easily. He just didn't know what they were armed with. His first priority would be to clear the top floor. He tried the door handle slowly and gently and felt the resistance of the locking mechanism. Giving a little extra effort, the handle moved more until it clicked open. Presumably, it had been overlooked, deemed secure due to its height.

The room was silent and dark. There were no sounds of breathing, no sign of movement. He was alone. The bedroom door was open, so he carefully moved closer and peered around the corner. It was cool from the air conditioning and the stairway at the far end of the tiled hallway was partially lit from the lighting downstairs. Harvey considered how he'd manage a hostage situation in this house. If he had help, he'd have the hostages locked in a bedroom with a guard. But all the bedroom doors were open with no lights on. So if everybody was downstairs, perhaps that meant that the number of men controlling the situation was small, possibly just one or two. One or two men with at least three hostages meant that Melody and her fellow prisoners would likely be tied up.

He stepped out into the hallway and stood at the top of the stairs, listening, breathing, absorbing the atmosphere. He waited a full minute before he stepped onto the top stair and then heard footsteps on the tiled floor downstairs. Pulling back, he glanced at his escape route, a dark bedroom adjacent to the stairway.

A man appeared in the downstairs hallway. Harvey saw only the back of the man, grey-haired, dressed neatly, and not ready for any combat in brogues and suit pants. The man opened a door. Harvey judged it to be the inner entrance to the garage. It was to the front of the house beside, what looked to be, the main front doors. A jingle of keys a few seconds later confirmed Harvey's suspicions.

The man returned, closed the garage door and strode back to the rear of the house. Harvey began to get a feel for the layout of the building; all the activity seemed to be at the back. Again, he considered what he would do. He would have a man at the front, near the window, to raise the alarm should an armed response unit close in.

The vibration of his phone in his thigh pocket caused him to stop. He couldn't risk reading the message now. It could only be from Reg. Lighting up his phone might catch the eye of some-body, a reflection or a shadow. It could wait.

Harvey crept silently down the sweeping staircase, all the time alert for any changes in sound from below. He was two steps from the bottom when he caught a narrow glimpse through the rear of the house. Two women were tied to the wall. Both naked. One was clearly dead. Harvey had seen enough death to know that a human body lost its natural sheen and colour after a day. The second woman was either asleep or had recently been killed. Her skin was alive and bore red patchy slap marks.

Another step.

The body of the man he'd killed lay on the floor behind a couch in a small pool of blood. Harvey could only see the back of the seat as it faced away from him. Why hadn't they moved the body away to another room, or outside? Again, with few men to watch the prisoners, they wouldn't have that luxury; the body would have to stay there.

Harvey could see through to the curtains that had shielded the rear doors. The room opened up to the right and to the left, out of his sight. If there were couches to the right, perhaps the area on the left was a dining area. He was in full view now, and anyone who walked into the hallway would see him. The kitchen was halfway along the hallway. Harvey hoped for a wooden block of sharp kitchen knives, maybe even a carelessly stored gun. But a knife would suffice. If he acted fast, he knew he could take down two or three armed men with just a knife given the right circumstances, circumstances that he'd have to instigate.

Harvey took the last step.

It was then he heard Melody's whisper.

"How do you plan on getting out of here alive?"

"I presume by your aggressive posture, and the fact you didn't even knock before entering, that Mills is now a prisoner inside the Turvey house and that Stone is somewhere close by ready to land himself in hot water," said the old man in his reclining leather office chair.

"Correct, sir."

"And you're mad at me for putting her in this situation?"

"I'm annoyed that you put *me* in this situation, sir," said Jackson. "We now have another hostage and a potential political nightmare on our hands and all because you want Stone out of the picture."

"I don't want Stone out of the picture, Jackson. I want him out of every picture. He's wild, he knows too much, and besides," said the old man lazily, "he's a lunatic, a torturer. He needs to go."

"There are other ways of achieving that without endangering the lives of good people and my career."

"So you're doubting me? You're scared. I'm beginning to question if I chose the right man for this job, Jackson. Do you want to step down? Because I can tell you now, it's a big step and an awful long drop. Keep talking like you're talking and no-one will even hear you hit the floor. Do you understand what I'm saying, Jackson?"

"I know what's right and wrong, sir," said Jackson.

"You said yourself that Stone needs locking up. He only got away last time because Mills tricked you. That tells me two things. Mills is good, possibly smarter than you, but Stone is better and definitely smarter than you. Right now, we have three hostages, including Mills, and we have an unofficial but extremely capable asset on the ground, who is not about to let the love of his life die in some feeble hostage attempt. Mills will be okay. Even if she's locked up, we can get her out. Stone will either be shot dead by Dubai police when our asset calls it in, or he'll spend the rest of his life sharing a cell and a bucket with twenty other guys in the middle of the desert. Turvey dies. You and I both move up the ladder. We both get rewarded for averting a political nightmare, and all you have to do is keep your mouth shut, and do what I tell you."

The old man reached for the bottom drawer of his desk and pulled out two tumblers and a small bottle of brandy.

"You have it all planned out, don't you? But you never told me why you want Stone so badly anyway." said Jackson.

The old man finished pouring two healthy measures of brandy. He twisted the cap on and left the bottle on the desk.

"You don't get to sit in this seat without having a few things in place." He passed Jackson the second glass and took a sip from his own. His tongue ran around his lips, savouring the bitter flavour. "First of all, you need to know people. It's a generation thing. Age and maturity tend to instil a little more confidence in people. You make new friends. You learn things. One of the things you learn fastest is who you can and can't trust. Stone and Mills were assigned to an old friend of mine, Frank Carver. Tenant was on the team too. Now *he's* an intelligent guy. But *not one* of them ever questioned Carver's integrity. Not one of them ever did a background check on him. It took a full internal investigation with MI5, and yourself, to catch him."

He took another long sip of the brandy and continued.

"No doubt, if Tenant had thought to run a background check on Carver, he'd have seen that Carver and I go way back. We started out together. We were often up against each other for promotions, and we ended up having a healthy respect for each other's skills, tenacity and ability to minimise risk." The old man smiled. "Risk management, Jackson. You need to be able to identify risk and eliminate it. Right now, we have a lunatic out there who knows too much about Carver. And if he knows too much about Carver-"

"Then he knows too much about you," finished Jackson.

"That's the way it all works. That's a risk. Do you understand?"

"You're covering your own backside."

"I'm eliminating risk. Understood?"

"However you want to word it, you're just getting even because you think Stone killed your friend. Now you're worried because you were also up to no good." Jackson paused. "But yeah, I get it."

"Good. Now go eliminate Stone."

CHAPTER TWENTY-ONE

Jackson walked into the ops room. His team were all hard at work finding a hole in Crowe's plan, searching for allies who could step in without publicising the operation, and formulating plans. The tension was electric; the stakes were high. The operation was close to home; it was personal, and the team were throwing everything they had at stopping it.

The effort was apparent. Even at a glance, Jackson could see how determined people were. It made him proud. Jackson himself had handpicked a lot of the team when he'd made the move from MI5 to MI6, and his decisions were now bearing fruit. Even Ladyluck, who could be emotional, brash, and sensitive, was pulling out all the stops only to hit the same walls as the rest of the team. But she kept going, undeterred.

Jackson took the spare seat next to Tenant and watched as the tech guru's fingers danced across the keyboard. Tenant wore large headphones, had his feet on a cushioned stool under his desk and stared up at the screens in front of him. Jackson was about to tap him on the shoulder when the door opened. Framed by the harsh corridor lights was Bernard Turvey.

Jackson stared at the shell of his boss. Turvey's strong exterior mask couldn't hide the pain and sleepless nights in his eyes, nor the slump in shoulders.

"Team," said Jackson, alerting them of Turvey's presence.

Slowly, keyboards stopped tapping, mice stopped clicking, and all heads turned to the man at the door.

An uneasy silence filled the room like a noxious gas. It stopped everyone in their tracks. Whatever they were thinking about was snatched from their minds. Bernard Turvey's life and death, and the choice he had to make, filled the void in their heads.

Bernard looked around the room. He swallowed frequently, fighting to maintain his composure. Finally, he stepped inside and let the door swing shut behind him.

Jackson broke the silence.

"Take a seat, sir."

Turvey smiled weakly, but held his hand up, indicating he was okay.

Bernard cleared his throat. "Looking at you all in here makes me proud," he began, "prouder than any of you will ever know." His steely resistance to breaking was clear. The team looked on with admiration at the strength of the man who stood before them. His leg shook uncontrollably, yet he didn't try to hide it. His lower jaw wobbled the moment it unhinged itself from the safety of its upper counterpart, yet the man continued to speak, unashamed and resolute. His wet and shiny eyes shone from the glow of the computer screens in the relative darkness of the room.

"You all have fine careers ahead of you," continued Bernard. "You are *all* at the top of your games, the peak of your abilities. And long may those abilities run free as you all continue to defy possibilities and stretch the boundaries of British intelligence and security on a daily basis."

Bernard looked around the room. He held the admiring

stares of each and every person in the room then stopped on Jackson.

"No doubt that all of you have something to say, questions to ask, feelings you want to convey. I know you do. Many of us have gotten to know each other very well, that's what comes of being surrounded by extremely capable people, and achieving incredible things together. I only wish I had the time to talk to you and to get to know you all a little better."

Bernard began to pace the room, walking alongside everyone and offering them all their own smiles in return for unsaid goodbyes. Bernard put his hand on Ladyluck's head as she broke, unable to hold her tears anymore. Angela Finsbury, the research assistant who sat beside her, put her hand on her back and rubbed gently. They spoke no words; there was nothing to say.

"What I am about to do, the decision I have made, although it seems difficult and it's hard for many of you to empathise, is the easiest decision I've ever had to make. The lives of my wife and daughter carry far more weight in the world than my own. I know I'll be remembered well, and I'll die knowing that they will live on. It'll be hard for them at first, but Anya will grow to be strong, knowing that I'm watching over her."

He paused as he completed a full circle of the room. "The truth is that, while you see it as a decision, I see only one choice. I couldn't go on living knowing that my cowardice killed the two most important people in my world. And that's the truth."

The door opened and a man wearing a suit and an ear-piece leaned in. One hand held the breast of his jacket closed, a habit formed from years of armed security. "Sir," he said in a strong, confident, Mancunian accent, "it's time."

"I'll be right out," replied Turvey. Then, as he held the door open, he paused. He turned back to face Jackson. The door seemed to be all that held him upright. "Get them out, Jackson.

Make them safe." Then he nodded his final goodbye and left the room.

The room sat stunned by the unexpected and heart-warming speech. Ladyluck cried into her sleeve. Jackson caught the attention of Angela Finsbury who was consoling Ladyluck and gestured with his head to take her to the washrooms.

"Alright, people, you know what we need to do. We have one hour before Bernard's speech. The strategy is changing. We need options on how to control this." He paused and thought about his next words carefully. "Stopping it may no longer be an option, and if that's the case, we need to control it."

Jackson turned to Tenant, who had removed his head-phones and put his feet down, but still frantically attacked his keyboard and flicked his head from screen to screen.

"Tenant," said Jackson, "where are we?"

"I have a way into the building's internet-leased line, so should the worst-case scenario look inevitable, I can cut the line. We have men on the ground ensuring that the media aren't using their own connections, and we have a high-frequency signal jammer in place just in case somebody tries. There's an armed guard on all the hotel entrances, and a third party has been brought in alongside uniformed police to handle the collection of mobile phones and tablets."

"Must be quite a scene?" said Jackson.

"It's all covert, sir. All the audience will know is that they had their mobile phone taken from them. And given that the board comprises of several MP's, I doubt they'll regard that as anything but additional security."

"Good," said Jackson, nodding. "Now talk to me about Stone."

Reg's fingers stopped dancing. His eyes stopped flicking from screen to screen. "Sir?"

"Don't kid a kidder, Tenant. What's his location?" said Jackson in a hushed tone.

"I'm not sure I know-"

"Tenant, last chance, we don't have much time," said Jackson. "I know you got him out there, but right now, we need him. Get a message to him. Can you do that?"

"Sure," said Reg, with a surprised yet ashamed expression. "What do you want me to tell him?"

"Tell him..." Jackson pondered briefly. "Tell him Jackson said to go get his girl out. Tell him to do whatever it takes to get Melody and the Turveys out of there."

"Are you okay, sir?" asked Jackson.

Jackson waited as if doubting his own thoughts. "Yeah. Yeah, I'm fine, Tenant. I just had a moment of clarity."

"Clarity, sir?"

"Also tell him..." Jackson looked over at the old man's office door hesitantly. "Also tell him to get out of there as soon as possible when it's done."

Reg looked up at him, surprised. "Jackson?"

Jackson sighed, shook his head and looked back at Reg. "Just trust me on this one, okay?"

CHAPTER TWENTY-TWO

"Melody, I know you can't respond. But you should know that we're all here for you," said Reg over the comms. His crackled and faint voice came over Melody's ear-piece. Somehow, his soft tone carried with it despite the poor connection. "Listen, we're running out of time but we're pulling out all the stops. You should see the guys here, I've never seen them so invested. What I'm trying to say, Melody, is, well, don't feel alone. No matter how hard it is, no matter what Crowe is saying or doing, we're with you, and we're coming for you." The connection dropped until Reg began speaking again. "We do need help though, Melody. Do what you can. Don't take any more risks, you've done enough. But if you can, try and get him to talk. There must be something we're missing. He's too confident. It's like he knows something we don't. See if you can bridge that gap."

Melody looked around the room. Exhaustion had overcome Angie Turvey, and she hung from her wrists, her head resting on the dead woman's head. Anya slept the deep sleep that only children seem to enjoy. Crowe sat at the dining table working on the laptop.

"How do you plan on getting out of here alive?" whispered Melody. "You know you're surrounded. So what's the plan?"

"Like I said before," began Crowe, "I'm smarter than the average bear."

"You think you're going to walk out of here? You saw what happened to your friend. You won't get two steps. There's a sniper over the water and there are snipers out front."

"I'm quite certain the British government won't be taking me down, not on Emirati soil anyway. I like my chances."

"How about a wager?" said Melody. "To give the girls a chance?"

Crowe laughed. It was an honest laugh. Not feigned, not cruel, it was genuine.

Melody continued to stare at him. "*I* bet Turvey doesn't pull the trigger," she said.

Crowe raised an eyebrow. "What's at stake here?"

"If he doesn't pull the trigger, you release the woman and the girl. Shoot me instead. Bernard doesn't have to know. He'll either do it or he won't, but that little girl and her mother have no part in this. I'm ready. Are you, Crowe?"

"It's not enough. What do I stand to win if I'm right and Turvey goes through with it?"

"What do you need?" asked Melody.

"Nothing, not from you anyway."

"Are you sure about that? I'm a resourceful girl with all sorts of things up my sleeve. You want weapons? You want a passport?"

"No way. It's not going to happen," said Crowe. But Melody caught the intrigue in his eyes.

"If I'm right," said Melody, "and Turvey doesn't kill himself, you let the girls go, and I get you out of here no questions asked. If I'm wrong, well, you do what you have to do. But right now, you don't have anywhere to go from here, and you can't stay here forever."

"I don't need your help, young lady. If he doesn't pull the trigger, his family are dead. What would *you* do? He doesn't have options."

"So you kill his family. Great. Then what? You just stroll out of here and into the arms of waiting police. They still have the death penalty here you know?"

"Young lady, do you honestly think I haven't thought of that? Do I look like the type of man to go into something like this blind? No, I do not."

"So what then?" asked Melody, "Your options are slim, and the boys outside will pull the trigger and ask questions later."

"Turvey dies. If it's not during his speech, his family dies. After that, he gets one more chance. One more chance to save lives, missy. I imagine by then he'll want to join his family anyway."

"And then what? You're out here. Do you have men in London? Is that it? If he doesn't do it, you send them in to do your dirty work?"

"Turvey is a man of many faces. I tried to tell his poor wife over there. But would she listen? Oh no. Sure, he loves his family, and he's done well. But do you know what he's had to do to get there? I'll tell you what he did. He tore my family to pieces. He killed my wife and daughter to get at me and still failed. I'm still here, and they're not. So as for your little bet, as tempting as it is, they die."

"You didn't answer the question," said Melody. "What then?"

"He's bent, as crooked as they come, in fact, in more ways than one. But one thing I do know is that he's patriotic."

"So what? Being patriotic won't help him here."

"No, you're right, it won't. But it helps me."

"How?" asked Melody.

"Let's just say that it's a matter of understanding politics over the value of a human being."

"Politics? Really, you're doing this in the name of politics? There are easier ways. Hold a sign up outside parliament or something."

"Do you know how delicate relationships are between nations right now?"

"Relationships are always delicate."

"Ah, you talk from experience," said Crowe.

"I've dabbled."

"You got burned?"

"I learned a lot," replied Melody.

"Would you do it again?"

"In a heartbeat."

"Why do think you were sent out here?"

"Who do you think is waiting for you to step outside?" said Melody.

"Nobody probably," said Crowe. "You see, if the Dubai government found out about you, not only would you be shot for espionage, but the UAE would undoubtedly sever ties with the UK. That would have a huge effect on oil and energy in the UK. And well, let's face it, where else are us Brits going to land our planes around here? It's the friendliest place for miles. If the UAE severed ties with the UK, then so would Saudi. And if that happens, then who would want to be friends with the UK? We have nothing to offer. It would be a political nightmare which would likely destroy the economy, and one the British govern- ment aren't keen to risk."

"So?" said Melody. "What's your point?"

"Well, missy, what do you think would happen with that very delicate relationship between the UAE and the UK if a bomb were to detonate, say in a mall or somewhere public?"

Melody's eyes widened.

"Or maybe if someone very important was killed in the blast?"

Melody struggled against her bindings, trying to force herself free.

Crowe smiled at her struggle. He leaned forward to face her. "Now what do you think would happen if that bomb were to be planted by a British undercover operative?"

CHAPTER TWENTY-THREE

"Listen up," said Jackson. "This just got very real."

The team all looked up from their stations.

"We have new intel, a bomb, somewhere public, possibly even targeting the Sheik's family. Ladyluck, get onto our assets. We need to know every known movement of anybody worth targeting. Finsbury, find Tenant a list of every possible public location worth bombing and tie it in with whatever Ladyluck finds. We need a crossover. Tenant, you can't do this alone. I need as many eyes as possible on every CCTV camera in whatever location Ladyluck and Finsbury come up with. Gordon, I need comms plans. If this goes south, we need to be able to pre-warn those upstairs of what is happening, and we need to be able to get a message to the British embassies in Dubai and Abu Dhabi."

"You're still keeping this under wraps?" asked Gordon.

Jackson stared at him from across the room. "I don't see what choice we have, Gordon. If we raise the alarm now, we'll be ordered to cut our losses. We'll lose Mills and the entire Turvey family."

"It's a huge risk for one family and an operative that no

longer operates," replied Gordon. "If that bomb goes off, the Turveys will be the last thing on our minds. It would destroy everything the UK stands for, sir."

Jackson took a deep breath and nodded. "You're right, but we need to give them every chance we can."

"Sir, I have eyes on Turvey," said Reg. "He's inside the hotel."

"Is he carrying?" asked Ladyluck.

"The weapon is taped to the underside of his seat. We had someone on the crew take care of it," said Jackson. "Tenant, make sure you hit that kill switch on the internet line."

"It's all ready to go, sir," replied Reg.

Jackson took a step closer to him. "Any news?"

"No response, but he's close. See this icon here?" Reg pointed discreetly to a red dot on a map displayed on one of his screens.

"That's Stone?" asked Jackson.

"Yep. Judging by the difference in signal strengths, he's on the roof or upper floor, and Melody is inside. See how weak her signal is."

"Can we talk to him?"

"No, he didn't get the standard issue ear-piece."

Jackson checked his watch. "We have thirty minutes before the speeches start."

"How long is his speech?" asked Reg.

Jackson frowned at him. "Not long enough, Tenant."

"Ladies and gentlemen, welcome to the DWC's forty-fifth annual gala dinner," began the Master of Ceremonies. He was stood in a black tuxedo on a small stage with a decorated wooden lectern, from which a single microphone protruded. "I'm sure you're all keen to sample the wonderful meal that has been prepared for you. But if I may, I'd like to let you all know the order of events for the evening, so you can all plan your getaways." The crowd offered a weak mumble of humour. "And where better place to start than with the entrees? While we savour those delicious morsels if you care to look up at the screen behind me, you'll see the live result of this fundraiser. I'll take this opportunity to remind you that twenty-five countries are participating in this year's appeal, and we hope to be able to raise a donation toward the DWC in excess of five hundred million dollars."

The MC paused while the audience gasped. Then, with the timing of a professional, he continued his speech. "Yes, ladies and gentlemen, that's half a billion dollars with which, I'm sure you can imagine, we would be able to change the lives of not hundreds of people, not even thousands, but millions of individuals out there who need our help."

The audience applauded. The MC raised his hands to calm them. "Following the entrees, we will be honoured with our first speaker of the evening. He's come all the way from Australia just to be here tonight. So please do give a warm British welcome to Mr Augustus Derby, who is also here with his very beautiful wife. For those who aren't aware, Mr Derby is responsible for bringing us all together here tonight. If you'd like to catch a glimpse of him, he's the one on the top table. Can't see him? Okay, here's a clue, he's the one with the tan."

The crowd laughed again, but the MC stopped them short. "We'll then break for the main course. I shall not spoil the surprise, but I hope you brought your doggy bags because we have managed to get twice-awarded Michelin star chef Patrick Du Priz to come to our little gathering and cook us up some of his finest flavourful offerings."

The crowd murmured. Most of the audience would frequently dine in some of the world's top restaurants. But they all knew that to recognise and appreciate the chef was the way to befriend him and be invited to his own restaurant at a later date.

"It is then, at exactly eight o'clock, ladies and gentlemen, that the clock will be stopped. The phone lines and internet donation service have been open now for twenty-four hours. But from that point on, no more donations will be accepted, and our guest of honour, Mr Bernard Turvey, will take over the microphone to reveal the final figure. So without further ado, let's see just how close we are to that final figure. And remember, we're looking for five hundred million dollars. Are we ready?" The MC held the microphone out to the crowd, and though many cheered, a few preferred not to make such vulgar displays of immaturity in public.

"Okay, let's count down," said the MC. "Three, two..." There was hushed silence, and then he whispered into the microphone. "One."

A huge two-hundred-inch screen above the Master of Ceremonies lit up with displays of fireworks. The lights in the room dimmed slightly, and lasers fixed to the ceiling carved their way across the room in wild, erratic circles. The display was designed to build the tension in the room, and to great effect. Then, in the centre of the screen, in massive figures above him, the number three hundred and eighty-four million appeared in bold red letters.

"So, there we go, ladies and gentlemen," continued the MC. The lights were slowly brought back up. The lasers were faded to off. "There we go. Just shy of eighty percent. We have an hour still left to run. So call your wealthy uncles, phone your friends, sell your kidneys, do whatever it takes. Let's make this year count. Let's hit that half a billion dollar target. Thank you for your time, ladies and gentlemen, please do enjoy your entrees. I shall return shortly to introduce the first of our guests. But, for now, bon appetit, everybody."

CHAPTER TWENTY-FIVE

"Okay, everyone, this is it," said Jackson to the room. "You all know the situation. Those of you looking for the bomb, carry on looking. Time is running out. Those of you not involved in the live event, keep going. Shout out anything you find, no matter how insignificant. And those of you researching the audience, keep your eyes peeled. Tenant, how many cameras do we have on the audience?"

"Dozens, sir. I've got the live feed of all the major news channels and broadcasters."

"Good, get them up on the screens. People, we need to be watching the audience. We have men at every door. If you see anything suspicious, call it out. We'll have someone take them out of the room. There's a strong chance that Crowe has someone there to make sure Bernard goes through with it. We cannot let that happen," said Jackson. "You can all see the table plan on the wall behind me. If you see someone acting suspect, call it out, gender, age, description, table number. We need to keep it as low key as possible."

Jackson approached Reg as soon as he saw the team get their

heads down. The noise in the room returned to its low hum of discussion and frantic clicking of keyboards.

"Tenant, what's the news with Dubai?"

"Harvey won't read my messages. I believe he's on the attack," replied Reg.

"You believe? We need confirmation. At no point here can we let any of this roll without our understanding."

"Affirmative, sir. I've sent him two messages. If he won't read them, I have no way of contacting him."

Jackson huffed loudly through his nose. "You know him. What's he likely to do?"

"He's a good guy, sir, despite what you've heard or read."

"You think he can stop this?"

"I think he'll rescue Melody. In fact, I have no doubt about that." Reg paused. "I can't comment on Mrs Turvey and the girl."

"You think he'd leave them there?" asked Jackson.

"I think he'll read the situation and do whatever he can with Melody as his priority."

"Mills is not our priority. She knew the dangers."

"With all due respect, sir, Harvey is not an operative. He's just a capable man looking out for his girl."

"How much does Stone know?" asked Jackson.

"He knew where to find Melody, and he knows she's in trouble," replied Reg. "What he's found out since is unknown."

"So he doesn't know about the bomb?"

"I don't know. Maybe?" Reg shrugged.

"But he knows about the demands and the repercussions?"

"Your guess is as good as mine."

"Tell me he knows that the local government need to stay out of the picture."

"I may have missed that out during my covert briefing with him on the underground, sir."

Jackson shook his head in disbelief. "Does Mills know Stone is there?"

"Bit of a risk, sir," said Reg. "It might alter her mental state. She might act before Harvey is ready, change his plan."

"Plan, Tenant?" said Jackson hopefully. "He has a plan?"

"Oh, believe me, sir; Harvey will have a plan A, B and C. Why do you think nobody ever caught him?" Reg smiled at his boss. "He's the best at what he does, sir."

Turvey stood from his seat. He winced at the sudden arrival of four large spotlights that illuminated him and followed him to the centre stage. He felt the weight of the handgun he'd pulled from the underside of the top table and stashed in his inside pocket. It felt heavy, heavier than any gun he'd carried before. It wasn't until he laid eyes on the first camera that his public speaking experience kicked in, and he straightened, suddenly aware of his posture.

He stepped up to the lectern, and the room slowly fell silent in anticipation of his speech. He heard the individual claps gradually stop, and could place the last clapping person beyond the bright lights. There was no escape now.

Turvey took a deep breath.

"When DWC was formed, I wasn't even born," he began. "In that first year, I think I'm right in saying that the equivalent value of the donation was a mere five thousand dollars, which, in those times, was a grand sum of money. But resources were low and medical research was technologically limited compared to the wonders we can achieve in today's world. That's evolution, some say, it's a natural progression. But I beg to differ. Let's consider the natural progression of the human race. Learning to walk, for instance, took us millions of years. Learning to communicate, again, took us millions of years. The difference between five thousand dollars and five hundred million dollars in only forty-five years cannot be disregarded as a natural progression."

The audience murmured, and Turvey, a practised public speaker, allowed them the chance. He knew it would add to the impact of what he was about to say.

"Forty-five years ago, one percent of the world's population was richer than the rest of the world. And guess what? That hasn't changed. We're not all wealthier. The population has grown exponentially in forty-five years, but that ninety-nine percent of the remaining wealth has just been diluted."

The audience was intrigued by the direction of his speech. Turvey spoke well. He was clear and had the nuances of a leader who guided people's imaginations.

"So if it's not a natural progression that can spark such a rise in generosity, then what is it? Do you know what I think, ladies and gentlemen in this room, and all the incredible people out there that have donated tonight to help save these poor people from a life of misery and pain?" He paused once more.

"I think it's desire."

Three hundred people sat at the tables in the room, and another hundred people stood around the edge as security, cameramen, media reporters and events crew. Not one person made a sound.

"Forget about natural progression, I want you to visualise something new. Desire. Visualise a job you once wanted. It was a job you had wanted for a long time, a great step in your long career, whatever that may be. How many other people went for that job? Ten? Twenty? Fifty? Heck, with today's internet recruitment channels, some companies see thousands of people applying for a single job. And the company gets to choose. They get to select the best of the best. But the reality is that thousands of people desire that job. And the result? The company ends up with the best person possible for that company. If they do their job right, that person will make positive changes. That person might mean the difference between a good year and a great year. That person might mean that others that were not invested in their jobs suddenly grew to become invested because that one person led them effectively. And what happens? The company lifts up a notch. It might be a small amount, it might be a great lift, but the company makes progress."

Turvey stared out at the crowd beyond the lights, not focusing on individuals, but scanning the heads in the room.

"Progress," he said. "One word. Sure, you might think the company makes progress from all those positive changes. But ladies and gentlemen, progress is not the reason. Can you see? It is the desire. It was the desire of all those thousands of other people that brought the best of the best, the cream of the cream, to the interview room. It was the desire of the organisation to progress. The organisation desired to hire the best of the best. And ladies and gentlemen, if you haven't seen the analogy, it is the desire of mankind, right here, right now, to help millions of people around the world. It is the desire of every single person who donated, no matter how big or small the donation, to make sure that those who need help get the help. Desire, ladies and gentlemen. If you want something badly enough, *you will make it happen*."

The audience burst into applause. Chairs scraped back as they stood to clap, and Mr Turvey looked down unsmiling at the praise. He had completed his work. All that remained was for him to flick the switch and display the final amount on the massive screen above.

"Before I hit this switch, ladies and gentlemen," he continued. "Before we see the final figure, I'd like to say just this. It won't be me standing here next year. I won't have the pleasure of seeing the delight in all of your smiling faces or enjoy the company of so many generous people. But I hope this charity continues. I hope that at each future gala dinner, year by year, the line from five thousand dollars to five hundred million dollars becomes even more vertical. I hope that one day, that number will be a billion dollars. And the way we do that is by raising the desire. The more people we have that want to help, the closer we'll get to our target. But you know what? More than anything, I hope in the not too distant future, maybe next year, maybe the year after, that we don't raise a penny."

Bernard said the last sentence with a cruel snarl and allowed time for the comment to be absorbed by his captive audience.

"I truly hope that in less than five years' time, this room is empty, or hosting a dance or a wedding or some other event than this one. I don't want the ninety-nine percent of the world's population having to put their hands in their pockets to help the sick. I don't even want the richest one percent of the population to pay out. Because one day, ladies and gentlemen, I believe we will break this illness, and wipe it from our planet. Every penny we've raised tonight is one step closer to that goal."

Once again, the room exploded in applause. Bernard pulled the handkerchief from his top pocket and wiped his brow. He knew his time was coming. He'd bought as much time as he could have hoped for. But his ear-piece had not burst into life to inform him that Crowe had been taken down as he had hoped. That meant that Angie and Anya were still prisoners, and all that remained was to save his family's lives.

"And now we come to the part we have all been waiting for," said Bernard. "In a moment, I shall hit stop on the clock, and the donations will cease to be accepted. The final figure will be shown on the screen above me, and we'll have a fairly accurate measurement of just how much the population of the world desire to help those that so desperately need our help."

Bernard moved his hand to the switch and noticed for the first time how unsteady his hands were. Fear gripped him. He knew with each passing second that he was one step closer to death. He glanced at Gordon at the edge of the room and was met with a saddened expression and a gentle shake of the head.

Gordon's hand raised to his ear, and suddenly, Bernard's own ear-piece crackled into life. "Just stall, sir. Take as long as you need."

Bernard regained his composure. He wiped his brow once more, and then addressed the audience who sat forward attentively.

"Shall we have a countdown?" he said. The number ten appeared in bold, colourful figures on the screen. The audience began to count down.

"Ten."

"Nine."

More people joined in the countdown, and the room felt like an Olympic stadium.

"Eight."

"Seven."

The lasers danced around the walls. Spotlights flashed from person to person, lighting up a member of the audience before moving onto the next person.

"Six."

"Five."

"The screen began to display its fireworks, as the bright red and blue numbers increased in size.

"Four."

"Three."

Bernard held onto the lectern as he looked up hopefully. He willed the money to be there. He desired it so much. If his last act could be something as significant as a half-a-billion-dollar donation to help the cause, he would at least be remembered for the occasion.

"Two."

"One."

The screen went dark. The audience hushed. The spotlights went out and the lasers died.

Then the smiling face of a man in his fifties appeared on the screen.

"Hello, London."

CHAPTER TWENTY-SEVEN

"How?" shouted Jackson at Reg, who sat with his jaw hanging open.

"I, I don't know, sir," stammered Reg. "I didn't see that coming."

"I thought you said you had control over the internet line?"

"Yes, I'm in total control of what's being sent out. But I can't see anything coming in, certainly not video traffic," said Reg.

"So how come we, and a few million other people, are staring at Caesar Crowe's face?"

"He has to be using another line. There must be-"

"Find it," snapped Jackson. "And stop it." He turned to another tech operative a few desks along from Reg. "Bailey, get the volume up on that screen."

A few seconds later, the cold voice of Caesar Crowe had filtered through into the heads of every single person in the room as they watched him captivate and bemuse the guests of the forty-fifth DWC Annual Gala Dinner.

"I realise that I am not a listed speaker at the event tonight, and I feel I should add that I did not donate this year or the year before. Perhaps that's one of the reasons I wasn't invited?"

He smiled at the camera, and the audience felt the chill of his tone.

"Alas," continued Crowe, "it is not for me to decide the audience of such a gratifying affair. I can only imagine the audience with you tonight are all very wealthy, very naïve, but very well connected. It's not what you know, it's who you know, right?"

The audience murmured and looked confusedly between Turvey on stage and the Master of Ceremonies who stood to the side.

"Speaking of knowing people," said Crowe, "the reason I have decided to hijack the final speech of tonight's charitable soiree is to allow you all the opportunity to get to know Mr Turvey. I listened with glee at his speech, and I must say, Bernie, you know how to get the crowd going, don't you?"

Bernard looked aghast. His eyes flicked from the crowds behind the glaring lights and back to the screen.

"You see," continued Crowe, "Mr Turvey here may have an exterior worthy of a place beside the Lord himself behind the pearly gates of heaven for his saint-like emotions, and heartfelt *desires*. But he does, in fact, have a few secrets of his own, and tonight, ladies and gentlemen, as a finalé, we shall reveal those secrets. So you can make your own minds up about Saint Turvey and his spot in heaven."

Crowe was as much an experienced public speaker as Bernard and held his tongue for a moment for the crowds to exchange confused chatter.

"Did you know, good people of the DWC, that your guest speaker tonight, the man that chairs the entire DWC operation..." Crowe put his hand up to his mouth as if revealing a secret. "Did you know he's actually a senior member of MI6? Now you do. It's true, you know. How can any of God's angels lie? Look at him. He cannot deny it. Can you, Bernie?"

Bernard straightened. His career was top secret, but there was nothing he could do to prevent the exposure now. Instead, he stared resolutely at Crowe.

"Some of you may have had ideas about Mr Turvey's career in law enforcement. Some of you may have no idea. But the best secrets are the ones that come with a surprise, don't you think? Some of you may even wonder how a man such as Bernie here actually makes it into MI6, and I would wonder too, if I didn't know the truth. You see, ladies and gentlemen, the man who stands before you tonight is a very, very bad man. But tonight, we shall give him the opportunity to resurrect his soul. I'm not talking about the five hundred and fifteen million dollars that have been raised tonight. Yes, five hundred and fifteen million dollars, people. You beat your target by fifteen million dollars.

"But I digress. I'm not talking about Bernie saving his soul by being an empty voice and flicking a switch to create a snowball effect whereby thousands of volunteers work for nothing in the most God-awful places on the planet to save a bunch of ungrateful, lazy and unintelligent people from a life of suffering, as their sins decreed. No. I'm talking about the man behind the facade. I'm talking about the rotten, stinking soul of Bernard Turvey and his so-called *desires*.

"You see, a long time ago, before the internet, and seemingly when the world was a larger place, it was impossible to reach out to people across a fibre optic network to ask for help. It was impossible to make a call on your mobile phone to raise an alarm. However, it was possible for people like Bernard Turvey to torture and kill innocent people and go unnoticed."

Crowe allowed a few seconds for the crowd to become inquisitive. Turvey stood straight on the stage, but the glares and horrified stares began to find his flesh. He began to sink. He knew what was coming next.

"You see, Bernard Turvey was once a mere foot soldier, an

apprentice among the best. Britain's finest. He had ambition. He had desires, ladies and gentlemen. He'd smelled the glory and seen people rise quickly in the ranks; he wanted that for himself. Myself, I was a criminal. I'm not ashamed to say it, not because it's in my past, but because, well, to be frank, the opinions of those of you listening matter to me not. I stole, not from the poor, no, I was raised better than that, but I carved earnings from institutions. I shaved pennies from organisations, unnoticed. I stole from that one percent of people your fabled guest speaker spoke of earlier, not the ninety-nine percent of the population who had to share the petty remains of the global wealth.

"I did well, but over time, I admit, greed took hold of me. Eventually, I made a mistake. It was catastrophic. One might say my desires outgrew my capabilities. One day, I woke up staring at the painful end of Mr Turvey's gun. Not at first, but as my eyes adjusted to the morning light and my brain began to understand that it was all over, I began to accept it. I'd been caught. I was ready to stand, dress and be taken away. And had it been another member of Britain's finest and not a power-hungry, ladder-climber such as Bernie, that is exactly how the next few moments would have played out. I had no gun in my hand. I made no attempt to get away, and neither did my wife. It was as she woke, and rolled over to kiss her husband on the cheek, that she saw the gun. Frightened, as you can imagine, she jumped up and began to scramble out of bed."

Crowe's voice broke, slightly, a play on the memory aimed to bring the audience to his side.

"That was when old twitchy fingers Turvey here shot her dead."

The crowd gasped.

"Not once, ladies and gentlemen, not twice, but three times. Once in the back of the head and two more to finish her off while she lay on the floor. I thank God that she was dead before the second and third bullets touched her."

Crowe gave a sombre, downcast look, and then continued his story.

"Then I made a run for it. This was no longer a game of cops and robbers. I was no longer going to say that it was fair cop guv'nor, and allow myself to be handcuffed. This man was out for blood. I made it as far as the bedroom door when the first bullet hit me in the shoulder. I still have the scar. But as I snatched open the bedroom door and let it crash into the wall beside me, I looked down for a brief moment. I saw the face of an angel staring back at me. My child."

Crowe silenced, and the room silenced with him.

"Then her face just seemed to cave in, as the bullets tore her apart in front of my eyes."

The audience noise shot up and Bernard clasped his eyes closed, wishing this nightmare would end.

"I ran, of course," said Crowe. "I ran for all I had, and by some misguided fortune, Bernard Turvey here wasn't arresting me as part of a crack squad of MI5 agents. He was, in fact, operating alone. He was seeking the glory he so very much desired. So I made my escape. The tragic deaths of my family were covered over, and the blame put on some crazed burglar who was never found. Ladies and gentlemen, does that sound like the type of man who would sit beside God himself and command the angels?"

People began to stand to leave the room. But Crowe raised the volume of his speech and caught the attention of them all.

"And then there's poor Mrs Turvey. Oh yes, the story continues. You see, as shambolic as my previous story was, there's more. Oh yes. He wasn't content with his elevated position in the prestigious MI6. He wasn't content with chairing one of the world's largest charities."

Crowe's voice dropped to a caring whisper.

"He wasn't content either with being lucky enough to have the support and devotion of the very beautiful Angela Turvey, and their even more beautiful daughter, Anya Turvey. No, he had to get his thrills elsewhere. He had to fulfil his desires, you see?" Crowe paused and looked around the room. "How do I know all this? How do I know that Mr Turvey's family are so worthy of gratitude and respect? How do I know they're so beautiful?"

Crowe smiled.

"They're right here with me."

CHAPTER TWENTY-EIGHT

Crowe moved away from the camera and allowed the global audience a view of the Turvey's Dubai holiday home. To the left was Angie Turvey, stripped naked and tied to what looked like the corpse of another woman, who was tied to fixings in the wall. In the centre of the screen sat Anya Turvey. Her wrists and ankles were bound with duct tape, and to the right of the screen was another woman dressed in black. She had also been bound and was unable to move.

The three women stared at the screen, and the horrified audience gasped collectively. An elderly woman dressed in a flowery dress and her finest pearls fainted and slipped from her chair. Two men either side rushed to tend her.

"Stop," shouted Turvey. He held onto the lectern as if his life depended on it. "Enough is enough. I'll do it."

"You'll wait and do exactly what you're told," replied Crowe, coming back into the camera's view. "These people deserve to hear the rest of my story. These people deserve to know the truth about the monster behind the shiny, idyllic illusion you cast. You see, good people of the DWC, Mr Turvey has a whole range of tastes. I'm in his home now and I can tell you, it is exquisitely designed and finished with the finest materials money can buy. The table that this laptop rests on is worth more than ten thousand dollars, and that's just the table. If you sold the art in this house, you could feed a village of starving children in Asia for a month. So, when Bernie here tells us all about his so-called heroic attempts at destroying the terrible affliction for what DWC stands to quell, ask yourself this: how much did he actually donate tonight?"

The crowd had fallen silent again. Bernard Turvey leaned against the lectern, unable to face the screen and look into the eyes of the man that had destroyed his family and his reputation. It no longer mattered that the charity had smashed the target. It was all over.

"Nothing," spat Crowe. "Zero. That's how much he donated to the cause he so strongly believes in. Yet he pleaded with you all to make sure you gave whatever you could afford, didn't he? Desire, ladies and gentlemen. Let's talk about Bernie's desires and his tastes, as I believe that for this next part of my speech, they are most appropriate."

Crowe's face was moved out of focus, and a printed photo of Bernard Turvey with two young and expensive-looking prostitutes was placed in front of the camera.

"That's not Angie Turvey, I can assure you all. Angie here has far more class than that. No, these girls are nothing but high-class prostitutes sought from a high-class escort agency. It may seem as if they are simply enjoying dinner with a well-dressed, tanned businessman. But on that particular night, the fun didn't stop there."

The photo was replaced with another. The second image showed Bernard Turvey in bed with the two girls. The room was disgusted. A man at the front shouted an insult at Bernard and made to leave with his wife. But Crowe stopped him with a loud and old command. "*Sit down.*"

The man looked up at the screen.

"Yes, you, the one with no hair and the suit that looks like your grandfather bought it before the war, *sit down*."

The man reddened and sat, looking indignant and wholly embarrassed.

"Would you like to see more?" Crowe addressed the entire room again. He then replaced the image with one of Bernard Turvey tied to the same bed, but in a state of submission and humiliation. He was clearly aroused as the two leather-clad girls wore various arrangements of strap-on sex toys.

"Shocking, isn't it?" said Crowe. "This is the man you all came to see. The man you all came to hear talk about how wonderful this charity is. Look at him squirm on the stage in front of you all."

Many of the women in the audience had looked away from the screen, horrified at what they had seen.

"We all know these things happen. We all know that there are people out there who enjoy a fruitful sex life. But do you all honestly think that Mrs Turvey here deserves to be so mistreated?" Crowe moved to one side to allow the audience a view of the woman who stood behind him, tied to the corpse of her neighbour. "However," he continued, "I regret to inform you all that our dear friend, Bernie, is even sicker than you might quite imagine."

Crowe looked sorrowfully at the camera as if the news he was about to deliver was against his own will. "Ladies and gentlemen, I give you Bernard Turvey in all his glory."

Once more, Crowe's face disappeared from view as the final photo crept into the frame.

CHAPTER TWENTY-NINE

"Oh my God," said Jackson. "How do we stop this?"

"I can't stop the video traffic going into the event. But I can stop the traffic from leaving the Turvey house where it's originating from," said Reg.

"Do it," replied Jackson.

"Once I kill it though, we'll have no way of getting back in there, and we won't have eyes on the family." Reg leaned back in his chair. "It's your call, sir. We've been trying to get a handle on what's going on in the house for two days. We now have eyes on the inside."

Jackson dropped his head into his hands and peered through his fingers in despair.

"Let's face it," continued Reg, "it can't get much worse, can it?"

Suddenly, Crowe's cold voice tore through the speakers. "I think we've all seen enough of our friend, Bernie, haven't we? I hope that you can all see that the man stood on the stage before you is not all he seems. I also feel that now is the time to let the rest of the world know exactly what's coming next."

The ambient hum of the audience dropped once more as

the outraged and disgusted people turned their attention back to the face on the screen.

"Mr Turvey, do you want to tell the rest of the world what you are going to do?" said Crowe. "Or should I?"

Bernard Turvey stood rocking on the stage. He stared unblinkingly at the floor for what seemed like an eternity before raising his head and speaking to the audience. Lowering his mouth to the microphone, he looked out at the horrified faces then took a deep breath.

"I could stand here and defend myself, defend my honour, and defend my family name. I could stand here and plead with you all for forgiveness and try to regain your trust. But the fact of the matter is..."

He paused, as if the words he spoke next would strike him down.

"Yes?" said Crowe. "Go on, Bernie."

Bernard's eyes flicked up to the screen and back to the crowd; they were wet, glistening with the high-powered spots that seemed to burn right through him.

"It's true," he said. "It's all true."

As if the audience doubted Crowe's allegations, they gasped in unison once more, Turvey's words somehow cementing the facts.

"And what are we going to do about it?" asked Crowe. "What do you have to say to all these nice people that were sucked in by your cruel and perverse desires?"

"Words cannot describe how I feel right now," said Bernard. "To the audience and the public, I am truly ashamed. I abused my position, I abused my power, and I abused my wealth for my own satisfaction."

"That's a start," said Crowe. "Who in the audience wants to see old Bernie here suffer?"

The room remained quiet for a while. Then somewhere near the back of the room, a man shouted out, "Make him pay."

Another joined in. "Yeah, make him donate all his money."

"Make him resign," shouted another.

"All good ideas," said Crowe. "But I was thinking of something a little more permanent. You know, a payment so true that even God himself couldn't undo the changes, even if he wanted to."

"Send him down," cried a woman from the front of the crowd.

"Yeah, lock him up."

"Send him where?" asked Crowe. "To prison? So you can keep paying for him with your hard-earned taxes. Is that what you really want?"

The room quietened once more.

"No, I didn't think so," said Crowe.

In the operations room, Jackson calmly addressed his team. "This is it. Be ready to-"

"I've lost my connection," said Reg. There was a sudden urgency in his usually calm voice.

"You've what?" asked Jackson.

"I can't get on. I'm being kicked out of the firewall."

"Well, can't you get back on?"

"I'm trying but-"

"But what?" cried Jackson. "You know what comes next, don't you?"

"Of course I know what comes next," snapped Reg. "But we're being attacked ourselves. He must have bots. It's a denial of service attack."

"Now is not the time to play games, Tenant."

"He's right, sir," said the girl beside Reg. "We have a dedicated line, and it's as much as I can do to fend off the attacks. They're coming from everywhere."

A woman's scream brought the focus back to the event, and all eyes returned to the live feed from the dinner.

Bernard stood in the centre of the stage with a gun in his hand. He pulled the cocking lever back and let the mechanism collect a round from the magazine. Then he placed the weapon against his temple.

CHAPTER THIRTY

The startled audience winced as Angie Turvey screamed at her husband from behind Crowe. The shrill high pitch caused the speakers to crackle, and Crowe spun in his seat.

"That's right Bernie, you get the idea," said Crowe, turning back to the screen. "Is there anything you'd like to say to Angie before you go?"

"Mummy," yelled Anya from the couch. "Mummy, I'm scared."

Angie ignored her daughter and yelled at the laptop. "Bernie, *no*."

Bernard Turvey's face was bright red. His sunken eyes were like black holes, as the adrenaline, fear and horror of the past few days approached its climax.

"Angie," he called, his throat thick with shame, "Angie, I'm so sorry. I never meant for this."

Angie pulled at her restraints and Julie's body rocked limply with her attempts. "Don't do it, Bernie. Please, don't do it."

"I don't have a choice, baby," replied Bernard. His hand shook with the weapon, and he forced the muzzle into his head. "There's no way back from this."

Two armed policemen approached the stage, but Crowe saw them at the edge of the screen and called them off.

"Baby, no," screamed Angie. Her knees gave way, and she fell against her bindings. Julie's head bounced softly against her naked chest.

"Mummy." Floods of tears streamed from Anya's eyes as she looked at her mother's stress. Her voice trailed off to a high-pitched whine, and then loud, uncontrollable crying.

"Angie, I'm sorry," said Bernard. "I have to do this. For you." He broke and sobbed loudly. The stress of the situation had blinded him to the audience. He pulled at his hair with his free hand, and jerked his head into his chest, then with a loud, agitated groan, he straightened.

"I'm sorry, baby," said Angie. "I'm sorry I put you through hell. I'm sorry I wasn't a better wife. We can work it out. I understand. I don't care what you did, just put the gun down."

"Bernie?" said Crowe, interjecting. "You know what you need to do, don't you?"

Bernard was sobbing uncontrollably now, along with his daughter who had her face buried in the cushions of the couch, unable to move.

"Bernie, are you ignoring me?" said Crowe coldly.

"You sick son of a bitch," replied Bernard.

"Pull the trigger, Bernie."

"No, baby, no," yelled Angie. "We can move away. We can start again."

It was at that moment that Crowe pulled his own handgun from his waistband, and moved from the laptop toward Angie.

The crowd was deathly silent. Women cried and turned away. The armed police all looked for direction from a man at the edge of the room, who held one hand up to halt them and, with the other hand, held his finger to his ear, talking to his own bosses on his ear-piece.

Crowe stood behind Angie, whose face was buried behind Julie's cold and stiffening legs. He grabbed a handful of hair and pulled her head back, turning her face to the laptop.

"Look at him," he said. "I want you to watch him."

"Get your hands off her, you coward," snarled Bernard, aggression cutting through the fear.

"Bernie," wailed Angie in a long hopeless whimper. "I love you, Bernie. I always did, and I always will."

"Now, damn it," snapped Crowe. "Pull the God damned trigger."

The audience's eyes flicked back to Turvey in anticipation.

Bernard's entire arm shook involuntarily. The gun hit his head each time until he pressed it firmly into his skull again.

"Do it, Turvey," shouted Crowe. "Or I'll do it."

Bernard's arm folded firmly as if all the effort it took him to pull the trigger came from his shoulder.

Crowe slammed his handgun into the side of Angie's head, and she crumpled along with Julie's body, unconscious. He stepped across the room and grabbed the back of Anya's top with his free hand.

Melody launched herself on the couch to stop him, but Anya's legs were already in the air as he hoisted her over the back of the chair to stand beside her unconscious mother. She didn't scream. She was visibly crying, but she didn't whimper. Anya just stared at her mother's face, as if looking up at her father on the screen would somehow make it worse.

"Now, Bernie, would you care to re-think that?" said Crowe.

"Anya," said Bernard. His desperate voice shook Anya from her gaze, and she looked up at him as if guilty of some childish action. "Anya, it's me, baby. Everything's going to be okay. I promise you. Are you hurt?"

Anya stared at him on the screen with the audience behind him.

"Anya, baby, are you hurt?

She shook her head slowly then lowered it again.

"That's it, baby. I want you to look away. Close your eyes and remember the day we had on the beach. You remember that, don't you? Don't you baby? The house at the beach. Remember how we swam and all the little fishes came to us?"

The girl looked up at the screen again and nodded.

"Good, I want you to close your eyes, and think of that day. Can you do that?"

The girl's face crumpled into a loud sob, and she shook her head. "No, Daddy, I'm scared."

"It's okay. You don't need to be scared, baby. You can do this. You're a big girl now, aren't you?"

Her wide eyes glistened on the large screen above Bernard, and a woman in the audience called out to Crowe, "Take her away, you monster. She can't see this."

Crowe sensed the audience's growing impatience. "Bernard, you have precisely ten seconds to say goodbye to your daughter. Or I'll finish them both."

"Anya, baby, close your eyes. Please just close your eyes, okay? I love you baby, more than anything in the world. Please just close your eyes, and I'll be with you forever. Wherever you go, I'll be by your side, baby. Okay?"

The girl nodded at the screen.

"Okay, are you ready to close your eyes?" asked Bernard. His voice trembled as he said goodbye to his daughter.

She nodded once more.

"Okay, baby. I love you, remember that."

Anya closed her eyes.

Bernard raised the gun to his head for the last time.

"Okay, Turvey," began Crowe, "the world has seen who you really are. The evidence is irrefutable." He smiled cruelly at the camera and placed the gun behind Anya's head. "Pull the trigger, Bernie."

Bernard's face was a mess of sweat, tears and emotion. His hand quivered for all to see, so he moved the gun to his mouth and tilted his head back. The packed hall was as silent as it could be.

"*Do it,*" shouted Crowe. He opened his foul mouth once more. But instead of another onslaught of bitter, cold words, a trickle of blood ran across his lower lip and dribbled onto his chin. His eyes opened wide. Then slowly, and as if it grew from deep inside him, the shiny point of a nine-inch carving knife emerged from his mouth.

CHAPTER THIRTY-ONE

Confusion spread throughout the audience, and people stood as if sitting somehow obscured the truth behind the unbelievable turn of events.

The man in black twisted the blade to the right with a crunch of gristle and bone. As the life slipped out of Caesar Crowe's body, and gravity took effect, he slipped slowly off the blade and crumpled to the floor at the newcomer's feet. The shadow stood tall over Caesar's body, emotionless, a dark silhouette against the now-moonlit curtains. He remained motionless for what seemed like an eternity, but the struggles of the woman on the couch caught his eye, and he turned the blade on her. He stepped over Caesar Crowe and slit the tape that bound the woman. The crowd sighed collectively, a deep sigh of relief. The trauma was over.

The woman pulled her wrists free, flung her arms around the stranger, and kissed him hard on the mouth. This time, chairs scraped against the floor, and the noise in the room grew from the hushed silence of the shocked but captivated audience to a deafening roar of applause and cheers. Even the media presenters who had also been enthralled by the night's events clapped.

She pulled away and took the blade from the man in black. After cutting her own ankle restraints, she began to free the little girl and her mother, who had to be calmed down as she frantically tore herself away from the corpse. The second she was free, she reached down and scooped up her daughter. She then sat on the couch with the girl on her lap and began rocking gently back and forth, smoothing the child's hair.

The stage was rushed by armed guards, who took the weapon from Bernard Turvey and held him upright as his knees gave way. They dragged the ruined man away, and the ever-professional Master of Ceremonies took to the stage in an attempt to control the riot of people trying to leave the hall.

A dark-haired man remained seated, while others fought to leave. He stared coldly at the large screen that, by now, showed the woman pulling a blanket around Mrs Turvey and the little girl and lowering herself to her knees to console the distraught pair. The man, in his late forties with a crooked nose and cleft lip, stood, straightened his bow tie, downed the remains of his drink, and then joined the queue of people at the doors.

CHAPTER THIRTY-TWO

Jackson fell back into the chair that was behind him. The room full of operatives had not cheered, had not clapped; they hadn't broken a smile. The sequence of events that had played out so dramatically in front of theirs, and a million other people's eyes, had merely altered the plan and set a new objective.

Melody's voice, controlled and calm, began to ring loud and clear through the speaker beside Reg.

"Reg, do you copy?" she asked.

Reg gave a tight smile at the girl, Jess, who sat beside him, and then pushed the push-to-talk button on the microphone. "Loud and clear, Melody, loud and clear. It's never been so good to hear your voice."

Melody waited a few seconds, and then replied, "Yeah, it was getting close there for a minute."

"Okay, you sound like you have everything under control there. But I need you to help me with something."

"Sure," said Melody. "What do I need to do?"

"Was he on a laptop? Was that where the video feed was coming from?"

"Yeah, it's right here. You need me to shut it down?"

"No," said Reg, a little sharper than he needed. "Are there any other programmes running on it?"

Melody was quiet then she said, "Not much. But wait, there's a remote session. Looks like a black box with red and blue lines of code or something."

"That's it," said Reg. "That's what we need to stop."

"I just closed the black box," said Melody. "Did that work?"

Reg glanced up at his screen then across at Jess, who nodded with a smile and mouthed the words. "We're back online."

"You did it," said Reg. "Good work. You may want to shut the laptop down; you still have a pretty large audience."

Melody turned the camera off and was about to shut the laptop down when Reg hit the push-to-talk button again. "Melody, are you still there?"

"Of course, you're in my ear," she replied.

"We may have a bit of a problem," said Reg.

The sentence roused Jackson from his daze. He sat up and stared across at Reg who was looking worriedly at Jess.

"Are you sure no other programmes were running?" asked Reg.

"Of course I'm sure," said Melody.

"Well, don't make yourselves too comfy there," continued Reg. "I think you just set the timer on the bomb."

CHAPTER THIRTY-THREE

"How do you know?" asked Melody. "How long do we have?"

Harvey sensed the sudden urgency in Melody's voice. "What's wrong?"

Melody looked across the room to where Harvey had begun to drag Crowe's body beside Omar's. "Reg thinks we just triggered the timer on the bomb."

"There's a timer?" he asked.

"Here's what I see," began Reg. "It looks like there was a constant exchange of traffic between the laptop and another device. It's not uncommon. They're called keep-alives. They're normally set to ping one another at set intervals to make sure the other is still alive. However, if for some reason, one of the devices fail, the one that's still alive can be programmed to carry out a certain function, such as search for the device, shutdown, or-"

"Detonate?" said Melody.

Harvey heard only Melody's side of the conversation and leaned on the back of the couch with his arms folded. "Can you get Reg up on the screen?" he asked.

Melody fired the laptop back up, and Reg continued to talk.

"It looks like when we shut the program down, the keep alive was met with a final command. One word. Begins with D."

"Hey Reg, are you able to get on the laptop so we can all talk?" said Melody.

"Yeah sure, I'm just getting on now," he replied.

A few moments later, Reg's face appeared on the screen. Melody saw that he was sat in his usual position with his feet up under the desk, a can of soft drink in front of him and his keyboard on his lap.

"Good evening, Dubai," said Reg.

"Reg how do we stop this?" asked Melody.

"We've no way of knowing where it is," said Reg. "It could be in the house. It could be anywhere."

"What about his phone?" said Harvey. "If we gave you his phone, could you trace where it's been?"

Reg thought on it. "I can only see where it was when it made calls. The interaction would be logged. So as long as he made a call somewhere close."

Harvey began to rifle through Crowe's pockets and retrieved his phone.

"It's here. What do you need us to do, Reg?" said Harvey.

"Pull the SIM out. What's the number?"

Harvey read the printed number on the SIM card out loud and waited for Reg's confirmation.

"Okay, here we go," said Reg. "It's a burner, but it's loaded with data. And hey, look." Reg caught the attention of Jess beside him, and the two tech gurus smiled and high-fived.

"Are you guys celebrating?" asked Melody.

"Sorry, Melody," said Reg. "But Jess here has been working on a program that dissects the historical data saved in the maps function inside the search engine."

"That's awesome. But how does that help us?" asked Harvey.

"Well, if I just share my screen with you both." Reg clicked his mouse a few times, and the camera view of London was replaced with a live view of Reg's screen. It displayed a map of Dubai. "Do you see all these little dots here that form a long red line?" asked Reg.

"Yeah, we see them," said Melody.

"Okay, so in GPS talk, they're called-"

"Way-points," finished Melody. "That's Crowe's movements. He doesn't know his way around Dubai, so he used the maps app on his phone."

"All the data we need is here," said Reg.

"So where's the bomb?" asked Harvey. "It looks like he's been all over the city."

"It looks like he has, but in most cases, he was just passing through," said Reg.

"Where has he spent the most time?" asked Melody.

"Hi, Melody, Jess here," began Jess. "I hope you don't mind me jumping in on this?"

"Hi Jess, you do what you need to do. Just find us that bomb."

"Well, I can't find you the bomb itself, but I can show you this. You see this dot here?" Jess circled the dot on the map that represented the house on the Palm Jumeirah.

"Yeah, sure," said Melody.

"Now watch. If you click on the way-point, you can see that he was there for forty-eight hours."

"That makes sense," said Melody.

"Okay, so now let's go all the way over here." Jess dragged the mouse across the screen, away from the blue that represented the ocean, past the mass of buildings that represented the city, and into the flat yellow space that represented the desert. A thin trail of way-points led from the Turvey house and meandered into the desert, stopping at an area on the map that looked to be the very edge of civilisation. The buildings came to a halt with wild desert behind them. The dot was in the centre of a large walled villa, on a street with other large walled villas.

"I know that place," said Melody.

"What?" said Reg. "How?"

"Remember the safe house I had to go to before I came here?" asked Melody. "I had to meet a guy called Bob."

"Yes, but that was an operative," said Reg. "Why would he-"

"Well," said Melody, "either Crowe wasn't who we thought he was, or Bob isn't who he says he is."

"We do have one more problem," said Jess.

"Go ahead, Jess," said Harvey.

"It looks like when you woke up Crowe's phone, it had a message waiting to send."

"Okay, so what?" said Harvey.

"Well now it's sent," replied Jess, matter-of-factly.

"So what did it say?" asked Melody.

"It's a distress call," said Jess, "to the Dubai police."

CHAPTER THIRTY-FOUR

Jackson slipped out of the operations room and took the fire escape stairs to the next floor. He found the old man in his office staring out the window with his chin resting on his joined fingers.

"Did you see it?" asked Jackson.

"I doubt anyone with a TV or a laptop in the UK missed it, Jackson," replied the old man. "It'll probably get an award for the highest rankings in history. Hostages, a live suicide attempt and a murder, that's about as good as it gets."

"It was all part of your plan, wasn't it?"

"You catch on quick, Jackson."

"What about the bomb?"

"Not part of the plan," replied the old man.

"It could destroy us."

"It probably will destroy us. So why aren't you downstairs finding it?"

"I can't see your angle on this. It's all just a game to you, isn't it?"

The old man span in his seat slowly to face Jackson. "If this is a game, Jackson, then I'm happy to say that Turvey just lost,

Crowe is out, and Stone is about to die. Not a bad result if I do say so myself."

"If that bomb goes off, sir, then we're all out," said Jackson. "Dubai will think it was us, all ties will be severed, and nearly a million Brits will be trapped in a suddenly very hostile place." Jackson stepped forward and placed his hands flat on the old man's desk. "And that's just the best-case scenario. Do you understand?"

"Jackson, firstly get your hands off my desk. Secondly, if the bomb detonates, do you think it will be me in the firing line?"

"Firing line? What are you talking about? We're talking about people's lives here."

"Answer the question, Jackson." The old man eyed him with the satisfaction of his own cunning.

"No. I doubt it," replied Jackson.

"Who do you think it will be?"

"Stone, I guess, and Mills. It'll be them who won't be coming home."

"True, but I doubt the PM will be overly excited about a relationship with the safest place in the Middle East being destroyed over an emotional ploy to rescue a man's wife and daughter without his consent. And who was it that made that decision, Jackson? Who organised the mission to rescue the Turveys? It wasn't me."

Jackson shook his head in disbelief.

"So will he come after me?" asked the old man rhetorically. "I don't think so."

"You're framing me?" said Jackson. "After all this, it's me who's going to carry this?"

"Framing is such a negative word, Jackson," said the old man. "I prefer to call it schooling."

"Are you insane? This is international relationships we're

talking about here. We're not in the playground arguing over who broke a window."

"I know precisely what we're talking about, and it is what you make it. If you want to make it international, here." The old man slid the desk phone across the shiny, wooden surface. "Use this, call the PM. I have his number if you want it. But if you want to make it in this world, Jackson, stop being so emotional, get yourself downstairs and lead." The old man sat back in his chair. "Oh, and as for best-case scenario, I'll tell you exactly what you should be hoping for. Stone finds the bomb before it detonates. The police find Stone and nail him for murder. The Dubai government remain totally unaware of the bomb and any involvement with British MI6."

Jackson stared disbelievingly at the old man. He couldn't believe that after all he had done to climb the ladder, the risks he had taken with his life, the arses he had kissed, and the crap he had to put up with, he was given a choice, and neither option was good. He could either get Stone and Mills out, potentially devastate the ties between the UAE and the UK and destroy his career, or he could play the game.

"You know what to do, Jackson," said the old man. "Do it well, and you might even find yourself in Turvey's office. The seat is still warm, I hear."

CHAPTER THIRTY-FIVE

"We need to go," said Melody. "Now."

"Hold on," said Reg over the webcam. "Take the laptop with you. It will tie the murder directly to the UK."

Harvey dug through Crowe's pockets again and found the car keys he'd heard rattling earlier. He glanced across at Melody and, with an unspoken gesture, told her they were taking the car. He walked calmly toward the garage.

"Get me on the comms, Reg," said Melody as she slammed the lid of the laptop and followed Harvey out of the room.

Melody stopped and caught Angie's attention. "Hey, are you coming?"

Angie glanced up with tired eyes and pulled the blanket around her. She shook her head. "No. No, I think we'll stay."

"Are you going to be okay?" asked Melody. "The police are-"

"On their way," finished Angie. "Yes, I know."

"What are you going to tell them?"

Angie cast her eyes to the floor, as memories of the previous few days ran through her mind. "We came into the house and were taken hostage," she replied. "It's the truth."

"What about these guys?" asked Melody, gesturing at the two dead men.

"We were saved." Angie looked up at Melody once more. "It's Melody, right?"

Melody nodded softly.

"Go, Melody, get away from this place. You don't know what they'll do if they catch you. I'll handle it. I always do."

Melody began to say something but stopped herself. Instead, she turned and followed Harvey out the door.

"Melody," called Angie.

Melody stopped once more and turned to face the woman, who looked down at her sleeping daughter in her arms.

"Thank you," said Angie. "For everything."

Melody smiled, then turned and left the room.

Harvey stepped into the garage and found a little blue Porsche beside a BMW SUV. The key fob had a Porsche symbol on, so he hit the unlock button and the door locks popped open. Melody climbed into the passenger seat beside Harvey, as he hit the button for the garage door to open.

The dark night was giving way to a fresh new day, and traces of reds and oranges began to show between the high-rise buildings on the mainland. Harvey drove steadily, not wanting to catch anybody's attention. The road off the Palm Jumeirah was already growing busy. Residents of the apartment blocks that lined the trunk of the Palm were beginning their morning commute.

The little Porsche seemed to be at home among the expensive SUVs and sports cars on the road. Harvey soon found that driving slowly and carefully was getting him nowhere. So as soon they reached the mainland, he pulled out into the fast lane and joined the speeding motorists.

Melody held the tiny button on her ear-piece for a few seconds until she heard the beeps indicating that the channel was closed. Communication with Reg would now require her to push the little button, but she wanted to talk to Harvey.

"What are you doing?" asked Melody.

"Blending in," replied Harvey. "Are you going to tell me where we're going?"

"I didn't mean the driving, Harvey," snapped Melody. "I meant what are you doing here?"

Harvey didn't reply.

"Don't play the silent card with me, Harvey. How did you find out where I was?"

"Intuition," said Harvey with a smile.

"You followed me?" she asked. "Is that it? Why? Did you think I couldn't handle it anymore?"

Harvey didn't reply.

"You told me to go, remember? I could have just left it for someone else."

"It's what you wanted," said Harvey. "I was holding you back."

"That's *my* choice," Melody yelled. "It's not your choice to make." She lowered her voice and spoke softly. "You gave me an ultimatum. How do you think that makes me feel?"

"How do you think you'd have felt if you hadn't come and helped?" said Harvey. "Do you honestly think that we'd still be in France playing happy families? You'd have spent the past two days regretting it and probably ended up resenting me. You needed a kick start, so-"

"So you kicked me?" finished Melody.

"Yeah, and I'd do the same again if I had the choice."

"I'm not the type of girl that appreciates being kicked, Harvey. You can't just tell me to go and then show up three thousand miles away. It doesn't work like that."

Harvey dropped the car into third gear, popped the clutch, and carved across the four-lane highway onto the shoulder. Cars honked their horns and swerved to miss them, but Harvey was unmovable.

He slammed on the brakes and the little sports car slid to a stop.

"I don't know what I'm doing, Melody," he began. His voice was raised, but he didn't shout. Harvey never shouted. "I've never done this, I've never felt like this, and I've never wanted someone so badly in all my life." He sat back in his seat and faced the front. "If I did it wrong, then so what, I did it wrong. But at least I did something. And if there's a next time, you know what? I'll probably get it wrong again, but I'll still try."

Melody leaned across the small centre console and put her hand on his cheek. Then she kissed him. Harvey returned the kiss and then pulled her away. He just stared at her.

"You didn't do too badly," said Melody. "Now let's go and stop this bomb."

CHAPTER THIRTY-SIX

"There you are. I thought we'd lost you there for a while," said Reg when Melody opened up the channel on her ear-piece again. Jess saw the smile on his face when Melody's voice came through the speaker.

"Technical hitch, Reg," said Melody. "We're back, so tell us where to go." Her voice was tinny and weak over the satellite comms, but she was recognisable.

"Okay, so we've got two choices," said Reg. "The villa in the desert is a twenty-mile drive. Jess pulled up the data, and it looks like Crowe spent a few days there before the Turvey house."

"Have you run a background check on the Bob guy?" asked Melody. "Is he in on this? Is he dirty?"

"I'm waiting for Jackson to get back. He got the contact from higher up. There's a chain of command here, you know?"

"You mean there's more red tape?" asked Melody.

"Oodles of it," replied Reg.

"You said we had two choices. Where else did Crowe go?" asked Melody.

"Well, he's certainly been sightseeing," replied Reg.

"So it could be anywhere?" said Melody.

"My money is on Dubai Mall," said Reg. "It's a huge tourist attraction."

"That's a big mall," replied Melody. "Are we looking for a needle here?"

"Yeah, it's a small needle in a very large haystack. But it's the safest bet."

"How do we know he wasn't shopping or meeting someone?"

"Well, unless he was shopping for six hours."

"Six hours?" said Melody. "What was he doing there for six hours?"

"Planting a bomb probably," said Reg. "But hey, I've been thinking."

Jess slapped his arm suddenly and gave him a stern look.

"Okay, Jess and I have been think-"

"Jess and you?" said Melody, grinning over at Harvey who smirked back. "Have you found your match, Reggie?"

Reg blushed, and Jess turned back to her screen, too embarrassed to face Reg.

"Anyway," Reg continued, "we were thinking that wherever he placed the device would need a fairly strong signal for the keep-alives. He wouldn't risk it detonating accidentally while he was still in the country. He's a British citizen. He'd be locked in, just as you would be and all the other Brits."

"So that rules out the basement parking, and probably the lower floors as well," said Melody.

"Agreed. But it would also need to be small enough to carry in a pack or something. Security is tight. You can't just drive in with a delivery, they're booked in advance. We did the research."

"Okay, so it's backpack size?" asked Melody.

"Has to be," said Reg. "But also, the mall is spotless. It's hit by an army of cleaners every night. They'd find a backpack lying around easily."

"So what is it? In a shop?"

"We don't know. But we're looking for somewhere on the upper floors, somewhere accessible by the public, and somewhere a small backpack could be hidden."

"Not much to go on, Reg."

"Isn't that always the case?" he replied.

"Any idea when this thing is supposed to go off?" asked Melody.

"No clue. But we do know that the mall opens to the public at ten in the morning. So you have four hours to get yourselves in there."

"I just found something," said Jess.

Reg span back to face her.

"Shoot, Jess. What did you find?"

"Something is happening in the mall this morning. It's on the website."

"Like what?" asked Melody. "What's the connection?"

"Someone important is visiting," said Jess, reading off the website. "Someone called Sheikha Alia bin something."

"Sheikha what?" replied Melody. "You *do* know what a Sheikha is, right?"

Jess looked at Reg, who looked equally as confused. Reg typed the name into a search browser.

"Oh God," he said.

"What?" asked Jess? "Who is it?"

"It's one of the Sheik's daughters."

Harvey and Melody ditched the Porsche on the seventh floor of the mall car park and walked swiftly but calmly to the entrance. The glass doors slid back silently, and the pair were hit with sandalwood-perfumed air conditioning in the lobby. Another set of glass doors opened, and they stepped into the huge expanse of the mall. The stores that ran left and right were all closed. A huge atrium filled the centre of the space.

Melody spoke quietly to Reg. "Hey, this place is huge. Have we got any idea at all where to look?"

Reg's tinny voice came back, calm as ever. "Not as yet, Melody. We're looking here, but we don't have much to go on."

"Okay, keep looking," said Melody, shaking her head at Harvey. "We're going to split up, see if we can get into the maintenance areas."

"Splitting up is fine, Melody," said Reg. "But we ran some calculations, and a rucksack full of explosives would need to be fairly close to its target. The further away from the public space, the less effective it will be."

"Yeah, copy that. The stores are all closed. The only things open are the coffee shops, I guess so the store workers can get a coffee before work."

Melody joined Harvey, who was leaning against the handrail of the atrium, looking down at the six floors of shops below.

"Why here?" asked Harvey.

"Why not? It's a public place, lots of damage."

"Yeah but look around. There's nowhere to hide it," replied Harvey.

"Reg said that a rucksack full of explosives would need to be fairly close to its target to be effective. The staff areas behind the scenes would be too far away to do much damage. If the target is the Sheikha, she wouldn't go behind the scenes, I'm guessing."

"So why here?" Harvey asked again.

"Because she's shopping I guess," said Melody.

"And is it usually made public knowledge when somebody like the Sheikha goes shopping?"

Melody thought on what Harvey said. "No, probably not. What are you getting at?"

"I don't know. It just seems odd to me that Crowe knew in advance about a shopping trip."

Melody turned away and closed her eyes, focusing on the issue. The what, why and where didn't add up. As she turned away and took a step, a tiny rush of wind lifted her hair slightly, along with the familiar sound of a bullet rushing past.

"Down," she said and hurled herself to the floor. Harvey ducked down and slid away from the glass handrail.

"Somebody's on to us," she called as she slid herself over to Harvey.

A quick look at the ceiling far behind them told Harvey all he needed to know.

"Three things. He's got a silencer, he's below us, and he's not a cop."

Melody glanced behind them and found the damaged plasterboard ceiling. Gypsum powder still fell lightly from the impact. Harvey chanced raising his head to get an idea of the shooter's position. He saw nothing and no shots were fired.

"He's down there somewhere," said Harvey, "waiting for the perfect shot."

Reg's voice came through, broken and distorted. "You want the good news or the bad news?"

"I'm lying on the floor being shot at," said Melody, "I'll take the bad news. Give me something to look forward to."

There was a short delay. "Sheikha Alia is opening a chain of designer handbag stores, and the one in the mall where you are is apparently the flagship store. It's being opened today at ten am."

"Oh great," replied Melody. "So we can assume the bomb is set to detonate at that time too. What's the good news?"

"There's twenty-five percent off for the first ten customers of the day."

"It's a bad time for jokes, Reg. We've got about three hours to find this bomb and being shot at is not helping."

"Okay, my bad. But what if I told you that there's a long corridor beside a massive electronics store on level six?"

"How did-"

"Jess is on the CCTV system. We can't see the name of the store, the camera is at a funny angle, but we can see movement down there."

"Reg, you're a star," said Melody. Catching Harvey's attention, she explained, "Sixth floor, next to an electronics store. The Sheikha is opening the flagship store of her new designer handbag chain this morning."

"That's why the bomb is here then," said Harvey. "That's how Crowe knew the Sheikha would be here."

"How about I stay up here and keep him occupied, and you

go down and finish him?" said Melody. "There's a fire escape stairwell behind us."

"Saving your backside again, right?" said Harvey.

"You can always stay here and let him shoot at you while I go down and take him out."

"Choices, choices," replied Harvey, as he slid across the tiled floor towards the fire escape.

Melody popped her head up and peered through the glass to try to find the shooter. No shots were fired. She moved along to a large pillar, periodically popping her head up to let the shooter know she was still there.

"Melody," said Reg, "you might have a little problem."

"Go for it, Reg," said Melody. "What on earth could go wrong now?"

"There are two more men heading your way."

Jackson stepped back into the operations room and took a cursory glance around to make sure everyone was working, not because he micromanaged, but because his words to Tenant had to be kept confidential. He touched Reg's shoulder and gestured at the small glass meeting room.

Reg asked Jess to keep an eye on the mall CCTV and alert Melody to the two newcomers' movements. He then followed Jackson to the fishbowl, pulled up a seat, and sat down, interlocking his fingers on the table. "This'll need to be quick, sir," he began. "Melody and Harvey have company, and we're their eyes."

Jackson looked back over his shoulder at Jess, who was flicking from screen to screen.

"Do you have an update for me? Has there been any progress?" asked Jackson calmly.

"We tracked Crowe's movements, where he'd been, where he'd spent the most time, and where a likely target might be."

"And where do you think the target is?" asked Jackson.

"It wasn't easy, sir, and right now, we have no concrete

evidence," said Reg. "But if Crowe wanted to really implicate the UK in a bombing, the target would need to be substantial."

"Agreed," said Jackson.

"One of the places he spent the most time, six hours to be precise, was the mall."

"You think he's going to maim the general public? Get them against us too?"

"No," said Reg, "well, yes, but they'll be collateral. We think he was targeting a Sheikha, the daughter of some Sheik." Reg heard how ridiculous and exaggerated the words sounded when they left his mouth. "I know it sounds far-fetched, sir, but the evidence is stacking up."

"The Sheikha will be in the mall?" asked Jackson. "And how would Crowe have known that?"

"She's opening a chain of stores, designer stuff. This one is the flagship store and she's opening it today. It's in the media, has been for two weeks."

"Okay, good work. So where do you think the bomb is?" asked Jackson.

"The store itself. She'll be right outside."

"In range?"

"Exactly, sir."

"Tenant, I have to tell you something. But it goes no further than this room."

Reg didn't reply. He just raised his eyebrows, waiting for Jackson to deliver the blow.

"I've been to see the old man," said Jackson.

"So far, nobody knows about this, sir. If he's worried about-"

"He's not worried about anything, Tenant. It's me that needs to be worried."

"How come?" asked Reg, leaning forward in his seat. "I don't see how this affects you."

"I've been put in a position, Tenant. I can either get Mills and Stone out of there and hide them away, though God knows they'd be in hiding the rest of their lives..."

"Or?" asked Reg, his brow furrowing.

"Or, we give them up. Let Dubai arrest them, kill them, whatever comes first. Deny all knowledge of them and avert the whole situation."

Reg was stunned. "Give them up? They're-"

"Expendable. It was the plan all along. The old man wanted Stone out of the picture, and he isn't too fussed if Mills goes with him. They're just pawns to him."

"Pawns? I don't see that we have any option, sir," said Reg. "We get them out."

"And the bomb?" asked Jackson.

Right then, Jess stuck her head in the room. "Sorry to interrupt. Reg, we have a problem."

"Do you want to tell me why I just had the Prime Minister on the phone, asking me why we're monitoring Dubai traffic and private CCTV cameras?"

Jackson pulled his phone from his ear, closed his eyes, took a deep breath then lied.

"We're not, sir. I made it clear that the team were not to use intrusion methods. They know how sensitive the situation is."

"Sounds like somebody didn't understand you, Jackson," said the old man. "Apparently, some Dubai official just issued a formal warning. He told us to cease and desist."

"Cease and desist? What is this, a war?"

"It damn well will be, Jackson, if you don't get your team in line."

The old man hung up, and Jackson stepped out of the fishbowl.

"What's the problem, Tenant?" he asked.

"We got a trace from Dubai. They know we're on their systems. They kicked us off twice, but we found a back door."

"Are you still on there?"

"Officially, sir?"

"Tell me straight, Tenant," said Jackson. "Now is not the time for fluff."

"We got kicked off, so we rerouted the connection to make it look like we're someone else. Hopefully, by the time they figure it out, we'll be out of there."

"Should I ask who we're masquerading as?"

"Probably best not to, sir. Least said, soonest mended, and all that."

Jackson shook his head in disbelief. "You're going to start World War Three, Tenant," he hissed.

"Sir, if we can't see what's going on in the mall, we could lose Melody and Harvey."

"Tenant, if you get caught on their systems, we'll lose a lot more than two bloody operatives."

"Understood, sir," said Reg. "But there's one thing I don't get."

"Go on," said Jackson.

"See the two guys here," Reg pointed to two men dressed in casual clothes. Both men were walking either side of the atrium, closing in on Melody's position.

"Yeah, I see them," said Jackson. "Who are they? Does she know they're coming?"

"I just told her. But, well, sir, there's a third, and he's been shooting at Melody and Harvey."

"Who are they? Do we know yet?"

"They're clearly not local, but they are tanned," said Reg. "Also, we showed Melody a house, right out in the desert. It was where Crowe had been staying."

"So what?" said Jackson, confused as to how the information was relevant.

"She said she'd been there already. It was where she met that Bob guy."

"Bob? The operative?"

"So he *is* an operative then?" asked Reg.

"Officially?" said Jackson.

"I'll take that as a yes, then," said Reg. "You think he's dirty?"

Jackson lowered himself onto one knee to the side of Reg and spoke very quietly. "I think there's a lot more at play here than we know about. Tell me, Tenant, do you trust Jess?" he asked.

Reg's eyes widened. "Of course. She's like a third hand for me right now."

"I need her to do some digging for me."

CHAPTER FORTY

The last thing the sniper felt were Harvey's hands gripping the side of his head and then snatching it to one side. Harvey had run down the fire escape and seen the man lying prone in the narrow alleyway designed as both a fire escape and entrance to the rear of the stores. A door led off from the main alley into an even narrower corridor, painted lime green with six-inch red pipes fixed to the ceiling.

Harvey dragged the body through the door and into the service corridor. He heaved the man into a large plastic bin on wheels and covered him with a few black rubbish bags.

It was as he closed the lid and readied himself to go back out to get Melody that something he'd seen caught up with his racing mind. He turned back and reopened the lid of the bin to confirm exactly what he'd seen. Inside was loose trash, as well as bags of used packaging, the same as any other bin in any other mall. There was a flattened cardboard box, and printed on the side was the word, 'Princess.' Then beside it was, what Harvey guessed to be, the Arabic equivalent in a long swirling font to the right of the English spelling.

He checked the doors either side of the bin. One was the

electronics store, but the other had the sign removed. He tried the door. It was locked. There were no cameras along the corridor so Harvey tested the top and bottom of the door, pushing and feeling for where the locks were. If the door was the main exit, and the actual store was locked from the inside, then it could be the only way in. He gave a shove with his shoulder and felt the door give, but it didn't open. So he stepped back, and with all his strength, kicked out at the door. The heel of his foot slammed into the wood beside the lock and splintered the frame. One more kick and the door popped open and banged against the wall behind.

Harvey checked the ceiling corners for cameras or alarms and saw nothing. He stepped inside.

The warning Reg had given Melody had been timely. As the two men closed in on her, one from either side, she checked around and had no escape except one. Melody was out of sight behind one of six columns that bordered the circular atrium. She watched from her spot on the floor as the two men walked slowly and casually toward her. As soon as they were both behind a column, she quietly got to her feet, pulled herself over the handrail, and lowered herself down, hanging over the seven-floor drop with her fingers barely gripping the smooth tiled floor above.

It seemed like an eternity until the two men met where she had been lying, and spoke in clear English.

"What the-?" said the first man.

"Where did she go?" said the second.

"I didn't see anything," said the first man. "Okay, keep cool. She's got to be around somewhere. Keep your gun holstered unless you have to. The last thing we need is the plod turning up."

"She was just here, Jim," said the second man. "Try the fire exit. I'll stay here and keep an eye out."

Melody's arms began to tremble with her weight. She edged across to get her fingers into a better position and swung her legs toward the column to take some of her weight. The smooth concrete upright had no footholds, but the grip on her boots eased her hands enough to get some strength back.

Pulling up into a chin-up position, she chanced a look back through the glass. The man had his back to her and was just one metre from the handrail. She saw the fire escape door in the distance and knew she had to take the chance. Melody quietly swung her leg up then switched her hands from the tiled floor to the underside of the smooth glass. She waited to make sure the man hadn't heard her then pulled herself up behind him. Holding the glass with one hand, with the other, she slowly removed her belt, made a loop, and quickly slipped it over the man's head, pulling back with all her weight.

The man was caught off guard and slammed into the glass handrail. His neck was pulled back at a horrific angle. Melody kept her weight on the belt. With her free hand, she reached over, grabbed the front of the man's belt and heaved him backwards over the top of the glass.

She watched him fall. His face twisted in fear at his futile attempts to grip something, anything. Less than two seconds later, he was seven floors down with two broken legs, a smashed pelvis, a broken back and a crushed skull. It took three more seconds for him to die.

Melody pulled herself back over the glass handrail and looked down to the sixth floor in time to see the first guy heading towards the sniper, where Harvey would be.

More store employees had begun to file into the mall. It was no longer an empty space, and pretty soon someone would find the body seven floors below. She ran to the fire escape and down the stairs three at a time, then stopped at the door to the sixth floor. Peering through the window, she saw the back of the man on the far side of the mall, heading into the alleyway where the sniper had been. Two shops down from the alleyway, she saw what they had been looking for, a brand new shop with Princess written in glittery font like it had been hand-scrawled. Beside it was the Arabic translation in the same style. The man disappeared through a door to the right, so Melody took her chance.

She bumped into an Asian girl as soon as she stepped into the mall. Apologising, she turned and made her to the alleyway. Her watch said seven forty-five. The shops were all still closed, but the staff were growing in numbers. Various uniforms, various nationalities. As casually as she could, Melody scanned the people, looking for somebody out of place. But she saw no-one.

Reg's voice came loud and clear through her ear-piece. "Melody, are you there?"

"Not a good time, Reg. What's up?"

"Well, if you look up to your right, you'll see the camera I'm looking through, and luckily for you, I saw everything and managed to stop recording."

"Lucky for me, not so lucky for the fella I just threw off the seventh floor."

"It's not all good news, Melody," said Reg, with caution in his voice. "I'd say you have about five seconds to get out of sight."

Melody stopped and turned around instinctively. "Why?"

A scream, loud and piercing, filled the atrium.

There was no need to walk quietly along the narrow service corridor, Melody heard the sounds of the two men fighting before she'd even opened the ruined door. It opened up into the backroom of the Princess store, and the first thing Melody saw was Harvey smashing a fire extinguisher into the man's face.

The shelves that had been neatly fixed to the wall gave way under the man's weight, and he crumpled to the floor.

"We've got about two minutes to get out of here," said Melody.

Harvey stood poised with the extinguisher in his hand and saw the look of urgency on Melody's face.

"What did you do?" he asked.

"Nothing you wouldn't have done," said Melody defensively.

"Just messier, yeah?"

"Kinda," replied Melody.

"I'm not going anywhere until he wakes up and tells me who put him up to it."

Melody looked down at the man on the floor. He was out

cold and his bloodied nose was already swelling. "I'll search the store."

She stepped past Harvey who had bent down to tie the man's shoelaces tightly around his ankles and then together in a firm knot.

Melody worked methodically from left to right, taking down every bag and garment. She first felt for weight and then checked inside. The search took just five minutes and did nothing but prove that the bomb wasn't in the front of the shop.

"Nothing," she called, as she stepped into the back room to find Harvey stood over the man with an aerosol can and lighter in his hand.

"What are you doing?" asked Melody.

Harvey didn't reply.

"Harvey, listen to me, you can't do that."

Harvey tested the spray.

"Squirt him with the fire extinguisher," said Harvey. "Wake him up."

Melody did as instructed. She knew Harvey better than anyone and knew he would go through with it. She slapped the man and sprayed water from the extinguisher over his face until he began to come around.

"Move back," said Harvey.

Melody did as she was told.

Harvey lit the lighter and aimed the spray at the man's face. He gave it a short blast, not enough to injure him, but enough to wake him up quickly. He looked up at Harvey, dazed and confused, then realised he was bound. Harvey gave a test burn into the space beside him.

"Who?" said Harvey.

The man's throat issued a croaky and weak mumble.

Another test burn.

Another feeble murmur.

This time, Harvey didn't hold back. He gave a full second, directly into the man's face. The smell of burning hair and scorched skin instantly filled the small room. Through gritted teeth, the man bucked and rocked, but couldn't move.

"You have five seconds between each burn. If you talk, you earn yourself another five seconds," said Harvey. "Starting now."

"Go fuck yourself."

Harvey lit the lighter and counted down.

He sprayed, and the man rocked back into the wall in agony. But still, he didn't cry out. Instead, he just growled through his teeth.

"Five," said Harvey.

The man was panting, controlling the pain.

"Two."

The man prepared himself for the oncoming pain.

Harvey sprayed.

"Don't make it hard on yourself. You're not scarred yet. Let's start again," said Harvey. "Five. Who's controlling you?"

"Crowe."

"Three," said Harvey. "Crowe's dead, and I'm not stupid. One."

Harvey sprayed.

"I can do this all day," said Harvey, reaching down and pulling the man back upright from where he'd fallen onto his side.

"Who? Five."

"I don't know his name."

"Three," said Harvey. "You get your orders from someone."

"No, I-"

Harvey sprayed.

The smell of burning skin was thick in the air, so Melody closed the door as best she could. The man pulled his knees up as far as they would go and buried his face in his thighs, trying to ease the pain, trying to wipe the hot evaporating liquid from his face.

"Five. Who gives you your orders?"

"I can't say."

"Three."

"No, not again. Okay, okay it's Bob."

"You're learning," said Harvey. "You just earned a bonus round. Who's Bob?"

"I don't know. He's the team lead."

"Is that his real name?"

"No, none of us have real names. I'm Jim."

"Five," said Harvey. "Keep talking."

Jim was fighting for breath. His eyes were closed tight against the pain. "You don't know who we are. If you did, you wouldn't-"

"Wouldn't what?" asked Harvey.

Jim opened his eyes and flinched at how tender they were, but looked up at Harvey, somehow managing to pull a wry grin. "You'd run a mile if you knew."

Harvey sprayed.

"Tell me where the bomb is."

Jim's shave was scorched. The skin on his face had turned an angry red. "I've said too much already. You're going to have to kill me."

"Three," said Harvey.

"No, no more," pleaded Jim.

"One."

"Okay, okay, I'll talk."

"Five. Is the bomb in here?"

Jim shook his head.

"Three. Where did you hide it?"

"*We* didn't hide it."

"Who did? Crowe? He was at the mall all day."

"Do you honestly think he would bring it here himself?"

"So who did?"

Jim didn't reply. He just laughed, a low, painful laugh. His face was too scorched to move his jaw, but from somewhere inside him, a laugh emanated.

"Five."

"You fool."

"Three."

"Don't you see?"

"One."

"You did."

CHAPTER FORTY-THREE

"Sir, I've found something. I think we should go somewhere private," said Jess.

Jackson gave the rest of the room a cursory look and then held the door to the fishbowl open for her. "Reg, are you joining us?" he said.

Jess and Reg sat opposite Jackson, who sat with his hands clasped, ready to listen.

"I did as you asked, sir," said Jess.

"How did you get on?"

"It felt wrong, I feel like a traitor."

"What did you find, Jess?" asked Jackson, ignoring her morality.

She gave Reg a sideways glance, and then spoke clearly, but softly, as if she thought the room was bugged.

"It took some digging, but I managed to go back four weeks," began Jess. "The data is saved incrementally, with the newest data overwriting the oldest each thirtieth day of the new cycle."

Jackson nodded, as if already aware of how the disaster recovery system worked.

"First of all, I looked for patterns in his movements, and

then highlighted the anomalies. He's in here six days a week, plays golf on his day off, and goes to his local pub on the way home from work on a Thursday."

"No deviation?" asked Jackson.

"Not much. He took his wife shopping, but he stayed in the car while she went and shopped."

"What else?"

"I have a friend in facilities, sir," said Jess. "I know it was wrong of me, but I had no choice, I asked him to talk to accounts and get me the phone records."

"Mobile phones? We can get that information here."

"Landlines, sir," said Jess. "His desk phone."

"Are you going anywhere with this?" asked Jackson.

"I managed to get three months of records for his extension. Actually, I got the whole department's. I didn't want it known that I was investigating him."

"Good call. And?" said Jackson.

"Well, sir, I wondered what he does here on Saturdays. We're only in the office if an operation is live, and this is the first major operation we've had for a while."

"Let me guess, he wasn't just catching up on his paperwork?"

"No sir." Jess paused. "He was on the phone to Dubai."

"Anywhere else?"

"No, just Dubai, eight am every Saturday until four weeks ago, when he presumed the data would be overwritten. But the landlines don't work like that."

"Does anybody else know about this?" asked Jackson.

"You said to keep it quiet."

"Good. Here's what we're going to do."

CHAPTER FORTY-FOUR

"My office. Now."

The old man had a way with words, and Jackson's experience had taught him that time was running out. When men with as much power as the old man wanted something, they typically got it.

Jackson disconnected the call, nodded to Reg and Jess, and left the operations room.

He didn't knock on the old man's door, but he did take a breath when he stepped inside and saw the two well-dressed officials standing in front of the old man's desk. They both turned to watch Jackson as he closed the door, reading his movements, looking for guilt.

The old man was sitting back in his chair. His hands were placed on the leather-clad arms, showing his signet ring on one finger and his wedding ring on the other.

"Jackson, this is Mr Marsh and Mr Fowler. Are you aware of who they are?" said the old man.

"Expensive suits, well-tailored, royal crests on your cufflinks, I'd say Downing Street?"

"Close," said Marsh. "We represent the foreign office."

"Are you selling something?" asked Jackson. "I'm very busy, so-"

"Get your team out of Dubai's security systems, Mr Jackson."

Jackson cocked his head. "We're not inside Dubai's security system."

"The debacle with Mr Turvey has caused a plague of viral media. Although Dubai was never mentioned in the incident, the information has come from somewhere, and the talk of the bomb, well, naturally the Dubai Government are keen to get to the bottom of this. So imagine their surprise, Mr Jackson, when they then find an intruder on their satellite systems, monitoring the very mall where Sheikha Alia, who is a very public figure, is opening a store today."

Jackson opened his mouth to talk, but Fowler spoke first.

"We have not come here to *ask* you to get out of Dubai, Mr Jackson. We have come to inform you, personally, that you are no longer operational." Fowler handed over a brown envelope stamped with the official crest. "Following this conversation, you will leave here and inform the rest of your team that they are to go home. They'll be assigned to other duties, details of which will be disclosed once this torrid affair has been dealt with."

"You're shutting us down?" said Jackson.

"Frankly, Mr Jackson, if I were you, I would be grateful that it's Mr Marsh and I standing before you now, and not the foreign minister or the PM himself. Luckily for you, both men are far too busy trying to repair the damage you're causing. Firstly, by operating on foreign soil without instruction. Secondly, by managing an operation so poorly that the entire world saw a live kidnapping of an operative's family and the downright outrageous murder of the perpetrator. And thirdly, by allowing the announcement of a potential bomb to be broadcast to the world. How on earth you thought you would get away with it without us finding out is beyond me. But mark my words, Mr Jackson, your career in British Intelligence is finished."

"Do you have any questions?" asked Marsh.

"No, sir," said Jackson.

"Then we bid you good day, and good luck finding a new career."

The two men left the room, and the old man opened his desk drawer. He placed two glasses on the desk and began to fill them.

"I told you to leave it alone," said the old man.

"You told me to send Mills in the first place," replied Jackson.

"If you had done as I had told you, this would all be over by now."

Jackson sat on the edge of the guest seat. His career sat even more precariously on a knife-edge.

"I pulled the team off before I came up," he lied. "You were right, Stone and Mills are a lost cause. It seems futile now. I guess we'll see what the news has to say about it."

The old man nodded. "So you're coming around," he said. "Finally learned the hard way, did you?" He sat forward and leaned on the desk. His cuff-links knocked heavily on the wood. "Don't fight it. You'll be demoted, but I'll see to it that you don't have to wear a uniform. But you'll still start near the bottom."

"You can do that?" asked Jackson.

"Like I said before, you don't get to sit here without knowing a thing or two, and knowing how to play the game. You're not the first, and you won't be the last, to learn the hard way."

"What about Stone and Mills?" asked Jackson.

"Forget about them. They're history. Right now, they'll either be being arrested or being shot. It's a shame about Mills, she could have been good. I looked at her record. But with a liability like Stone, it was destined for failure."

"And the bomb?"

"Not our problem."

"But it's British made."

"We'll deny it. Stone will take the blame. We'll show Dubai the media footage. Crowe makes it clear he was setting us up. Our ties may be fragile, but there are two hundred years of history that one man can't destroy."

"So that's it then?" said Jackson. "It's all over."

"Turvey will be replaced. It would have been you, but you're out now. So someone else will fill your shoes. This place changes. You have to roll with the punches."

"You'll stay?" asked Jackson.

"I have a year or so left in me. I'll see it out until the end."

"I'll see you before I go," said Jackson. "I'll go give the team the good news."

Jackson stood and made towards the door.

"Jackson," called the old man. Jackson turned and watched the old man relax in his chair like a fat cat that knew he'd get the mouse all along. "Don't be hard on yourself, just learn from it. Morality is a good thing to have, but playing the game is the key."

Jackson closed the door behind him.

CHAPTER FORTY-FIVE

"We need to move, now," said Melody, as two policemen ran past the store front.

Harvey tossed the empty aerosol can on top of Jim and left him writhing on the floor to suffer from his burns. He followed Melody out the door. The pair stopped at the end of the service corridor and peered through the small glass window.

"You heard what he said?" asked Melody.

"It was in the Porsche all along, and we delivered it," said Harvey.

"It wasn't the bomb itself that was traceable back to Britain," said Melody. "It was us who delivered it. It feels like we've been set up."

"Jackson?" asked Harvey.

Melody tried to get Reg on the comms. But all that came back was static. She looked at Harvey, grim-faced.

"We're on our own," she said.

"Let's get the Porsche out of here," said Harvey. "We might just get out of Dubai alive."

"And take it where?"

"I have an idea about that," said Harvey, pushing the door

open. The movement surprised an armed cop who was standing to one side of the frame. Before he could react, Harvey had twisted his arm up behind his back, disarmed him, and landed a forehead into the man's nose. Melody took his radio and used his own cuffs from his belt on his wrists.

They bolted through the fire escape door, checked up and down then ran to the seventh floor. A security guard stood at the top of the second flight of stairs, so Harvey launched an uppercut into the man's groin, and helped him on his way down the concrete stairs. Again, he peered through the small window in the door that led out to the mall.

Harvey glanced back at Melody. His knack for communicating his thoughts without words, something he'd learned from his mentor as a child, came in handy. Melody instantly knew that there were obstructions.

They remained unobserved as they edged around the perimeter wall to the exit, where two armed policemen stood smoking and chatting outside. Melody went through alone and caught their attention.

"Hey, excuse me, guys. There's a man on the floor." She pointed vaguely into the mall. "Help him."

The two men threw their cigarettes on the floor and brushed past her. By the time the first one had seen Harvey standing on the inside of the doors, it was too late for them both. In a matter of seconds, they were disarmed and bound just like their colleague on the floor below. One had a broken nose, and the other had a broken forearm from Melody's over-zealous arm lock.

Harvey drove, while Melody found the house in the desert on her phone's map app. She pulled her seatbelt on as Harvey swung the little sports car onto the ramp as fast as he could. He found the balance of clutch and accelerator, and the Porsche gripped the rough tarmac easily. Finally, they hit the ground floor, bumped over a speed bump, and accelerated out onto the main road.

"How much time do we have?" asked Harvey.

"Until the bomb goes off or until we're shot dead?"

"Bomb," said Harvey.

"Forty-five minutes," replied Melody.

"How far is the house?"

"Fifty-five minutes."

Harvey dropped the clutch and slammed the gear stick down into third as a helicopter flew past in the opposite direction and a line of police cars tore overhead on the elevated section.

They were free of the city in less than ten minutes and joined the tail end of the morning traffic.

CHAPTER FORTY-SIX

Reg, Jess and Jackson walked down the steps of MI6 together. Jackson carried a box containing the items that had decorated his office. Reg and Jess just had their laptop bags.

"I'm sorry it had to come to this, sir," said Reg.

"You don't have to call me sir," said Jackson. "Not anymore anyway." He looked both ways on the street and took a breath. "I just wanted to say that it was nothing you guys did, and I appreciate you trying. I just wish we could have got Mills and Stone out of there. They were good people."

"Don't talk like they're dead," said Reg.

"Well, if they're not dead, they'll be locked up for the foreseeable," said Jackson. "I tried. We tried, I mean. We did our best."

"I just don't understand it," said Reg. "It was just a quick job for Melody."

"There are forces at play here that go way above our pay grades, Reg."

"Like what?"

"Oh, come on, I can't think about it now," said Jackson. "It's over."

"For you, maybe, but not for them. They're out there still. They may be alive."

"Reg, don't get mixed up in this. It's a dangerous game. Trust me; I just learned the hard way."

"You have no idea what I'm capable of, what I've done," said Reg. "Come on, I can handle the truth, and if you're not going to do anything about it, maybe I will."

"See how far it gets you, Reg. I'll tell you if that's what you really want, but trust me when I say stay away."

Reg stared defiantly at Jackson.

"You're serious about this?"

Reg didn't reply.

Jackson stepped in closer to Reg and Jess and spoke quietly. "Think about this, Reg, who gave the order to get Melody out there? And who is the only one who hasn't been moved from his office?"

Reg's mind clicked into place. Jackson saw the realisation hit home.

"Now think about who's next in line for Turvey's job."

"The old man," said Reg. "The old man set them both up. But why? They saved Turvey's life."

"I told you, don't go there. He's a dangerous man. Keep him on your side, but look for a transfer behind the scenes, both of you. He'll take down anyone who stands in his way. That's all you get from me."

Reg nodded and gave a tight-lipped smile. "Good luck, Jackson."

Jackson stared back. "You know what? I suddenly feel like I can do anything I want."

"So what are you going to do?" asked Jess.

"Live a little," said Jackson. "Live a lot." He gave them a final admiring look. "Goodbye, Reg. Goodbye, Jess."

The two nodded, and Jackson turned to walk away.

"That's not a happy ending," said Jess to Reg as they turned to walk in the opposite direction. "Hey, are you okay?" she asked.

"I'm just thinking about Melody and Harvey. It can't be it. It can't be that cut and dry."

"Can you reach them at all?" asked Jess. "On LUCY?"

"You heard what Jackson said, any attempts to reach them will be deemed as a criminal offence. They'll throw the book at me. How can anyone be so callous, Jess? How can anybody in this day and age get away with doing what the old man did?"

"Power and positioning," said Jess.

"Well, he underestimated Harvey, that's for sure. At least Turvey is alive."

They crossed the main road and stepped up onto the pavement. The sky was already dark, and a light rain had begun to fall. Jess linked her arm through Reg's. She didn't speak, and he didn't pull away, but it felt nice, a semblance of warmth in an otherwise cold world.

"What if we could help Jackson at least?" said Jess.

"How do we help Jackson?" asked Reg. "He's out on his ear already."

"What if we somehow got a message to someone up top, you know?"

"You mean send the foreign minister an email?" said Reg. "What are the chances of him paying that any attention?"

"Maybe. But what if he had no choice but to see what we had to say? And what if what we had to say told a few home truths?"

Reg caught where she was heading with the conversation. "You're talking about-"

"Biblical, Reg," said Jess. "I'm talking about the hardest hack you ever did with the biggest risk you've ever taken. But it'll shake up British intelligence, and clean out a few cobwebs at the same time."

CHAPTER FORTY-SEVEN

Far out in the desert, Harvey stopped the Porsche at the end of a street, five hundred yards from the villa. His arm rested on the open window and the cool desert air washed through the car.

"How do you want to play this?" asked Melody.

"The way I see it, we have three choices," replied Harvey. "Drive the Porsche through the gates, leave it for Bob to find, hopefully in less than ten minutes' time. Option two, drive it through the gates, find Bob, and strap him to the bonnet."

"And option three?" asked Melody.

Suddenly the car rear-view mirror filled with light, and the roar of a heavy pickup truck accelerating towards them filled the quiet street. There wasn't time to move. There wasn't time to get out. Harvey reached across Melody and took hold of the door handle, locking her against the seat.

The truck slammed into the back end of the much smaller sports car, shattering the windows. Harvey slammed the car into reverse, lifted the clutch and pinned the accelerator to the floor. Smoke filled the car as its tyres fought the truck's massive torque. But the little car's weight was no match for the much heavier Ford. Melody leaned out the window and fired two rounds at the driver, but he had an MP5 aimed directly at her. The side of the Porsche was chewed up, the mirror smashed into pieces, and the windscreen shattered into glass pieces that fell around them.

The truck was pushing them towards a wall in an empty piece of land between two abandoned villas. The Porsche left the tarmac and began to slide easily across the sand on the wasteland.

"Option three?" asked Melody, eyeing the wall fifty feet away.

"Do you trust me?" asked Harvey.

"Do I have a choice right now?"

Harvey's legs were almost straight as he put as much weight on the brakes as possible. He was heaving on the handbrake.

"When I let go of the brake, this car is going to fly forward. When that happens, we need to be as far away from this car as possible. How many in the truck?"

"Just one. It's Bob," said Melody.

"Good, he's going to get what's coming to him. On my count, jump from the car and give him everything you've got."

"What?" cried melody. "He has a-"

"Three."

"Harvey."

"Two."

Melody pulled the door handle.

"One," said Harvey.

Harvey opened his own door, pulled his foot from the brake, and instantly felt the speed pick up. Jumping out, he rolled across the ground onto broken bricks, glass and sand then sat up on one knee and emptied the handgun he'd taken from the cop into the truck's cab.

He watched as the realisation dawned on Bob's face, but by then, the Porsche had its own momentum. Both Harvey and

Melody dived for cover as the bumper hit the wall, which folded the car's chassis, designed to absorb an impact. The storage compartment under the bonnet of the little Porsche crumpled, crushing the sports bag hidden inside.

Harvey lay across Melody behind a mound of sand and bricks and waited for the explosion.

Instead, they heard the creak of the old Ford's driver door open.

Harvey raised his head and saw Bob standing by the side of the truck forty-feet away. Bob held the MP5 like a seasoned pro. He hit the magazine eject button and let the empty fall to the floor. Then, like a predator who knows his prey is trapped, he slowly pulled a fresh magazine from his cargo pants.

After the grinding of steel on steel and the screech of brakes, the sound of the magazine being loaded was loud in the empty street.

Then came the sound of heavy boots approaching on the sand and gravel as Bob made his way across the wasteland.

Harvey remained lying across Melody. He was waiting for his opportunity, and his window was getting smaller and smaller with each step Bob took.

He looked over the pile of sand and bricks one last time to see Bob taking aim and froze as Bob raised the gun to his shoulder. Harvey's window of opportunity had gone.

Bob's lip curled in hatred as he lowered his face to the weapon's stock and closed one eye. Harvey ducked back down.

Melody had opened her eyes and stared up at him. Their faces were inches apart.

Neither of them moved. No words were spoken. Harvey nodded a silent goodbye and took three deep breaths. He brought his knees up underneath him, ready to jump up and take the gunman down. He knew he'd be hit, but if Melody could have a chance at running, she could get away.

A small tear rolled out of Melody's eye. She knew what he was about to do.

The cocking lever on Bob's MP5 snatched back, metallic and crisp.

Then the timer on the home-made incendiary device inside the sports holdall in the front of the Porsche hit zero.

CHAPTER FORTY-EIGHT

By the time Harvey and Melody had arrived in central London, Dubai police were announcing the failed bombing at one of their prestigious malls. A successful operation undertaken by Dubai's elite undercover unit was how the media had been told to phrase the incident. The statement was designed to reassure the public that they had been in no danger at any time.

It was around the time of that initial press release that Reg was waiting precisely where he'd been told to wait, on the roof of the MI6 building overlooking the River Thames.

He wore his usual duffel coat, buttoned up to his chin to stop the chilled breeze that rolled off the river from attacking his very core. He was met at exactly ten am, not a minute before, not a minute after, exactly as he was told.

"Thank you for coming, Tenant," said the old man as he walked across the rooftop.

"It's okay, sir," said Reg. "Perhaps next time we could use a meeting room though?"

"What I have to say goes no further," said the old man. "Are you trustworthy, Tenant?"

"I've been on the force for ten years, sir. Nobody has ever doubted my credibility."

"That's what I thought, and I'm glad to hear it." The old man shuffled his feet. "About Jackson," he began, "it's a shame. The man had potential. But, as you know, you don't win the game by doing what's right, you win by doing what you're told." The old man eyed Reg up and down. "Can you do what you're told, Tenant?"

Reg listened intently. He wondered how the lies came out of the old man's mouth so easily.

"Of course, sir," said Reg. "There's no emotion. It's black and white."

"Black and white?" said the old man. "Yes, that's what it is. It's a shame Jackson didn't see things that way."

"He was a good operative, sir. But you did what you had to do."

The old man's face tightened, and his whole demeanour changed.

"Tell me, Tenant, how did you do it?" The old man pulled a handgun from inside his jacket.

Reg's body tensed. He straightened from his lazy slouch to bolt upright. He'd been surrounded by danger for most of his career, but it was the first time a gun had been pointed at him.

"Don't play games with me, Tenant. I'm far better, and my armies are a lot stronger than yours."

"I, I-"

"You nearly ruined me, Tenant, with your meddling. I had a nice visit from the minister of foreign affairs thanks to you."

"Really?" said Reg, collecting himself. "Did you have a nice chat?"

"Your cheap sarcastic wit is as cheap as your childish attempts to bring me down, Tenant. Fortunately for me, I've been playing this game a lot longer than you have, and I know the rules better than anyone."

"There are rules?" said Reg. "Seems like you make them up to suit yourself and it's everyone else that suffers."

"It's the losers who suffer, Tenant," said the old man. "And you just lost. Game over."

The old man gave a hand signal, and suddenly Jess was pushed into view by a masked gunman who stepped up behind her, his gun firmly planted into her temple.

"*Jess,*" called Reg. "*No. Leave her out of this.*"

"I thought you said there was no emotion, Tenant? I hear the pair of you are growing close."

"*Let her go.*"

"No," snarled the old man like a spoiled child. "You're the last two loose ends. I thought you were trustworthy but clearly, you're a liability, a risk. Just like the other loser, Jackson."

"You'll never get away with this. What did you expect us to do? Isn't it bad enough you killed Melody and Harvey?"

"*That's* an allegation, Tenant. *I* didn't exactly pull the trigger."

"No, but you left them to die. You might as well have killed them yourself. And *what,* now you're going to cover your tracks? Is that it? We're the last ones left to testify against you."

"I had this conversation with Jackson," said the old man. A British Army Westland Lynx helicopter rose up behind Reg. The down-force flapped at Reg's coat. Its fuselage was painted British Army green, and the pilot nodded at the old man before setting the bird down to rest on the helipad beside them. "I'll tell you what I told him," called the old man over the thunderous noise of the rotors. "It's called minimising risk, and I'm damn good at it."

The pilot of the Lynx kept the blades turning, and the old man stepped up closer to Reg. He gestured with his gun at the masked man who held Jess by her hair in front of him. "He'll take care of you both," said the old man. "Goodbye Tenant."

The old man stepped back towards the helicopter, keeping his gun trained on Reg. Then he climbed up into the rear compartment of the Lynx and motioned for the pilot to get airborne. It was as the blades began to pick up speed and the helicopter began to lift off that the masked gunman on the roof pulled the balaclava off.

A mass of long, dark, naturally curly hair bounced softly onto two strong feminine shoulders. Melody Mills released Jess and smiled up at the old man. The three of them began to wave.

The old man was outraged. As he turned to the pilot and shouted to be taken back down, he caught sight of the man beside him. He hadn't seen him when he'd climbed into the chopper. Harvey Stone sat in the far seat with a SIG Sauer P226 aimed at the stunned old man.

Harvey made a circular motion with his finger pointing upwards, then reached across and disarmed the old man. The pilot gently pulled the collective up, taking the helicopter higher and higher.

"Stop," shouted the old man. "Where are you taking me?"

The pilot didn't respond, so the old man took a headset from where it hung and pulled it on. Harvey sat watching and smiling.

"I said, take me down this instant," said the old man.

The pilot didn't reply.

"Who are you?" asked the old man, ignoring Harvey's weapon.

Harvey didn't reply.

"Will somebody damn well tell me what's going on here?" shouted the old man. Spit flew from his mouth in rage.

The pilot eased off the collective at eighteen thousand feet. The air was too thin at the altitude for the helicopter to hover.

By that time, the old man was panicking, struggling to close the door that Harvey had locked in the open position.

"Somebody tell me what the bloody hell is going on."

The pilot spoke for the first time through the in-flight comms.

"Welcome aboard the flight, sir."

"Who are you? Where's *my* pilot?"

"We hope you enjoyed the ride up, and we apologise for the delay. But rest assured the descent will be much faster."

"Take me down," screamed the old man.

"Oh, you'll be going down shortly," said Harvey. "But first, there's a score to settle."

"Who are you?"

"You don't know my name?" said Harvey. "You left me in the desert to take the rap for a murder and a bombing, and you don't even know what I look like?"

"Stone," said the old man.

"You're worse than I imagined," said Harvey. "Killing people sat at your desk. I could almost respect the men you sent after us. At least they had the courage to stand and fight."

"You don't know the half of it."

"Oh, I know," said Harvey. "We have a mutual friend. He told me all about how you never really wanted Melody in the country, and how she was only sent there so I'd go after her willingly. You didn't have the guts to ask me yourself."

"Yeah, well, the plan worked, didn't it?"

"Nearly," replied Harvey.

"It was a shame about your friend Jackson," said the old man, hoping for a rise from Harvey. "But he never would have made it. He's too weak."

Harvey didn't reply.

"How well exactly do you know him?" asked the old man.

"You know he's the spineless coward who left you there? I gave him a choice, you know?"

"Yeah, he told me about the choice you gave him," said Harvey, "and Reg told me about the choice he made."

"It's their word against mine," spat the old man. "Take me down. This is a joke."

"And what about Turvey? You didn't really give him much of a choice, did you? Die or watch his family be killed?"

"Turvey was in the way," snarled the old man. "I knew he would never let his family die."

"In your way?" said Harvey. "You wanted his desk, his job. Is that all this was about? But to get there, you were willing to kill innocent people? You make me sick."

"You don't know the rules of the game," said the old man. "I do. I saw the bigger picture."

"I don't care about *your* bigger picture. It's *my* turn to give *you* a choice, old man," said Harvey.

"Is that right? Just because you're holding a gun, you think you can manipulate me? You have *no idea* who you are dealing with, you impetuous-"

Harvey leaned forward and tossed the gun out the open side door. The weapon span away through the air and disappeared from view.

"What was you saying?" said Harvey. "I don't need a gun. I'll kill you with my bare hands."

"So what?" asked the old man. "What now?"

"Option one," began Harvey, "you jump."

The old man looked nervously out the open door. At eighteen thousand feet, London appeared extremely small.

"Or?" he asked, holding onto the back of the seat and the large u-shaped handle beside the door.

"Or you die an extremely painful and slow death." Harvey

leaned closer to the old man. "And when it comes to slow deaths..." He grinned. "I wrote the book on it."

"Pilot, this is nonsense. Take me down at once. How do I call ATC from here?"

The pilot looked behind him and tapped the cushioned headset that covered his ear.

"*Who are you?*" demanded the old man.

That was when Jackson turned in his seat, raised the visor on his helmet, removed his sunglasses, and winked at the old man.

Jackson brought the helicopter down in a small paddock which sat beside a disused barn near the town of Epping in Essex. Harvey knew it was disused. The area had been his old stomping ground. It was where he had honed his skills under the watchful eye of his mentor, Julios.

"Out," said Harvey to the old man.

The old man looked terrified. He clung to the handrail beside the door of the Lynx and wept.

Harvey stepped past him and jumped to the ground as the rotors slowed to a stop above him. A car sat thirty feet away. Its single occupant had been waiting for them to arrive.

Jackson joined Harvey as he unlocked the old barn, and they began to prepare.

The man in the car waited, controlling his temper and keeping hold of his emotions.

The old man sat in the chopper sobbing to himself.

Harvey pushed the big doors to the barn open to let the light in and the roosting pigeons out. The space was empty, save for the wooden beams that formed the roof truss and a workbench that ran along one side of the room.

In the far corner was a pile of old farm tools, a tractor wheel and other items, with a tarpaulin stretched across to keep the weather from getting to them.

"What first?" said Jackson.

"We need a hole in the ground, three feet square," said Harvey. "There're some shovels under the tarp. Have the old man dig it, it'll keep him busy."

Jackson did as instructed. He pulled a shovel from the corner of the room and strode outside to face the old man, who looked up as Jackson approached with disdain in his eyes.

"It's time to get out," said Jackson, without a quiver of hesitation, emotion or sorrow in his voice.

"What are you going to do to me?" said the old man, eyeing the shovel in Jackson's hands.

Jackson said nothing. He handed the old man the old, heavy shovel, and pointed to a spot in the centre of the paddock. "Dig."

"My own grave? Is that it? You're going to kill me and bury me here, wherever we are."

Harvey stepped out of the barn, looked up into the sky, and then leaned on the barn door. "Not very imaginative, are you?" he said to the old man.

"What do you mean?"

"I thought you would have credited me with a bit more creativity," replied Harvey. "But we're not here to discuss it. You'll find out soon enough. Now go dig the hole."

The old man opened his mouth to say something, but the look on Harvey's face changed his mind. He held the shovel with both hands and took a slow walk to the middle of the small paddock.

"Just there's fine," called Harvey.

The old man stopped, removed his long overcoat, which he

folded and placed on the ground, and then slowly set about digging.

"What do you have planned, Harvey?" said Jackson, once the old man was out of earshot.

Harvey didn't answer the question. "We need firewood and lots of it."

CHAPTER FIFTY

Before long, the old man was waist deep in a grave-shaped hole. Harvey and Jackson had spent two hours gathering the wood while the man in the car had sat and watched. A pile of broken branches, old pallets and dead trees stood six feet high to one side of the hole. Harvey carried a sledgehammer, a long iron stake and a length of rope to the scene and dropped them to the ground.

"What's that for?" asked the old man, leaning on the shovel from deep inside the hole.

Harvey didn't reply.

He hammered the stake into the soft ground a few feet from the hole and fastened one end of the twenty-foot rope to the eyelet at the top end of the stake.

"What are you doing?" asked the old man, becoming very scared. "Tell me. What are you going to do?"

"You ask too many questions," said Harvey.

"I thought you would just shoot me and be done with it. But, but this all seems so dramatic."

Harvey swung the sledgehammer over his shoulder and looked down into the hole. "You earned this. You deserve far more than a quick bullet in the head, and I'm known for making sure people get what they deserve. So shut up and get out of the hole. It's deep enough."

The old man half rolled and half climbed out of the hole on the far side, away from Harvey, the stake and the rope.

Harvey gave him a look.

The old man took a deep breath and gingerly stepped around to where Harvey stood.

"Strip," said Harvey.

"Strip?"

"Strip," Harvey repeated, his diction clear, leaving no room for the old man to question him. The old man removed his clothes and folded them neatly in a pile beside him. He stood with his hands over his genitals and held back his tears.

"Hands," said Harvey.

"Hands?" said the old man. His voice had changed from his authoritative grumble to the high-pitched song of a child.

"Hold them out."

The old man held his hands out for Harvey to begin tying them together. Harvey bound the old man's wrists in a neat series of loops and then wound the rope around his ankles. He completed the binding with a sturdy knot which was neat, with barely any excess rope.

"You've done this before,' said Jackson.

Harvey didn't reply.

"It's cold," said the old man.

"You want us to light a fire?" said Harvey. He began to pull wood into the hole that the old man had dug and then turned to Jackson. "Let's build a fire."

In the distance, the car sat with its engine running to keep the man warm. Before long, the driver saw that the time was approaching, and wiped the tears from his face.

Harvey waited for the fire to get going. He stood motionless, his arms folded across his chest. He stared at the old man.

"I've killed many people," said Harvey. "They all deserved it in one way or another, some more than others. But none of them were mindless murders."

"Is this a confession?" said the old man.

Harvey ignored the old man's comment and continued, while Jackson stood and listened, oddly in awe of Harvey's presence.

"Over the years, I've done some very bad things to some very bad people," said Harvey. "I've learned a thing or two about death and how it works."

Harvey began to walk in a tight circle around the old man, who followed Harvey with his eyes. But when Harvey disappeared behind him, he closed his eyes tightly, too frightened to move.

"There are a series of emotions that most men go through," said Harvey, "when they know death is coming. It's almost like some deep psychology that's ingrained in all of us. Firstly, there's the denial, the anger. Do you remember how you insulted us on the ride here, old man?"

The old man didn't respond.

Harvey stepped up directly behind the old man and whispered into his ear. "Then comes the fear."

The flab on the old man's stomach wobbled as his entire body shuddered.

"The fear brings the tears and the shame, as the human mind spins all sorts of horrific scenarios to a vivid imagining. That's where you are now."

Harvey walked around the front and stood between the old man and the fire.

"You're going to die a very slow and painful death. But know this, old man," said Harvey in his chilled, emotionless tone, "you'll suffer far beyond that which your imagination can conjure up. So whatever you think we're going to do to you, cast the image aside, because it's not even close."

The man's face was shining with tears, and snot ran freely across his wide double chin. Then, with the finality of death itself, he broke. Loud sobs came from deep inside his gut. His body shook with adrenaline and the cold, and urine began to stream down his inner leg.

Harvey glanced across at Jackson, who stood wide-eyed at the way Harvey had broken the man he'd once looked up to, just with words.

Harvey gestured with his head for Jackson to follow him to the barn, and as they stepped inside, Jackson caught Harvey by the arm. "Hey, Harvey," he began, and then removed his hand, "listen. I don't know what you have planned, but are you sure you want to go ahead with this?"

"I'm not going through with anything," said Harvey. "I'm just facilitating, helping a friend."

Jackson looked solemnly back at Harvey's cold eyes and nodded.

"Help me with this," said Harvey, and he pulled back the tarp from the corner of the barn.

Melody, Reg and Jess walked down the steps of the Secret Intelligence Service building on London's Southbank. They turned right and followed the road around to walk across Vauxhall Bridge. The slight rain had eased off, but a bitter wind blew off the river and bit into their faces.

They were halfway across the bridge when Reg stopped and leaned on the handrail. He looked down into the murky water below then turned to Melody and said what they were all thinking. "Why don't you come work with us, Melody?"

Melody gave a laugh. "I don't think so, Reg," she said. "I've hardly had a break these past few days."

"How about an office-based job?" said Reg. "You'd still be awesome at it."

"Can you honestly see me stuck inside an office for the rest of my life?" replied Melody. "It would drive me insane."

"So, what? You're going to sit in Harvey's farm for the rest of your life?" said Reg. "And do what?"

Melody smiled. "It's such a beautiful place, Reg. We walk to the beach, through the forests and across fields. We eat at stunning French cafes and quaint little restaurants. It's so different from, well here, and don't get me wrong, I love London, but there's something about the green, the quiet and the ocean that just sets your mind at ease. I love it there, Reg."

Reg smiled. The three of them stood side by side leaning on the railing, watching the water flow past beneath them.

"Sounds idyllic, Melody," said Reg. "But don't you get bored?"

"Not bored, Reg," said Melody. "Just…"

"You miss it all, don't you?" said Reg.

"It's complicated," said Melody,

"Reg, don't press her," said Jess. "If she wanted to come back, she would."

Melody looked up at them both then gazed across at the rest of the city.

"It's Harvey, isn't it?" said Reg. "You feel like you have to make a choice."

"Reg," said Jess, "leave her alone."

"It's okay, thanks, Jess," said Melody. "He's right. At least, he's kind of right." Melody put her hands in her jacket pockets and turned to lean her back on the railing. "When Gordon came to find us, and when I had to decide if I was going to come, we had the chat. He doesn't want to hold me back. So it's not him that's holding me, it's me that holding me. Does that make sense?"

"That makes perfect sense to me, Melody," said Jess. "But can I ask you something?"

"Sure, I'm in the spotlight now, might as well get it all out," said Melody.

"I'm sorry, but I have to ask, and I'm sorry if it comes out wrong, but well, it seems to me that Harvey is…"

Jess hung on her last word, searching for the right way to describe Harvey without insulting Melody or Harvey himself.

"Different?" suggested Melody.

"Yes, different," said Jess. "And honestly, I don't mean that negatively, but, well, I've heard the stories, and, if they're all true, then-"

"The stories are all true," said Reg. "But things done in the past don't make him a bad man. In fact, as shocking as some of the stories are, there's honour inside him. He's a good guy."

"Yeah," said Melody. "He has his moral compass that guides him, and he's not as hard as you think. There's a soft side to him."

Reg raised an eyebrow. "A soft side, yeah?"

"Yeah," continued Melody. "I know it's hard to believe. But he makes me coffee in bed, and you should see him with Boon."

"Boon?" asked Jess.

"Boon is their dog," said Reg. "Harvey rescued him when his owner was killed by-"

"I think that's a story for another occasion, Reg," said Melody. "But you'd have to see it to believe it. Harvey is genuinely a sweetheart. He'd do anything for me, and he'll always be the first one to stand up to a bully. I think that's one of his most endearing qualities."

"So this new soft Harvey you met," said Reg, smiling, "what do you reckon he's doing to the old man right now?"

"I don't know, Reg," said Melody. "But I'm sure whatever it is, his moral compass is guiding him." She flashed Reg a smile and turned back around to watch the water flow past.

The team were all sat in the operations room on Monday morning. Reg was beside Jess, and they'd enjoyed a weekend together, grateful to be alive, grateful to have jobs, and happy that Melody and Harvey had escaped Dubai.

Ladyluck, Gordon and the others were all at their desks, awaiting the briefing that was usually the starting gun for the week. Two people entered the room, a man and woman, both well-dressed and well-groomed. They stood at the far end of the room beside the glass walls of the fishbowl with their hands folded in front of them.

"People, heads up," said the man. "My name is Mr Thorn, and this is Miss Finch. We're sorry to interrupt your morning. I'm sure you're all aware that there have been some changes around here, and we'd like to thank you for your patience. The past week has been a trying time for us all. But we're pleased to say that we're through it, and well, in short, that's entirely down to the professionalism and aptitude that this team demonstrated. And, believe me, it has not gone unnoticed."

The team shared confused glances but smiled at the praise.

"I'll leave the details of Mr Fox and Mr Turvey out of this, and we would appreciate it if you could all treat the entire incident as confidential. If you're approached by journalists, say nothing."

Mr Thorn eyed the room and saw nothing but courteous nods from the men and women who all sat attentively listening.

"We'd also like to introduce you to your new head," continued Thorn. "But before we introduce you, I'd like to say that the gentleman in question has risen through the ranks, and showed the exact attitude and traits that we look for in all our staff. I have no doubt that he will lead you to success. The door opened once more and Jackson stood in the door frame. He hadn't taken a step when everyone in the room stood and applauded him.

The man in the suit cut the clapping short, and the team sat back in their seats.

"Mr Jackson will be seated in the vacant office upstairs and, if anything, you should take note and use him as an example of what hard work and determination will get you."

Reg stepped forward and shook Jackson's hand. "Pleased to have you back, sir."

"I believe it's you I have to thank for that, Tenant," said Jackson. "And, of course, you Jess."

Jess beamed at the recognition, and, as was her habit when she was the centre of attention, she began to clean her glasses with her shirt.

Reg returned to his seat as Miss Finch, who stood beside Jackson addressed the room. "That does, of course, leave a hole in the operations room, and quite frankly, Mr Jackson leaves behind some very big shoes for someone to fill. But after careful consideration, which may have been swayed by the sheer courage this man displayed during recent events, along with his ability to remain focused and calm under severe pressure, we have decided to award the role to Mr Tenant. If he'll take it, of course." She turned to face Reg and smiled a warm but professional smile.

Reg was taken aback and stared disbelievingly at Jess, who held her hands to her face with joy and leaned forward to hug him. A few seconds later, Reg stood, shook the hands of the man, woman and Jackson then returned to his seat.

"Well?" said the smartly dressed man. "Do you want the role or not?"

Reg, ever the introvert, laughed at the sudden attention. "Of course I want the role. But I do have a few conditions."

The beach and the small village in Argeles-Sur-Mer hadn't changed in the few days that Harvey and Melody had been away.

In the morning, they drank coffee and breakfasted in the small cafe where Gordon had been waiting for them. While they waited, Harvey had pulled the only British paper from the pile of newspapers by the door and flicked through the news, uninterested in any of it.

Melody had skimmed through the paper herself. There was an article about how the Dubai government had averted a near crisis when their special armed response unit had carried out the controlled explosion of a car bomb in a rural street out of town. She flicked past the story. However, she was interested in one particular article about a man who had been found tarred and feathered and been dumped on the high street of Epping town centre. The man was named Augustus Fox and had recently been shamed from a senior role in the British government. Fox, who was still alive but severely burned, faces life imprisonment and extradition to the United Arab Emirates. The story continued to describe how the British have not extradited anybody to the Arab nation since 2011, due to possible torture practices. But, considering the levity of the crimes, and in an effort to maintain peaceful relations with the Emiratis, the Crown Prosecution would be pushing for the extradition ban to be lifted.

Melody peered over the top of the paper at Harvey, who stared back stony-faced. She turned her attention back to the newspaper, deciding not to bring the story up. It was nice to be home. Normality was a long way off, and a lengthy discussion about Harvey's idea of acceptable levels of punishment could be saved for another time.

Boon had been pleased to see them when they'd collected him from their neighbour's place. Although the neighbours had pushed for details of their trip, they had managed to avoid going into too much depth. Melody had bought them flowers and chocolates as a gift and had been forced to accept the invitation to dinner.

As they walked along the beach, Boon ran full pelt along the sand, as if showing off in front of Melody and Harvey, reminding them of how fast he could run. Melody took Harvey's hand in hers and held her flip-flops in her other hand. She loved the feeling of the soft sand beneath her feet.

"About what you said," she began.

"When?" replied Harvey.

"In the car, the Porsche, you told me you'd never felt this way before. Is that true?"

Harvey didn't reply.

"Come on, you were doing well in Dubai, really letting go."

"What do you want me to say, Melody?" said Harvey.

"The truth, Harvey. Where do we stand?"

"I told you how I feel. I don't have to say it over and over, do I?"

"No."

"Well, what then?" said Harvey. "I flew to Dubai to bring you home, and now you're home, I'd like to get back to the way things were."

"The way things were?" Melody said. "And how were things, in your mind?"

"You know, the normal stuff. Morning coffee, training, working on the house," said Harvey. "You wanted to grow some vegetables, right? Well, let's do that." Harvey paused and thought about what he was asking of her. "Unless you still want-"

"No, Harvey, you just said it."

"So you don't want to go back to work?"

"Part of me does, I can't lie," said Melody. "But all of me wants to be here with you."

Harvey began a slow walk and Melody walked beside him, scooping up damp cold sand in her feet with each step.

"You really want to go back?" asked Harvey.

"I just said, I'd rather-"

"But part of you does? Because it's fine, we just have to absorb it."

"Absorb it?" asked Melody.

"Yeah, we have to flex. You know, it doesn't have to be all or nothing."

"So if I worked the odd job, you'd be totally okay with it?"

"Yeah, I guess so," said Harvey. "I did a fair amount of thinking when you left and when I was on the plane, and then again when I was sat on the balcony while you were set up for the shot."

"You what?" said Melody. "You were outside? Four feet from me?"

"The whole time," said Harvey. "I could even smell your shampoo."

"I was there for hours and you didn't think to let me know you were there?"

"I didn't want you to lose focus."

"I have to say," said Melody, "that was a great shot you made from the villa."

"Had a good teacher, didn't I?" replied Harvey. "I'd do it again, you know?"

"Do what?"

"Come and get you, you know, if you were in trouble."

"Yeah, I know. It's nice to know too." Melody opened her mouth and let the words slip away.

"Would it help if we were married?" asked Harvey.

"You what?" replied Melody.

"You know, us. Would it help if we were married? Would it feel more stable for you? To know that you had someone to come home to and to know I'd be there waiting?"

Melody stopped dead in her tracks. "Is that a proposal, Mr Stone?"

Harvey stopped and stared back at her. "Yes. Yes, it is."

Melody laughed and put her hands up to her face. She peeked through her fingers. "You're serious?" she said.

Harvey didn't reply.

"Yes, I'll marry you, Harvey. But you don't get away with it that easily."

"What do you mean?" asked Harvey.

"I want a proper proposal. You're going to have to get romantic on me, Mr Stone," said Melody as she walked past Harvey, who watched her walk, shook his head then followed behind.

Being married didn't scare Harvey, and Melody *had* changed his life. She'd even taught him a few things too. He felt good. He felt like normality was coming. They laughed as they made their way to the lane that led to their little farmhouse. But the laughter came to a stop when Harvey saw the car waiting for them on the road.

It was a black saloon, parked where the lane met the beach road. One man stood to the rear of the car with his hands inside the pockets of his long overcoat.

Boon saw the man and issued a low growl. He looked up at Harvey, waiting for his command.

Harvey stopped ten feet in front of him; Melody stood alongside him. They both stared the dark-haired man up and down. They both noted his crooked nose and cleft lip, and both observed the bulge in his pocket from his sidearm.

"You're a hard pair to find," said the man, as he lit a cigarette and slid a shiny lighter back into the inside pocket of his suit jacket.

"How would you like to come and work for me?"

Harvey didn't reply.

The End

STONE RUSH

CHAPTER ONE

In the darkness of the night, the calm, inky-black waters of the Mediterranean offered Bella one of very few choices.

She peered over the side of the boat as the water gently licked at the wooden hull below, and listened to the slurp and splash of the water as the vessel met the oncoming tide.

Bella searched ahead into the night for a sign of the first option: Greece. She'd been told that when the mountains appeared on the horizon, her journey would be coming to an end. But that did not guarantee her safety or the safety of her unborn child; even *she* knew that. A new journey would begin with new dangers, but it would be a journey of hope.

Behind her, Turkey had long since disappeared from sight, taking Bella's only friend, Yana, with it; there may be a chance that Bella could return, but it was very slim.

Yana and Bella had travelled from Syria together, huddled in the back of a truck under heavy canvasses that smelled of oil, dirt and urine. That seemed an age ago, when Bella had had only two options: stay and be killed or leave and head into the unknown. Their chances of survival as the pair had begun their journey from Aleppo had been very small but they had made it, just.

Bella wished Yana had joined her on the boat. She wished that someone had answered her prayers, but the greed and lust of man had been no match for the two young girls.

As children, Yana had always been the prettier of the two, although she'd downplayed it, and had always told Bella that she would meet a great man who would care for her and provide her with many children. But Yana's fair skin and large, clear eyes had steered her away from Bella in the end. Their journey had been fraught with danger and controlled by men along the way. The two girls had merely been garbage floating in the sea, this way and that, pulled by the tides of cruel men and pushed by their will to survive.

Bella knew that they would never meet again.

In front, somewhere in the darkness, lay the uncertainty of another journey by road, through Europe and finally to England, where she had been told she would be welcomed, fed and sheltered. Behind her was certain death, but the chance to see her friend one last time.

Bella's third option lay beneath her. It was the easiest option and the one with the most certain outcome.

The boat creaked and swayed in the water, and the heavy diesel engine popped quietly somewhere at the back, near the doors to the lower deck where the other refugees were kept.

She wouldn't be missed.

Militants had been moving in even as Bella and Yana had escaped the city, and they'd heard from other refugees that people had been slaughtered like animals on the street. A young man who they had met in Turkey had told them that the thousands killed were the lucky ones; the ones who survived with no chance of escape were now living in hell.

She longed to be with her family again.

Bella timed her climb over the handrail with the gentle sway of the boat and then stood to peer into the welcoming black arms of death.

She gave a final glance ahead, yet did not see the mountains that supposedly surrounded Athens. Behind, Turkey had become a distant memory. Below her was where she would end her journey, on her terms.

Bella leaned forward with both arms outstretched behind her, clinging to the rail. Tears rolled silently from her eyes, but she did not sob.

It was time.

She offered a small prayer to her God, to her family and to Yana, and spared them all one last thought.

Bella closed her eyes, released her grip on the handrail and waited for the deep, cool water to embrace her.

But she did not fall. She hung in the air, suspended above death. Once more, her journey had been halted by choice: heaven or hell.

Life or death.

A strong hand reached from behind. She felt herself being hoisted back over the handrail and carried in the air like a sack to the back of the boat, back to the others.

And then down.

She was unceremoniously dumped on the floor at the feet of her silent and scared companions. Then darkness engulfed her once more, as the wooden doors slammed shut.

"Where did you go?" whispered the young man that Bella had been sitting with before. "You know they will kill you for this?"

She didn't reply.

"Bella? We must play by their rules if we are to survive, and we must stick together."

"What if I do not *want* to survive?" she replied. "What if it is death that is the most inviting?"

"But, Bella, think of England. It is a safe place for us. There will be opportunity."

"Is that what you believe? Do you think that our safety or opportunity lies in England? It is just another unknown. It is just another journey."

There was silence in the small cell below deck.

"But, Bella, what about the baby? Think of the baby."

"My baby stays with me, and all the time it lives and breathes inside my body, it is with me," said Bella, clutching her swollen tummy with both hands. "If I die, my baby dies with me. I will take it to a place where no harm can come to us anymore."

"Bella, you have to understand," said the young man in the darkness. "When you escape, they punish us *all*. I am sure that now we will not be given our ration of water. But when you say these things, God himself will punish you alone. Your baby may enjoy the paradise of heaven, but I am afraid that *you* will not."

As if the spoken words were heard by something far greater, the low rumble of the diesel engine stopped and Bella heard the lick and slurp of the water once more.

She wondered if she would get another chance.

Men's voices, loud but muffled, came from outside. Bella felt the boat bump against something larger than itself.

Another boat? Or was it land?

Had they arrived in Athens already?

The others remained silent, waiting for the doors to open, and for their chance at freedom to begin. Nine frightened pairs of eyes stared at her in the dim light, clinging to hope.

Bella sat in silence, waiting for death to take her by the hand.

But it wasn't the hand of death that reached in and grabbed

her by the hair; it was the hand of the man with the big crooked nose and the wandering hands of the devil himself. Fernando.

She was yanked from the cell and briefly saw the stunned faces of her fellow refugees return to darkness when the door slammed shut again behind her. Up on deck, Fernando forced her to board another boat, and then stepped across to join her.

"Call me when you reach Athens," he called to two men who stood at the boat controls. He then shoved Bella down three small steps, once more into darkness.

"But Fernando, what do we tell the boss?" one of the men replied.

The man with the crooked nose closed the two small doors, leaving Bella once more with just the darkness to keep her company.

"Tell him, I have other plans for her and to be grateful it is only one I am taking," he called out.

Other plans?

Bella found a fishing net in the darkness and curled up as best she could within her new surroundings. Once the boat had started moving, she knew Fernando would not come for her. She even managed to sleep a little, a benefit of her willingness to die. With the worry of what *might be* put to one side, her dreams of what was certain provided a dark yet welcome finality.

A peace.

Time passed neither slow or fast; it just passed. But when the two little doors were eventually yanked open, and Fernando stepped down into her cabin, she knew the gates of hell had been opened.

CHAPTER TWO

"Morning, handsome," said Melody. "How's the weather there?"

"It's okay," replied Harvey. "It's not raining."

"It's not raining? Is that your only description of the weather?"

"What do you want me to say, Melody?" he said with a smile. "The sky's blue and the birds are singing? It's the south of France, the weather is always nice."

Melody sighed. "I guess that's about as much as I should expect from you, isn't it?"

Harvey didn't reply. He continued to lean against the doorframe looking out over their small plot of land, which Melody had begun to use for growing vegetables, and which doubled as her rifle range.

"London's nice, in case you were wondering," said Melody, pushing for conversation. "I love the fresh morning walks from the station to the office, wrapped up in a scarf and warmed by my coffee."

"Is that your way of saying it's cold?" asked Harvey. "What's the case about? What's Reg got you working on?"

"Come on, you know I can't tell you that," replied Melody. "But it does seem to be going well."

"How long do you think you'll be in London for?"

"Until we're done. Reg thinks he's on to something and we have ground units in place, so hopefully, it's a hot lead and we can wrap it up."

"Sounds interesting," said Harvey. "Another solve for your diary, eh?"

"Stop digging for clues. I can't give you any more details. I had to sign the secrets act again and all sorts of non-disclosure agreements. Anyway, what are you doing today? Will you be hitting that roof you've been meaning to fix?"

"The roof?" said Harvey.

"Don't play games with *me*, Harvey Stone. You've been telling me you'll fix that roof for a *year* now."

"I'll tell you what, Melody, you go and play at being James Bond with your mates in London, and I'll take care of things over here in the sunshine. How does that sound?"

Melody laughed. "You're so non-committal."

"Are you going to let me finish my coffee in peace?"

"Okay, enjoy yourself over there," said Melody. "I miss you, Harvey."

"Speak soon, yeah? Take care."

Harvey hit the disconnect button and placed the phone on the kitchen table. He had a habit of placing things perfectly symmetrical to their surroundings. It was a practice that he wasn't sure if he'd picked up from his foster father, who was always meticulous about such things, or his mentor, Julios, who had explained that remembering how you leave things, a room, a phone, or a pen, is an easy way to see if an intruder has been. Either way, Harvey had been able to shake off the life of crime, but never the habits that were the core of his success, and often the reason he was still alive.

Boon, Harvey's dog, sat expectantly on the tiled floor, looking up at his master and waiting for breakfast. Harvey poured out some dry food and stood at the open door of his little farmhouse looking out at the fields beyond.

Harvey usually started his day with a run. Then he would chip away at the jobs that needed doing to the house before either heading to the beach or for a ride on his motorbike along the winding French country lanes. The house had come a long way since he'd bought it. He'd sealed the windows and painted the woodwork, but Melody was right, the roof needed doing before winter came around again.

Harvey swallowed the remainder of his coffee, rolled his head from left to right with two satisfying clicks of his neck, and then called to Boon. "Are you coming?"

Boon's ears pricked up, and he sprang to his feet.

"Come on then," said Harvey.

Boon's paws tapped across the tiles and he scampered through the doorway, ready for his morning run. Harvey gave the house a glance, taking a mental image. Then he pulled the door closed behind him and locked it.

His run varied from day to day. Another thing he'd learned long ago from his mentor was to try and avoid using the same route twice. Habits made it easier to catch people, a fact he'd exploited many times himself while forming plans to take down his own targets.

Harvey ran across his land and into the thick forest that stood on the boundary of the property. He hurdled fallen trees and picturesque streams then burst through an overgrown hedge into the adjacent, freshly-ploughed fields that bore the signs of early spring. The paddocks, fields and forests that surrounded his home allowed him ample opportunities to try different routes.

As easy as it was to run a new route each day, Harvey

always finished at the beach near his home. He knew it was a mistake, and each day he did it, Julios' words came to life in his mind. But the beach was perfect for a final sprint, and in some weird way, by going against what Julios had told him to do so often, Harvey confirmed that his old life was over. Now he trod a new path where habits were allowed, his enemies were either dead or far away, and in the criminal world, Harvey Stone was a mere memory to the few that ever laid eyes on him and survived; a new generation of villains had emerged.

Harvey walked the last hundred yards along his private dirt driveway, a small muddy track between his own land and his neighbour's. He used the walk as his warm down, and it gave him time to stretch his legs.

Stopping halfway along the driveway, he reached down to his feet, folding himself in half and gripping his toes between fingers and thumbs. Then he worked his head lower, stretching his back and glutes until, by holding the back of his legs, he could place his forehead against his knees.

That was when he saw the fresh tyre tracks in the mud.

They were of an SUV or bigger, judging by the width. Melody drove a little sports car and she'd been gone a few days already. Harvey's bike had hybrid tyres.

Someone else had driven along the drive.

Harvey's senses pricked. He took a quick look around. He hadn't seen any cars on the return from his run. It was early morning for the sleepy, coastal village; the tourists would come later. Harvey wasn't expecting anybody. Visitors were rare.

He checked the house. The front door was shut and bolted from the inside as it always was. The windows looked intact, locked and exactly how he'd left them. Nothing seemed out of place.

Except for the tyre tracks.

He moved to the rear of the house, taking a wide arc and surveying his land. It was seemingly devoid of life.

It was when he reached the back door and found the envelope pinned to the wood that he knew trouble had come knocking.

CHAPTER THREE

"How's the progress going?" said Jackson, as he stepped into the operations room.

"Radio silence, sir," replied Reg. "We have Gibson and Sharp in the country, but so far, neither has made contact."

"So what's the protocol?"

"They have trackers, sir, so we can see where they are."

"But you can't talk to them?"

"Not as yet. We're trying but have had no response. They have comms kits, but right now, it's unknown if these are being blocked by the Greek authorities."

"And do we have any idea of who is running the show yet?"

"Not yet, sir. That's why the two operatives were sent. They were both briefed and told not to engage. We're expecting a report back in two hours' time. If we don't hear anything, we'll send in some backup."

"Okay," said Jackson. "Nothing heavy. This is a straightforward investigation. I had hoped we'd have straightforward answers by now."

Jackson stepped out of the operations room and closed the door behind him.

"He's on your case," said Ladyluck from the far end of a central row of tables.

"Thanks, Ladyluck, I'll deal with Jackson. You just find me Gibson and Sharp," said Reg.

He turned back to his screen and ran another ping test on the two men's comms kit.

"I know that look," said Melody. "You're worried about them."

"Of course I'm worried, Melody. I sent three men to Athens to carry out some surveillance, one of whom has been missing for a week, the other two we haven't heard from for eight hours."

"But we can see them on screen," said Jess. "That's something, isn't it?"

"I think we all know that doesn't mean they're alive," said Reg. "How many times have we chased after Harvey only to find a pile of clothes in a field?"

"Oh, come on, we can't compare these two guys to Harvey. These are trained men. They know the protocols. They know the moves."

Reg shoved his keyboard away and sat back.

"Reg, take it easy," said Jess.

"Yeah, I'm sure they'll be fine."

"I just don't want to have to make those calls, Melody," he whispered. "To their wives, you know? We already lost Harper. We can't afford to lose another."

"Harper knew the risks, Reg," said Jess. "He was the first man in, and instead of doing what he was told, he went off-piste and landed himself in hot water. If he'd just done what he was told in the first place, first of all, he'd still be alive, and secondly, they wouldn't know we're on to them. We'd have eyes on the ground feeding us information so we can intercept the delivery. How much simpler could it get?"

"But he didn't, Jess, did he?" argued Reg. "No. He used his

own judgment without our support, got caught and now anyone I send out there is in danger from the moment the wheels hit the ground."

Jess turned away, clearly displeased with Reg's reaction. She was the baby of the team. Her last name, Jones, was never used. When an operative went to Jess with a problem to be researched, they didn't address a cold last name. Instead, they sat with a Jess, a real person who understood what they were trying to achieve. Everyone knew Jess well enough to use her first name. She'd helped them all at some point. Although she and Reg had been an item for over a year, work was work, and she sucked up Reg's snappy comment with professional distaste.

"So send more men," said Melody.

"Excuse me?" said Reg. "Did you just hear what we said?"

"I heard," said Melody. "Send two operatives to track down Gibson and Sharp. Who are the two new guys?"

Reg glanced at the far end of the room.

"You mean Derby and Barnet?"

"Yeah, send them. Let them prove themselves," said Melody.

"It might come to that," replied Reg. "I don't like it though."

"Where'd they transfer from anyway?" asked Melody. "They look like they know what they're doing."

"Can't really say, Melody," said Reg. He turned his head to face her. "Even if I knew."

"They don't tell you? Don't you get their career history?"

"I just run the operations, Melody."

"So?"

"So what?"

"Are you going to send them?"

"I know you're right, but let's hang on," said Reg. "I don't want to jump to conclusions until we know Gibson and Sharp are definitely in some kind of trouble."

"By the time Gibson and Sharp are found, it'll be too late. We've already lost our eyes on the ground."

Reg leaned back in his chair and gave a loud exhale of frustrated air.

"Derby," he called to the other side of the room.

"Sir?"

"Get yourself set up," said Reg. "You and Barnet are going to Athens."

"What do you mean they got in your way?" Fernando shouted into the phone. "You're a smart guy, aren't you? Or do I need to find someone smarter?"

Bella tried her hardest to hear the voice on the other end of the phone, but Fernando had moved away and was pacing the boat.

"Undercover agents? So take care of them. We have a boatful arriving in Athens in approximately thirty minutes. Make sure they reach the lorry or-"

Fernando's voice lowered to almost a growl.

"Listen to me, Streaky, if the agents stand in your way, get rid of them like the last one. We need to get these people through, or the boss will have us all dumped in the sea, and hey, *I* am not going to be the one to take the rap. Take care of it." Fernando paused. "What do you mean where am *I*? Don't you worry so much about what I'm doing. You just concentrate on getting rid of those agents, and getting those trucks ready."

From where Bella lay below deck, Fernando seemed to be getting angrier and angrier. She couldn't face any more of the man's temper. He was like a coiled spring.

"I don't care what Jimmy told you, Streaky." Fernando's voice had risen again to an excited yell. "I took *one* as a guarantee, and I'm keeping her safe. There's nine more in Jimmy's boat. Lock them in the workshop and see to it that they make the truck tomorrow."

He disconnected the call.

Bella heard Fernando walking above her. He was confident on the boat, walking naturally with the movements of the waves as if he'd been at sea for many years. She also noticed that this new boat rocked much less than the other one. Maybe Fernando was more skilled than the previous captain.

She lay in darkness on the scratchy, smelly fishing nets, listening to his footsteps. Her body tensed each time it sounded like he was close by, near the back of the boat.

She was dreading the doors opening again.

Bella wondered what would happen. Her English wasn't perfect, but it was good enough to understand the one-sided conversation Fernando had spoken with somebody called Streaky. The others were going to be loaded onto another truck. That had been the plan for her; that was what she had paid for. The last leg of her journey.

Would she be going too? Would she be reunited with them eventually? Or had *her* path now changed?

She would choose her own path when the time was right.

"Boss?" she heard Fernando say. He was using the telephone again, but this time his tone was different, more submissive.

"No, I've told him to take care of it. The boat should be arriving any time now."

Fernando paced above her once more. He took long, slow steps instead of the shorter more agitated ones he had taken before.

"Yes, I have taken one for security," said Fernando. "No, boss, she is *not* for my own pleasure. This one is a troublemaker."

The pacing stopped. Bella listened intently to the one-sided conversation.

"Yes, it's a girl."

"What do you mean is she pretty? What do you think I-?"

"No, boss. I'll keep her on my boat. I have an idea."

"Yes, boss."

"I know. They will send more men and they will just keep coming."

"I don't know how they found us. In fact, as I remember, it was your job to see that our operation remained invisible, but now I see even you aren't able to stop their meddling. We'll need to find alternatives in the future. Athens is no longer safe for us. But most of all, it is important that we encourage Harvey Stone to join us here. We will kill two birds with one stone. Or should I say all the birds and the Stone."

"Oh, he will come. It's what he does. In fact, I have already reached out to him. But I think maybe he will need some gentle persuasion."

"No, boss. I asked him to join us a few months ago. But he's retired now, so he'll need convincing. I'm sure I have the means."

"I'm so sure because his moral compass is his weakness. Give me one of the refugees and I'll have him for sure."

"Yes, boss, I know I already *hurt* them. But clearly, he needs further encouragement. I think perhaps one of the younger ones. It will be a small sacrifice to pay for such a grand finale to Mr Stone's life."

Fernando disconnected the call, sighed out loud, and took four slow, deliberate steps towards the back of the boat.

No harm will come to her. That's what he'd said.

Bella clung to that thought as the two small wooden doors opened. Fernando stooped low and peered inside. He stood silhouetted by the dawn sun. Bella couldn't make out his features or his expression but saw that he was removing his belt.

She huddled herself against the wall and tucked her bare feet into the dirty nets.

"What do you want?" she cried.

"Bella, Bella, Bella," he said with a mock soothing voice.

"Leave me alone," she said. "Please. Just don't touch me."

Fernando stood over her with his belt in his hand, rocking the leather strap back and forth. His other hand was slowly unfastening the buttons on his trousers.

"We can do this the hard way, Bella," he said. "Or we can do this the even harder way."

CHAPTER FIVE

"Sir, you might want to see this," said Jess, leaning back as she moved her computer's video output to one of the large wall-mounted screens above them.

"Who's that?" asked Reg. He tracked the little red icon that moved across the satellite imagery screen.

"Gibson, sir."

"He's in a boat?" asked Reg, a little surprised.

"Looks like it. He still hasn't checked in though."

"And Sharp?" asked Reg. "Any news from him?"

"Not a dicky bird, sir."

"Do we have him on screen at least?"

"Nope. He disappeared last night," replied Jess. "He was by the boatyard for a while, but then just vanished while we were in the meeting."

"Vanished?"

"Vanished, sir," said Jess. "Could be two reasons-"

"He's underground-"

"Or he's underwater," finished Jess.

"Or he's just plain old had everything stripped off him and dumped in the sea," offered Melody. "It wouldn't be the first time that had happened, would it?" Melody raised an eyebrow to Reg. She was referring to an incident where Harvey had his clothes stripped off his body, leaving the team clueless about his whereabouts.

Reg fell silent and stared at the red dot on the screen as it moved slowly out to deeper water, away from the mainland into the Mediterranean.

"I know where I'd put my money," said Ladyluck under her breath.

Reg span around and immediately realised that the whole office had been watching the screen too. One of their colleagues, who had been missing for two days, was very possibly being led out to sea to be dumped in the ocean, and another one was missing.

"Keep your thoughts to yourself please, Ladyluck," muttered Reg.

"Jess, can we try to get hold of him?" asked Reg. "Just keep trying."

"I've had an open call out to the pair of them for nearly forty-eight hours now, sir," replied Jess. "Sat phones are off and the comms aren't being responded to. We ran some network tests and the devices are responding, so they're operational, but neither of the men are responding."

"Can we get a live satellite feed on that boat please, someone?"

Jess's fingers sprang into life. Within a few moments, the large wall-mounted screen beside the satellite tracker displayed an aerial view of the world. Then the image zoomed closer and closer until the continents became countries, and countries became cities, until finally Athens and the Mediterranean filled the screen. The image zoomed in at the satellite camera's maximum range and the city was pushed off screen. A pixelated image of a tiny boat surrounded by the ocean remained on the screen.

"Is that the best we can do?" asked Reg.

"That's the only satellite we can access in the region right now, sir," said Jess, "without drawing attention to the operation."

"I feel so helpless," said the woman beside Ladyluck. "I mean, can't we call the Greek authorities or something?"

"And tell them what?" asked Reg. "That we're sorry but we seem to have misplaced two of our secret service agents in your lovely city, and we think another might be about to-"

"Don't say it," said Jess.

"It doesn't need saying anyway," said Reg.

The boat had stopped. The satellite image grew a little clearer, but was still not clear enough for the team to identify individual people. It was just a blurred picture of two men struggling with something heavy. Within a few moments, there was no need to watch.

The red dot on the overhead screen blinked off and a tiny beeping alarm started on Jess' central computer. The entire team stared at the two screens in silent disbelief.

"Switch that off," said Reg. He lowered his head. "Let's all take a moment, team, to remember Gibson and spare a thought for his family."

Reg stood giddy on his feet while around him his team dealt with the blow in their own ways. Some of them closed their eyes. Some looked at the floor. Manners, who sat beside Lady-luck, mouthed a silent prayer to herself.

"Thank you, everyone," said Reg. "Jess, follow that boat. We need the identification mark. There must be a port authority number on it. Ladyluck, start making arrangements."

"Arrangements, sir?" Ladyluck replied. "What for?"

"We're relocating the operations team," said Reg. "We're not going to catch this lot sat here. We're *all* going to Athens."

CHAPTER SIX

Harvey took a slow climb down the ladder with a pile of broken roof tiles on his shoulder and dumped them in a rubbish skip. He'd been slowly filling it over the past few months. Behind his garage was a stack of new tiles that he'd bought. It wasn't many, but enough to replace the broken ones dotted around the roof. Winter would arrive before he knew it. Anyway, where better a place to keep an eye on his property than on the roof? The note had jarred Harvey. The work took his mind off the note, but his senses had been pricked.

He collected two of the new tiles, walked back to the ladder and began the long climb up. Slotting them in was easy on the lower rows. He'd just hooked the lowest tile over the roof baton when he caught sight of a black SUV travelling very slowly along the lane towards the beach. It was nothing; cars used the lane all the time. But Harvey noted the make and model and eyed it as it drove past.

The driver stared back at him.

It took another two hours to replace the broken tiles. The sun was rising high, the day heading into peak tourist time.

More cars began to venture along the lane, but not the black SUV.

The beach was just two minutes away. Although the town of Argylles did not see as many tourists as places like Marseille or Montpellier, which were both a few hours along the coast, many people who hunted for the quieter coastal spots eventually found the place Harvey called home. The cars became frequent as the morning grew later, but he kept his eye on the traffic. An old habit.

Soon after Harvey had finished the roof, he stood in his kitchen at the back door with a coffee in his hand. Boon was sleeping somewhere inside the house.

The photo on the kitchen counter drew his attention once more.

Why would someone want him?

The photograph felt sticky as if it had been recently printed. It showed a young girl in a small, poorly lit room. Her hands and feet were tied, her nose was bloodied, and her eye swollen. She had clearly been beaten. It wasn't the most shocking thing Harvey had seen. In fact, he'd done far worse to people himself. But what did the photo mean?

He tried to recall the face, but it was nobody he knew or remembered, and he thought himself to be pretty good at remembering faces. Scribbled on the back had been a small cryptic message. *You can stop this. FF.*

The message was correct; Harvey probably could stop whatever was happening. But why would he get involved in what looked like it could be a lot of trouble? Someone else's trouble. He'd had enough of his own adventures. He didn't need to go and fight someone else's battles.

But who was it? And how did they know where he lived?

The note had been signed *FF*.

The fields behind his little farmhouse were perfect for

thinking, just wide, open fields that stretched on forever, dotted with small forests. The scene allowed the mind to wander where it wanted, almost as if it was itself walking in the fields.

Maybe someone had gotten his name from somebody else. Someone fighting for beaten housewives, perhaps? Maybe the photo was just generic or staged as a trap. But he knew it wasn't. Harvey had seen enough to know that it was a real photo with a real girl in a real room.

With real blood on her dirtied face.

Harvey picked up the image up for the twentieth time. "She's foreign," he said aloud. "The clothes, the skin, the headscarf."

He studied the photo further.

"That's a fishing net that she's lying on."

Harvey held the photo into the light.

"The walls are wood and the..." Harvey stopped. He pictured the scene. It was suddenly clear in his mind.

It was a boat. The girl was on a boat.

Was it in France? Was it close by? Was that why someone had asked him to help?

Footsteps crunched on the loose stones to the side of the house. Harvey pushed the back door closed and stepped into the shadows. The footsteps grew closer and slowed; whoever it was knew to be quiet.

An arm reached out, ready to pin another photo to his door. Harvey wrenched the door open and grabbed the wrist tight.

"Non, non. S'il vous plaît. Ne me blessé pas," cried the young French boy, his eyes wide with fear.

Harvey dragged him inside and continued to grip his arm. He snatched the photo from him. "Where is this?" he asked.

The boy just shook his head.

"Où?" shouted Harvey.

The boy instinctively glanced towards the lane and held up

a five-euro note. Harvey pulled him through the house to the bedroom where the windows looked out onto the long drive and the lane beyond. He pulled the edge of the curtain back. A glimmer of light reflected off a car window parked in full view at the end of his drive. Before Harvey could react, the car pulled off abruptly.

It was the black SUV he'd seen earlier. Harvey recalled one man driving alone, no kids, and he hadn't seen any baggage.

"Go," he said to the kid. He released his grip and pointed to the door but remained staring at the new photo.

The boy ran back through the house, past Boon, who had woken and ventured out from the couch to see what was happening, and out into the field. The door crashed closed behind him.

Harvey watched through the window as the boy ran the length of his driveway without looking back then turned right, heading inland towards the village.

The photo was a similar scene, but with a different girl.

He turned away in disgust. It was clear that she'd been more than just beaten.

Harvey sat the new photo beside the old one in the kitchen then flipped it over face down.

The party has started. Your presence is required. FF.

CHAPTER SEVEN

"So you expect him to make contact soon, do you?" said Fernando.

Bella was amazed that the pig could take a phone call so calmly after what he'd just done to her. She wiped her eyes with the back of her hand and pulled her dress down to cover herself, thankful for the darkness of the cabin. She couldn't bear to look at the damage he'd caused.

Bella had been horrified when he'd used his phone to take a photo while he hurt her. She'd hidden her face with her hands, but he'd just pulled them away and told her to smile. Then, he'd seemed proud when he sent the photo to somebody.

Am I being sold?

She dry heaved at the thought of him inside her. Never would she forget that sickening sensation. His odour, his breath and his crooked nose would always haunt her. Bella had worked herself up. Her breathing had quickened, and her dry throat rasped. But not for long.

"We need him here in Athens, Rascal. Don't let him run away with the idea that hurting you is going to achieve anything," said Fernando. "I've seen him in action. The man's a beast, and if you're not careful, he'll take you down before you even know he's there. Stay local, stay visible, and get him on your side. I'll take care of him when he's here."

Even from outside on the deck, Fernando's voice nauseated Bella. There was no going forward for her now. A few hours ago, she'd had a choice: life or death. Now all she had was the hope that Fernando got her to England where she may be able to put the terrible journey behind her and start afresh, somehow.

But even if he did...

Bella knew she wouldn't be able to live with herself now. She was dirty. Her timing needed to be right. It would need to be soon before they arrived on land.

I'm carrying the child of the devil, she thought.

Bella pushed herself up onto her knees and winced at the pain he'd caused, sharp like daggers below her dress. Something had torn and she'd bled.

She tried the doors but they didn't budge. She peered through the crack between them and saw that Fernando had pushed something through the handles to stop them from opening, a piece of wood maybe. Bella fell back onto the nets and curled up into a ball.

"Keep me posted, Rascal," said Fernando, his phone call coming to an end. "If he doesn't reach out today, I'll send another photo, and this time, he'll respond for sure."

Bella's heart sank. She would need to find a way to die before then. But in the darkness and with the doors locked, she would have no chance. If Fernando needed another photo, worse than before, then perhaps an opportunity would arise.

She would take the devil child with her.

What he'd done to her had been excruciating, but it was the ease at which he'd done it that had seemed to make it worse. The man had no remorse. He was pure evil. His footsteps on the deck above acted as a reminder that the devil walked close by.

Bella thought back to happier times, desperate to push the bitter taste of him out of her mouth. Her body. Her mind.

She thought of her mother. She remembered how they would sit and talk for hours about all the things that had been and all that might be. Her mother had warned Bella that she would need to find the right man, a kind man, to enjoy her life with. Some men, her mother had warned, would take everything and give nothing back. But the right man would wait until it was offered and when the time was right; that would be the man to bear her children for.

Fernando had taken what he'd wanted with ease.

Had he done it before?

He would do it again, for sure. Maybe Bella could finish them both, herself and Fernando. Her own life might be over, but maybe she could help and save the lives of others. Perhaps she could sink the boat. Perhaps the deed would work in her favour as she stood on the cusp of heaven and hell, a tainted woman carrying the devil's child, unworthy of heaven's grace.

The boat's engine started up again. She hadn't even noticed it had stopped, but thinking back, it had fallen silent just before he'd opened the door. At least he wouldn't touch her while the boat was moving.

She moved again to the two doors and peered through the tiny crack. It was daylight still, and the blue sea and sky seemed to merge.

Bella had seen the small canopy above the wheel. It had been about halfway along the boat. If Fernando was steering, would he hear if she broke out?

She pushed gently on one side of the doors.

It didn't move.

She pushed a little harder.

The corner gave a little.

Harder still.

She could feel the cool air on her hands.

Bella grasped the other door and applied pressure. She found that it flexed more than the first.

Hope peered tentatively from the darkness.

The door seemed to be made of long wooden panels. If she could just break one free, maybe she could get an arm out then remove whatever Fernando had wedged between the handles.

Her heart pounded. If he caught her, who knew what else he was capable of doing.

Bella laid on her back and put the heel of her right foot against the first wooden panel. She raised her arms above her head and held onto the wooden wall.

She pushed.

The door flexed but remained.

Deep breaths and hope filled her thoughts. She would have limited time if she managed to break through.

On a count of three, she told herself. Her breathing began to quicken.

Strength.

Three.

Freedom.

Two.

Mother.

"Right team, let's get ourselves ready," said Reg, as the private jet taxied along the airfield towards the awaiting cars.

"We'll take the van, sir," said Derby. "Barnet and me."

"Good," said Reg. "That leaves four of us. Jess, Melody, Ladyluck, you ride with me in the car. I want to get to the safe house and get surveillance set up, and I want to be set up by nightfall."

"What do we have for a safe house?" asked Melody, looking around at the team. "A villa?"

"It's a two-bed apartment opposite the boatyard, maybe thirty to forty minutes' drive from here," said Ladyluck. She was pleased with her ability to organise the plane, the safe house and transport in under two hours.

"And presumably we're not going to blaze through Athens in an unmarked black BMW?" replied Melody, donning her sunglasses and letting her hair fall over her tight leather jacket.

"There's a financial crisis, Mills," said Ladyluck, reaching for her small case from the overhead. "Arriving in the industrial area in a BMW would be like painting targets on our backs."

Melody ducked down and peered through the window. An

old car and a beat-up van were parked beside each other at the furthest end of the private runway. They stood away from the buildings and sheltered by stationary planes.

"They look like they won't even make the forty minute journey," said Melody.

"So they're the perfect disguise. They'll fit right in." Ladyluck smiled as she sat back down in her seat. "Passports out everyone. We'll be greeted by officials and then left to our own devices. He's friendly, but if he tests you, we're on a business trip."

"A business trip?" said Derby, from the seat behind her. "We have a flight case full of automatic weapons, and enough rounds to start world war three."

"This is Greece, Derby. If you want me to put it into perspective, *you* have more money than Greece in your savings account," replied Ladyluck in her best authoritative tone and clearly loving being the centre of attention. "You'll be surprised at the questions they don't ask when you cross their palms with silver."

Derby laughed. "Yeah and paper notes with the Queen's head on."

"You can be sure of that." Ladyluck smiled and gave him a wink.

"We'll load the van," said Derby. "You guys go ahead and get the place secure. We'll follow up with the gear."

Reg nodded his appreciation.

The private jet jerked to a stop, and Ladyluck stood again to be the first to exit.

At the bottom of the stairs stood two men, one in an ill-fitting cheap suit and one in a fine, light suit with a brown leather belt and shoes. A pair of sunglasses finished his polished look. Behind them were two cars and the old van. One of the cars was a nearly new silver Audi; the other was an old black

Peugeot. Melody could easily guess which vehicle belonged to which man, and which one was the official taking backhanders from the British government.

Melody stood third in the queue to disembark and then stepped out into the beautiful Greek sunshine. The feeling of warmth on her face was a pleasant change from the bitter London wind. It lifted her spirits immediately. The man with the shades and fine suit inspected their passports. He waved them on without so much as a hi or goodbye, unashamedly holding the brown envelope that Ladyluck had passed him under his arm as he did.

Melody had been missing Harvey. It was always the same while she was away. She wasn't full time with Reg's team and hadn't taken on too many jobs for him, but when she did, she missed home. She missed Boon and the house. The Greece operation had escalated from a simple human trafficking case to something far more sinister, and when agents had begun to disappear, Reg had asked for her help.

Maybe when it was over, she could stay out there for a while, she thought, and ask Harvey to join her for a holiday. As long as the plan went smoothly, they'd all be out in a few days. Some quality time with Harvey in Greece might be just what the doctor ordered.

It was Melody's first time in Athens. She sat silently looking out of the car window during the ride from the airfield, noting the simple houses and visible poverty. Despite Greece's ongoing financial situation, the forest-covered hills and glorious sunshine conveyed a sense of peace. It was a reminder that money wasn't the answer to everyone's happiness.

They crested a hill and looked down over the sprawling city of Athens. From above, it seemed to fill every space the valley floor had to offer, from the mountains that surrounded it to the beautiful blue sea below. Generic low-rise buildings stood side by side in pastel whites, blues and yellows, while the older, grander and often ancient buildings commanded the open space around them. In the centre of the city, atop the tallest rocky outcrop, stood the remains of an ancient citadel and landmark: the Acropolis.

The drive through the vibrant city gave a clear picture of life in Athens. Small squares hidden in backstreets teemed with life, where coffee shops and boutique clothes stores were hives of activity. Narrow streets with graffiti-covered buildings fed like river tributaries into larger roads with open squares, often featuring a central statue or monument. Melody recognised international chains and high-end designer stores in small pockets of affluence. Other areas housed tiny shops and street stalls, crammed with second-hand furniture, paintings, clocks, and anything that might raise a few euros.

The apartment that Ladyluck had organised was on the south side of the city at the north end of the coastline. There seemed to be much less traffic on the roads, fewer people on the streets and less wealth invested into the poorly maintained buildings.

"Mobile two, this is mobile one. Come back," said Reg into his radio.

"Mobile two," said Derby from the van.

"Mobile two, what's your ETA?" asked Reg.

"We're loaded and just coming down into Athens now. About thirty minutes behind you."

"Good," said Reg. "Mobile two, go find some coffee and maybe pick up water and supplies. We'll go in and set up surveillance. We don't want six people seen carrying boxes and bags into the apartment, so we'll arrive in batches."

"Copy," came the reply.

"Melody, can you check the roof? We need eyes all around, and that'll be your perch with the sniper rifle," said

Reg, as he flicked through some photos of the boatyard in his folder.

"Yep," said Melody, snapping out of her daydream.

"Are you okay, Melody?" asked Ladyluck. "You seem quiet."

"Yeah, just missing home, I guess," replied Melody without turning away from the window.

"I'm sure this will be over in a few days, Melody," said Reg.

The driver stopped the car outside a rundown apartment block facing a row of boatyards. The area bordered an industrial part of town. Chain link fences opposite the building acted as a perimeter for the boatyards.

"Is that our boatyard?" asked Melody.

"Yes, the middle one," replied Ladyluck.

"Security is pretty dire. Shouldn't be too hard to get inside."

"We need to see what they're doing before we send any more agents in, Melody. I can't risk anyone else."

"Copy that," replied Melody.

She scanned the grounds of the boatyard. Vast, open areas were dotted with scrapped or decrepit boats on trailers. Engines and loose parts lay scattered in the spaces between the trailers, and wild dogs patrolled the area in their perpetual hunt for food.

Melody peered up at the apartment building. It looked completely empty. "Looks nice, Ladyluck," she said. "Who's your travel agent?"

"It might not be a five-star hotel, Melody," replied Ladyluck. "But it's facing the boatyard, and I think you'll find it has all the amenities we need."

"I'm sure it's fine," said Reg, as he pushed his door open and climbed out of the car. "Two at a time. Jess, you're with me. Melody, Ladyluck, wait for my signal then follow."

Melody observed as Reg held the door open for Jess then followed her inside. Ladyluck caught Melody watching them.

"Cute, aren't they?" she said.

"She's nice," said Melody. "He deserves someone like her."

"He tells me you used to work together, full time, I mean."

"Yeah, we've spent the best part of ten years on various teams. Reg is a solid guy."

"And what do you think about him *running* this team?" asked Ladyluck. "You think he can handle it? I mean, he was just a researcher, a tech guy."

"Reg has seen more action than he lets on," replied Melody. "And he's capable of a lot more than you think. Are you having trouble with him?"

"No," said Ladyluck. "But I do doubt his ability to handle the decision making. It's a tough job."

"Do you?" replied Melody. "On what grounds?"

Ladyluck knew she'd overstepped the mark. "Well, he's not-"

"You don't know what he is or what he isn't," snapped Melody. "And all I've seen from you so far is negativity and pessimism. So why don't you keep your opinions to yourself? Give Reg a chance and, who knows, you might even learn something from him."

"Well, I-"

"Conversation's over, Ladyluck. Move on."

Melody pushed the car door open and climbed out with her rucksack.

"Hey," called Ladyluck, as she climbed out of her side. "He said to wait, right?"

"I'm done with waiting."

Melody pushed open the door to the old apartment building and stepped inside the fresh but very basic granite-clad foyer. A single, narrow set of stairs led off to her left and a small lift door stood in front. No concierge waited to take their bags. No plants were dotted around to cheer the place up. Just cheap decor, yellowing paint and the lift door. Any sign of previous tenants lay beneath a thick layer of dust.

The door opened behind her and Ladyluck stepped inside. Melody turned to glance her way, but Ladyluck averted her eyes.

"It's the top floor," said Ladyluck, hinting at the small lift.

Melody hit the button and a single door squeaked to one side, revealing a space ample enough for two people, but no more.

"Cosy," said Ladyluck.

Melody didn't reply. She stepped in and hit the button for the top floor. The doors struggled but eventually closed. The elevator's mechanism groaned into life and slowly began to rise.

It was nearly a full minute later when the ride stopped. There were two apartments in front of them, two doors and a strong, unpleasant odour of cat urine. To Melody's immediate right was the narrow staircase leading down to the foyer. An even smaller set of stairs led up to the roof.

"They're both ours," said Ladyluck, as she stepped out behind her. "One is for sleeping, one is for working."

Melody pushed the door of the right-hand apartment, and it swung open.

"Oh jeez, is that-?"

"Cat piss," said Melody. "I'm guessing we'll be sleeping in the other one."

She nudged the left-hand door and let it swing back to hit the wall.

"Reg?" she called.

There was no reply.

Melody stepped inside the apartment. There was a small kitchen to the right with a bathroom beside it, and then three larger rooms off the small corridor. Bright light spilt through the large west-facing windows into the lounge.

Melody stepped into the hallway.

"Reg? Jess?" she called, louder than before.

"Maybe they're on the roof?" asked Ladyluck.

Melody reached for her radio. "Tenant, come back."

No reply.

"Say that again?" said Ladyluck, cocking her head to one side.

Melody gave the call again over the radio.

"Sounds like it's coming from in here," said Ladyluck, opening the door to one of the bedrooms. "It is. Look, it's his radio. He must have dropped it."

"Reg wouldn't drop that," said Melody with urgency. "Check the other apartment. I'll check the roof."

Melody ran to the stairs. She hadn't even reached the roof when the entire top floor filled with Ladyluck's chilling scream.

CHAPTER NINE

There were few places to hide in the village of Argylles. Finding a rental car was easy for Harvey, as he rode his motorbike along the little high street. There were no hotels, just two bed and breakfasts and a few campsites.

Harvey found the SUV in under thirty minutes and found the owner less than five minutes afterwards. He was a short man. Either he was wearing a bad attempt at blending in as a tourist, in his khaki shorts and sleeveless top, or he was simply happy to be in the sunshine, where he could show off his toned arms.

To Harvey, he stood out a mile.

Harvey watched him from a distance as he emerged from one of the village's two little cafes. He was typing a message into his phone. Then he lit a cigarette and took the short walk to his car.

Harvey sized him up and began to formulate a plan. He didn't have time or energy to waste on these people. They'd somehow found him, but Harvey was sure they would leave him alone once they had heard what he had to say.

And did what he had to do.

The black SUV pulled away from the curb and took the road out of the village towards the beach, a long and winding stretch of tarmac that hugged the coast for miles. Harvey waited a full minute, and then followed.

As predicted, the man stopped the car a few miles further out of the village in front of a small cliffside bed and breakfast. Harvey assumed that staying in the centre would have been too close to Harvey's house, and any lodging further away would be inconvenient to deliver the messages. The next village was some way down the road, and even quieter than Argylles with even fewer bed and breakfasts.

The driver's door opened as Harvey approached. Harvey slid his visor up on his helmet, and came to a stop in front of the SUV to stop him from driving away. But Harvey's arrival was apparently part of the man's plan.

"I was wondering when you'd show your face," he said, smiling, as though Harvey had finally succumbed to the offers on the back of the two sick photos.

Harvey stepped off the bike, turned the engine off, and turned to face him. "What's with the pictures?"

"They say a picture says a thousand words, Mr Stone," he replied.

Harvey put the accent at European, but couldn't pinpoint the origin. He didn't reply.

"We need your help, Mr Stone. We have some people we need you to take care of."

"What makes you think that I'm looking for work? And why can't you sort them out yourself?" said Harvey. "I don't know you, I don't need money, and I certainly don't appreciate you sending little boys to my house to do your dirty work."

"Ah, the boy."

"Yeah, the boy. What are you, *nuts*? What do you think he's going to do now? He's going to tell his dad that some bloke in a black car gave him money to-"

"He won't tell anyone. I made sure of that."

Harvey didn't reply.

"So?" asked the man.

"So what?"

"Are you coming with me, or will you stay? I can assure you, the photos will only get worse." He lit another cigarette and breathed the smoke out in a long silver plume that carried in the wind. "Only you can stop the suffering, Mr Stone."

"Who do you work for?" asked Harvey. "Who's FF?"

"Ah, come on now."

"Do you know who I am?" Harvey asked.

"Well, my boss tells me great things."

"You've got the time it takes for me to count to ten before that becomes your last cigarette. Who do you work for?"

"Mr Stone-"

"Ten." Harvey took a step closer.

"You don't have a gun. You're just-"

"Nine."

Another step.

"If you hurt me, more will die."

"I don't care about anyone else," said Harvey. "Eight."

"Not even little girls?" said the man, stepping backwards. "I'm told you have morals."

"Seven."

Harvey matched his steps to maintain the distance.

"Don't you want to stop them being raped, Mr Stone?" said the man. "I can't believe you would just let them suffer."

"Six."

The man glanced backwards at where he was going and saw the cliff edge growing closer. He had nowhere to run.

"Five," said Harvey. "What do you need me to do?"

The man stopped walking backwards and held his hands up as if to stop the drama.

"Okay, okay. We have an operation. It was going well," he began. "But as you know, these things don't last. There are men, they make it hard for us, they stop our lorries."

"Four."

"We go here, they follow. We go there, they go there. They stopped our trucks. It costs money." The man's voice was becoming panicked.

"Three. Who are these people?"

"We don't know. Maybe competition? But they have to go, and my boss says good things about you."

"And who is your boss?"

The man inhaled, and his large chest rose with the air.

"Two."

"Fernando," he said finally. "Fernando Ferez."

A memory hit Harvey, and he immediately understood.

"He told me that he spoke to you a few months ago, here on the beach. He offered you work," said the man.

"And I told him I don't want work."

"Well, he-"

"What's the job?"

"I can't say, Mr Stone." The man looked apologetic. "We have to keep things tight, you know."

Harvey didn't reply.

"So you'll do it?" said the man. A wry smile crept onto his face. "You'll come to Athens with me?"

"I didn't say that," replied Harvey. "But now I know where it is and who it is for."

Harvey rolled his neck left and right.

"What? *What?*" The man glanced behind him at the cliff edge. "You won't kill me."

"Wouldn't I?"

"No. No, you won't. You want to stop the girls from being hurt, and only I can take you." He gave Harvey a smug look, lowered his hands and straightened his vest top. "So how should we do this?"

"Like this," said Harvey. He took a step forward.

The man stepped back in defence into thin air.

"One."

CHAPTER TEN

"One."

Bella spoke the final count aloud then slammed the heel of her foot into one of the wooden panels, which splintered and broke away from the frame. But the gap was too small for her to climb through.

She tried again on the next panel along. It took two more attempts, but eventually, she broke through.

Bella stretched through with her arm. The gap still wasn't wide enough for her body, but she could reach the chunk of wood that Fernando had wedged between the handles. She tugged on it and hit it until it clattered to the deck.

Sunlight and air washed over her, and the wake of the boat spread out before her like a winding road to the horizon. As fast as she could, she pulled herself from the cabin. Holding onto the handrail, she took a final glance back to check Fernando hadn't seen her.

Suddenly, the engine stopped.

Fernando was nowhere to be seen. The raised cabin blocked her view of the rest of the boat. She checked the narrow gangways that ran along each side.

He must be at the front.

Seizing her chance, Bella took a tentative and painful step over the handrail with one leg. She then paused to check behind her.

Fernando's eyes locked onto hers as a lion might peer from long grass. He swung a long gaff in a wild arc. Bella couldn't move. She was stuck; her dress was caught on the old handrail. The long wooden pole caught her square in the back, knocking the wind out of her. She tried to free herself and pull her leg back, but Fernando swung the long pole once more. Bella felt the sharp hooked end of the gaff rush past just inches from her face.

Bella toppled and fell to the floor.

"You little bitch," said Fernando, seeing the damage she had done to his boat. "You're nothing but an ungrateful whore." He kicked out at her and connected with her lower back.

Bella rolled into a ball then saw her chance. If she could just stand up, she could make the leap over the side rail.

"Come here, you little-"

Bella sprang to her bare feet, took one step, placed her hands onto the stainless steel tubing, and leapt into the air. Then, with a sudden jerk to her throat, she was yanked backwards by the neck. Fernando's gaff held tight around her throat. She hit the hard deck flat on her back in a confused state of shock and pain. She writhed as her body sought to understand.

Fernando stepped across and stood over her. His nose seemed to be even larger and more crooked from where she lay, looking up at him.

"You're beginning to be more trouble than you're worth," he said. "It's a shame."

Bella didn't reply. Her chance had gone. He would surely make her suffer now.

"Why do you want to die?" he asked. His voice softened.

"You spent so long running from your home to get to England and look." He pointed to the land on the horizon. "It's not far now, maybe two days once we hit land. So why do you do these things?"

"There's nothing left for me now," she whispered. The fight inside her had dissipated, and she prepared herself for pain.

"There are many things left for you if you want them bad enough." Fernando lowered himself to a crouch beside her. "You're pretty," he said. "You just need a chance, a helping hand."

"And who is going to give me a helping hand now?" Bella replied, cradling her stomach.

Fernando dropped his eyes to her belly.

"I can help you there. I know a man."

"No. It is forbidden."

"It is forbidden?" asked Fernando. "It is forbidden to destroy the life of one to save the life of another?"

Bella shook her head. "It's over. My life is over. Do as you wish to me."

Fernando smoothed her hair and tucked the loose strands behind her ear. He ran his dirty finger along her cheek and dropped it to her neck. Then she allowed his hand to move to her chest. Bella shuddered at his touch, her breathing quickened, and she clamped her eyes shut tight.

Fernando rested his hand on her stomach.

"So precious," he whispered. "You carry a miracle inside."

Bella didn't reply.

"Why do you fear me?"

She opened her brown eyes, and he met her gaze with curiosity.

"You could have it all," he said. "Everything you need. Everything you desire."

"My life was over when I left Syria."

"No, no, no," said Fernando. "Your life has only just begun." He slid his hand away and traced the outline of her belly with his finger.

Bella tensed as his touch ran along the outside of her leg to her dirty toes, and then began its journey back up the inside of her thigh.

"The way I see it, Bella, you are at a crossroads, a junction, if you will." He stopped at her knee and rested his hand. "One path leads to certain death, a long and painful death, in which you will not find martyrdom." His finger began its journey again, pulling with it the hem of Bella's torn dress. "The second path leads to a long and fruitful life with all the luxuries a girl like yourself could dream of, the softest bed you ever saw, the finest foods you ever ate, and the prettiest dresses money can buy. But only for you, you understand? You will bear *my* children and *my* children alone." His finger stopped at her stomach once more. He had revealed her nakedness beneath the dress.

"You carried this baby from Syria?" he asked.

Bella nodded. She knew it was a lie. She knew the child was his; it could only be his.

Fernando bent to her and began to kiss her neck with soft, gentle touches of his lips on her skin.

Small tears leaked from Bella's eyes and ran freely into her hair. She heard him inhale her scent, felt him feel her breast, and tasted his foul breath that hung heavily in the air.

"Tell me, Bella," he whispered. "Tell me what path you choose and I will see to it that you get everything you deserve."

Fernando positioned himself on top of her, forcing her legs apart with his knee.

"Of course, for you to get what you desire, in return you must give me what I desire."

Bella felt him, hard against her body, but was unable to move.

Fernando bent to whisper in her ear. "I can be soft and gentle if you let me. I can make you happy."

She felt sick. Her throat had closed with fear and panic. She tried to speak, but no words came.

"Tell me which path you choose, Bella."

Fernando's breathing had quickened. He pressed into her in a slow rhythm.

"Bella, give me what I want," he said. "Look how far I've brought you." He kissed from her neck to her ear. "I can take you all the way."

"I..." Bella began. Her voice was raspy from her bone-dry throat.

"Yes?" whispered Fernando, pressing harder and breathing faster.

"I choose..."

Fernando gave a soft groan. "Choose life, Bella."

Bella opened her mouth to finish her sentence, but a small vibration from Fernando's pocket pulled him away. He sat up, and Bella saw his eyes widen with anger and frustration at the incoming call.

He pulled the phone from his pocket, hit the green button to connect the call, and sat back on his haunches, straddling Bella so she could not escape.

"Tell me you have him."

CHAPTER ELEVEN

"All units abort," called Melody into her radio. "I repeat, all units abort. It's a trap. We're compromised."

"Who would have done this?" said LadyLuck; tears streamed from her eyes.

"Let's get out of here, Ladyluck," said Melody. "Take the stairs, it'll be quicker."

Ladyluck couldn't peel her eyes from Sharp's body.

"I said, let's *move*," said Melody, grabbing Ladyluck's arm and pulling her towards the door. She hit the push-to-talk button on her radio again. "The safe house is compromised. Wait for further instructions."

One short, sharp message returned with confirmation that mobile two had received and understood the message. "Copy that," said Derby.

"Down," said Melody, pushing Ladyluck towards the stairs.

"But what about Tenant and Jess?"

Melody stopped and took a quick look up the stairs to the roof.

"Stay here and scream if anyone comes," said Melody. She checked the digital readout on the decrepit elevator. "The lift is on the ground floor. Keep an eye on that readout. If it starts to climb, shout for me. If you hear anyone on the stairs, shout for me. You got that? Anyone at all."

Ladyluck hugged herself and stared at the floor.

"Ladyluck, did you hear me?"

She looked up at Melody.

"Anyone comes and you call," said Melody. "I'll be right there. I'm not going far."

Ladyluck gave an almost imperceptible nod and blinked away the tears that had begun to pool in her eyes.

Melody sprang up the little stairwell. At the top was a small door with a push-bar fire exit handle and a tiny frosted glass window with steel mesh reinforcement. The glass was old, scratched and dirty. Melody couldn't see through it.

Pulling her Sig from her waistband, Melody loaded a round. She nudged the handle, and the door opened effortlessly.

The rooftop was covered in terracotta tiles with a thick layer of dust. Fresh footprints led from the door to the low wall that ran around the edge of the building.

"Ladyluck, are you still there?"

There was a brief pause then a scared voice came back. "I'm here, but hurry. I don't like it."

"Okay, just hang in there."

Melody stepped out onto the tiles. The prints weren't clear. It was as if someone had walked from the stairs to the wall and back several times, each time along the same route, and each time making an individual footprint harder to read.

She checked left and right, but the rooftop was empty. Keeping to the pre-made footprints to avoid making her own, Melody walked to the parapet wall and glanced down at the road below.

The car was gone.

"Shit."

A few moments later, she was bounding down the stairs and found Ladyluck stood rooted to the same spot, her eyes firmly on the elevator readout.

"Let's go," said Melody. "Stay behind me."

"What did you see?" asked Ladyluck, as she followed Melody onto the stairs.

Melody turned back to her and held her index finger to her lips to quiet her then continued to sidestep down the stairs with her back to the wall. They found the foyer empty. Melody pulled Ladyluck to one side of the two main doors.

"When we get outside, we need to run, okay?"

"Run?" said Ladyluck. "But where? Why? The car-"

"The car is gone," said Melody.

"What's happened?" asked Ladyluck, beginning to panic.

"Mobile two, come back. Do you receive?"

"Loud and clear, Mills," said Derby.

"The safe house is compromised. Avoid at all costs. We lost Reg and Jess, and we're running blind."

"Copy that," came Derby's reply. "Do you have an RV point?"

"We'll find you. Radio silence from here on in," replied Melody. "Emergency calls only."

She clipped the radio to her belt and looked Ladyluck up and down.

"You're going to need to lose those," said Melody, gesturing at Ladyluck's heels.

"These?" said Ladyluck. "But everything I had was in the car."

"Well, the car's gone, so you need to lose them."

Ladyluck gave an indignant groan and removed her shoes one at a time. She stood with them in her hand, her handbag hanging neatly off her shoulder.

"Where are we going to go?" she asked. "What's happened to the others?"

Melody peered around the corner at the doors, and then faced Ladyluck. "Reg and Jess are missing. We can assume that whoever took them was responsible for Sharp's death. Seeing as the car has gone too, we have to assume the driver was in on this too, and that Ferez knows our position. They probably came down the stairs with Reg and Jess while we took the lift up."

"But who-?"

"Whoever you contacted to arrange the cars and the apartment is in on this too, so that seems like a good place to start. Who was it?"

"I just have a number. Everything is on my laptop."

"In the car?" said Melody.

Ladyluck shrugged and held her hands palm out to indicate that she wasn't carrying anything but her bag and her shoes.

"You remember who your contact was?"

"It was a safe number. We only use trusted sources from the database. I didn't just find them on the internet," said Ladyluck, her tone becoming defensive and irritated.

"You ran checks? They were qualified?"

"Yes, of course. Jackson gave us the contact. We haven't had any issues before."

"Ladyluck, do you trust me?" asked Melody.

"Do I have a choice?"

"Right now, you have *two* choices," said Melody. "You can stay here and hope they don't come back."

"Or?" asked Ladyluck, dreading the next option.

"You can trust me. But it's going to be dangerous."

Harvey didn't watch the man fall to his death. He didn't even imagine the man's body being torn apart and spread across the jagged rocks for the bloody, red sea to consume. Instead, Harvey strode casually to the black rental SUV, opened the door and looked inside.

An old smartphone sat in the centre console under the over-spilling ashtray. A cable ran from the cigarette lighter to the glove compartment where Harvey found a small photograph printer and a pack of photo paper. A few empty drink cans and sandwich wrappers littered the car floor, and all the surfaces had a layer of cigarette ash.

He took the phone and scrolled through the recently dialled numbers. There was only one number. Harvey hit the green button to initiate a call.

"Tell me you have him," came the answer.

"This stops now," said Harvey.

"Ah, Mr Stone," replied the voice. "You met my friend, I see."

Harvey recognised the voice of the tall man that had approached him on the beach months earlier. The whistle of a gentle breeze crackled through the phone's tiny speaker.

"I told you once before, I'm not interested in working for you. Consider this the second and last warning. There won't be a third, Ferez."

"Ah but, Mr Stone, a man of your talents is wasted on that little farm of yours. You could be so useful. What is it you grow there anyway? Memories?"

"If I'd have known you were going to pester me with pictures of your dirty little hobbies, Ferez, I'd have cut your throat the first time I met you."

Ferez gave a soft laugh. "I believe next time, Mr Stone, you won't have a choice *but* to help me."

"What's that supposed to mean?"

"You are a man who is guided by his moral compass, are you not?" said Fernando. "You just can't help yourself, can you?"

Harvey didn't reply.

"I imagine, in your childhood, you were the boy who defended the little ones against the bullies. Am I right, Mr Stone?"

Harvey didn't reply.

"You're remembering it now, aren't you? All those sweaty tumbles with other prepubescent boys. You enjoyed the looks on their surprised faces, didn't you? You defended the wimps who lacked the courage and strength to fight their own battles. You enjoyed the power it gave you to overcome the selfish little boys." Fernando paused. Harvey's mind filled with featureless faces of his childhood that he'd destroyed and left behind.

"But most of all, Mr Stone," Fernando continued, "I believe you enjoyed the fear, the smell of the hunter becoming the hunted, the predator becoming the prey. There's a beast inside you, Harvey, and you need to exercise it."

A silence filled the airwaves between the two men.

"I'm right, aren't I, Harvey?" Fernando's tone took on a cruel, discriminated timbre. "Your silence is louder than you credit it for. You don't scare *me*, Harvey Stone. You won't smell my fear. You won't look into *my* eyes and allow the beast you nurture so lovingly inside your soul to grow and rise up. It won't strike *me* down, Harvey. You're no better than the bullies themselves.

"Is that right?" replied Harvey.

"You condescend me, Harvey?" said Fernando. "You talk as if you're surrounded by an indefeasible wall that nobody can climb, as if the beast inside chaperons you as you amble through your wasted life."

Harvey didn't reply.

Fernando had worked himself up. His breathing had quickened, and Harvey imagined his dark eyes widening with adrenaline.

"You'll come, Harvey," he continued. "You'll come when I ask you to come. You'll do as I ask, beast or no beast."

"Have you finished with the speeches?" asked Harvey.

"There's a hole in your defences, Harvey," said Fernando. "There's a hole so big I could park my boat in it."

"So it's a stalemate then," said Harvey.

"It seems that way. But whose move is it?"

"I don't care whose move it is, Ferez," said Harvey. "I already explained once; it ends here. Find someone else to do your dirty work."

"Oh, but I want *you*, Harvey Stone," said Fernando. "I need you, and I'll have you. I believe *you* called *me*. So that makes it my move, does it not?"

Harvey didn't reply.

"Start the clock, Mr Stone." Harvey almost heard the grin on Fernando's face in the shadow of his crooked nose. "Start the clock because this will be a move to remember."

CHAPTER THIRTEEN

"An old friend," said Fernando, as he disconnected the call and pocketed his phone. "I think you will meet him soon. I hope so."

Bella didn't reply. She gazed up into the sky at the white clouds that rolled overhead, free.

"Have you decided which path you will take, Bella?"

Bella lowered her gaze to look at Fernando.

"I have thought about it," she murmured softly.

"And?" pushed Fernando. "Do you choose death?" He reached behind him for his knife. "Or do you choose life?"

Fernando was perfectly silhouetted by the sun. His face was lost in black shadow. The slightest cock of his head as he waited for her to answer was the only sign she could read.

"If I choose death..."

"Yes?" said Fernando. He span the knife in his hand and then rested the sharp point on her stomach.

"If I choose death, how will it be?" she asked. Her breathing turned hard and fast as she sucked in her stomach away from the blade.

"Slow," said Fernando. "Just like I told you."

"But how?" she asked. "With that?" She lowered her eyes to the knife.

Fernando shrugged.

"Maybe," he said. "Maybe a little with the knife, maybe a little with the water. I can be very creative, you know."

"And you will do it here? Now?" she asked.

"No," said Fernando with a cruel laugh. "This is no place to die. Think of the blood. Who will clean it all up when you're gone?"

The boat rocked as the strengthening wind picked up.

"And my baby?"

"Your baby?" he said. "You think I am an animal?" He seemed to grow angry at the statement. "Your baby will not suffer, if you live or if you choose death. But you are testing my patience, Bella. If you choose life, you will go to see my friend. He will take care of everything, and you will return to me clean. But if you choose death, it will be *your* choice, and therefore, you will be the murderer of your own child."

"But, not-"

"There's no buts, Bella," spat Fernando. "I'm offering you more than you ever dreamed of when you left that hole you came from. You dreamed of England, but what do you think you would get? A house, a car, a job? You people make me sick. There's no house waiting for you, no car, no job. You would be sheltered and fed, and that is all, while you wait in the system to be processed like a dog. Are you a dog, Bella?"

"No."

"What I am offering you, you must understand, is far beyond what England has to offer a refugee. You are a refugee, are you not?"

Bella nodded.

"A house, it is a nice house, with a garden where you will

plant flowers and a kitchen that you will keep clean and cook in. You can cook, can't you, Bella?"

She nodded once more.

"You will have freedom, money to go shopping and buy clothes and food." He paused for a moment. "Money to buy clothes and food for our children."

"Our children," she repeated.

"Our children," said Fernando. His voice had calmed and softened as if coercing her with his gentle side. "Our children will be beautiful, Bella. Two boys and one girl. Two to carry my name and one to carry your beauty."

Bella turned her head to one side and stared out to sea. She quickly became mesmerised by the rolling tide and sideways sky.

Fernando reached down and smoothed her hair once more.

"Bella," he whispered, "from the day I first saw you, I knew. Such a pretty thing, far prettier than the other girls. Your mother was pretty too, yes?"

Bella didn't reply. She held the thoughts of her mother at bay in the depths of her mind, while hope showed itself in fleeting glimpses of what could have been, and what still might come.

"And you are strong, with a heart like a lion, yes?"

She turned to face him.

"We would marry then?" she said, as if the realisation of having children had only just fallen into place.

"We would marry, yes," replied Fernando. "You would be my wife, and I would be so proud, Bella."

"But I have to give you what you want?"

"And I have to give you what you want in return, Bella. I will provide. You will not go without. You will not be hungry, and you will bathe in soap and creams, and lie in the softest sheets."

"And what do you want from me?"

"There are many things I want, Bella," said Fernando, as he once again lowered himself on top of her. "But one thing at a time. I do not want to fight. I do not want to take." He stared into her brown eyes. "I want you to give it to me freely, as a man's wife should."

Fernando wiped a tear from Bella's eye and kissed her cheek. She lay still, unable to move, and unwilling to try.

"Do you choose life, Bella?"

She nodded. The small movement of her head sealed her fate, and Fernando smiled.

CHAPTER FOURTEEN

"Where are we going?" asked Ladyluck, as she stopped running and fell in behind Melody, who was peering around the corner of a wall.

"We need to find mobile two. They have all our gear," she replied.

"Can't we just chance getting them on the radio?" asked Ladyluck. "Just once. My feet are getting torn to shreds."

Melody turned and looked at her feet. "Are they bleeding?"

"Not yet," replied Ladyluck. "But-"

"When we get deeper into the backstreets, we'll be able to slow down. But right now, we know that someone is out there with Reg and Jess. We don't know how many there are, or how heavily armed they are, but what we do know is that they aren't afraid to kill."

"You think we'll find them?" asked Ladyluck. "Tenant, I mean, and Jess?"

"It's been less than twenty minutes. Given the traffic in Athens, they can't be more than three miles away, and given that the people we're after operate from the boatyard, it's a safe bet that they've been taken there."

"So why are we running away from the boatyard into the city?"

Melody exhaled with frustration and put her hands on her hips.

"Because, Ladyluck," she said, "you have no weapons training or field experience. And you have no shoes. I have a handgun with one magazine. We need to find Derby so I can off-load you and get some hardware."

"Off-load me?" said Ladyluck. "So I'm slowing you down, am I?"

"Not really, Ladyluck. But trust me, if there was even the remotest possibility that I could take you into the boatyard so you could talk them to death while I escaped with Reg and Jess, we'd be running towards it and not away from it. But as it stands, you're an MI6 *researcher*, you're one of the team, and I'm not going to lose anyone else."

Ladyluck nodded at the assessment, and Melody turned back to the corner of the building.

"Do I talk too much?" asked Ladyluck.

Melody closed her eyes and took a breath.

"I mean, I can stop if you want. I just talk when I'm nervous. I don't really know why."

Melody turned back to her, ready to snap, when the front end of a black saloon car began to turn into the street.

"Move." Melody dragged Ladyluck around the corner into the side street, then pushed her into the entrance porch of an old shop with a boarded up doorway.

"Is that them?" asked Ladyluck. "Did they see us? Do you think they have Tenant in the car?"

Melody drew her Sig and ignored the questions. The sound of the engine approaching grew louder and the car's suspension squeaked on the rough cobbled street. Melody had noticed the sound on the journey from the airfield.

"It's them. Keep back," said Melody.

The car slowed then stopped, but the engine continued to run. They seemed to be waiting for something. Melody didn't dare to look around the corner. The car could only be ten metres away at the most, and they had nowhere to run. She studied the boards across the doorway.

"Ladyluck, see if you can open the door."

"It's boarded up," she replied. "How-"

A bullet ricocheting off the ground two feet in front of them cut her off.

Melody caught a glimpse of light from a nearby rooftop.

A scope.

She turned, shoved Ladyluck out of the way and planted a heel kick firmly into the door beside the lock. The old wooden frame splintered and the door crashed into the wall behind.

"Go. Now." Melody pushed Ladyluck into the dark space.

She glanced behind her in time to see another glint of light in the scope. Another round took a chunk of concrete off the building above her head. Dust and stones rained down, and she heard the car's engine rev.

Melody shut the door as best she could, and grabbed the top of an old wooden dresser.

"Help me," she called to Ladyluck. "Pull it over."

The pair heaved on the piece of old furniture, and let it crash to the floor. Then, seeing what Melody was trying to do, Ladyluck joined her in pushing it against the broken door.

"Now go," said Melody. "Look for a back door."

The boarded door began to splinter with holes and they heard the slamming of car doors. Then the door began to bang as men on the other side called to each other.

"There's no back door," said Ladyluck. "We're trapped."

"The stairs. Go."

The pair bounded up the four flights of stairs and heard the splintering of wood and crashing below, just as they broke out onto the roof.

Melody ran to the edge and looked across at the neighbouring rooftop. It was only a two-metre gap but at least a three-metre drop.

"No," said Ladyluck. "I can't do that."

Melody ripped a piece of timber off an old wooden pallet and forced it between the door handles.

"That should buy us some time," she said, just as the sniper found them on the roof and another bullet bounced off the doors.

"Damn it," she said, diving to the ground. "Can't we catch a break here?"

The two women rolled to the parapet wall that ran around the edge of the rooftop. The doors began to splinter as the men behind them fired into the wood.

"Handguns," said Melody. "That's a Glock."

"You can tell?" asked Ladyluck.

"Remember how I said you had two choices, Ladyluck?" said Melody, aiming at the doors, ready to take down whoever broke through.

"I chose wrong, didn't I?" replied Ladyluck.

"You can't change that now," said Melody. "But you do now have two more choices. The first one isn't great."

"And the second one?"

Melody glanced back at the low wall they would need to jump to reach the neighbouring building. "Even worse."

"No, Melody. I can't," said Ladyluck.

"Do you want to stay here and let whoever that is take you?" said Melody. "It's just a jump. It's not far. Just land and roll. You did gymnastics at school?"

"Twenty years ago, Melody."

More gunshots tore through the wood, then a boot burst through.

"You have seconds to decide, Ladyluck," said Melody, scrambling to her feet.

Immediately, a wild shot from the rifle on the far rooftop pinged off the parapet wall. Ladyluck moved into a crouch and peered behind her.

"Don't worry about him. He hasn't come close once," said Melody. "Are you ready?"

The wood that Melody had wedged between the door handles began to crack with the weight of the men ramming it from behind.

Ladyluck stood.

Another wild shot sang through the air close by.

"We're going to run and jump. Right foot on the wall, land with both feet, and roll. You got that?" said Melody, reaching for Ladyluck's hand.

The door finally burst open to their right.

"Now," screamed Melody. She pulled Ladyluck the first few steps. As soon as her right foot hit the wall, she let go and pushed off with everything she had, clearing the gap easily and landing with both feet. She tucked her head and rolled on one shoulder straight back up to her feet. Then she dove for cover into the open staircase.

Chancing a look back, Melody saw Ladyluck stood frozen with one foot on the parapet wall, her face a picture of fear, bewilderment and pure horror.

A man appeared behind Ladyluck, forced her arms behind her back then covered her mouth with his hand. Another man appeared, aimed his MP-5 at Melody and let off a three-round burst.

The last thing Melody saw before she made her escape

down the stairs was a blow to Ladyluck's head, knocking her senseless. Her knees buckled, and she fell like a rag doll into her captor's arms.

CHAPTER FIFTEEN

Harvey was agitated.

Boon sensed his master's unrest and retreated to the bedroom to curl up on the warm bed, something Melody never allowed, but Harvey never noticed.

The two photos sat side by side on the coffee table. They seemed to stare at Harvey, almost beckoning him. He stood and opened the door to the wood burner, picked up two small logs to keep the fire going for a while, and then shut the door.

Harvey loitered by the fire for a few seconds then reopened the door and cast the two photos inside with the logs. He shut the burner and peered through the glass as the heat immediately took hold of the polythene coating and began to melt, turning the already agonised faces into warped and perverted faces of horror.

He took his place on the couch once more and stretched out. The peace and quiet of their French home had been a dream of Harvey's for many years, and laying on his couch in total silence, except for the crackling and occasional hiss of the burning wood, had all been a part of that dream.

He'd often imagined how his future life would be during the times he'd sat waiting for a target, in the dark corner of a house, an alleyway, or a park. The hours had been long and silent with only his thoughts for company. His dreams of the house in France had accompanied him on so many of those occasions. And now, the dream had finally come true.

Except it hadn't.

Two voices sang in his head. Two faces haunted his imagination. His perpetual need to stand up to bullies tickled the nerves in his fingers; they twitched of their own volition. The movement caught Harvey's eye as if they belonged to someone else. He clenched his fist, closed his eyes, and tried to focus on the crackling and popping wood.

But the voices of the two beaten and abused girls in the photos chorused in his ear. Their faces morphed into one within the confines of his imagination. The photos were now one, and black and white as if ancient. Tears were the only movement in the scenes.

Harvey had seen it all before, pain, suffering, abuse. He'd seen suffering, instigated pain, avenged violence, and delivered retribution in too many cold, hard and drawn out deaths. Each murder was dispatched with the precision of a surgeon to ensure that the victim's last moments were filled with the misery that their own victims would endure for the remainder of their lives.

The photo in his mind now played like a showreel. The scene remained the same, but the faces changed like credits on a screen.

He remembered them all too well.

They haunted his dreams still. He occasionally woke in a sweat; not through guilt, he understood that his victims had all deserved every ounce of misery they suffered. But his dreams were fuelled by his hatred, a reminder of the good that he'd done, and the peace that he'd brought to others.

Recently, the dreams had become heavier and more vivid as if he was reliving the killings, and now, those twisted characters entered Harvey's waking mind through the medium of the two photos. The man he'd skinned alive. The man he'd glued down and whose stomach he'd slit open. The perverted rapist Harvey had buried alive with nothing but a hosepipe to encourage a futile glimpse of hope in the dying man's mind. The gargled chokes of a college lecturer who had abused his position; he'd walked into Harvey's trap as a fly might land in a web. Harvey had pinned him to the ground in a morbid crucifix with stakes that Harvey had carved while he waited. The man had slowly drowned in his own blood from the slightest of nicks to his windpipe from Harvey's blade. All of their screams howled inside Harvey's head.

In the past, long before France had become a reality, his dreams had woken him as a calling. Each target had satiated his thirst for retribution. But only for a while.

A temporary fix.

Harvey swung his legs off the couch, let his head fall into his hands, and forced the screams and tortured faces from his mind's eye. A method that had worked before had been to concentrate on the good things, the beach, his home, Melody and Boon. Melody had been a blessing for him. He'd never imagined he'd deserved someone like her, someone who knew about his past and understood him, or at least tried to. They'd started a life together which seemed to have eased the haunting dreams for a while. But now that the home in France and their lives together had become normality, the itch in his conscience had awoken the beast inside.

He reached for his phone and hit redial. He only ever called

Melody, so her number was the only number on the list; she answered on the second ring.

"Hey handsome, I can't talk right now," Melody answered, sounding rushed. "Everything okay? You don't normally call at this time."

"Yeah, it's quiet here," said Harvey. "Can you run some checks for me on a number?"

"Ah, Harvey, we're right in the middle of a case. Can it wait?"

"I guess," said Harvey. "I just keep getting messages from a number. I thought you might be able to get me a location."

"As soon as I'm back in the office maybe, but hey, listen, I have to go," said Melody.

"Where are you?" asked Harvey.

"We've been through this, I can't talk about it. But I'll make it up to you when I get home, okay?"

Harvey didn't reply.

"Okay, stay out of trouble. See you soon."

Melody disconnected the call.

The light outside was slowly giving way to the night. The birds that tuned the peace had quietened, and the warm air from the wood burner seemed thick with memories in their small house. He thought of Melody and wondered what she was doing, what case she was working on. She had been an excellent operative, a highly skilled sniper, and a born leader. She never quite managed to think like a criminal, but instead, she was able to feel as they do, using some kind of criminal empathy that allowed her to be one step ahead. Harvey was proud of her. The frequent trips to London to work a case had been her own need. Much like Harvey, Melody had an itch and Harvey just couldn't stand in her way; he couldn't stop her from scratching it.

It was fully dark when the phone he'd found in the car earlier that day pinged a single sustained chime. Harvey reached for his leather jacket, pulled the phone from his pocket, and clicked on the message displaying another photo. This time the image resided on the phone. This time the man had gone too far.

Harvey turned away from the poor girl in the photo.

It was then that his own itch returned with a vengeance.

As land grew nearer, Bella's heart grew heavier. When the sound of the engine died down, and Fernando coasted the boat to a stop beside the dock, her body tensed. The realisation of her situation became a reality. It wasn't the empty boatyard or Fernando's smiling face behind the Perspex at the boat's controls, it was the massive expanse of Athens that spread out before her. The city was a sea of dirty white buildings wrapped in the arms of tall hills and mountainsides.

Escape now would be impossible. Where would she go? She didn't know the language; she knew only Arabic and the little English she had learnt. Being alone didn't scare Bella, being alone would be welcomed, being alone was better than giving her body to Fernando and his pig breath.

Somewhere in the city, she would spend the rest of her days and bear the children of her captor. Somehow, through all the turmoil, the loss and grief she had endured so far, it was possible that it would be a better life than she would have in England.

Bella took a breath. As Fernando stepped up to the dock and tied the bowline, she too stepped up, disembarking of her own fruition as if she was free to make those choices now. She stopped and waited for Fernando so as not to anger him.

"Welcome to my city, Bella," said Fernando. "I hope we will both be very happy here."

Bella stared at the city before her, and then back to the sea. She knew she would never see Turkey, or her friend, again. But the next step she took would be a step into a new life.

Freedom.

"Is it far?" she asked. "Your house?"

Fernando finished tying the boat to the dock and came to stand beside her.

"No, it is *our* house, Bella," said Fernando. "I want you to start to think like that. I want you to make the house your own house." He turned her roughly towards him. "I want you to be happy, Bella."

"Is it close?" she asked. "I would like to sleep."

"It is not far, and you can bathe and sleep as you wish soon. We will be home in a while. I have a busy day tomorrow, but when I am done, I will show you the city."

"What is there to do here?" asked Bella. "Do you have places to walk?"

"There are many places to walk, many thousands of years old."

"Thousands of years?" asked Bella. "It is an old city?"

"One of the oldest" replied Fernando. "Do you see the big hill in the centre of the city?"

Bella nodded.

"This is the Acropolis. It is a marvellous construction, and surrounding it are churches and buildings and statues, with fine restaurants and wine."

"Wine?" said Bella. "I cannot drink wine."

"Then I will drink it for you," replied Fernando. "But you

will love the food, and I will teach you to cook the way the local people do."

"You was born here?" asked Bella.

"No, Bella, I was not. I was born in Portugal, but I moved here when I was a child."

"Por-tu-" said Bella, trying to pronounce the word.

"Port-u-gal," said Fernando. "It is close to Spain but prettier." He gave her a little wink.

"Do you miss Por-tu-?"

"I remember few things about my home. Most of my memories are here in Athens." Fernando placed his hands gently on her shoulders and turned her to face the hills on the south side of the city. "It was in those hills that I used to walk with my uncle, and in the sea below where I learned to swim and to catch fish."

"Then," began Bella, "you are refugee also?"

Fernando's face hardened at the comment. "No, I am not like you, Bella." He seemed to spit the words out. "We had everything we needed, my family, but bad fortune."

"You ran," said Bella, "like me. We both ran. You are refugee."

"My father was killed. I did not run from a war into the arms of *anyone* who would take me. I came here to live with my uncle and to seek my fortune."

Bella lowered her head and closed her eyes.

"*My* family will be dead now, and I also did not run into the arms of just *anyone* who would take me, like you say. I *had* no choice."

"Well," said Fernando. His voice softened. "You have a choice now. The city is yours."

Bella opened her mouth to talk, but Fernando pulled away and answered his phone.

"Yes, boss," he began. "I am here now in Athens."

Fernando opened a door to a small building with what looked like boat engines in front of it and pieces of wood laying on the ground. Bella walked behind him into the building, and before Fernando had the chance to stop her from following, she saw the people inside. But they weren't just refugees. Alongside the refugees were white people. By their clothes, their faces, their hair, they were English, and they were chained to the walls. They were clean as if they had only just been taken there, not like Bella, who had grown used to being dirty, or the refugees, who cowered in the corner of the room.

A small part of Bella wanted to go and sit with the people she had travelled with for so long, to share the final leg of the journey with them. But she was different now.

She belonged to Fernando.

The white man croaked something. Her mouth fell open in pity, and the anguished looks of appeal on the faces of the man and two women were all too familiar for Bella.

But Fernando had seen her. He shoved her hard, back out of the room and into the night with an angry look. He followed, locking the door behind him.

A part of Bella wanted to know who he was talking to, who his boss was, and what he was like. But the numbed and deadened part of her didn't care. His boss would be the man who had the money Bella's family had gathered for her to take the journey to England.

Her father had sold most of what they had, aware of the approaching army and the trail of destruction, and fully aware that someone as young and pretty as Bella would not stand a chance against the cruel soldiers. They would take what they wanted and leave the remains with nothing but a dead family and no chance of escape.

"How can you say that?" said Fernando. His voice raised as if his boss had triggered his defences. "*I* brought them from Syria, and *I* will get them to England. I've done it before, and I will do it again."

Bella thought of the others she'd travelled with and wondered what chances of life they really had. In the back of the boat, in the darkness, they had spoken often. But it seemed as if they had been brainwashed. There had been no doubt that England would be like a haven for them with free food, money and a roof over their heads.

Bella had been the one to question the truth. Bella had listened to them with their dreams of beautiful clothes. Omar, the silent man who had sat in the corner, had even spoken of getting a car so he could drive to see the famous green hills in the English countryside, where food grows in rich fields that roll on for as far as the eye can see.

He'd silenced again when Bella had asked him why England would give free food, money and homes to refugees. She hadn't doubted that England would help. But she was aware that it would be a hard time, and perhaps many years before they could have jobs that might pay enough for them to be independent.

"So how come you are here?" the older lady had asked.

Bella had replied, "Because no matter how hard the work is, no matter the suffering, there will be life and a future. I just cannot describe that future. It is all too uncertain."

Fernando was in the midst of an argument with his boss. His raised voice snapped Bella back to the present.

"You cannot replace *me*," he said. "I have helped you from the start. The contacts we use are all my own, not yours."

A pause.

"Yes, you funded the boats, and I agree; you also supplied the bribe money. But without my contacts, not one of them would have made it through."

Fernando silenced while his boss seemed to give him an ultimatum.

"Trust me," Fernando replied. "I will get them out of Athens and into the UK, and if I don't, then fine, we will go our separate ways."

He was about to disconnect the call when his boss seemed to have one more thing to say.

"Yes?"

Fernando's frown relaxed, and a broad smile spread across his face as if his skin was made of clay. His nose was the only feature that remained impassive to the news.

"How many of the interfering agents are left? How many do we need to worry about?" A pause. "Three?"

Bella wondered what he was talking about. How many of who were left? She continued to listen to the one-sided conversation.

"Two men and a woman?"

"I am about to send him one last photo," said Fernando. "He will be here by morning. He can't ignore me forever."

"Yes, I am sure." Fernando turned away and lowered his voice, but Bella heard him whisper in the quiet night. "It will be perhaps the most tantalising photo yet. In the morning, Mr Stone will be our newest employee."

Fernando disconnected the call.

"Is there trouble?" asked Bella.

"No, Bella," replied Fernando, his smile still intact. "In fact, I think things just took a turn in the right direction."

"It *sounds* like trouble," said Bella.

"Ah, my sweet Bella," said Fernando. He smoothed her hair with a dirty hand. "Why don't you wait in the car?" He gestured at the silver Mercedes parked behind the workshop. "I have some business to take care of, and it's something that someone as pretty as you should not have to see."

CHAPTER SEVENTEEN

From the doorway of the neighbouring house, Melody watched three men load Ladyluck into the back of the black Peugeot. Two climbed in either side of her, and the other took the front passenger seat. The sniper was nowhere to be seen, though he was clearly untrained and a poor shot. But if he saw Melody, he could easily give away her position.

The car pulled out slowly. Melody considered that several gunshots had been fired, and although the area was almost derelict, somebody could have heard them and called the police. The men had seemed unconcerned. Melody realised that she had, in fact, not seen another person or car since their arrival at the apartment building, other than the men and the black Peugeot.

She desperately needed to find Derby. She needed to find Reg. She also needed a weapon. But, first of all, she needed to get away from where she was.

Keeping to the backstreets, Melody meandered through the narrow alleyways in the general direction of the city centre, using the behemoth Acropolis as a guide. The further away from the industrial area she walked, the more people began to fill the streets. Cars became more frequent; at first, this put her on edge and caused her to slow down to study every individual. But after a while, the crowds grew busy enough for her to blend in. Thoughts of stopping in the quaint little stores or wandering the markets were far from her mind. Her focus was finding Derby, Reg and Jess.

Finding Reg and Jess wouldn't be too hard; Melody had a plan for that. But overcoming the gang on her own could be extremely difficult with just a handgun. Finding Derby would mean she would have her rifle, and she could then find a perch somewhere to pick them off by one by one.

While walking, she gave Derby a lot of thought, trying to empathise with him to work out where he'd be. If she was him and she had been told to wait in Athens until further notice, what would she do?

Given the fact that he had a vanload of equipment, including rifles, surveillance gear, computers, scanners, and satellite comms, Derby wouldn't leave the vehicle unattended. This gave Melody an idea. Derby wasn't a tech guy, but they all knew how to work the frequency scanners. If Melody were sat in a van full of tech gear waiting for someone to find her, she'd use the scanners to dial into the police channel and wait for the action.

Melody needed to create some action.

She came to the end of a street and turned left up a long hill. A tiny old church stood in the centre of the road, splitting the wave of tourists into two, left and right. The tourists merged again on the far side of the church, but the variance in the flow of foot traffic was an ideal spot for pickpockets.

Melody spotted them easily enough. Congregated around the edges of the junction were drug addicts, the jobless and the homeless, drinking cans of strong lager or cider, and smoking cheap cigarettes or joints. The pickpockets stood to one side of them, ever watchful.

Melody made herself an easy target.

She pulled a ten-euro note from her cargo pants and tucked it so that it was half in and half out of her back pocket. She walked past the intimidating crowd as if she were lost, turning herself around, and checking the streets signs. Then she walked on and waited.

Less than two minutes later, she felt the tug on her cargo pants and span on the spot to find the thief running away at a full sprint down the hill. He looked to be a skinny man, unshaven, with tattoos and a green mock army jacket.

"Stop, thief," she screamed, then pulled her Sig and placed two careful shots over the man's head harmlessly into the air. The thief ducked into a side road. Tourists dove for cover into shops and one local man fell off his bicycle in an effort to stop quickly. The busy street emptied in seconds.

As planned, it took less than a minute until she began to hear the sound of approaching sirens, so she made her exit into the shadows of a tiny side street. Once out of sight, Melody too ran at full speed away from the scene. She found the entrance to an apartment building between two tourist shops, sprinted up the stairs to the rooftop, and looked down at the street.

The police had arrived and had begun to question tourists, who described the events and illustrated their stories with wild gestures of their hands. A woman holding a child pointed in the direction of the pickpocket then mimed Melody firing her weapon. Another man pointed roughly in the direction that Melody had run. The policeman spoke into his radio.

That was when Melody's plan looked like it would fail.

From her vantage point on the roof above, she could see down at the intersection of four small streets. Near the church where she had fired the shots, more police congregated, and then a chief gestured at the officers. To Melody, it was clear what his instructions to his team were without hearing.

They were to check the surrounding buildings and go door to door.

Melody crouched behind a parapet wall for the second time that day, and seriously doubted her plan. She hadn't thought it through properly. It had been a hunch, and it was looking as though it might have been a terrible decision with dire consequences. She chanced another look down. There were two officers on her street stepping into the building beside hers. Melody estimated the time to search the four-story building; two apartments on each floor and then they would check the roof space, where they would look across and see Melody. Ten minutes, maximum.

A few tense minutes passed. Two more policemen were in the adjacent street, coming out of one building and straight into another. They spoke casually, seemingly bored. One of the cops smoked a cigarette. The other was overweight and disinterested. Melody hoped they represented a standard fitness level across all Athens police force. If she had to run, she might just stand a chance.

Melody heard banging on the roof access door of the neighbouring building. The door was locked. Maybe that would stop them. Maybe not.

She took another look over the wall to the street below. More police had joined the effort of checking the buildings. They were closing in.

But then she saw what she was looking for. Melody started for the stairwell just as the policemen broke through the door on the next building. For the tiniest of moments, Melody held his surprised gaze. Then she ran.

"Edo," the first one called, immediately seeing her run. He pulled his weapon and fired two rounds just as Melody dove into the stairwell. She landed painfully on her side, half rolling and half falling onto the first few steps. As momentum picked up, she continued to bounce hard on her back to the floor below.

Melody heard the shouts from above as she lay slightly dazed on the floor, winded and bruised. She bound down the remaining stairs, pulling her radio from her pocket. She had just one chance.

"Mobile two, stop where you are," she said and prayed that Derby had heard. She'd just kicked the hornet's nest, and if her timing was wrong, she was about to get stung.

Melody jumped the last few stairs. The jolt was like a dull kick to the fresh bruises on her back, but she carried on with gritted teeth and burst through the single entrance door onto the street.

A group of four policemen saw her, but it took them a few seconds to realise that she was their suspect. By the time they had engaged their brains, Derby had slammed the van brakes on and crawled alongside her. The side door slid open, and Melody fell into the rear cargo area.

A few sporadic gunshots dotted the back of the van, but Derby easily slid around a few tight corners and gunned the engine, leaving the unsuspecting police behind.

The ride in the taxi from the airport to Athens took around thirty minutes. Harvey sat in the front passenger seat, as he always did in taxis, and focused on the facts.

The girls in the first two pictures had clearly been beaten and abused, but the captors were obviously capable of a lot more, judging by the last photo. It had shown a girl surrounded by old boats on trailers hanging naked by her feet from the type of gantry that mechanics might use to hoist a boat from a trailer. Harvey pictured the girl. There was no need to open the phone to look at the photo again. What he'd seen was beyond abuse. It was an image he'd never forget.

Harvey asked the driver to stop as soon as the coast was in full view. He didn't carry a bag or a gun, or even his knife. Worse than that, Harvey didn't have a plan.

That would be his first port of call.

The sky was growing dark, and the sun began to sink into to the Mediterranean, lighting up the mountains that surrounded the city. The same mountains would help Harvey find where the captives were being held. Harvey had noticed that behind the girl in the last photo, the ridgeline of the peaks that cradled

Athens was just in view. There was nothing particularly outstanding about the rocky features, but their shape would be distinct enough for Harvey to work out the rough direction of the boatyard. Then he would just need to wait and watch the activity.

He took a walk down to the beach and considered his options. The first pictures of the girls had been taken inside a boat, possibly a fishing vessel. It hadn't been a new yacht with a white fiberglass hull and stainless steel bimini, rails and stays. Instead, it had been a dark and dirty boat, possibly with nets and bundled up canvasses, and with random fishing gear dotted around. Harvey had an image in his mind of what he was looking for.

He remembered Ferez's statement.

"You have a hole in your defences so big I could park my boat in it."

At the coast, there was a large marina with expensive yachts and bay-liners for water sports. There were no old fishing boats moored there. He was in the wrong area.

Harvey had checked a map of Athens on the internet before he had left France. He'd seen that the coastline was relatively short and that in the north and south, a small range of mountains sat like arms around the city. He'd also seen what looked to be dry docks or boatyards at both ends of the coast, the type of place where a mechanic might need a gantry to raise and lower a boat off a trailer.

Harvey studied the mountains to the north and to the south then took an educated guess at the location being at the north end of the coastline. The peaks looked right, and the gradient of the mountains seemed to match the image in his mind. But he wouldn't know for sure until he got there.

He acted like any other tourist walking along the coastline, carrying his leather biker jacket slung over his shoulder and wearing sunglasses. As he made his way north, he took in the sights, while passing groups of teenagers, couples and occasionally a foursome of retired people. Harvey assumed that they were visitors from the cruise ships that stood proudly in the port to the north.

Gradually, the tourist restaurants and souvenir shops became less frequent. Life on the streets began to quieten. Large cruise ships stood in line to dock at the port, patiently waiting for the hungry and cash-rich tourists.

It was as he passed the entrance to the docks that a flashing blue light ahead caught Harvey's eye. Two police cars and an ambulance sat outside what looked like an old rundown apartment building a few hundred yards along the road. Harvey crossed the street to be on the same side when he approached.

Four fat and lazy-looking policemen stood waiting beside their cars, smoking and talking loudly, each one fighting to be heard above the other with wild expressive gestures of their arms and faces. Then two men emerged from the building carrying a stretcher, which they loaded unceremoniously into the ambulance before closing the doors.

Harvey knew a dead body on a stretcher when he saw one. The childhood memory of his sister being carted out of his foster father's house had been ingrained into his mind. It was one of the catalysts for who he'd grown to be. Ironically, it was also the reason he found himself in Athens.

He approached the building as the convoy of emergency vehicles moved away. There was nothing to see from the outside, just an old dirty building opposite three rough and dirty boatyards.

Harvey walked to the corner of the building and looked up the hill at the receding police cars. In front of him was a perfect view of the mountains, clearly bearing the features he'd seen in the photo. He was in the right place.

All that remained was to identify which of the three boat-yards belonged to Ferez and had the refugees inside. For that, he'd need to find a high spot where he could sit and watch. Harvey glanced back at the dirty old apartment building that he'd just passed. It was ideal for his needs. Plus, something about it didn't sit right; four policemen had attended a crime in a deserted neighbourhood and then stood outside smoking while the EMTs had dealt with the body.

It had all seemed a bit too easy.

Harvey checked around him with a subtle glance left and right, then walked back to the entrance of the building. The names on the intercoms had faded to nothing, and a thick layer of dust lay on the granite floor of the foyer, recently disturbed.

Given the choice of a tiny elevator and the stairs, Harvey opted for the stairs, climbing straight to the top floor, where he was immediately hit by the stench of cat urine. The smell seemed to come from the apartment on the right. The door was open, and from a quick glance inside, Harvey saw that it, like the rest of the building, had been abandoned.

The apartment on the left had police tape across the door but stood ajar. Harvey gave it a nudge, and let the door swing open. He listened for movement or breathing. A novice killer would have adrenaline coursing through his veins; it was the hardest thing to control. But he heard nothing. Harvey lifted the tape, stepped inside, and pushed the door closed quietly behind him. He waited for a full minute in silence before moving further. Old habits.

The view from the empty living room gave him a perfect view over the boat yards, exactly as he'd hoped. Though the light was fading, he could see that they were all individually fenced off with chain link fencing. A tiny strip of wasteland separated one from the next. Each boatyard had a collection of small buildings amid the random boats and vessels.

Then a familiar shape caught his eye. In the pale light, standing tall beside an old workshop building, he found the gantry that the girl in the last photo had been hanging from; a few old oil drums stood beside it, along with a wooden reel of what even at that distance, Harvey knew to be barbed wire.

"Found you," he whispered to himself.

CHAPTER NINETEEN

"This is your home?" asked Bella, as she closed the door to Fernando's old Mercedes.

"No, Bella," replied Fernando. "This is *our* home. That's how I want you to think of it now, as our home."

Bella's heart sank a little. The house and garden walls were crumbling, and the bright blue window frames did little to bring any joy to the sorry-looking building. The terracotta roof sagged in the middle as if it would collapse in a strong wind, and the forecourt was strewn with leaves from nearby trees and rubbish that either Fernando had discarded or passers-by had dropped into the property; probably both, thought Bella.

Wild vines covered the front of the small one-story building, bearing red flowers, which were bright against the dirty white walls, but not bright enough to distract from the deep cracks than ran from the roof to the ground. The barred windows grinned at Bella's arrival. Bella wondered if the bars were to stop robbers getting in or people like Bella getting out.

The property stood at the centre of a steep hill, with houses spread out below and above. From the lofty heights of Fernando's house, the rows of buildings below seemed to occupy every available space.

"I like the view," said Bella.

"You wait until you see inside, my sweet," said Fernando. "It needs a little work, but I'm sure you'll manage just fine."

Fernando lifted the gate open, rather than swung it, and then waved for her to follow him to the front door.

I could run now, while his back is turned. It might be my last chance.

She glanced to her left back down the hill. So many alleyways, perfect for hiding.

"Bella?" said Fernando. "Are you coming?"

She turned back to him, nodded and feigned a smile, then followed obediently.

Inside, the house bore the aroma of dirty clothes, unwashed bodies and stagnant water. The smell seemed to warm the air. Bella forced the front door closed behind her, and had to turn sideways to move along the hallway past boxes of magazines, newspapers, lamps and all sorts of bric-a-brac. Fernando, it seemed, had hoarded everything he'd ever seen, bought or found.

She remembered clearly a discussion she'd had with her mother, during one of their chats.

"We might not have everything we want, Bella," her mother had said. "But your father works hard to make sure we have everything we need, and those things, we need to take care of so they see many years."

"But the other children have televisions," Bella had replied.

"Do not concern yourself with the things that other families have, Bella. When you walk into our home, you smell fresh clothes, clean floors, and homemade cooking. I have seen the houses of other families. They are no better than the vermin that feed from the garbage." Her mother had spoken with distaste.

Bella had found it odd that the families of her friends, who had more money than Bella's, would choose to live like that.

Fernando's house reminded her of her friend's house.

"Are you coming?" asked Fernando from the end of the hallway. "I want to show you the kitchen."

Bella snapped out of her memory, and dreaded seeing the state the kitchen.

"It needs a little cleaning, but can you see past that?" said Fernando. "Can you see yourself here with the children running around your feet?"

"And where will you be?" asked Bella. "While I am cooking and looking after the children?"

"I will be working, or relaxing after a hard day." He looked confused, as if her question had been rhetorical. "You will be happy here, Bella. I promise you."

"I would like to use the washroom," she said under her breath.

"I will show you," said Fernando.

"No," said Bella, a little too sharp. "No, I am sure I will find it."

The fact was that Bella could smell the bathroom above the stale body odour, rotting food and stagnant water. She wasn't prepared, however, to walk into a bathroom quite so bad as it was. Bella immediately gagged as the stench clung to her throat. She ran from the tiny room and stomped into the kitchen.

"Bella?" said Fernando. "You look upset. What is wrong? Do you not like the house?"

Bella was incredulous at how Fernando could not see what she saw, or if he did, how he could even imagine that the hygiene was acceptable.

"I must say what I am thinking," she said, "or I will not say anything all."

"So speak, Bella," said Fernando. "You are free now, remember?"

"You..." She tried to sugarcoat the words, but there was no use. "You live like a *pig*, Fernando. You have insects crawling on the dinner things. You have *never* cleaned your toilet, and something, somewhere, has died inside this house. It is foul. I *cannot* live here."

She closed her eyes and waited for the attack.

Fernando crushed his cigarette into a dirty dinner plate with hardened food encrusted onto its surface. He spoke quietly but was clearly insulted.

"For somebody who has just escaped a war zone and lived in the very pits of trucks and boats being fed by whoever would feed you and drinking from a bowl like a dog," said Fernando, catching his breath as his temper began to soar, "you have a very big mouth."

"This is *filth*," Bella began, almost pleading.

"*This*," snapped Fernando, his index finger pointed into the air, "is your home. And this..." He spread his arms out as if presenting the hovel as some kind of grand palace. "Is your kitchen." He lit another cigarette and left the room leaving Bella staring at her feet, expecting another blow.

"Oh, and Bella?" Fernando continued, as he opened the front door to leave.

She looked up at him, ashamed of her ingratitude.

"If you do not like its present condition, you should clean it. I'll be back shortly, and I shall be hungry."

CHAPTER TWENTY

The van door slammed. Melody sat bolt upright in a panic. It took her a few seconds to realise where she was.

"Hey, you were out cold," said Derby, reaching from the driver's seat into the back of the van to pass Melody a coffee.

"What time is it?" she asked.

"It's morning, but more importantly, it's time we ditched the van. We were lucky to find this place to hole up in last night, but we can't go driving around the streets in it all day."

Melody moved from the nest she'd made between the boxes and flight cases, and sat on the wheel arch.

Barnet turned around from the passenger seat. "We did a few drive-bys yesterday. The place is deserted. It's like the tourists still plague the city centre, but that little industrial area is a ghost town."

"Yeah, I noticed that," replied Melody. "It's the perfect place to bring in a bunch of refugees. No-one is snooping around."

"It's not just refugees, Melody," said Derby.

"What do you mean?"

"I mean, yeah sure, it's the refugees that sit in the back of the truck and get driven across Europe. But you don't think that any enterprising people smuggler is going to leave money on the table, do you? He's not going to miss out on any opportunity to get a bit more bang for his buck."

"Drugs?" asked Melody. "Is that it?"

"I would imagine so. We've seen it before," said Barnet. "There's usually a guy that'll escort a bunch of refugees out of the war zone, guide them through Turkey and land them here in Athens or somewhere else in Europe for the final leg of the trip."

"At which point the refugees' options are minimal, and they'll do anything that's asked of them," Derby cut in. "I mean, Athens isn't exactly thriving, is it?"

"So," said Melody, falling in with what the two men were saying, "instead of being taken on the final leg of their journey as they had paid for-"

"They're given an ultimatum. Stay here, or become-"

"Mules," finished Melody. "These poor people have been through enough. They've lost their families and starved from hiding in trucks for months to get here."

"And the worst thing is, Melody, most get caught going into Britain and wind up being thrown in the slammer-"

"At Her Majesty's pleasure," finished Barnet.

"Do we have proof of this?" asked Melody.

"That's what Sharp and Gibson were doing. You don't think we'd be involved if it was just a people smuggling case, do you?" said Derby. "No, this lot are bringing in ten or twenty people every week, and if each one of them is carrying a kilo or two of heroin or coke, or both, each of the refugees would be worth a fair old amount to the smuggler."

"Heroin is about seventy pounds a gram on the streets of London, maybe more, give or take, and that's probably cut too. But seventy pounds times a thousand grams is-"

"Seventy thousand," said Melody.

"Multiply that by, let's say, ten refugees," said Derby.

"Seven hundred thousand," said Melody.

"Now factor in anything else they can carry or put inside them," said Barnet.

"That all sounds a bit far-fetched, boys," said Melody. "Don't you think?"

"Yeah, it does sound like a movie plot," said Barnet. "But think of it this way, each of those refugees pays ten or twenty grand to get through Europe and into Britain. What's that? One hundred grand, maybe two hundred? Now to some, that's a hell of a lot of money, to most in fact. But is it enough for someone to kill a couple of MI6 agents over?"

"Gibson and Sharp?" said Melody.

"Yeah, why kill them?" said Barnet. "Whatever they found and whatever the smugglers are doing is worth considerably more than a few hundred grand, isn't it?"

Barnet turned in his seat again and smiled at Melody.

"Why didn't the whole team know about this?" asked Melody. "Why were we all led to believe that it was just a people smuggling case?"

"It's all speculation, Melody," said Derby. "What we need to do is catch a real live mule in the hands of a real live smuggler. Then, and only then, can we link them to all the other mules we have locked up back home."

"No," said Melody, "you're missing the point."

"What point is that?" asked Barnet.

"Reg and Jess are *missing*, plus three other operatives. Rescuing *them* is our new objective. If we can take the smuggler out in the meantime, then fine, but our focus needs to be on getting the team back. With them, we'll stand a much stronger chance of taking the smugglers down."

"And you think we can just walk in there and rescue them, do you?" asked Derby. "You saw what they did to Gibson, and I know you saw what happened to Sharp."

"That's nothing compared to what I'm going to do to these bastards," said Melody.

CHAPTER TWENTY-ONE

"I told you to stop sending me photos," said Harvey into the phone. "For someone who says he knows me, you don't seem to know me very well, do you?"

"Good morning, Mr Stone," replied Fernando. "It's a shame, you know. She was such a nice girl. But you know how it is, in every game, there has to be a loser and there has to be a winner. We do not like to be losers."

"Is she dead?" asked Harvey.

"Maybe," replied Fernando. "But maybe not. She may have pulled through the night. They are strong, these people. They have suffered very much."

"Let them go, Fernando," said Harvey. He began to pace the room.

"Oh, but we're only just beginning. The game is just warming up."

"What is it you want, Fernando?"

"Straight to the point, eh? You're a man of few words."

Harvey didn't reply.

"I imagine you're holed up in some grotty little apartment building overlooking our little boatyard. Am I right, Mr Stone?

Or can I call you Harvey? I imagine you followed the clues. Such a good dog, maybe I'll throw you a bone."

"Call me what you like, I'll be cutting your throat soon enough."

Fernando ignored the threat, and continued with his synopsis. "I also imagine that you found somewhere empty, easy to access with all the doors unlocked. Am I right, Harvey?"

Harvey didn't reply.

"And I imagine you wouldn't want to spend the night in a room that smells like cat piss, so you took the left side apartment."

Silence.

"I'm right, aren't I Harvey?" said Fernando with a chuckle. "I usually am, and you're so predictable."

Harvey immediately felt the trap. He began to search the other rooms.

"Have you checked the other rooms?"

Harvey sighed. "Of course."

"I hope my boys didn't make too much mess?" Fernando gave a soft groan. "Sorry about that. I did tell them to keep the place clean for our guests."

"Who was it?" asked Harvey, remembering the body bag.

"Oh, you know what? The name escapes me. I've always been bad at names," said Fernando. "Just one of those meddling men."

"Are you going to tell me where I come into all of this? It sounds like you and your boys have things wrapped up."

"Sadly not, Harvey. We have a truck leaving our little boatyard this afternoon and it's worth a considerable sum of money to us. But we still seem to have some loose ends that are trying to stop our little operation. So annoying, don't you agree?"

"Right."

"Well, we've exhausted our own resources, and I would like

very much for my men to get back to work. Production cannot stop because of one little set back, you know."

"So?"

"Well, we didn't quite round them all up," replied Fernando. "A few slipped through the net, and we do like to do a proper job. No loose ends."

"And?"

"If you can stop the rest of *them*, then maybe *we* won't have to hurt any more pretty girls." Fernando smiled. "It's a simple game, Harvey."

"How many?"

"Three. Not many for a man of your calibre. But the ones we've managed to capture so far don't seem to be very talkative, so we can't be too sure."

"And that's it, is it?" asked Harvey. "I stop the men, you get your truck out, and you leave me alone?"

"Something like that, yes."

"No, Fernando," said Harvey. "We need clear terms and conditions. It's a transaction. I stop the men, you get your truck out, and you leave me alone. Any deviation from the plan and it's game over."

"I can hear your mind ticking over," said Fernando. "You give away far too much. Perhaps that's why you rarely say anything. Am I right, Harvey?"

"Do we have a deal, Fernando?" said Harvey. "I don't have time for games."

"You think you can fool me with some sort of verbal agreement, hoping that I will relax, thinking that you will take these men down. But really, you're coming after me, aren't you? You want to free the refugees don't you? And by that admission, I'd say that you also want to kill me."

Harvey didn't reply.

"I'm right, aren't I?"

"Do we have a deal, Fernando?"

"Here's the deal. Bring me the bodies and get our trucks through, and I'll see to it that the refugees reach England, although I can't guarantee they'll all be completely unscathed. One, in particular is in a bad way. It's a shame, she's such a pretty thing, and our night security is a little bit...Well, let's just say he doesn't get out much, and the sight of her in such a weak and vulnerable state might just have been enough to send him over the edge. Do you catch my drift, Harvey?"

Harvey didn't reply.

"You can reach me on this number when you've made your choice. Oh, and by the way, Harvey, welcome to Athens. I knew you'd come eventually."

Fernando disconnected the call.

Harvey pocketed the phone and began to pace the room. The abandoned apartment building allowed him a birds-eye view of the boatyard. He saw the salvage boats lined up for scrap, the mobile gantry that the girl had been tied to, and what looked to be a workshop in the centre of the plot. The chain link fence that ran around the perimeter would be easy enough to scale, and there was enough vegetation in the wasteland surrounding the yard for someone to sit and watch.

Harvey began to formulate a plan. Save the refugees, and kill Ferez. If he had to go through with Ferez's demands to do so, then so be it.

He considered his approach.

If his old team were to launch an attack on the workshop, they would have placed a sniper up high, and then sent in a few men to coordinate an attack from all sides. It would help if Harvey knew who he was up against. Was it just a team of vigilantes? Was it an enemy of Fernando and his boss? A turf war, maybe? Or was it some kind of authority? The police would have helicopters and wouldn't be sitting around waiting for things to happen. Plus, the four lazy policemen Harvey had seen hadn't seemed too bothered by the body. Maybe the police were on the payroll.

Harvey stood over the bloodstained screed floor in the bedroom of the apartment and hit redial on the phone.

Fernando answered the call with a chirp.

CHAPTER TWENTY-TWO

"Harvey, so have you made your decision then?" said Fernando. "So quickly too. That's what I like to see."

Bella lay on her side with her back to Fernando, pretending to sleep and fighting back her stinging tears. She'd barely slept all night, kept awake by the evil presence of Fernando who lay beside her and his incessant drone.

Only a man with no conscience could sleep during times of such atrocities, she had thought.

She had remembered where she was as soon as she had awoken from one of few exhaustion-induced sleeps. The reality of her stupidity had hit her hard, just as the nasty smell of the bed sheets choked her throat.

Bella felt Fernando's wandering hand reach around and cup her breast and she fought not to open her eyes. At least if he thought she was sleeping, he wouldn't force himself on her again.

"Now, now, Harvey, there's no need for that kind of talk."

Whoever this man Harvey was, Fernando obviously thought he was a dangerous man. Bella clung to the hope that he would rescue her. She longed to be in that workshop with the other refugees and the people she had seen the night before. Although they had been tied and left in the dark, at least they were together.

"As long as our trucks can get out without being stopped, then I see no reason to worry about us hurting anybody else." Fernando paused as the voice replied. "No, Harvey. I want to see the bodies. This might be a game, but I make the rules."

Fernando pinched Bella. She opened her eyes with a start and rolled over to face him, so his hand was away from her chest.

"Let's make it interesting," said Fernando into his phone. "Our truck leaves at four pm. I want to see three bodies before midday. That gives you five hours to take care of them, or the truck will be slightly lighter, if you get my meaning."

Harvey didn't reply.

"There's not many rules in my game, Harvey." His hand moved to Bella's backside. "You finish them however you see fit." He paused again.

"Calm down, calm down, Harvey." Fernando began to stroke Bella's back. She shuddered at his gentle touch, somehow preferring it when he was rough and more genuine. She knew his soft touches were just for show, especially following his previous night's demonstration of power.

"Maybe once this is over, we can have a little chat. Who knows, you might like working with us."

Bella heard the phone's tiny speaker emitting the other man's voice. He sounded angry.

"Right now, you don't have the power to make those kind of statements, Harvey. You should remember that I have some very nasty men at my disposal, and one of those girls, in particular, will please the boys very much."

Fernando paused.

"That's right, Harvey, you stay silent. That's the best way."

Fernando lifted the bed cover and pushed Bella's head down. She resisted at first, but he grabbed her hair and pushed harder.

"Now I have your attention, Harvey. Bring me the bodies by midday today, or another girl dies. We have enough refugees; we can afford to lose one or two along the way."

Fernando disconnected the call and put the phone down beside Bella.

She looked up at him.

"Oh Bella," said Fernando. "You have a lot to learn."

He slid out of bed and walked naked to the door. "Unfortunately, today is a very busy day for both of us, so we will resume our lessons later."

Bella covered herself with the dirty covers.

"And what it is we are doing today?" she called out.

"You don't need to know the details, Bella. But know this, until you prove yourself to me, you shall either remain locked inside this house, or you'll stay by my side." He lowered his tone again. She was beginning to hate and fear his gentle tone as much as she hated his gentle touch. Cruelty usually followed both.

"I want to trust you, Bella," he continued. "I want you to be happy. But until I can trust you, I'm afraid I must insist that you stay by my side."

"Then you should tell me what it is I should do to make you trust me. Tell me what I should do and I will do them," Bella lied. "I want so much to be happy. I want to walk in the glorious hills and breathe the fresh air."

Fernando eyed her with caution then eased into his tight, thin-lipped smiled. "You just carry on doing what you did for me last night and this morning, and I'm sure we'll be just fine."

"This is what you like?" asked Bella, as innocently as she could fake it.

"This is what all men like, Bella. But you, my dear, are fortunate enough to be with a patient man who will teach you." He nodded as if even he believed his own words. "Just wait, Bella, your time will come. Now get dressed. We have a busy day."

"But I have only the clothes I was wearing," said Bella, "and they are ruined."

"So?" replied Fernando.

"So, I want to look my best for you. I want you to be proud, as I am." She mumbled the words and looked away at the barred window.

Fernando was silent for a moment then stepped back into the room. He pulled open the small wardrobe. On one side were his own clothes, a mix of various coloured shirts and pants. At the other end of the rail were three dresses. They were old, and not Bella's style.

"Choose one," said Fernando. "It is a gift to you, my Bella."

Bella wrapped the dirty bed covers around her and edged off the bed to look closer at the dresses.

"You should not cover yourself, Bella," said Fernando, tugging at the material.

Bella held the covers tight. "Please, allow me some privacy."

"Privacy?" asked Fernando. "Why?"

Bella could not answer. She just held the covers around her and stared blindly at the dresses.

"Get dressed," said Fernando, and left the room muttering to himself.

Bella swayed. She felt light-headed. She leaned on the wardrobe and took a few deep breaths, then reluctantly pulled out the first dress that was hanging on the rail. It was a white dress with floral patterns. To her dismay, it barely came to her knees. The other dresses were the same length.

"They are too small," she called out.

Fernando stepped into the room again, quicker than Bella

had imagined, as if he'd been waiting. She wondered if he had been watching her through the gap in the door.

"I do not want to disappoint you," she said.

"What's wrong with it?" he asked. His hand automatically began to smooth Bella's hair behind her ear. "You look so pretty wearing it."

His wandering hands began to pull the dress up behind her, but she manoeuvred away.

"It is too short," she said. "Look." She gestured to her legs.

"My dear, Bella," Fernando began, "you have a lot of things to learn about Athens and Europe. You look beautiful, and I am sure that all the men will be looking at you when we are outside."

"But I do not want them to look at me."

Fernando sighed and checked his watch. "I think we have time for one quick lesson before we leave."

CHAPTER TWENTY-THREE

"So we have all this tech gear but no-one to operate it?" said Melody.

They were parked up in a maze of back streets away from the city centre.

"Just take what you need and what you can carry," said Derby. "The rest can all be picked up later."

"I wouldn't count on it still being here," said Melody, glancing over her shoulder at three homeless men sat on the steps of a rundown residential building behind them. They sat and watched Melody and the two men as they sorted through the gear.

"The laptops are encrypted, the v-Sat is useless without the network credentials, and we're taking the weapons," said Barnet. "So what? They'll get a bunch of stuff they can't use, and a van that the police are looking for in conjunction with a shooting in the city centre." He pulled his pack over his shoulder.

"Agreed," said Melody, and hoisted her own pack off the van's wooden floor.

"We could torch it," said Derby. "It would destroy the prints."

"It would also give the local police a range. They'd know we were here and probably slip the hobos over there a few euros. They'd tell them when, and that would give the police a radius."

Barnet began to walk off down the hill. The view of the sea above the houses added serenity to the otherwise tense morning.

"Barnet?" said Derby. "Where are you going?"

"You two can argue all you like about what we do with that piece of junk," he called back. "But I'm out of here. The clock is ticking."

"He's right," said Melody, collecting her peli-case with her Diemaco rifle held snugly inside in its foam inserts.

Derby slammed the van door shut and locked it. The two of them joined Barnet, who had continued to head down the hill with his head held firmly to the phone in his hand.

"So what do we have?" asked Melody. "I have my Diemaco. I can find myself a perch and cover you two if you want to find a weakness in that old fence?"

"I have my Sig, plus we both have MP-5s in our packs," said Derby. "There's a strip of wasteland between the boatyard and the next one. I suggest Barnet and I take a side each. Can you cover us both?"

"Shouldn't be an issue in daylight," replied Melody.

"You have a perch in mind?"

"The apartment building," said Melody. "It's perfect."

"But what about-"

"Sharp?" asked Melody. "I'm sure he won't mind me. Besides, I'll be up on the roof."

"You don't think it's a bit close for comfort?"

"Derby, from up there I can shoot the first person who steps out of that workshop. If you two are inside the perimeter, you'll have free rein of the outside. But once you're on the inside, I'll lose all visual, and you'll be on your own. That MP-5 will be your only friend. Remember, priority one is to get Reg and Jess out, the second is to save the refugees. The only way we're going to accomplish that is by taking down Ferez and his men."

"One thing bothers me, Melody," said Derby. "If there were enough of them to take Reg, Jess and all the others, we're going to need to be pretty tight for three of us to get through them."

"I thought about that too," said Melody. "But Reg and Jess aren't exactly trained killers. It was only you, Barnet and me that were ever going to go tactical and take them down anyway."

"Like I said, Melody," said Derby. "If they took Gordon and Sharp down-"

"Then we'll just need to make sure it's us that comes out on top," said Melody. "We're the last line of defence here. Reg and the others will be depending on us."

"Okay, let's split up," said Barnet, who stood waiting on the corner of a small intersection in the backstreets. "Derby and I will take the flanks. Melody, if you get yourself up on the roof, we'll give you ten minutes to put your weapon together before we move in."

"Yep," agreed Melody. "It should be enough time to get set up. We don't have comms so do as much as you guys can in the open, and I'll pick them off as they appear."

"Got it," said Derby. "Right, move now. I'll mark ten minutes. Be ready."

CHAPTER TWENTY-FOUR

Harvey studied the boatyard, committing the layout to memory, and then left the apartment building by the stairs. He took the fire exit door that led to a warren of alleyways to the rear of the building, thinking that the front door would be monitored. The old fire escape looked as though it hadn't been used for years.

For Harvey's plan to work, his assumptions needed to be correct. He had no real facts. He didn't know who the men were, or how trained they would be.

Expect the worst.

Harvey's assumptions were based on stealth. If two men tried to enter the boatyard, they wouldn't walk through the gate; they'd use the wasteland to either side of the yard. And they'd split up. One team on the right side, one on the left, leaving a sniper somewhere to call the shots.

They'd go in on foot, and for that, they'd need to prep somewhere quiet before they stepped into the open, somewhere like the maze of backstreets in which Harvey now found himself.

If his assumptions were wrong, it would be a big mistake. He'd left the boatyard wide open.

Harvey turned a corner quietly. He saw the first man,

crouched down in a doorway, rummaging through a backpack. He moved quickly but controlled.

Harvey took one step at a time, slow and silent, keeping out of the man's peripheral vision as much as he could. Only when Harvey got up close behind him, he saw the man was assembling an MP-5 from the parts in his pack, and that his Sig stuck out of his waistband.

"Don't move," said Harvey, quiet but firm. "Don't turn around."

The man froze.

Harvey whipped the Sig from the man's belt.

"Hands," said Harvey.

The man raised his hands.

Harvey checked the MP-5. It was still missing the bolt and magazine. No danger there.

"You have cuffs?"

"In my-"

"No talking," said Harvey. He kept three steps back. A trained man could spot an opportune moment to turn the tables.

"Cuff yourself," said Harvey. "Tight."

He waited and checked all around him as the man pulled a pack of plasticuffs from his bag, and began to put them on.

"Tight," Harvey reminded him.

The man gave a sharp jerk to demonstrate how tight they were.

"Okay, time for answers," Harvey began. "Where's the rest of the team?"

"Mate," said the man, turning his head.

Harvey slammed the butt of the handgun into his temple.

"I said, don't turn around."

The cuffed man knelt on the ground and winced at the pain. A small trickle of blood began to run from the fresh wound.

"Where's the rest of you?" asked Harvey.

"Rest of who?" the man replied.

"You don't know me. You don't know what I'm capable of. So I'll give you that one," said Harvey. "Any more lies or cheap attempts at stalling for time, and I'll cut your throat."

Harvey remained totally calm. The man had begun to sweat, a sure sign of fear. Adrenaline would be surging through him, and fight or flight would kick in. Harvey needed to control that. He needed the fear.

"Do I need to ask again?" he asked the man.

"I don't know. We split up."

"So what's the plan?" asked Harvey.

"What plan?"

"I warned you once."

The man sighed. "You don't know who you're dealing with here, mate."

"Can I presume judging by the fact that you're on the north side of the boatyard that your mate is somewhere back there on the south side also assembling an MP-5?"

The man didn't reply.

"I'll be honest with you," said Harvey. "In four and a half hours, I'll be dragging your body into that boatyard along with your friend's. I can kill you fast or slow, and that all depends on what you tell me."

Harvey felt the man's body relax, a sign of defeat. His next reaction would determine Harvey's. He would either break down, deny knowledge and beg, or he'd be aggressive.

"Go fuck yourself," said the man.

Harvey smiled and raised the gun to the back of his head.

An approaching car caught Harvey's attention. He kicked the man forward through the open doorway into the abandoned shop. Harvey followed him inside then helped him to his feet by pulling on the back of his shirt.

"Up," said Harvey, shoving him towards the staircase. Harvey looked around. The room was a mess with smashed furniture across the floor and the door hanging off its hinges.

"To the top," said Harvey, following at a safe distance.

"I'm telling you, mate. You don't know who you're dealing with here."

Harvey didn't reply.

At the top of the stairs, the man paused and turned back to Harvey.

"Do you really want to do this?" he asked.

Harvey kicked him through to the roof but noticed as he followed that the doors were riddled with bullet holes. He scanned the small roof space as his prisoner struggled to get to his feet.

"Talk to me," said Harvey. "Tell me what you're doing here."

"Same as you mate, earning a living," he replied. Harvey caught him searching the surrounding rooftops, probably for one of his team.

"Do you know who I am?"

"Why would I know you? Are you famous?"

"I try not to be," said Harvey. "Who do you work for?"

"I deliver pizza."

"With an MP-5?" Harvey began to circle the man. He stopped behind him.

"It's a rough neighbourhood," said the man, and started to turn.

"Face the front," said Harvey. "Don't move."

"Are you going to tell me who *you* work for?"

Harvey ignored him.

"What do you know about the girls?"

"*Girls?*"

"The refugees," said Harvey. "What do you know about them?"

"Not a lot. Did they order pizza?"

"You know what? I really didn't want to have to kill you, but you are beginning to piss me off."

"Am I supposed to be scared?"

Harvey was impressed. All too often, he came up against men that crumpled when they faced death. This man was behaving differently. It was something beyond training.

Harvey moved in. He placed the muzzle of the handgun into the base of the man's spine and searched his pockets for his wallet. He found it with his phone, a small folding case with some euros and an ID card.

"Your name's Barnet?"

"That's with a capital B."

Harvey saw the back of the man's ears lift as he grinned with sarcasm.

"Well, Barnet," said Harvey, tossing the wallet to the floor, "on your knees."

"I prefer to die standing up if it's all the same to you."

Harvey kicked out at the back of the man's legs. He immediately fell to the ground.

"Knees," said Harvey.

Barnet rolled over to his front and managed to shuffle onto his knees with his hands still bound tight by the plasticuffs.

"I prefer it when you kneel," said Harvey. "I get less blood on my clothes."

He raised the weapon once more to Barnet's head and saw the defiant man squeeze his eyes shut. It was make or break time. Harvey had seen even the toughest men break just moments before they were about to die. Harvey paused just long enough to give Barnet that chance.

It was during that decisive few seconds when his life hung in the balance of Harvey's intuition that Barnet's phone began to vibrate.

CHAPTER TWENTY-FIVE

"You look pretty in that dress," said Fernando, as he pulled the car away from his house. He reached across and put his hand on Bella's exposed thigh. She shuddered at his touch.

"It won't always be like this," he said, removing his hand. "One day soon, you will be more willing. It will be easier."

Bella stared out of the window, seeing Athens for the first time in daylight.

"What do you think of my city?" asked Fernando.

"I haven't seen much of it," she replied.

"But from what you see now, it's pretty, no?"

"The flowers are colourful."

"And look at the ocean, Bella." Fernando held his hand out in front, presenting her with the Mediterranean. "See how it sparkles like thousands of jewels. It has always captivated me."

"Captivated?" asked Bella. "What is this?"

"It is when a person is so fixed on something, they cannot bear to turn their head and look elsewhere."

"And what is the opposite of captivated?" asked Bella. She remained watching the houses pass by, but she wasn't really looking.

"It is repulsed," said Fernando.

"Repulsed?"

"Repulsed."

"So if a person cannot bear to look at something, they are repulsed?"

"Yes."

"And if they cannot bear to turn away, they are captivated?"

"Yes," said Fernando. "Where did you learn English? It is very good, I have to say."

"My father was strict. He made me learn," began Bella. "He said that one day I would use English more than my own language."

"He's a smart man," replied Fernando. "Is he-"

"He's dead," snapped Bella. "Can we leave it there?"

"Yes," said Fernando. "Yes, we can. I'm sorry. I just want to know you, Bella. I want to learn you and hear about your past."

Bella bit her lip and fought back the tears, but her throat choked, and she gasped then sucked in a deep lungful of air.

"Bella?"

"You raped me, Fernando," she said, her voice thick with emotion. "You raped me in Syria, you raped me in Turkey, you raped me on the boats, and now you rape me in your home. But still, Fernando, still you tell me you care. You say that I'm pretty and that you want to know me, and want me to be happy." She dabbed at her eyes with the back of her hand, and Fernando passed her his handkerchief.

"I can't do this," she continued. "I cannot lie to myself. I cannot do the..." She struggled with the words. "Disgusting things you want me to do. You *repulse* me, Fernando. I cannot bear to look at you. So tell me how I'm supposed to marry you. How am I supposed to wait patiently at home all day with your children, and smile when you come home? How am I supposed to raise children when I am not happy? Our children will be unhappy. I just don't know-"

"Have you finished?" said Fernando, his tone bored as if he was tired of her whining. He pulled the car to the side of the road, cracked the window open for some fresh air, and pulled the handbrake up.

"Listen to me," he began. "I took you away from Syria. I saved your sorry little life."

"I paid you."

"You ungrateful bitch. I took you in good faith. You think four thousand dollars even comes close to what it costs? Wake up, Bella."

"It was everything we had."

"And I took it in good spirit."

"You took it because I was pretty, you told me."

"And I stand by that. I was..." Fernando searched for the word. "Captivated. I was captivated, Bella."

"And what about the others? You weren't so captivated by them, were you? I didn't see you giving them any special treatment, no wandering hands."

"I knew I wanted you, Bella," said Fernando, "from the first day I saw you, and you told me you wanted to run. I knew I could help, I knew it was my chance, and I prayed that nobody offered you a cheaper ride."

"You took all we had."

"I had to take something, Bella. It is a business. What am I supposed to say to my partner?"

"You mean your boss?"

"He's not my boss. We are partners."

"But he pays for everything, while you take all the risk?"

"We have an agreement," said Fernando.

"It doesn't matter anyway. You raped me. I can't even remember how many times now." The tears came back and

Bella fought to suck air in between her loud sobs. "How can you say you care when you did that to me? You hurt me."

"But Bella, you have to understand," said Fernando. "Being on that boat with you after so long, seeing you every day, with those big brown eyes." He lowered his head. "I am ashamed, Bella. Forgive me."

"But in Syria, in the truck, it was the first time."

"I was captivated, Bella."

"It was my first time, Fernando," spat Bella under her breath. "Do you even know what that means?"

There was a silence. Bella rested her head on the cool glass and closed her eyes.

"The baby?" said Fernando, his voice soft with understanding. "The baby is mine?"

Bella nodded.

"We have a baby?" said Fernando. "Oh Bella, this is wonderful."

"The baby is the devil," she spat. "How can I bear a child that was born of rape? How can I love a child that-"

"But I can make this right, Bella," said Fernando, his voice pleading. "We can make it work. We can go to the shops and get the things you need. Let me show you, Bella."

Bella shook her head. She let the tears roll across her face without wiping her eyes.

"We can do this, Bella," said Fernando. He took her hand in her both of his then held it to his mouth and kissed it softly. "We can do this."

His manipulative words span around in Bella's head. It was like he had two faces, two minds. When he was soft, he could truly be gentle, but when the dark side appeared, he could be so cruel.

She opened her mouth to reply, but suddenly the windscreen shattered in their faces, and the roof of the car collapsed with a deafening bang.

Bella screamed and fought with the door handle as the body of a man in black slid slowly down onto the bonnet and stared at her with a deathly gaze.

CHAPTER TWENTY-SIX

Melody crouched with her back to the parapet wall. She was on the rooftop of the old apartment building where they'd found Sharp's body. She moved fast. Flipping the lid of the peli-case open, she quickly pieced together her rifle. She could do it blindfolded and had done several times, both in her training and as part of her ongoing practice.

A loud thud broke the silence, followed by shattered glass raining down onto the concrete below. Melody finished attaching her scope before she stood and peered over the side. An old silver Mercedes roared away with a body on its bonnet. The driver didn't let off the accelerator as he swerved the car onto the main road, and the body of the man slid off onto the street. Melody crouched low and brought her rifle up to see through the scope.

It was Barnet.

"Shit."

The car tyres squealed again, and Melody moved the rifle in time to see the old Mercedes mount the pavement and burst through the gates to the boatyard. The car screeched to a halt outside what looked like a workshop building.

In all the chaos, movement caught her peripheral vision, and she just saw what looked like Derby diving for cover in the wasteland to the south side. She scanned the narrow strip of sand and trees for movement then moved across to the boatyard.

Everything happened so fast. Melody couldn't find the driver in her scope, but he'd left the door open. There was no movement. It had been a few seconds of chaos, then nothing.

She moved the rifle in horizontal layers across the huge expanse of the boatyard, stopping at each salvage boat before marking them as clear and moving on. It was her methodical way of clearing an area. The wasteland to the north was empty as far as she could see.

They were down to two now, just Derby and her, and the only protection Derby had was Melody. She suddenly realised how vulnerable she was on the roof. There would be no escape if somebody burst onto the rooftop, and by the time she swung the long Diemaco around, she'd be dead.

Melody reached for her Sig in her waistband and placed it on the parapet wall. Then, as an extra precaution, she wedged the door shut with a heavy coping tile that had fallen from the parapet wall. It wouldn't stop anyone for long, but maybe long enough for her to get the upper hand.

Melody returned to the wall and swung the rifle to the south side wasteland. She knew Derby would be low, looking for a weak spot in the perimeter fence.

She just had a few minutes, and then Derby would be inside and making his way to the workshop. But he'd still be expecting Barnet to come in from the far side. She scanned the boatyard again just as the door to the workshop was kicked open.

A man appeared at the door, peering around cautiously.

It was Fernando Ferez.

Melody had him in her sights. He lit a cigarette. Melody calmed her breathing. Her finger touched the trigger.

Fernando had seen Derby. Melody could see him peering between the boats.

She breathed in once.

He was calling to Derby.

Melody exhaled. She waited until the very end of her breath then squeezed the trigger.

But Ferez had ducked inside, and the round found the concrete in a puff of dust. Melody moved the rifle across to Derby's position.

"Yes," she said when she saw Derby had broken through the fence and was making his way towards the workshop. "One hundred and fifty meters, Derby. You can do this."

Derby got himself within range of the workshop and crouched down, brought his MP-5 up on its sling, and tucked his Sig into his waistband.

"Come on, Derby."

Melody moved her weapon and focused on the door to the workshop.

"Come on, you bastard, show yourself."

Time seemed to stand still.

She moved back to Derby. He'd repositioned by the side of a boat to give himself a clearer view of the workshop door.

Melody wished they had comms but it had been too risky to use since the initial abductions. She swung the Diemaco back to the workshop for a moment, then returned to Derby to see a figure in black step up behind him and drag him out of sight behind a boat.

"*No.*" She almost screamed aloud. "Shit, shit, shit."

The workshop door was kicked open again with a crash. Melody kept her rifle on Derby's position but turned her head to see Ferez running from the workshop using two hostages as cover.

It was Reg and Jess.

"What's happening?" Melody whispered.

Melody looked back through the scope to find Derby. It looked like a fight was taking place behind the boats. The two men rolled on the ground with the MP-5 between them. Derby's head appeared just briefly, and Melody moved her finger away from the trigger as soon as she saw him.

"Keep your cool, girl," she told herself.

Then the fight came to an abrupt halt, and the man in black stood over Derby's unmoving body.

"What the...?"

The man in black then moved towards the workshop.

"Come on, one more step and you're mine."

He stepped into view, edging slowly along the side of the boat.

"I've got you now."

Melody's finger found the trigger. She relaxed her breathing, felt the wind, and adjusted half a click on her scope as the man emerged.

She began to squeeze the trigger then felt the familiar thump of the rifle's kickback into her shoulder. Reloading quickly and collecting the spent round, Melody watched the mystery man tumble away and hit the ground as if some invisible force had hit him.

"Gotcha."

Melody's spirits lifted; the tables were turning. She refocused on the man, hoping for the kill shot. But neither he nor Derby were anywhere to be seen.

"Where have you gone?"

She scanned the boatyard once more.

Was Derby alive?

If he was, now they had a fighting chance. Then things took a turn for the worse.

"Give me a break."

Fernando had led Reg and Jess to a waiting boat at gunpoint. He cowered behind Reg. Again, Melody had no clear shot. He shoved Jess onto the deck, followed by Reg, who stumbled and fell onto her.

Fernando quickly untied the bowline and threw the rope onto the front of the boat. He then stepped off the dock, suddenly in clear view. Melody fired. But it had happened too fast. She'd rushed. The shot went wide and careened off the boat's bimini frame.

Fernando realised he was being shot at and ducked out of view behind the boat's central controls. He fired up the two big on-board engines and immediately pulled the throttles into reverse.

Derby suddenly came into the view of her scope. He'd run from between the boats with one bloodied hand on the back of his head, waving his other arm at the boat.

What was he doing?

Melody's heart was racing. She felt useless from her perch. Too many obstructions had blocked any chance of her getting a clean shot.

Then, just as Fernando was making his escape with Reg and Jess, the man in black staggered out behind Derby carrying his MP-5. The shot was clear as day with no obstructions.

Melody lowered her head, slowed her breathing, and at the peak of her exhale, she began to squeeze the trigger.

The man turned and stared directly up at Melody as if he'd felt himself in her sights. His white t-shirt was stained red across the right-hand side, and though he clutched his shoulder, clearly pained, he stood tall and fearless, cradling Derby's MP-5.

She knew that look too well.

"Harvey?"

Only when Harvey had slammed the man's face into the hard concrete, felt his body fall limp and then rolled him onto his back, did he see whom he'd been fighting. Harvey had met him just briefly the previous month in London. He worked with Melody and Reg. He was one of the new guys that had joined the team in a small bar for end of week drinks. Suddenly, it all made sense.

He was Barnet's partner.

It wasn't a rival gang trying to stop Ferez; it was the British Government. More accurately, the guy was one of Melody's team. Or at least, he was posing as one of the team.

Which meant that Melody would be out there somewhere, and she'd be alone.

"Derby?" he said. "Wake up."

Harvey slapped him.

Derby was alive, but his head was bleeding, and he was out cold. Harvey checked around him, but the cannibalised boats on the trailers surrounding his position blocked his view of the workshop.

Harvey took Derby's MP-5 and stood with his back to the

side of the old Bayliner. He edged along slowly to get a view of the workshop. But then, like the silence before a car crash, he felt a pang of voyeurism; he was being observed.

The feeling lasted just a fraction of a second before something red-hot slammed into his shoulder with the force of a hammer. He stumbled and fell over Derby. Immediately, he felt the warm trickle of blood soak his shirt and cling to his skin. It had been a clean shot, in and out. Another inch to the side and it would have missed entirely. Harvey lay for a few seconds, clutching his wound, stemming the flow of blood.

He lay dazed on the ground and felt Derby stand behind him. He heard his boots walking away groggily across the concrete.

"Derby," he called out.

But he hadn't heard.

Harvey got his knees and forced himself to his feet, then staggered behind Derby, who was running towards the boat that Ferez was using to escape. Harvey followed behind him, running out into the open. He painfully raised the weapon.

He heard the unmistakable sound of a bullet ricocheting off metal. An image of the apartment flashed through his mind. It was the perfect building for a sniper.

And he knew the perfect sniper for the job.

He turned to face her. A tiny glint of light on the rooftop was her only tell-tale.

Harvey held his arms out as far as his damaged shoulder would allow, enough to show her it was him. He knew he'd be in her sights, and he knew he had seconds before she pulled the trigger. He smiled up at her, hoping she would recognise him through her scope.

But then the flash of a muzzle told him otherwise.

The clatter of Derby's Sig scraping across the ground caused

Harvey to spin and find Derby doubled over, clutching his hand in agony.

Harvey raised the MP-5 with his good arm.

"On your knees," said Harvey.

The man looked back

"Harvey?"

"Knees."

"Harvey, you remember me? I work with Melody. We met last month." Derby began to straighten.

Harvey set the selector to single shot and fired a single round into Derby's right foot, sending the man to the ground.

Derby screamed in agony. "What are you doing, you madman? I'm on your side."

"Is that right?" said Harvey.

"Of course I bloody am. I work with Melody." Derby pulled his boot off, wincing at the pain, and revealed a blood-soaked sock, inside which, Harvey could see there was a lot of damage. "Don't just bleeding stand there," said Derby, holding out his hand. "Help me up."

"You want a hand up?" asked Harvey.

"Don't mess about, mate," said Derby, breathless. "I'm in a lot of pain here."

"I can see."

"You know what? I liked you," began Derby. "Even when the guys at work told me stories about what you've done, I defended you. They spoke like you were some kind of monster, a law unto yourself, and unstoppable."

Harvey stared at him.

"They said you were crazy, and that most people are too afraid to even look at you," said Derby. "And when I asked them what you'd done and why you were like that, they just said that some people are born bad. It's in their blood."

Silence.

"You had a sister, right?"

Harvey didn't reply.

"She killed herself, didn't she?" Derby smiled. "It don't surprise me with a brother like-"

Quick as a flash, Harvey slammed the butt of the rifle into Derby's jaw. The large man fell back to the floor, his boot dropped to the ground by his side.

Harvey set to work.

He dragged Derby to the gantry, bound his hands with an off-cut of rope he found on one of the nearby boats, and hooked a chain around his neck. Then Harvey began to take up the slack with the chain hoist.

He glanced out to sea, but all that was left of Ferez's boat was the dissipating wake. With each pull, Derby raised a little further off the ground. His ruined foot dragged a trail of blood across the concrete.

Derby's feet slowly raised into the air. The lack of airflow shook him from his daze as his body fought to survive.

"Harvey," he choked.

Harvey continued to raise the man into the air.

"Stop it."

The chain was tightening with Derby's weight. His voice had become barely a whisper.

"Who put you up to it?" asked Harvey. "Don't hold out on me, Derby, I found Barnet and his phone. He's been talking to Ferez."

Derby's eyes were wide with fright.

"You're setting us up, aren't you?" said Harvey. "Melody and me. This whole thing is about getting us both here together. Who's running the show?"

Derby's panicked breathing came in short, sharp bursts.

"You're dirty," said Harvey. "Admit it, and I'll finish it."

Derby just stared back. His eyes had begun to bulge.

Harvey planted the heel of his foot hard into Derby's gut, sending his body swinging freely on the chain.

"I said, admit it," shouted Harvey, enraged by the traitor.

Derby tried to talk.

"Louder," said Harvey.

Derby tried to move his head but the chain held him tight.

"Blink once if you're a traitor."

Derby blinked.

"Blink once if you were out to kill me."

Derby coughed a spray of blood into the air. He blinked once.

Harvey nodded and raised the weapon to Derby's head.

"Blink once if you were out to kill Melody."

Derby tried to talk.

"I said, blink once if you were out to kill Melody," shouted Harvey, and rammed Derby's groin with the butt of his rifle.

Derby's face was a bright red mess of tears and blood. He blinked once.

"Last question," said Harvey. "Blink once if the order came from MI6."

Derby raised a vague smile, coughed once, and was then still. Harvey took a deep breath and fired the weapon into Derby's head to make sure. He tossed the rifle to one side and heard footsteps behind him.

"I wondered when you'd come," said Harvey, as he emptied Derby's pockets.

"What are you doing here, Harvey?"

Harvey was silent, as he thought about the answer carefully. "My moral compass," he said. "I never could turn it off."

"Do you know who that was?"

Harvey remained facing Derby, but the voice came from behind him, and he knew that at least one weapon would be trained on him.

"Yeah I know who he was," said Harvey. "The question is, do *you?*"

"Of course I do. That's why I'm wondering why you shot him and hung him out to dry."

"You shot him first," said Harvey with a smile.

"I shot his gun from his hand. He was about to kill you."

"Is that right?" said Harvey. "So why did you shoot me?"

"I didn't know it was you. Why didn't you tell me you were coming?"

"I tried to tell you."

"But I was busy?"

"That's right, you were busy," said Harvey. "Still, doesn't matter now, does it?"

"It still matters, Harvey. He was an MI6 operative. There's no going back."

"And Barnet?" asked Harvey. "I take it there's no going back from that either?"

"That was you?"

"Of course."

"What have you done, Harvey?" said Melody, her eyes wide. "Even Jackson won't be able to get you out of this."

"They were dirty, Melody. Didn't you hear him? How long were you stood there?"

"Seconds."

"So you missed the important bit," said Harvey.

"So tell me what he said."

"It wasn't what he said, Melody," said Harvey. "It was what he didn't say."

CHAPTER TWENTY-EIGHT

Fernando gunned the engine and the car roared out of the side street onto the main beach road. The body slid off the car as he wrenched the steering wheel left. The tyres squealed as if they would rip off the wheels as he swung the car again and burst through the gates of his boatyard, smashing off their hinges and sending them crashing to the ground.

Fernando didn't let off the throttle once. He swerved between the boats and slammed on the brakes outside the workshop.

"Bella, I want you to get to the boat, get inside and stay out of sight."

"But, Fernando, I'm scared. What's happening?"

His phone had begun to vibrate and he hit the green button to answer the call. In the silence that followed the previous chaos and above the pounding drum of Bella's heart, she heard the man say a single sentence.

"One man down."

The call was disconnected.

"Just do as I say," said Fernando, clearly shaken. "I have something to deal with, and then I will join you."

Fernando pushed the door open and ran into the workshop, leaving her in the car alone.

She sank down in her seat, afraid to move.

Shouting came from the workshop, but it wasn't Fernando's voice; it was an Englishman. Then Fernando kicked the door open and disappeared inside.

"What have I done?" she asked herself.

To her surprise, the tears didn't come. She felt them inside her, behind her eyes, but they refused to show. Instead, her breathing relaxed, and she sat calmly. Her world spun. Her mind was thick with regret, sorrow, loss, guilt. But still, the tears refused to come.

She had to get away. She had to find a moment to escape Fernando. But a part of her wanted to stay. A part of her felt an obligation to the other girls; maybe they were still escaping Syria, maybe they hadn't met Fernando yet, but Bella knew that more girls would cross his path in the days, weeks and months ahead.

"I can stop this," she thought. "It is my responsibility."

She had known a boy like Fernando at home when she had been a child, a boy called Azad. He'd walked God's world as if God himself had created it just for him, and as if every other man owed him something, like he was above everybody, even God.

But Bella knew that these people came crashing down sooner or later. Society doesn't tolerate people like that for long. Her community had grown tired of Azad's dealings. Too many children had complained to his parents, his father had dished out too many futile beatings, and one day, Azad had seriously hurt a young girl, so badly that she could never bear children. The fathers of the other children took it upon themselves to straighten the boy out, to teach him the way of God, of love and life.

Bella's father had been one of those men. He later spoke to Bella on the subject. It was one of the few times he had sat her down to talk as a father might talk to his child. Her father hadn't said what the men had done to Azad, or what lessons they had taught him. She'd found that out for herself from her friends.

Bella had asked her father why they did not show Azad kindness, as is God's wish that evil be met with kindness. Her father had simply replied that a man that wields the fires of hell must earn kindness.

A few days had passed until Bella had spoken to her friend, whose father had not been so tight-lipped about the lessons. Although nobody in the village spoke of the incident publicly, it was clear that all the villagers knew what had happened. Even at school, her teacher hadn't acknowledged the vacant seat where Azad had sat. Azad had been one of the oldest in the mixed class. He had always called out, louder than the rest of the children. There was a void in his absence, but nobody complained.

Bella's friend had told her that the men had taken the boy to the top of the jebel, a full two day's hike away. They stripped him and burned his possessions, then dragged him naked over the sharp rocks so his ruined feet would always remind him of his return journey. They cut away the boy's eyelids so that he could forever see the damage he had caused. Finally, they tied the boy to a fig tree with bark as white as the hair on her grandfather's head, and cut all but two of his fingers off, one on each hand. For this, they told him he could count the choices he had: redemption or perpetual castigation, an outcast forever.

Azad had never returned, and life had resumed as close to normal as it could have.

Like Azad, Fernando would come crashing down.

Gunfire woke Bella from her daze. A bullet hit the concrete

and sprayed a puff of dust into the air. Fernando was in front of her with a man and woman. They were running to the boat.

Bella reached for the door handle.

"Leave," she whispered, pleading to the empty car.

She heard the boat engine roar into life, and saw Fernando duck down as if someone was shooting at him, someone Bella could not see.

She sank lower in the car then looked across to the door Fernando had left open. If only she could close it and drive away. She heard the scuffle of feet, and another single gunshot close by.

Bella closed her eyes and considered running. But maybe she would be shot. She wondered if it was the man Fernando had spoken to, the dangerous man.

Am I safe now?

A few minutes passed. Bella watched Fernando making his escape on the boat. She revelled in the relief that washed over her.

A woman stepped from behind the workshop. She carried a large rifle, larger than the type her father had used for hunting.

Bella thought that she was pretty but tough. She stared at her white skin and dark features from the safety of the car. The woman looked perfect. She began to talk to someone behind the car; the dangerous man that Fernando had spoken to maybe?

All Bella heard was the mumbled murmurs, but the tension had eased. There was peace between these two people. Bella chanced a glance into the side mirror. She saw the back of the woman in her black clothes, and the back of the man. Blood ran freely from his shoulder. He'd been shot.

And a dead man hung from a big steel frame behind him.

CHAPTER TWENTY-NINE

The inside of the workshop smelled of countless years of oil spills, sweat and cheap cigarettes. The only light shone through tiny cracks in the walls and roof, sending laser-like beams to the feet of the seventeen prisoners that stood at the edges of the room tied to hooks fixed high into the walls.

"Melody," cried Ladyluck. "Oh my God, it's you. Thank God." She began to sob in the dark.

"Are we all here?" asked Melody.

She looked around the room and saw in the shadows the frightened white eyes of nine more people.

"What the-?"

"Refugees," said Harvey. "Ready for the truck."

"Is anyone hurt?" asked Melody.

"Over here," came a voice from the corner of the room.

"Who's there? What's wrong?" asked Melody.

"It's my friend. They beat her, and..." Her voice broke. "Please help her. She's dying."

"Harvey, find a light or a lamp or something," said Melody. She made her way towards the voice.

Harvey rummaged through the unorganised tools on the

benches and systematically emptied the shelves of the metal cabinet that stood near the door. Eventually, he found what he was looking for. He clicked the switch for the battery-powered lamp, and a dim light suddenly illuminated the frightened faces of the prisoners. They turned their heads to protect their eyes.

Harvey took the lamp over to Melody and saw that the girl's torn clothes were soaked in blood from the waist down.

It was the girl from the last photo he'd received.

"I'll take care of her," said Melody, moving to protect the girl's modesty. "What's her name?"

"Alia," said the girl who had called to Melody. "Her name is Alia."

"Alia, can you hear me?" said Melody. She searched for signs of life and felt the warm but soft brush of the girl's body exhaling.

"Alia, I'm going to help you. Can you stand?"

A single tear ran from the girl's eye.

Melody checked her legs for breaks by running her hands from the feet upwards to the thighs, but the girl flinched when Melody reached the dried blood on her bare skin.

"It's okay. I'm not going to hurt you," said Melody. Alia's eyes followed Melody's hands with a lazy flicker of exhaustion. Melody pulled the lamp closer and searched for the source of the blood. She found barbed wire around the tops of Alia's thighs. The rusty barbs had torn her apart. Melody continued her examination, moving up to the girl's stomach. She felt ribs, far too pronounced, and beneath her dress, she found more barbed wire wrapped around Alia's chest beneath her arms.

Melody looked away. There was no need to expose the girl with so many onlookers.

"She was hung from it," said Harvey behind her. "The barbed wire. Ferez sent me a photo."

Melody reached out and smoothed the girl's hair. "Alia, listen, we're going to get you to a doctor, okay?"

She didn't respond.

Melody felt the faint pulse on Alia's wrist.

"You're going to be okay. Do you hear me?"

But as she said the words, shock and loss of blood overcame the girl's fragile body.

"No, no," said Melody, feeling for a pulse on her neck. "Help me," she called to Harvey.

But Harvey just placed his hand on her shoulder. "Melody-"

"Untie her," she said. "Get that wire off her."

"Melody, stop."

The room was silent. All eyes were on Melody.

"She's gone," said Harvey. He gave her shoulder a squeeze.

Melody let her head hang in defeat. Then she pulled on the girl's ruined clothes to keep her covered. "How long do we have?" she asked, refusing to remove her gaze from Alia's face.

"She's not hurting anymore, Melody," said Harvey.

He rubbed her shoulder and pulled her into him. But Melody was resolute. Her determine had been triggered. Harvey knew the look.

"Ferez was here a while ago. He took Reg and Jess," said Ladyluck.

"We saw him get away on his boat," spat Melody. "Coward."

"He called someone when he was here. He was frightened. Somebody called Streaky. He told him to bring the trucks now. I think they are moving the refugees early."

As if the driver was waiting for his cue, they heard the distant sound of a heavy diesel engine pulling into the boatyard.

"Quick," said Melody. "Help me untie them. We can save them."

"No," said Harvey. "There's no time." He moved to the door

and watched as the truck drew closer, slowly manoeuvring through the array of boats and trailers.

"What do you mean, no?" replied Melody, reaching up to Ladyluck's bound arms.

"Leave them."

"Harvey?" said Melody. "Help me get them down. We can still rescue them."

"Do you trust me, Melody?"

"Of course I do. I-"

"I've got an idea."

Bella saw two trucks arriving in the car's side mirror. The man and woman were still in the workshop.

"This might be my last chance," she said to herself.

She slipped from the car to a space in the shadows between two boats. Then she climbed into one and pulled a heavy, oily tarp over her.

The squeal and loud hiss of the lorries' air brakes was followed by two engines shuddering to a noisy stop. Doors opened and slammed shut, and footsteps disappeared into the workshop.

Bella closed her eyes.

She wished for the thousandth time that she had just stayed in her village. She wished she hadn't travelled to Aleppo, and most of all, she wished she hadn't met Fernando. No matter how hard she tried, Bella couldn't put the image of her family being gunned down out of her mind. She tried to imagine herself there and indulged in a romantic thought of her and her family all holding hands. If they were to die, then they would die together.

The reality was that they'd never be given a chance to die as they wished. The stories that she'd heard of gunmen bursting into homes and just shooting anyone in sight in cold blood were more realistic.

Somebody screamed from inside the workshop. It wasn't a scream of pain, it sounded to Bella more like a scream of anger. Such cruelty, everywhere she went.

One by one, the refugees were led from the workshop to the second lorry. The scene played out before Bella's eyes. It was as if they were being led to the firing squad. It was just like the stories Bella had heard from Syria when the military had pulled entire families from their homes and slaughtered them on the streets. But the refugees would have a very different and more uncertain future.

Bella's chance of reaching England was slipping away. Perhaps it was gone forever now, for Bella at least. Uncertainty shrouded the faces of her people. Only fear guided them onto the truck.

The two men laughed and joked amongst themselves. One stood by the door to the workshop, counting the scared faces as they emerged from the darkness. The other stood at the back of the lorry, shoving the men up roughly and helping the two younger girls, rewarding himself with a grope of their chest as he did so.

From beneath the tarp, Bella could see directly into the cargo space of the truck. Large boxes stood to the sides with plastic sheeting draped across them. The refugees sat in a corner on the floor, just as Bella remembered them sitting on the floor of the cabin on the boat, huddled together for warmth and security.

It would be the last time Bella saw any of them. She tried to focus on their faces, to remember them. They would never meet again, but Bella thought she would think of them in the times to come and hope that they fared well.

More shouting emerged from the workshop. The cry was

brief and female. The man who had stood at the rear of the truck had moved inside and out of sight, his movements lithe and slow.

He appeared at the door a few moments later with a well-dressed woman with blonde hair. She was not a refugee but was equally as scared. The woman's bare feet were bound and she shuffled painfully across the hard and rough concrete.

She never said a word. Even when she was assisted in boarding the truck and wandering hands ran up her skirt, she was silent. A look of disgust that twisted her face was the only sign she even felt the man's sly gropes. She sat alone with her knees drawn up and her head buried in her legs until the last hostage was led from the workshop.

It was the lady in black, the pretty one with pale skin and dark features. Her wrists were also bound, and like the first woman, she was treated to the same inquisitive hands as she climbed onto the flatbed of the truck. But this woman was different. She immediately returned her leg to the ground, turned, and in an instant, landed her forehead onto his nose.

Bella smiled from the safety of her hiding place.

Outraged, the man repaid the assault with a hard slap, and forced the woman onto the truck while holding his bloodied nose with one hand.

He spoke to her. Bella couldn't hear the words, but some things do not need to be heard; there was enough in the way he spoke.

The shutter door of the first truck was pulled shut and locked with a padlock, trapping the two women inside. Bella wondered where they would be going. Not England. If they were going to England, they would surely be with the refugees.

The two men then moved to the back of the refugee truck. Bella tried to see the faces of the refugees for one last desperate attempt at contact with them, but they had all huddled too close together and averted their eyes from the two men outside. A few blankets were tossed inside and the man with the bloodied nose began to walk away.

To Bella's horror, he walked directly towards where she lay. She slowly lowered her head and pulled the tarp over her.

His footsteps were slow as if he had all the time in the world.

Then he stopped.

Bella dared not move. He was just a few feet away. She closed her eyes, just waiting for the tarp to be ripped back at any moment. But the moments grew longer. Was he watching her? She feared to make the slightest movement in case the tarp she was lying beneath made a sound and gave her away. Her breathing quickened. No matter how hard she tried to control it, her short breaths seemed so loud.

A trickle of liquid splashing onto the dry concrete was followed with a soft groan of pleasure. Was he urinating? Then he hacked up phlegm from deep inside him, a noise that Bella had hated even when her father had done the same.

The noise stopped.

"Fernando, where are you? We must leave if we are to make the border."

He was using the phone. Bella's heart sank when she thought of Fernando. He had escaped with two people, a man and a woman, but she prayed he wouldn't return. She doubted he would ever find her in the boat beneath the tarp. But Bella knew that a small twist of fate could align their paths once more, and her chances of escaping would be gone forever.

Bella was torn. Part of her wanted Fernando to return, to give her the chance of finishing him somehow. But she could never do it. Part of Bella wanted the men to drive the refugees away, to leave the boatyard so she could escape. But she didn't know where she would go. The most significant part of her wanted to end it all, for death to be on her terms.

"No, it's fine. It looks like there has been a war, but there's no-one else here, just the refugees, two hostages and a dead guy hanging from the gantry." He paused. "You left them on the island? Is it safe?"

Bella gasped, louder than she expected.

Another silence followed. Surely, he had heard. Bella's heartbeat on the boat's wooden floor pounded like a drum.

"Hold on, Fernando," said the man into the phone. "I thought I heard something."

Bella glanced up at the refugees inside the lorry and caught the eye of the young girl with whom she had once spoken. Her eyes widened with recognition. But Bella gave a soft shake of her head, pleading with her eyes for her to stay silent.

Time stood still.

The boat rocked slightly as he pulled himself up onto the trailer. Bella prayed that her feet could not be seen sticking out of the tarp. She prayed her breathing was not too loud.

"Ah, it's nothing," said the man, and jumped back to the ground.

Bella's gave a long quiet exhale. Her heart was thumping.

"The two women? We'll deal with them. I will do it personally. I will throw them from the cliffs. By the time their bodies are found, they will be unrecognisable."

The two women would be killed. Bella was sad for them. The second lady had been so strong with spirit.

"I'd say we need to clear out of this place, Fernando. Once we're gone, come and take what you need. We'll need to find someplace new to run the operation."

There was a silence while Fernando spoke to the man. Bella pictured his huge ugly nose and two-sided voice. Was he angry or was he gentle when he spoke to his men?

"No, I haven't seen your little plaything." He laughed a cruel sneer. "She has probably gone and joined the homeless on the streets of Athens by now. She'll earn her keep; she was pretty."

Bella realised they were discussing her.

Fernando has noticed I am missing?

"Don't worry. If we see her, we'll kill her."

The last refugee was led from the workshop, leaving Melody and Ladyluck alone in the semi-darkness.

"This isn't good, Ladyluck," said Melody. "I've got a bad feeling here."

Ladyluck raised her head. She was clearly exhausted from standing and hanging with her arms in the air.

"Why? Do you want to go with *them?*" she replied.

"If we were put with the *refugees*, we could have helped them escape on the way to the UK," whispered Melody. "If we're being kept here, it means they have other plans for us."

"Like what?" asked Ladyluck, loud and excited. "What other plans would they have?"

Melody shot her a glance to shut her up.

"Don't look at me like that, Mills. Your boyfriend got you into this. If you hadn't listened to him, we'd both be outside right now."

"I'm sure Harvey has a plan," said Melody, more to herself than to Ladyluck.

The light from the door fell into shadow, and one of the men moved into the workshop. He walked slowly like a predator, eying them both.

"See anything you like?" asked Melody.

He smiled back then returned his attention to Ladyluck, stepping closer to her.

"Don't you dare touch me," warned Ladyluck. Her eyes narrowed to slits and her mouth looked as though it was ready to bite. The defensive reaction from Ladyluck surprised Melody. Although Ladyluck liked to appear in charge and the focus of attention, almost as an alpha-female, she wasn't hardy enough for ground operations.

The man laughed and reached out with his hand, resting one finger on Ladyluck's throat.

"Feisty," he said with a smile.

"Pig," replied Ladyluck.

He ignored the comment and continued to stare at his finger then slowly let it slide from Ladyluck's neck down her chest. He stopped momentarily. Melody could see the rise and fall of Ladyluck's chest.

A deathly silence filled the room. Melody wondered how she would react if his hand ventured to the right or left. The man stared at Ladyluck with lust, his grin spreading.

Ladyluck stared back, almost daring him to go further.

"Streaky, what are you doing?" came the other man's voice from the doorway.

Streaky winked at Ladyluck and removed his hand.

"Just a bit of window shopping, Jimmy," he replied.

"Load the truck, Streaky," said Jimmy. He continued to watch his partner with suspicion, as though his wandering hands were a common occurrence.

Streaky reached up and unhooked Ladyluck's bindings from the meat hook that hung from the ceiling. Relief washed over her face when her arms lowered. But Streaky ruined her small moment of pleasure by whispering in her ear loud enough for Melody to hear.

"There'll be plenty of time later, girls."

Melody studied Streaky's face. He wasn't a pleasant looking man. His eyes were small and too close together, his skin was rough as if he'd spent his life at sea or in the open air, and the hair on his back and chest met his unshaven face with very little demarcation.

"Ladies first," said Streaky, presenting the way out to Ladyluck. He turned and winked at Melody. "You sit tight there, my lovely. I'll be back for you shortly."

"Can't wait," replied Melody, returning his stare.

Ladyluck shuffled out with her ankles bound but turned to Melody briefly before she was nudged through the doorway with Streaky's hand on her backside. Melody was alone finally. She wished she had listened to Harvey when he'd wanted to tie a fake knot so she could slip her hands in and out. But it had seemed too risky, and Melody had told him to tie the knot tight.

Melody focused on acting submissive. If Streaky wanted to play, she would tolerate him as much as she could. The last thing she wanted was for him to get rough and find the Sig tucked in the back of her waistband, or the knife strapped to her ankle.

Streaky stepped back in the room as if he was expecting her to be up to something. "There you are," he said, and seemed to slide into the workshop, sidestepping in front of Melody as a hunter might circle its prey.

"Where else would I be?" said Melody.

He disappeared from view behind her but made no sound. The only sign he was close was the stale smell of body odour that overpowered the oil and cigarettes ingrained into the walls.

"Are you going to be trouble?" he hissed, his mouth suddenly close to Melody's ear.

She closed her eyes and prepared for the worst.

"No," she said. "I don't want any trouble."

His hands landed on Melody's hips with an oddly gentle touch. He was dangerously close to finding the gun.

"You just wait until we're alone," whispered Streaky. His hands edged to her stomach and pulled her backwards. Melody grimaced at the feeling of his growing excitement.

"Streaky," called Jimmy from outside. "Are you going to load her up or what?"

Streaky took a final sniff of Melody's hair and ran his hands up her sides then her arms, where he unhooked her.

"No trouble, remember?" whispered Streaky. The feigned seductive tones had gone from his voice.

He nudged Melody forward. Harvey hadn't tied Melody's feet; there hadn't been time. So she walked slowly and calmly, and stopped at the back of the truck. Streaky was clearly too engrossed in thoughts of his later plans to notice.

Ladyluck was sat near the bulkhead behind the cab with her bound wrists over legs. She peered over her knees as Melody swung her leg onto the truck.

Streaky's hand found her backside, his fingers close to Melody's weapon. She immediately dropped her leg back down, span, and planted her forehead into his nose.

Streaky folded in half, clutching his face, and Melody started to climb up onto the truck as if nothing had happened. But before she could stand, Streaky landed his open palm against Melody's face. The blow stung, but Melody took it well; she didn't retaliate. If he found the gun, her chances of escape would be over.

Ladyluck looked on in awe and Melody dropped to sit in the

opposite corner. The shutter door was pulled down with a crash, leaving them alone in the darkness.

"Hey, Ladyluck?"

There was a short silence followed by her scared and shaky voice. "Yes?"

"You remember when I told you I had a bad feeling?"

CHAPTER THIRTY-TWO

Standing in the shadow of a tree, the roots of which had punched through the concrete, and an old wooden fishing boat sat dormant on a trailer, Harvey looked on with pride. Melody had handled herself well. But the problem remained that she and Ladyluck hadn't been loaded into the same lorry as the refugees. They were in a truck by themselves.

Harvey began to formulate a new plan.

He *could* walk out into the open and hope that the two men didn't have guns. But that was unlikely. The chances were they'd both be armed to the teeth, and if they didn't kill him, they'd shoot a refugee, or worse, Melody. He could wait to see if the trucks left the boatyard together in convoy. Either way, his chances of rescuing Reg and Jess were growing slimmer. Melody was armed, and he had to trust that she could handle herself.

One of the men began to walk towards Harvey's position. Harvey took three slow steps backwards until his back was up against the tree. He looked out of the shadows, ready to strike if need be.

It was the one called Streaky, the guy that Melody had hit.

Harvey had heard his name being called. Streaky stopped on the other side of the boat to relieve himself.

Now would be the perfect time, thought Harvey. But acting on an impulse would be hasty. He needed a plan, but at the forefront of his mind, he knew that time was running out and his window of opportunity was fading away.

Scenarios played out in Harvey's mind, each vital detail seemed to be highlighted, as well as each risk. Many plans fell by the wayside as the risk increased and the odds of saving Reg and Jess grew higher. Another plan seemed reasonable, but the risk of Fernando escaping was too high. His plan needed to save the refugees, save Reg and Jess, and save Melody.

Streaky began to talk to Fernando on his phone.

"I will do it personally. I will throw them from the cliffs. By the time their bodies are found, they will be unrecognisable."

Streaky zipped up and walked away, still talking to Fernando. Harvey stepped out from the shadows. The engine of the first truck started. The man called Jimmy was at the wheel and lit a cigarette to begin his long journey.

Streaky finished his call and spoke with Jimmy, but the conversation was muffled over the sound of the diesel engine. Harvey crept around the back of the boats. While Streaky's back was turned talking to Jimmy, Harvey darted the twenty yards and stopped behind the refugee truck. He dropped and checked their feet.

He hadn't been seen.

Harvey was counting on Jimmy leaving with the refugees, so he'd be left alone with Streaky. Jimmy slammed his door shut. Things were moving. Harvey crouched beneath the lorry and watched as Streaky took a lazy stroll to his vehicle, which had Melody and Ladyluck inside.

Jimmy began to rev the engine.

Harvey rolled his neck to the left, waited for the click, and then to the right.

He was ready.

But then, Streaky also started his engine, and the driver's door slammed. Harvey peered beneath the refugee lorry and saw Melody's truck begin to roll away. He dropped to the ground, rolled beneath the vehicle and pulled himself up, just as Streaky rolled past.

Harvey could do nothing except watch as Melody was driven out of the boatyard and headed north away from the city, along the coastal mountain road.

CHAPTER THIRTY-THREE

"Hold your hands out," said Melody in the semi-darkness. She reached for the knife strapped to her ankle.

"What? Why?" said Ladyluck, her voice thick with tears.

"Have you been crying, Ladyluck?"

"We're going to die, you heard them," said Ladyluck. "I'm not ready to die. Oh, why did I come here?"

"Pull yourself together," snapped Melody. "You're not dead yet, and all the time I'm here, you're not going to die."

Ladyluck was silent, except for a sniff. She wiped her eyes with her bound hands.

"Hold your hands out, Ladyluck."

Melody felt for her wrists and began to slice through the rope.

"You have a knife?" said Ladyluck. "But I don't see what good it will do. Didn't you see him? He had a gun."

"Yeah well, you make your own luck in life, and I'm not going down without a fight," said Melody. "Now take the knife and cut my wrists free."

Ladyluck did as she was told, fumbling in the dark. She then returned the knife to Melody.

"Right," said Melody. "Now to get us out of here."

"I heard him padlock the shutter," said Ladyluck. "We'll never get it open."

"Never say never," said Melody, running her hands across the shutter. It comprised of five-inch horizontal slats that were hinged together, which allowed the door to roll up and over along the steel rails.

Melody searched in the dark and found a screw head. She tested it with the point of her knife then felt the satisfying click of the screw unfastening.

A few moments later, she dropped it to the floor and smiled in the dim light at Ladyluck. "We're in business."

Just then, the lorry took a sharp turn and hit an incline. Streaky must have dropped down a gear to take a hill, and the two women were thrown to the floor.

"He's climbing a hill. We must be close to the cliffs," said Ladyluck.

Melody rolled off her and immediately got to work on the remaining screws.

"What are you planning, Melody?" asked Ladyluck. "You're not going to jump from a moving truck, are you?"

Melody tossed another screw to the floor and then moved to the other side.

"Whatever happens, Ladyluck," she replied, "you can be sure I'm not going anywhere without you."

CHAPTER THIRTY-FOUR

Harvey was thankful when the refugee truck turned left out of the boatyard and took the same road as Melody. But the first truck was already out of sight.

The harsh concrete rushed passed just two feet below Harvey. His feet were hooked over a strut. He clung with his arms to the spare tyre, using all of his core strength to keep his torso from dropping and scraping along the road surface.

The rear bumper, a single beam of steel that looked more like a step than a bumper, was designed to prevent smaller cars from being wedged below the lorry's undercarriage in the event of a crash; it was two feet away from where he hung.

Harvey reached out with his left leg and hooked his foot over the beam. The move stretched his body out and increased the pull on his stomach. His shoulders began to shake with the strain. He took a few deep breaths, and in one smooth motion, moved his right foot to join the left on the steel beam. His two feet stuck out from the rear of the moving lorry.

Then, using the momentum from the move, he swung one arm across to the rear beam. Suddenly, the lorry took a turn. It hit a hill. Streaky crunched down a gear, creating a considerable jolt throughout the lorry.

Harvey's right hand slipped off the spare wheel and swung dangerously close to the road below. His balance was off. But he used the swing to make the final move to the beam and clung to it with all his remaining strength.

The lorry was still climbing. It had slowed enough for Harvey to pull himself straight and stand up, holding onto the padlock with one hand and searching for a handhold on the smooth rear shutter of the truck with the other.

The vehicle crested a hill and began to cruise down a short stretch of road. Harvey used the opportunity to edge to the corner and peer in front. There was a space between the truck's body and the loose shutter; it was just wide enough for Harvey to slot his fingers inside.

To one side, tall cliffs whizzed past, and to the other, the world dropped out of sight over the cliffs.

Harvey reached up, sliding his hands inside the gap, and then placed his left boot against the smooth shutter door, ready to climb to the roof. He peered around the edge once more, just as the lorry reached the trough and began another uphill climb. He'd need to wait until a downward stretch to give him as much chance as possible of scaling the truck.

One of the wheels found a pothole, which sent a violent jolt through to Harvey's precarious position. His right boot lost its grip on the beam and Harvey fell, somehow managing to keep his fingers inside the sharp groove. But his boots slid and bounced on the road, wrenching his body backwards.

Harvey's body stretched out and twisted painfully. He couldn't even let go; the pull on his fingers had wedged his fingers tight. They slowed as they crested another small hill then began to pick up speed. Harvey's boots were quickly grinding away and getting hot.

Harvey clenched his teeth, took three deep breaths, his fingers burning with pain, and dragged his left foot closer to the truck, his right continued to drag along the road.

The moment his left foot hooked over the beam, he gave one final pull and dragged his right foot up out of danger then sat on the narrow steel beam while his boots cooled down. Harvey's feet were burning. The soles of his shoes had begun to melt. His fingers screamed in agony; they were wedged deep and uncomfortably into the sharp groove.

With a final push, he stood up against the flat back of the truck once more. He pulled his fingers from the gap, flexed them, and then pushed them back in, as deep as they would go, gripping onto almost nothing but sharp steel and fibreglass.

Harvey placed his foot against the back of the shutter and without hesitation, he pulled himself up, pushing against the truck with his leg and sliding his fingers deeper into the gap. Then he pushed with his other leg until he could see over the roof. One more agonising push with all his might and his hand reached over onto the smooth fibreglass roof of the truck. Harvey swung his leg and pulled his whole body up. He lay for a moment to let his fingers regain some blood.

But the break was a mistake.

A sharp right turn immediately sent him into a slide towards the edge. He slammed his boot down, trying to gain friction. The lorry entered a steep incline, which threatened to throw him off the back. Harvey forced his other boot down. But he still moved slowly. He was in an even worse position than before.

Seconds felt like minutes; gradually, both the back and the side grew nearer. There was nothing to grip, and Harvey could only wait until a downhill part of the road. Then he could use the same forces that were trying to throw him off to slide to the front.

His prayer was finally answered when the lorry hit another

crest and began to pick up speed. Harvey's planted feet started to work against him as he slid across the smooth surface, gaining momentum. He turned mid-spin to slide feet first and slammed his boots into the roof of the cab. Harvey felt secure for the first time since the lorry had driven off with him underneath it.

Jimmy immediately leaned out of the window to identify the noise. His eyes opened wide in surprise when he saw Harvey stood above him. Jimmy's reactions were faster than Harvey expected. He began to slalom up the next hill, forcing the lorry from side to side of the narrow cliff road. But Harvey had handholds now. He stood above the driver's window waiting for his chance.

As soon as Jimmy leaned out again to see the results of his sharp turns, Harvey slammed his boot down onto his head. Jimmy's feet lost the pedals. The truck surged as it lost momentum and Harvey was thrown forwards. He reached out as he fell and just managed to grab hold of the huge wing mirror, then swung around to the driver's door.

Jimmy had barely recovered from Harvey's kick but was reaching across to the passenger seat for his gun. Harvey, half in and half out of the window, took a firm grip on his throat. A lorry coming the other way sounded its horn and threatened to hit Harvey's legs, which hung out of the window.

Keeping his grip on Jimmy, Harvey dragged himself all the way into the cab. Jimmy had the gun. Harvey pinned his arm to the seat with everything he had. Jimmy was fighting to control the lorry with all the commotion. Keeping his eyes on the road, he reached forwards and clamped his teeth into the back of Harvey's neck, biting down hard.

Harvey felt the teeth pierce skin. He slammed his elbow backwards into Jimmy's face. The truck immediately began to veer across the road. It scraped against the barrier that ran along the edge of the cliff, sending a shower of sparks into the air.

Taking hold of Jimmy's hand, Harvey snapped his fingers backwards with a violent series of cracks until Jimmy released the gun and screamed in agony. The weapon fell back to the floor of the truck, and Harvey began to pound Jimmy's face with his feet. The truck swerved violently across the narrow road, and the passenger side slammed into the rocks behind Harvey's head, sending shattered glass raining down on him. A deafening roar of jagged rock tearing at steel filled the cab.

Jimmy held one hand on the wheel. The other rested uselessly on his lap. Harvey took a glance through the windscreen and saw his chance; another oncoming truck approached. He straightened himself while Jimmy fought to steer to the lorry then rugby tackled him flat against the inside of the door, slamming his head against the hard interior.

Jimmy fought back with a headbutt then spat blood in Harvey's face. Undeterred, Harvey grabbed Jimmy by the scruff of his neck and pulled him closer. Just as the oncoming lorry was about to pass, Harvey forced Jimmy's head through the open window of the cab and snatched the wheel to the left.

The force and violence of the oncoming lorry meeting Jimmy's head wrenched his body from Harvey's hands and sucked him from the cab, leaving Harvey alone to steer the lorry back onto the right side of the road.

He changed down a gear as he reached the top of the next hill then planted his foot firmly on the accelerator, giving it all he had. In the distance, and far below him on the cliff-side road, he caught a brief glimpse of the other truck.

Harvey had Melody firmly in his sights.

CHAPTER THIRTY-FIVE

Once the first panel of the shutter door was off, the rest came away easily. Melody and Ladyluck each grabbed onto the top of the panel down and heaved backwards. The strips of fibreglass flexed, worked loose from the shutter mechanism, and then snapped away. Within a few minutes, they had a pile of broken shutter panels and a gap large enough to step through.

"Are you ready to jump?" asked Melody, holding onto the side of the truck and peering out over the cliff that dropped down beside the road.

"Jump?" said Ladyluck. "I told you before I am not jumping from a moving lorry." She began to get agitated. "First of all, you want me to jump off a building, now you want me to jump from a moving lorry." She waved her hands in the air. "Where is it you're planning on jumping *to?*" she asked. "Have you seen the drop?"

"Ladyluck," shouted Melody, instantly silencing her colleague. "Just calm down." She smiled at her friend whose face was frozen in a look of sheer terror.

"*Calm down?*" said Ladyluck. "You're *nuts*, Melody."

"You want to be rescued?"

"Of course I want to be rescued," said Ladyluck.

"Well, shut up then, and get ready to jump." Melody smiled at her and pointed at the half-destroyed lorry that was catching up fast. The right-hand side of the cab looked like it had been torn off. As the driver took the corner far too fast, the two women saw a streak of red down the driver side that ran the full length of the truck.

"Is that-?"

"None other," finished Melody. She waved Harvey closer, but the engine was already at its limit, issuing out thick smoke from under the cab. Harvey was catching up, but it was slow progress. Streaky must have seen the ruined lorry in his mirror because his driving suddenly became very erratic.

Harvey matched him turn for turn, and when Streaky slowed for a bend, Harvey just forced the lorry around at maximum speed, scraping the cliffs on the inside turns and the barriers on the outside as he closed the gap. With each bend, he grew closer and closer. The two women stood either side of the cargo bed, holding on tight to the remains of the shutter for stability.

Melody saw Harvey look at the road ahead. She could just make out his nod to her. Melody poked her head around and saw the downhill approach.

"Get ready, Ladyluck."

"What?" she cried. "No, Melody. No."

Harvey had closed the distance to just three metres. The engine screamed in revolt, and Streaky was giving his truck everything it had. With the flexibility of a dancer, Harvey brought his left leg up to the dash and began to kick at the edges of the windscreen. It shattered on the first blow, but Harvey lost speed with his efforts and brought his leg down.

Melody instinctively knew what Harvey was trying to do and drew her Sig. She waved it at Harvey and caught his eye.

He nodded once more.

She let go of her grip on the side of the truck, spread her feet shoulder width apart, and fired four times, placing a round through each corner of the windscreen.

"What are you doing?" shouted Ladyluck over the racket of the half-destroyed truck and the wind that rushed past. "You're going to kill him."

Melody tucked her Sig back into her waistband and watched as Harvey then forced the ruined screen out of its retaining rubber seal. With a final push, it fell away to the road below.

The pursuit came to an incline. Harvey saw it coming; he changed down to third gear and slammed the accelerator to the floor. Streaky hadn't been ready. He lost speed as he hit the hill, and the front end of Harvey's truck slammed into Streaky's rear end.

"Jump," he shouted. "Now."

"No way," said Ladyluck. She was truly terrified, gripping onto the side of the truck with everything she had.

Melody edged over to her.

"Quickly," shouted Harvey. He peered out of the side windows. "We're running out of time."

"Get away from me," said Ladyluck, seeing Melody grow closer, but refusing to let go of the side of the truck.

"Come on. There's no other way," shouted Melody.

Harvey slammed again into the truck, but Melody balanced like a surfer. She reached out to Ladyluck.

"No. You go," shouted Ladyluck. "I'll stay. I mean it. Go."

"If you stay, I'll stay," called Melody.

"I can't do it." She looked petrified.

Melody grabbed her arm. "Ladyluck, he's going to kill you."

The lorries rounded a bend and Melody lost her balance. Ladyluck grabbed onto Melody to stop her falling away. As the truck straightened, Melody yanked her off the side of the truck and held her from behind.

"I told you, I'm not leaving you behind again," Melody shouted into her ear.

"No, Melody, don't."

Harvey must have seen what Melody was doing, and once more closed the gap, slamming the trucks together. Melody used all her weight to pull Ladyluck down. She launched them both off the back of the cargo bay and in through the empty windscreen space.

They bounced off the passenger seat and landed on the floor of the truck in a sea of shattered glass with Ladyluck on top. Harvey looked even more determined and maintained his speed.

"Stay down," he called to them, and then dropped the gear once more. Ladyluck peered over the dashboard. Melody pulled up and joined her to watch as Harvey loitered a few meters behind Streaky with a sharp bend approaching fast.

"Harvey," said Melody. "We're not going to make it."

Harvey didn't reply.

"Harvey?"

He slammed the trucks together one last time, span the wheel left then right, forcing Streaky to counter his push. As Streaky tried to slow for the bend, Harvey gave the truck everything it had, forcing him to drive faster and faster towards the turn.

A harsh squeal of brakes sung out over the din of the engines. Burning tyre rubber joined the stench of hot oil and smoke, and Streaky's truck burst through the steel barriers and launched off the edge of the cliff in a final crescendo to the performance.

Harvey hung onto the wheel with everything he had. They slammed into the barrier, past where Streaky had broken through. In a shower of sparks and a deafening grinding of steel on steel, he finally coaxed the vehicle onto the road.

A tense silence followed. Both Melody and Ladyluck held on for dear life. Melody tried to look behind to see Streaky's lorry descend into the valley, but it was out of sight. It would be destroyed on the rocks below in a ball of flames, along with its driver.

CHAPTER THIRTY-SIX

The truck limped to a stop in a small coastal village at the foot of the mountain range. It seemed to sense the end of its ultimate journey. The engine cut out without Harvey even touching the ignition key, and a great wash of steam rose from the engine bay.

"Oh, those poor people," said Ladyluck. "I do hope they're okay."

"Why don't you go take a look?" replied Melody. "Just give me a minute here with Harvey."

Ladyluck took the hint and disappeared towards the back of the truck.

"You okay?" asked Harvey.

Melody nodded. "I'm worried about Reg though. Ferez is going to be mad as hell about this. He might lash out."

"How's he going to find out?" asked Harvey. "As far as he's concerned, Derby and Barnet are dead, and you and Ladyluck are either dead or on the way to being dead with your mate Streaky. I've done everything he asked me to do."

"What happens if Ferez tries to call Streaky?"

"I doubt he'll be able to answer." Harvey smiled.

"He's not stupid. He'll know something's up," said Melody.

"Well, then we need to find them quickly."

"Sorry to interrupt your plans for world domination," said Ladyluck, "but there's a padlock, and I can't open the shutter door."

"It's okay," said Melody. "I'll help." She jumped down from the cab and walked with Ladyluck to the rear shutter. Harvey joined them. He always enjoyed watching Melody solve problems.

"Hey, Ladyluck," said Melody. "For the record, I'm sorry I threw you out the back of a moving truck. No hard feelings, eh?" She pulled her Sig and readied it to shoot the padlock.

"No hard feelings?" replied Ladyluck. "That was wild. It was the most exciting thing I've ever done."

Harvey smiled to himself.

"In fact," Ladyluck continued, "can I do *that?*"

"Shoot the padlock?" asked Melody.

"Yeah, can I do it, please?"

Melody offered the grip to her.

"I haven't fired a weapon since basic training, and even then, it scared the hell out of me."

"Okay well just keep-"

Ladyluck fired.

Bits of the padlock's mechanism scattered across the ground.

"Yep," said Melody. "Just like that."

Harvey shoved the shutter door up, and the three of them stared into the darkness. Sixteen eyes peered back from the shadows. They were bunched into the corner behind toppled boxes and scattered kilo parcels of greyish brown powder wrapped in clear plastic.

"Lower the weapon," whispered Melody, ignoring the drugs. "They're frightened."

Ladyluck did as Melody instructed.

Melody climbed up onto the back of the truck but kept her

distance. "Come," she said. "You're free."

The refugees didn't move. They just huddled closer together.

Melody waved her arm to the open shutter. "Come." She smiled at them, but the scared faces with wide eyes remained where they were.

"T'aallu l'hon ma takhafu," said Ladyluck, peering into the truck and offering a large friendly smile.

The man in the middle raise his head. His eyes squinted.

"Come."

Ladyluck waved them over. "Intu halaa ahraa."

He slowly got to his knees and seven pairs of eyes all turned to him in wonder. The man took a few tentative steps towards Ladyluck.

"You're free now," she said, and waved her arm to present the tiny village.

"Ladyluck," said Melody, "I didn't know you spoke Arabic."

"I speak a few languages," she replied. "I think I've worked out what happens to *me* now. I've had my fun, and I don't think that coming with you is an option, even for the new adventurous Ladyluck. It's probably going to be dangerous, isn't it?"

Harvey nodded. "You're going to take care of these people?" he asked.

Ladyluck nodded. "It's what I do, right?" she said softly. "I take care of things. I'm a fixer, after all."

Harvey looked down at Melody. "It'll make it easier," he said.

"I'll get rid of the drugs, and find these people somewhere safe," said Ladyluck, pleased that she finally had something to offer to the operation.

Melody reached for her phone, found the number she was looking for and hit dial.

"Jackson, it's Mills. We hit a few issues. Find me Tenant's location and ping me the coordinates."

CHAPTER THIRTY-SEVEN

"An island?" said Harvey. "What is he, a Bond villain?"

"Many of them here are uninhabited but the local fishermen would know of them."

Harvey began to scan the coast.

"What are you looking for?" asked Melody.

"Well, I was going to steal a car to get back to Athens."

"Steal?" asked Melody.

"But now, we need a boat," said Harvey. "So we're going to steal one of them instead."

"Borrow, Harvey. We're going to borrow a boat."

"Call it what you like, Melody."

The pair dropped to the beachfront. Heading away from the village, they found one of the many small marinas that dotted the Greek coastline. They stopped a few hundred yards from the entrance.

"We can't just walk in there and take whatever we want, you know," said Melody.

Harvey didn't reply. He was eying the boats that were moored inside.

"You see anything you like?" asked Melody.

"Yep," said Harvey. "But we're going to have to swim for it."

"Swim?"

"Well, there's a dozen little boats in the marina that would serve our purpose. But there are too many locals about, they'd know who owned the boats. The last thing we want is for them to call the police. It would take some pretty good explaining."

"So?" said Melody, following Harvey's eyes. "You want to swim out to that little speedboat?"

"See any other options?" said Harvey. "The clock is ticking."

"Right, let's get it over with," said Melody, pulling her phone out and ensuring the waterproof case, which she kept on as standard, was secure. The Mediterranean was warmer than cold, but colder than warm. Fully dressed, the pair walked into the sea.

"What if someone sees us?" asked Melody.

"If you keep looking around nervously like that, they will. But if you act naturally, you'll be surprised at what people don't see," replied Harvey. "Swim around to the far side of the boat."

They reached the little Bayliner tied to a buoy a few hundred yards out, and hung onto the side. Harvey pulled himself up. His clothes and boots were heavy with water. He rolled onto the white and blue bench seat and then dropped to the fibreglass deck. Melody followed suit, anxious to see what he had planned.

"Now what?" she asked. "There're no keys."

Harvey gave her a look as if to question her confidence in him and then slid forward. "Just keep your head down."

He reached behind the console and pulled three wires from the ignition then ran each of them across the earth strip until he found the live wire, which produced sparks. Then he touched the live wire against the other two wires one at a time. Touching the first caused the ignition lights to illuminate. He carefully twisted the bare copper end together with the live wire then touched the twisted pair with the end of the third wire.

The starter kicked in. Harvey pumped the little primer knob a few times, then touched the cables together again. The engine kicked into life and began to idle.

"I'm impressed. You didn't even have to destroy the boat," said Melody.

"An old friend showed me how to do it once before," replied Harvey with a smile. Then, staying low, he eased the throttles forward one click while Melody untied the rope to the buoy.

"You set?" he asked. "Don't look back. Act naturally."

Melody nodded.

Harvey eased the throttles forward a little more but stayed down low until they were far enough from the shore not to be identified. Melody slid forwards and took the seat beside him at the helm. She was smiling to herself.

"What?" asked Harvey. "What are you smiling about?"

"You," she replied. "You're such a criminal."

Once they were out of sight of the marina, Harvey gunned the engines. Melody enjoyed the views and guided Harvey, following the location that Jackson had sent through to her phone. The little sports boat skimmed the surface of the Mediterranean, leaving a wake that weaved between the islands.

"Dead ahead," called Melody over the loud engine noise. She pointed at a circular island in front of them. The land itself seemed to form at an angle, as one giant mountain rising from the depths of the ocean.

"There must be another way in," called Melody. "That's going to be impossible."

Harvey drove in a wide circle around it, seeking the best place to moor the boat at a safe entry point. On the far side of the island facing the sea, a small, welcoming bay enjoyed calm waters and rich sand. Inside, moored at the far end, was Ferez's boat. Harvey saw it, slowed, and steered the stolen Bayliner into the bay.

"You're just going straight in?" asked Melody. "Have you ever heard of stealth?"

"Reg and Jess are still alive, right? The team in London can see them here?"

"Yeah, they picked up the trackers," replied Melody.

"You don't honestly think that Ferez actually wants Reg and Jess, do you?"

"So why does he have them?" asked Melody.

"Because he knows *we'll* try and rescue them, Melody." Harvey drove slowly into the little, secluded bay towards Ferez's boat. Sheer cliffs rose up high on either side of them. In the centre sat a tiny beach. Behind it was a dense but small forest. It lay before the steep hills that rose up to meet the cliffs on either side, forming what looked to be a plateau.

"So, you think he wants *us*?" asked Melody.

"I do," said Harvey. "And if he does, coming in stealthily isn't going to help. My guess is that he'll be sitting up there hiding and waiting to take us out."

"So we're just going to walk into a trap, are we?" said Melody.

"No," said Harvey. "I'm going to walk into the trap."

"And what am I supposed to do while you do that?"

"You'll be figuring out a plan to save Reg and Jess, while I figure out a plan to kill Ferez."

Harvey tied off to Ferez's boat before the pair dove into the water and swam the short distance to shore. They reached the forest to the rear of the beach and began the steady hike up the hill.

"Is that the best plan you can come up with?" said Melody.

"What happened to your mantra? Patience, planning and execution?"

Harvey stopped and looked up at the long scree slope ahead of them. Melody stared at Harvey's back as he rolled his neck from side to side with a satisfying click.

"You see that cliff up on our left?" asked Harvey, without turning around.

"Of course," replied Melody. She followed the veins and cracks in the limestone from the sharp rocks that stood like daggers in the sea below to the precipice that reached out three hundred feet above them like a child's bottom lip.

"Look closer," said Harvey.

CHAPTER THIRTY-EIGHT

It took the pair more than an hour to climb the steep scree slope up to the plateau. The island's terrain was scattered with loose rocks and wild plants that had somehow managed to take root in the deep cracks of the limestone.

At the top, the plateau led left and right. It seemed that the island had once been a volcano. One side of it had crumbled away, leaving the arc of a c-shape remaining and standing tall amongst the surrounding islands.

The two tiny dots on the edge of the precipice that Harvey had pointed out to Melody had been visible from below. But from the top, Melody couldn't see either of her friends.

The plateau was more than a hundred feet across in places. Deep cracks had long ago formed caves that led down to darkness, and sheer drops at the edges led straight down to the sea. Reg and Jess were nowhere to be seen.

The Mediterranean breeze was warm and strong at the top. Harvey, still topless with his shirt tied around his shoulder, powered on for a few more minutes.

"This is where we split up," said Harvey. "You go find Reg and Jess. I'll take care of Ferez."

"No, Harvey. What if he has a gun?" replied Melody.

"He won't," said Harvey. "This is more personal."

"Here, at least take my sidearm." Melody reached for her Sig, but Harvey held her arm.

"No, keep that out of sight," he said. "You need it more than me. I'll be okay."

Melody began to protest, but Harvey turned away. He climbed up onto a large rock that must have stood there for all of time, and then surveyed the wild, harsh landscape in front of him.

He glanced down at Melody.

"Are you still here?" he asked. "Go find them and stay out of sight. I'm going to finish this."

Harvey didn't wait for a response.

The wind began to pick up as the late afternoon sun sank lower to the picture perfect horizon.

"Ferez," Harvey called out. He caught Melody in his peripheral vision ducking out of view behind him. He heard her moving across the rocks to make her way to the end of the ridge. "Ferez," he called out again.

No reply came.

Harvey continued to scan the plateau. He could see why the place was uninhabited. It stood on the edge of the islands, bearing the brunt of the elements that came across Europe from the Atlantic.

"Ferez."

He knew that he'd feel a gunshot before he heard it, but Harvey was ready.

"You want me?" called Harvey at the top of his lungs. "Come and get me."

During a temporary lull in the wind, Harvey heard the faint chink of rocks hitting rocks as Ferez climbed out from his hole. Harvey watched Ferez's lanky frame make his way to the centre of the plateau.

"Is this where you want to do this, Ferez?" asked Harvey.

Ferez stared up at Harvey on top of the rock. "This is where I dreamed of doing this, Mr Stone."

"It's your choice," replied Harvey. He slowly climbed down from the rock.

The two men stood twenty feet apart on a hundred foot squared piece of flat land at the top of a three hundred foot cliff.

"For a man with such a reputation, it almost seems like the ideal place to die, does it not?" said Ferez.

"Is that why you want me, Ferez?" replied Harvey. "Because of my reputation?"

"Yes and no." He began to walk in a slow circle around Harvey. But Harvey knew Ferez was looking to turn him around to face the sun.

"Do you always talk in riddles?"

"No," said Ferez. "But there're so many reasons why you need to die, and killing you, Mr Stone, has been the dream of many men."

"You mean you're doing this for someone else?"

"Again, Mr Stone, yes and no," replied Ferez. "You've upset many people."

"Name one," said Harvey.

"You need to understand the consequences of your actions, Harvey. Did your father never teach you that? Oh, yes, that's right; you didn't have a father, did you?"

Ferez smiled and continued his walk. Harvey refused to turn to face him.

"You killed a man six months ago in Dubai."

"Crowe," said Harvey.

"Yes, Crowe. I watched the whole thing live."

Harvey didn't reply.

"But the consequences of your actions, Mr Stone, have left a lot of men out of pocket, and well, if you keep on following this moral compass of yours, then I'm afraid sooner or later one of those men will seek some sort of punishment."

"You did business with Crowe?" asked Harvey.

"No. Not Crowe directly, Harvey," said Ferez. He was behind Harvey now, but the distance seemed to be the same. "We have a mutual friend. And well, something you didn't know about me, Harvey, is that I'm a lot like you."

"We're nothing alike."

"I used to be like you anyway, Harvey," said Ferez. "But I evolved. Killing isn't a career, you know."

Ferez moved into Harvey's vision on his right.

"You see, Harvey, I know you think you're doing a deed, and everyone knows how good you are at..." He paused as if finding the right word. "Redemption. All you seem to do is implicate people."

Harvey didn't reply.

"You sign other people's death warrants, Mr Stone, and now it's time someone signed yours. Who better for such a task than me?"

"You didn't summon me here to help you then?" said Harvey. "You should have been clearer."

"Oh, I invited you, Harvey, because I wanted to see you in action. I wanted to see you take on the big boys, the team who have had your back all these years."

Ferez continued his walk in another long circle.

"You see, I saw you in action in Dubai, and I saw the aftermath of your attempt at *retribution*, as you call it. But I still doubted it. I just had to see it for myself."

"So let's do it then," said Harvey.

"What's the rush?" said Ferez. "Are you afraid your precious little Melody will be in trouble and need your help?"

Harvey didn't reply.

"I thought to myself," continued Ferez, "that when two monsters collide, the one who prevails will absorb the energy from the fallen one. Not in a magical or a godly sense, you understand. I'm not a believer myself. Are you a believer, Mr Stone?"

"In magic?" asked Harvey.

"Or the gods," replied Ferez.

"I believe in black and white," said Harvey. "Things are, or they aren't."

"So predictable. You're living a cliché, Harvey."

"*Living* being the operative word."

Ferez disappeared behind Harvey once more. Harvey stood resolute.

"So when I considered how it might feel to be the one to take down the great Harvey Stone, I also considered the power it would give me. Can you imagine the fear I would evoke in people, Harvey?"

"Not really, Fernando."

"I can," Fernando continued. "I thought to myself, if I were to take down the great Harvey Stone, where better for the two monsters to collide in a final epic battle than atop the highest peak around, and overlooking my beautiful Athens."

"Like a god?" said Harvey, mocking Ferez's warped sense of reality.

"Like a god." Ferez stopped in front of Harvey and turned to face him. "One of us will die here today, Mr Stone." He smiled with confidence. "Are you ready to die?"

CHAPTER THIRTY-NINE

Melody knew that there was no arguing with Harvey when he had his mind set on something, especially when it involved revenge. She'd learned not to fight it a long time ago. So she ducked down behind the massive rock that he'd climbed up, and made her way along the edge of the plateau, where the cliff edge stepped down in a series of ledges before the sheer drop. By making her way along the ridge, she was able to stay out of sight.

Harvey called out in the distance for Ferez to show himself. She should have known that Harvey would never walk into a trap; he was too smart. But Melody also knew that Fernando Ferez had earned his bones as a young teenager, the same way as Harvey, and that he'd been a notorious face in the European scene. She had every confidence in Harvey, but if he fell foul to Fernando Ferez, neither she, Reg or Jess stood much chance of escaping, gun or no gun.

Melody put the thought to the back of her mind and set on the task of finding Reg and Jess. The ledge she was traversing seemed to grow narrower with each step. It quickly disappeared, leaving her searching for hand and foot holds to take her to a small platform protruding from the cliffside.

Being an experienced climber, Melody spanned the gap with four moves, keeping three points of contact with the wall at all times and letting her legs carry the brunt of her weight. The sharp limestone was brittle from exposure, but she found solid handholds and crossed the first gap in under a minute.

The second gap was harder.

The short and narrow ledge on which she stood once again quickly became nothing but space for her toes, and the cliff began to overhang. It was the lip of the rock she had seen from below. On the far side of the gap stood Reg and Jess, huddled together and clinging to the wall with barely enough room to move.

Reg saw Melody first. His face broke into sheer relief for a fraction of a second. But then he realised that they may as well be a thousand miles apart. The overhanging cliff between them was just too much. Melody read it in his face and desperation spurred her on.

"Melody, no," called Reg. "Don't try it. It's suicide."

Jess turned around, still clinging to Reg, and Melody saw the look of sheer terror in her red and swollen eyes.

"There must be another way," called Reg.

"How did you get there?" asked Melody, peering over the edge at the waves crashing onto the sharp rock below.

"He lowered us down on a rope," answered Reg.

The wind had begun to whip along the cliff face, pulling any loose grout and sand off the rocks into Melody's eyes.

"There's a rope?" she said.

Reg nodded and held up the loose end apologetically.

Jess broke into tears again, and she turned away, burying her face into Reg's chest. The girl was freezing and scared out of her mind.

Melody scanned the problem. She'd faced overhangs before, and there were plenty of handholds, but she'd never attempted a perilous climb before in her big heavy boots. With the added danger of a three-hundred-foot drop onto the rocks below, she'd only get it wrong once.

Her mind mapped the moves and she danced the sequence on the narrow ledge, fixing the prominent rock features and cracks in her mind. Then, putting all fear behind her, she reached out with her left leg and wedged her boot inside a deep crack.

"So far so good," she told herself.

Reg was calling out to her. But her concentration and the roaring wind muffled his voice.

Climbing shoes would allow the climber to feel the rock and use their toes to sense how secure the foothold was. But her boots gave her no sensation at all. Taking a firm hold with her right hand, she reached out with her left and placed her hand inside a crack just wide enough to take it but deep enough to swallow her wrist. She balled a fist and tested the hold with a pull.

She pushed off onto her left leg. Her balled fist held her body close to the rocks. Melody didn't stop. In one smooth motion, her right arm swung beneath her left. Finding a strong hold, she then brought her right leg across. Climbing, for Melody, was all about the flow and motion. Stopping the motion breaks the flow.

She switched legs and allowed her left to extend out to the next deep vein. It was a full stretch for her, but her boot connected well. In three more moves, she had made the over-hang. The next combination left her with an arched back, hugging the concave shape of the rock. She placed her entire arm into a crack, found a hold inside, and tensed her muscle, which locked her arm and allowed her to lean out to look for the next grip. One more combination and Melody would be within reach of the ledge. But it would be the hardest challenge yet.

The cliffside by Melody's feet undercut the overhang, and from her precarious position, she could see no more footholds.

She would have to hang.

The hand holds looked good. If Melody reached out with her left hand and grabbed the largest knot of rock she could see, her right hand could follow. It would leave her one chance to swing her legs up to the ledge. Then she would have no plan; she couldn't see that far. But she was already a few minutes into the climb and her forearm muscles had begun to tire.

"Reg," she called out.

"I'm here," he replied. He was on his hands and knees with one hand holding onto the rocks and one hand extended out to her. "I'm ready."

Melody gave him a quick look to catch his eye. Reg wasn't a strong man or a hard man, but right there and then, she knew she could trust him with her life.

CHAPTER FORTY

The first blow came from Ferez, a sharp jab that cut through Harvey's defence and slammed into his chest.

Harvey took the hit in his stride and let Ferez dance around the space. He was obviously a boxer or fighter of some description. But Harvey knew that Ferez would have a weakness.

A wild roundhouse kick that Harvey easily ducked confirmed Harvey's thoughts. Ferez was a kick-boxer. The roundhouse was followed up with a straight kick to Harvey's head, which Harvey sidestepped before slamming his head into Ferez's face.

Undeterred, Ferez regained his composure and began his footwork again. Then, with the speed of a cat, Ferez threw a combination of punches and kicks, the last of which caught Harvey in the side of the head and sent him reeling, with his ear singing a high-pitch wail.

Ferez didn't let off. The next blows came at Harvey's legs, perfectly placed kicks aiming to break Harvey's knees. Ferez was smart. As Harvey blocked the kicks, Ferez threw two jabs with his fists at his face. Both connected, and both felt like he had been hit with steel.

Harvey sized Ferez up. He was tall and lanky, but inside, there seemed to be an iron core. Ferez outreached Harvey easily. Longer legs and arms gave him a considerable advantage as well as being trained. Harvey too had been trained to fight in several disciplines, which had resulted in him developing a style of his own. It was a mixture of judo, aikido and taekwondo, all rolled together and polished with the sheer animal instinct that can only be learned on the streets.

"Come on, Mr Stone," said Fernando, smiling at his clear advantage. "You're not living up to your name here. At least give me something to remember you by."

Harvey's legs were pounding from the several blows, and his ear was still ringing. He rolled his neck to the left and to the right, waited for the satisfying click, and then turned to face Ferez.

"I'm not giving you anything, Ferez," he said. "Why don't you come and get it."

As predicted, Ferez immediately set at Harvey with a series of high kicks. Harvey's eyes followed Ferez's feet as he circled through the air harmlessly in front of him. But with each kick, he grew closer. Ferez was pushing Harvey back to the cliff edge. Harvey began to take small steps back, blocking the kicks as they came then absorbing the body punches, and using the opportunity to land three hard blows to Ferez's nose in succession.

Ferez collected himself, wiped his nose and grinned at the blood on his cuff. "There we go," he said. "But I expected more of you."

Harvey didn't reply. He was watching Ferez's every move, and stepping back out towards the cliff as another series of kicks came his way. He was learning Ferez's technique. A pair of double punches, left then right, followed a series of kicks. The kicks were to lower Harvey defence; the body blows were to wind him or break a rib. Ferez had yet to throw a power punch.

The time was coming.

Another six steps to the cliff edge. He was close enough. Harvey made his first attack on Ferez, who ducked and weaved, avoiding each blow and replying with a sharp uppercut to Harvey's gut. Harvey sucked it up and waited for Ferez's second reply. It came as expected. But instead of dodging or moving, Harvey grabbed the arm and twisted it in one smooth motion. He pulled Ferez off balance and slammed the heel of his boot into the taller man's knee.

The knee buckled and visibly bent the wrong way, but it did not break. Harvey increased the pressure on Ferez's arm, despite him raining blows with his free hand into Harvey's head and face. Harvey lost count of how many times he was hit by Ferez's iron fist. He carried on twisting until he felt the pop of the bone dislocating and the grind of twisted ligaments.

Ferez cried out. He kicked furiously at Harvey, sending him to the ground just a few feet from the edge.

Harvey couldn't have orchestrated it better if he tried.

Ferez hopped up and down and shook the pain from his knee. His arm hung uselessly at his side. "Get up," he shouted to Harvey, outraged. "Get up so I can finish you."

Harvey pushed himself up on one knee, and Ferez, seeing his chance, came at Harvey with a kick to his head. But with Harvey's arms raised in an attempt to block the kick, he was caught off-balance and toppled from his crouch. Once more Ferez came at him with relentless punches of his good arm. The punches came fast and strong, but Harvey absorbed them, reached out for Ferez's damaged knee and with one hand on the man's ankle, he slammed the heel of his hand into the knee joint. This time, he felt the crunch of bone and gristle.

Ferez reeled with agony. The blows to Harvey's head stopped as the tall man stood with his weight on his one good leg, and one arm hanging dormant. He raised himself to his full height to deliver the hardest punch he could. But Harvey reacted fast. With his core wound like a spring, he released and landed an uppercut to Ferez's groin, doubling the man over. Unable to balance on one leg and with just one arm, Ferez was going down.

Harvey seized the moment. He reached up, grabbing Ferez by his collar, and rolled back, planting his foot in Ferez's chest. He used the momentum to pull Ferez onto him. Then, with all his might, Harvey straightened his leg and sent the man over his head and onto the edge of the cliff. Ferez landed hard on his back, with his feet hanging in the air. His one good hand held fast with everything he had left to a fist-sized rock that was half embedded into the ground.

Harvey launched himself at Ferez, but it was too late. Ferez had heaved himself up, rolled, and pulled the rock from the ground. It swung in a wild arc at the edge of Harvey's peripheral vision and connected with his head with a thump that seemed to echo throughout Harvey's mind.

He dropped to the floor and let the shadows of unconsciousness envelope his thoughts.

CHAPTER FORTY-ONE

The ledge was only five feet long and two feet wide, with a crumbling edge. Jess stood with her back to the cliff, her hands gripping the sharp rock and a look of sheer horror on her face. She tried to call out to Reg, but all Melody heard was the rush of the racing wind in her ears.

Reg took hold of Melody's belt and heaved her up on her count of three. With just the toes of her boots on the ledge and her back arched toward the overhang, Melody's muscles screamed at her to let go. But her tenacious mind told her to hang on just a few more moments.

She timed the final push with Reg's pull, and let go of the rock. For the longest of seconds, Melody hung out above the sharp rocks below, with only Reg to keep her from falling.

"Grab onto me," called Reg.

Her arms flailed and her fingers brushed over the rock. She'd lost her chance.

At the very last second, when balance had tipped the wrong way, and Reg had given her all he had to give, Jess bravely stepped from the safety of the rock face. She grabbed onto Reg's belt, and heaved him backwards, pulling Melody with him.

Melody regained her balance, and Reg was able to grab onto her arm. She fell onto him, and rolled to the cliff wall, her eyes wide, and her breathing sharp and short.

Reg's moment of heroism was over. He suddenly realised how perilously close he was to the edge, and slowly eased backwards to Jess, calming only when he felt the rock against his back.

Melody wanted to laugh or cry, she wasn't sure which, but she felt the emotions surging through her veins in the wake of adrenaline. The three were silent. No words needed to be spoken.

Then loudly, even with the wind, came the sound of somebody clapping. Melody twisted and looked up to the plateau.

Fernando Ferez stared back at her.

Melody's heart sank.

He smiled.

"I see that look of disappointment on your face, Melody Mills," he called out. "He was never going to live forever, you know."

Melody closed her eyes.

"Even the great Harvey Stone isn't immortal," continued Ferez.

"You evil bastard," hissed Melody. "What have you done with him?"

"Now, now, Melody, I think you have your own little predicament to consider before you go making life even more uncomfortable. Although, while I'm on the subject, I have to say, you're almost as predictable as Harvey used to be."

The words hit Melody hard.

Harvey used to be.

"You saw your friends in trouble and couldn't resist it, could you?" He smiled down at the three of them. "It's almost like leaving a trail of candy for a child to follow."

"So what?" said Melody, holding back the tears that seemed to burn the insides of her eyes. "What do you want with us?"

"You?" replied Ferez. "I don't want anything with you except to watch you die."

Jess began to sob and sniff.

"Why?" said Melody. She was having to shout to be heard above the increasing wind. "What have we done?"

"Oh, Melody, Melody, Melody," said Ferez. He began to pace the cliff above, a near vertical eight meters of sharp rock. "I explained all this to Harvey before he..." He smiled again. "Well, you know."

"No," said Melody. "No, I don't. Why don't you explain it to me?"

"He said you have spirit," said Ferez. "He said you'd be trouble and couldn't go quietly, even without your boyfriend to save you. You can't just accept death, can you?"

"Who said?" said Melody. "Your boss?"

"He's not my boss," said Ferez. "He's more of a partner."

"So while you're up here in the biting wind, I imagine he's at home in the warm eating his dinner? In Athens, is he?"

"Not that it matters, Melody, but London actually. We've been watching you all for quite a while."

"So now you have us. Why don't you come down here and finish us?"

Ferez laughed. "I don't need to come down there, Melody. Not when I have this."

He produced a grenade from a small knapsack. Melody noted his left arm was hurt by the way he held it close to his body.

"My favourite," he called down. With a smile, Ferez put the pin in his mouth.

"Wait," called Reg.

"Ah, Mr Tenant, you've been so quiet. I wondered when I'd

hear some of your futile quips."

"What do you want?" Reg asked. "Immunity? I can arrange it. I can make you a free man."

"Think about it, Ferez," called Melody. "All of this will be behind you."

"It will be behind me if I pull this pin and blow my problems from the side of this mountain. So what's the difference?"

"We can guard you," said Reg.

"Reg, no," hissed Jess under her breath.

But Reg ignored her. "I can turn a blind eye to your operations, Ferez. I can even make you invisible." Reg stared up at him with defiance. He looked like a man who was used to bargaining for his life. But Melody knew that deep inside, Reg, the computer whiz and all-round tech guru, clung to every piece of hope he could muster up.

Ferez was silent. He was considering the choice. Even the wind seemed to die down at the weight of Ferez's next words. "Nice try, Tenant. But I think I'll take my chances."

Melody felt her knees go weak. Her shoulders slumped as if the tension had held her upright and now gravity pulled at her limbs and organs.

"Goodbye, Miss Mills," said Ferez, and he pulled at the pin with his teeth.

Suddenly, Ferez lurched forward. Confusion spread across his face. Blood seeped from the top of his head, and his leg seemed to crumble.

Ferez fell to the ground out of sight above them.

"What the...?" Melody began. But before she'd even finished her sentence, the tired and grimy face of a timid young girl peered over the edge.

"Who the...?" said Reg. But before he'd even finished his sentence, the tired and bloodied face of Harvey Stone peered over the edge beside the girl.

CHAPTER FORTY-TWO

"Her name's Bella," Harvey called down to Melody as he replaced the pin through the grenade's trigger handle. "She found me." He turned and smiled at Bella.

"Oh Harvey," said Melody, and buried her face in her hands. "I thought-"

"Well, I'm not. But you lot will be if that sun goes down," replied Harvey. "Throw me the rope."

Melody coiled the rope ready to throw to Harvey, swung it back and forth a few times judging her throw, then launched it. The rope uncoiled flawlessly and Harvey caught it but winced at his wounds. His shoulder was bleeding from Melody's gunshot, his neck was sore from where Streaky had bitten him, and Ferez had left his mark in several places.

"Who's first?" called Harvey.

"I've tied Jess on. She's the lightest," replied Melody.

Harvey sat on the ground, planted his feet behind a large rock, and began to take Jess' weight.

"Bella?"

She turned to him. Harvey indicated with his fingers for her to watch Jess.

"Help her, and tell me when she is close, okay?"

Bella nodded. She seemed to understand English.

Jess came up easily, though she barely helped. Instead, she hung with her eyes closed, and when Harvey could pull no more, Bella had to help her over the edge onto the plateau. Jess rolled and scampered away from Ferez's body as if it might jump into life. Then she lay flat on the ground, exhausted with emotion. Bella untied the knot, pulled the rope off her, and lowered it down to the ledge.

"Ask them who is next," said Harvey in slow, simple English as though talking to a child.

Bella nodded and leaned out over the cliff top and called down. "Who is coming next? The man, he wants to know."

Harvey smiled to himself. Her English was excellent.

It was Reg who followed, seeing as Melody was the only person on the ledge capable of tying a bowline knot. Although he was heavier, Reg at least took some of his own weight and semi-climbed. Harvey could feel the tension on the rope rise and fall. Once again, Bella helped him over the edge and removed the rope.

Harvey had a hard time keeping the rope tight when the time came for Melody to ascend. She free-climbed most of the way, and it was only when she got to the top and one hand reached over onto the plateau, did she look up and catch Harvey's eye. She gave him a look of gratitude then began to heave herself over.

Just as Melody was about to pull her legs up, Ferez's hand reached out. The movement caught Harvey off guard. Melody fell backwards off the edge, and the rope slipped through Harvey's hand. It burnt deep into his skin as he clamped his fist around the rope. Then he felt the line slacken. Harvey held it with all his strength, knowing that Melody had bounced off the ledge and was hanging unconscious in the air three hundred feet above the rocks.

Reg backed Jess away from Ferez as he began to stand, but Bella threw herself at him. Ferez caught her by the throat and threw her to the ground, where she rolled and curled into a ball.

"You're supposed to be dead," said Ferez, staring at Harvey with one hand holding the wound on the back of his head. The other arm hung loosely at his side. Harvey strained to hold onto Melody as Ferez began a slow limp towards him.

Then, Harvey saw Reg do something he'd never done before; he launched himself at Ferez. But it wasn't enough. Ferez didn't budge. He simply knocked Reg to the ground with the back of his hand and continued limping towards Harvey.

Harvey wrapped the rope around his left hand as many times as he could, and stood. But Melody's weight pulled him closer to the edge. He countered the pull and leaned away, using his weight to hold Melody.

"Now we both die," said Ferez, with his unwavering evil grin. He pulled the grenade from his useless dead hand, gripped the pin with his teeth then spat it to the ground with the finality and certainty of death. "There's no escape now."

Harvey backed away. He knew that as soon as Ferez released the trigger, they would all die.

"Jess, get Reg out of here. Go hide in the boat," said Harvey, never removing his eyes from Ferez. Harvey edged back, taking the fight and potential explosion as far he could away from the others. "Run," he shouted at his friends, who stood there aghast.

"Let them go. But you cannot run, Harvey," said Ferez. His voice was tired as if he knew it was the end. "Just accept your fate."

Harvey doubled back past him, switching the rope to his right hand. He chanced a glance down to Melody who swung lifelessly on the end of the line.

"Melody," called Harvey, backing up some more. "You need to wake up."

"It's no use to try and escape, Harvey."

Through the tight rope in his hand, Harvey felt the ping of the first broken strand. He looked down. The sharp rock edge was cutting through Melody's lifeline.

He needed to act fast.

"Melody," he shouted again. But still, she swung with the wind and Harvey's movements. "Okay, Ferez," said Harvey. "You want to die? You want me to die?" He felt his chest rise and fall with the adrenaline. The veins and sinew in his arms and neck stuck out with the weight of Melody.

He took three deep breaths.

"Come and get me."

Ferez's grin seemed to lengthen and form an arc that cut deep into his face beneath his huge crooked nose. He took a step forwards.

Out of nowhere, a shape rushed past Harvey's dizzied sight, collided with Ferez's damaged leg, and took him to the ground. Bella held onto the hand with the grenade, holding it shut tight with everything she had. Harvey stepped forward to help, but she rolled onto Ferez's leg. He screamed loudly and rolled on top of her just inches from the edge.

Harvey lurched forward to grab Ferez, but seeing him, Bella pushed with everything she had. She growled, finding her last morsel of energy, and shoved Ferez over the side. There was just time, the smallest fraction of a moment of acquiescence before she too was pulled down with him.

She dropped from sight.

Harvey fell to the cliff edge, still clinging to the rope, in time to see Melody's swinging body beneath him and the explosion as Bella and Ferez hit the rocks below.

CHAPTER FORTY-THREE

Melody woke with the gentle rocking of the small waves that licked at the boat. The gentle vibration from the engine formed a rhythm that seemed to pulse throughout her body.

She opened her eyes.

The boat was being steered by Harvey. Reg lay on the floor and Jess stared down at her, smiling, with Melody's head in her lap.

"Ferez?" she croaked.

Jess shook her head.

"Dead?" Melody asked.

Jess gave a gentle nod.

"You okay?"

Jess broke into a great big smile.

"Well you clearly are," said Melody.

"Why don't you worry about yourself for a change?"

Melody closed her eyes again until she felt the familiar touch of Harvey's hand holding hers.

"Are we dead, Harvey?" she said, without opening her eyes.

He bent and kissed her forehead.

"Not for a while yet," he replied. "How are you feeling?"

"Like I fell off a cliff."

"We're nearly back on land. We'll get you checked out."

Reg, who had taken over steering the boat from Harvey, called out to her. "You had us all a bit worried there, Melody. It's not like you to miss out on the action."

Then it dawned on her; Melody tried to sit up and look around. "Where's the girl?" she asked. "Bella?"

Harvey didn't reply.

"No," said Melody. "That poor girl."

"It was her that took Ferez down," said Harvey.

Melody shed a tear for the girl who had saved their lives twice and eventually given her own.

"It's over, Melody," said Harvey. He looked out over the waves to the approaching ancient city of Athens glowing in the dimming sunlight. "We'll remember her."

CHAPTER FORTY-FOUR

At the boatyard, Ladyluck was waiting for them with a beaming smile.

"I spoke to London. They tracked you," she said, as Harvey brought the boat in neatly alongside the dock. She hugged Reg and Jess as they stepped onto the deck. Harvey stepped ashore to tie the bowlines.

"Wait," said Melody.

Harvey stopped and turned.

"Hey guys, do you think you could give us a minute?" she said to the team. They nodded and began a slow walk to a waiting car that Ladyluck had arranged. Melody listened to Reg and Jess begin telling their story to Ladyluck. Their voices trailed off.

"You okay?" asked Harvey.

"I'll be fine," replied Melody. "I'm bruised, but nothing is broken, and my headache will go. How about you?"

"Not bad," he replied, "considering you shot me." He smiled at her.

"I was thinking," said Melody, as she made her way across the small deck of the boat to stand in front of Harvey.

"Sounds dangerous," he replied.

"Oh no," she said. "I was thinking I should probably make that up to you."

"It's a gunshot, Melody," said Harvey. "It's going to take some serious making up."

"That's what I thought." She reached up to kiss him.

Behind Melody, the reflection of the sunset sky danced in a slow and shimmering rhythm across the glittering evening sea. As the sun reached down to touch the horizon, the two forms melding into one, Harvey reached down and returned Melody's kiss.

They held it for the longest of moments then Harvey broke away. He'd forgotten how good it was to be with her.

"So what do you have in mind?" he said, beginning to fall in with her suggestions.

"Well, we have a boat, we're on the Med, and there's the most beautiful sunset I've seen in a long time right here. It seems like a good place to start our next adventure."

Harvey didn't reply.

The End

Also by J.D. Weston

Award-winning author and creator of Harvey Stone and Frankie Black, J.D.Weston was born in London, England, and after more than a decade in the Middle East, now enjoys a tranquil life in Lincolnshire with his wife.

The Harvey Stone series is the prequel series set ten years before The Stone Cold Thriller series.

With more than twenty novels to J.D. Weston's name, the Harvey Stone series is the result of many years of storytelling, and is his finest work to date. You can find more about J.D. Weston at www.jdweston.com.

Turn the page to see his other books.

The Silent Man

To find the killer, he must lose his mind...

See www.jdweston.com for details.

The Spider's Web

To catch the killer, he must become the fly...

See www.jdweston.com for details.

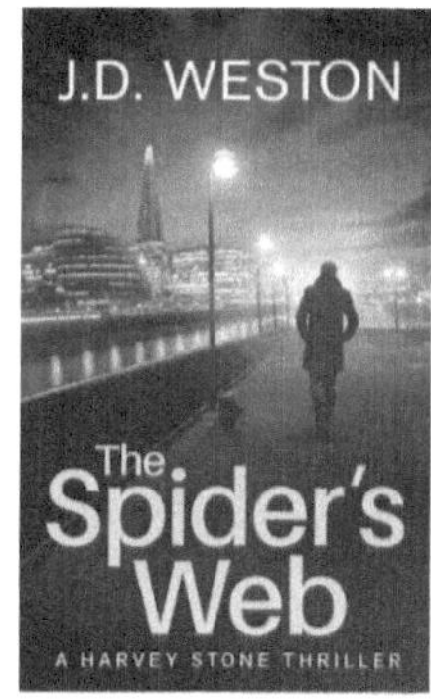

The Mercy Kill

To light the way, he must burn his past...

See www.jdweston.com for details.

The Savage Few

Coming 2021

Join the J.D. Weston Reader Group to stay up to date on new releases, receive discounts, and get three free eBooks.

See www.jdweston.com for details.

The Stone Cold Thriller Series

Stone Cold

Stone Fury

Stone Fall

Stone Rage

Stone Free

Stone Rush

Stone Game

Stone Raid

Stone Deep

Stone Fist

Stone Army

Stone Face

The Stone Cold Box Sets

Boxset One

Boxset Two

Boxset Three

Boxset Four

Visit www.jdweston.com for details.

The Frankie Black Files

Torn in Two

Her Only Hope

Black Blood

The Frankie Black Files Boxset

Visit www.jdweston.com for details.

ACKNOWLEDGEMENTS

Authors are often portrayed as having very lonely work lives. There breeds a stereotypical image of reclusive authors talking only to their cat or dog and their editor, and living off cereal and brandy.

I beg to differ.

There is absolutely no way on the planet that this book could have been created to the standard it is without the help and support of Erica Bawden, Paul Weston, Danny Maguire, and Heather Draper. All of whom offered vital feedback during various drafts and supported me while I locked myself away and spoke to my imaginary dog, ate cereal and drank brandy.

The book was painstakingly edited by Ceri Savage, who continues to sit with me on Skype every week as we flesh out the series, and also throws in some amazing ideas.

To those named above, I am truly grateful.

J.D.Weston.

Copyright © 2020 by J. D. Weston

The moral right of J.D. Weston to be identified as the author of this work has been asserted by him in accordance with the Copyright, Designs and Patents act 1988.

All the characters in this book are fictitious, and any resemblance to actual persons living or dead is purely coincidental.

All rights reserved. No part of this publication may be reproduced, stored in a retrieval system or transmitted in any form or by any means, without the prior permission in writing of the publisher, nor to be otherwise circulated in any form of binding or cover other than that in which it is published without a similar condition, including this condition, being imposed on the subsequent purchaser.